THE CURSE OF DRAGON TAIL ISLAND

Trusty Jack & the Salty Scoundrels

JONATHAN NEVAIR

For my father, who first took me sailing.

MAP (JEWEL ISLANDS)

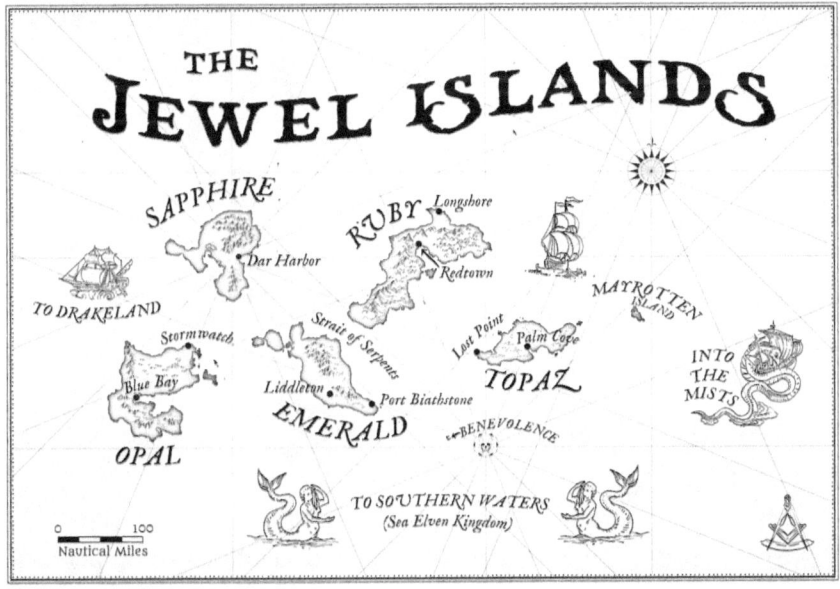

MAP (BENEVOLENCE)

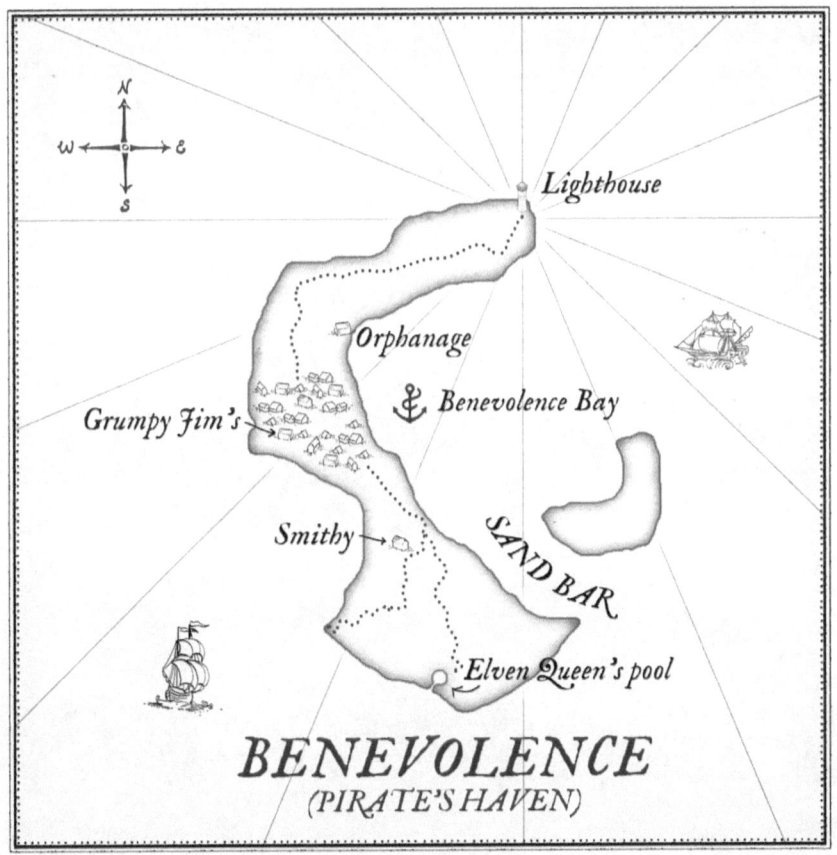

Lighthouse

Orphanage

Benevolence Bay

Grumpy Jim's

Smithy

SAND BAR

Elven Queen's pool

BENEVOLENCE
(PIRATE'S HAVEN)

PROLOGUE

A PIRATE'S LIFE

"**B**limey!" Trusty Jack exclaimed, peering through his spyglass. "That frigate captain looks like a toad!"

Raucous laughter erupted on the deck of the *Lady Luck*.

Jack spun the dial with his fingers and re-focused the eyepiece. With each rise and fall of the ship over the azure swells, warty constellations on pitted cheeks bounced in and out of view.

"Aye, he's a scurvy dog for sure, Captain." The voice was Dûr Riggins, aka Big Rig, *Lady Luck's* dwarven quartermaster, who approached the railing at Jack's side. "Been laid a festering spell by a Topaz mage, he has."

"And lived." Trusty Jack continued his examination of the frigate captain. Portly but solid. Mid-fifties and sea-seasoned by the look of him. He aimed the spyglass lower, focusing on his attire. The ruby-colored overcoat left no doubt of the captain's allegiance.

"What do you say, lads?" Jack barked, the potential prize whetting his appetite. "Shall we gut this ship and leave the nobles thirsty?"

Cheers and the stomping of boots rose from the ragtag crew of humans, dwarves, and half-orcs. Their riotous response drowned out the crashing of swells into *Lady Luck's* bow as they tacked southeast, bearing down on the frigate.

"Give 'em a taste of what it's like for common folk in the Isles," Big Rig said, voice as deep as a dwarven mine.

Trusty Jack swung the spyglass across the ship's deck. A crew of sea elves, their fin-like ridges unmistakable, hastened through tasks, securing items and tightening sails.

"He's making a run for the bay," Big Rig said.

"Aye." Trusty Jack narrowed his eye, tanned and leathery skin pulling at the dried salt on his cheek. He blinked, freeing his face from the mineral's binding. Well-seasoned crow's feet settled into familiar crevices from thirty-odd years of prioritizing laughter and freedom. By a curse of fate, he'd spent eight of those years behind bars lacking the very liberties he treasured.

Jack continued his sweep to aft. He kept the eyepiece steady as the frigate came about, reading the words that crossed the scratched lens. "*Merry Madeline...* now there's a fancy name."

"Full of gold and rum she'll be," Big Rig said.

With a slap of his palm, *Lady Luck's* captain shut the spyglass and eyed the quartermaster.

The dwarf's bushy eyebrows rose, crinkling the onyx skin on his forehead. He adjusted his eyepatch so it nestled in the empty socket.

"Hoist the colors, Mr. Riggins."

"Ha!" Big Rig whacked a thick hand against his leather-armored chest, rattling the twin axes in crisscrossed hilts. "Salty music to me ears!"

"Bring us broadside on the angle," Jack said. He double-checked the frigate's track, assessing the wind and its course. "We've got the weather gauge. They'll not make it to harbor before we intercept."

"'Tis no easy picking, Jack."

Big Rig was right about that. It wasn't that *Lady Luck* couldn't hold her own against a frigate; the sloop had taken down many a ship bigger and broader and had earned her captain a respectable reputation in the Jeweled Sea. Respectable for a pirate, that is. Among the handful of marauding, non-law-abiding vessels roaming the archipelago, *Lady*

Luck's skipper, one James R. Hawk, had been deemed a fair and kind-hearted pirate—if such a thing were possible.

What worried Jack wasn't maneuverability or the courage of his crew. *Lady Luck* was faster than most ships in her class, and his sailors were devoted and brave under pressure. This was about something else: magic. Until they closed the distance, he couldn't be sure what kind of spellcasting backed up the *Madeline's* physical arsenal.

Trusty Jack knelt and placed a hand on the quartermaster's shoulder. "Let's just say, I've got a trick up my sleeve, savvy?"

"Always full o' surprises you are, Jacky boy." Big Rig spat over the side for luck and made his way past the main mast barking orders to the crew.

"Lana!" Trusty Jack shouted.

A rotund half-orc, head shaved save for a plume of black hair atop her skull, strode forward. In the noonday sun, the first mate's green skin shimmered against her drab plus-size monk's robe. She cracked her knuckles and grunted.

"Get that damn mage up from below decks. I want a word with her."

"Aye, Cap'n." The half-orc grinned, exposing the line of sharpened teeth set between her two thick lower tusks that rose to her eyebrows.

"And be gracious about it, for jewel's sake," Jack added, aware of Lana's quickness to anger. "That elf is..." He left the sentence unfinished, eyes on the sailors above him trimming the canvas.

"A bit of a landlubber?" the half-orc said.

Trusty Jack winked in agreement. He removed his tricorne hat and wiped salty sweat from his brow. "Damn but it's bloody hot for noon." He billowed his loose-fitting cotton shirt and scraped away the fraying hairs from the blonde ponytail that clung to his neck. "When we make port in Benevolence, I'm getting me a proper barber."

"You'll make a pretty sight for certain, Captain," a dwarven sailor said, passing him with an armload of cutlasses.

"Cap'n's always a sight!" a human woman shouted amidships, pulling a rope arm over arm to raise *Lady Luck's* skull and crossbones. "He gets eyes when'ver we're ashore."

Trusty Jack waved off the comment, a tinge of heat tingling his cheeks. Well-built, and six feet tall with a square jaw and hazel eyes, he'd once been told by a highborn lady that if he wasn't so free-spirited and crude of dress that he could woo a royal court. That was, if he took a proper bath and learned how to dance.

"It'll never happen, my lady," he had said. "There's too much of the open sea around me to waste it standing and swinging about inside a hall of stone."

And where had he spent the next eight years? Locked inside a hall of stone at Longshore Prison.

Jack gripped the railing and gazed out to sea. Beyond the frigate, at the horizon's edge, he made out the green palms and white lighthouse of Benevolence Bay.

Memories of another lifetime. Long before he'd turned to a pirate's life. Before the scars and tattoos. Before the rum. Before he'd gone and lost the one woman who—

"Coming about!" Big Rig shouted.

Trusty Jack swung underneath the rotating beam as if it were his dance partner and the ship his ballroom. Twelve years at sea, seven of them as captain of *Lady Luck*, had made ship life more home than the solid ground of the Jeweled Islands.

"You called for me?"

Jack turned in time to grab the elf's robe before she went over the side from the heeling ship.

"I hope this is important," the mage said, ignoring her near disastrous tumble overboard. The elf pulled at the robe's fabric, straightening wrinkles from the pirate's strong grip. "I was in the middle of an alchemical—"

Trusty Jack swung the mage around and directed her gaze at the frigate, closer now as they cut the distance.

"A ship." The elf feigned a gasp. "At sea, no less. How unusual..."

"Not just any ship, Master Rin. Our prize."

The elf's eyes went wide, their icy blue growing colder against the tropical sea. "You mean to take her?"

"Indeed. Time to put your passage fee to use." Jack held out his spyglass. Scratched and worn, the dulled golden metal appeared crude against the mage's exquisite velvet robe.

With typical elven grace, Master Rin brushed back her silver mane that fell to mid-chest, placing it behind her shoulders. Delicate fingers, white as bone, opened the spyglass and aimed it at the frigate.

"Either I'm a troll's uncle, or that human captain's been fester-spelled," Jack said.

"Indeed," Master Rin said. "Topaz magic... powerful sorcery to survive. Looks like he's got a limp as well. Though I doubt its source was jewel magic."

Trusty Jack squinted and focused on the frigate. Shouts from the sea elves reached his ears and he made out the tiny form of the captain. The wart-stricken man strode about, barking orders.

The elf was right. He did walk with a limp.

"A blade to his starboard leg at some point," Jack said.

"How can you tell?"

"Ran a dagger through someone's thigh once."

"During battle?"

Jack bobbed his head back and forth. "More of a personal dispute..."

"Over a woman, I'm sure," the elf muttered.

"*With* a woman," he said. "One I hope to never see again."

Master Rin closed the spyglass and handed it back. "And of what service may I be to the most feared pirate in the Jeweled Seas?"

Jack scoffed. "Most feared? Nay, Master Rin. I can't claim that title. Another has their flag planted on that lonely isle. But no one knows the waters 'round the Jewels and how to sail them safely better than I do... be it weather, monster, or spirits in a ship's path."

The mage lowered her chin, acknowledging the statement.

"I assume you'd like me to enhance the accuracy of the archers?" she asked. "Perhaps add fire damage to their arrows? Or would you prefer I heat the cutlass blades of your crew?"

"On the contrary." Jack gazed at the frigate. "I request that you offer up a deception."

"Illusion is not my school of magic, dear Captain. I'm a red wizard."

"Come now, Master Elf. I'd wager you're capable of it." Trusty Jack's lips curved into a subtle smile. "I've an eye for these things."

The elf had been aloof during the voyage. Cloistered in her cabin, she had emerged only for meals and to take astronomical readings by moonlight. But a captain's crew has eyes and ears for things strange and new to a ship, especially when superstitions about wizards and their knowledge of the island chain's ancient powers ran rampant through pirate fleets.

"To call on opposite jewel magic is a dangerous gambit," the elf said.

"A pirate's life is always a gamble, Master Rin." Jack spread his arms wide. "You're on the *Lady Luck* now, so that makes you a pirate... for today." He rolled up his cotton sleeves, revealing a random assortment of crude tattoos—ships, skulls, rum bottles, and the names of vessels taken as prizes.

"They're turning, Captain!" Big Rig shouted from midships.

"Too late now, Master Rin. We're all in."

The toad-faced captain had done the math. A run for the bay was out of the cards.

"All hands on deck!" Trusty Jack shouted to the crew, who scurried about and responded with hoots and cheers.

"Very well, for the sake of lessening the slaughter," the mage said. "But I do so with your awareness of the risks."

"Thank you, Master Rin. Needless death, despite what you might assume about pirates, is never the answer." Trusty Jack strode past the elf and made for Big Rig who was kneeling with Lana and Grek, another half-orc.

"Bones speak of mixed fortune, Captain," the quartermaster said as he approached.

Jack's eyes passed over the hastily drawn chalk circle on the deck and the scattering of chicken bones and precious gems. Rubies, emeralds, and sapphires glittered in the noonday sun. The pattern meant nothing to him.

"Aye." Grek's low and scratchy voice was like sandpaper on wood. "Good and bad portents." He fingered the beaded necklace on his bare green chest in a practiced ritual.

"You've not steered us wrong yet, Seer." Trusty Jack knelt with the three sailors. "We have the weather and I've got a bit of magic up my sleeve." He winked at Big Rig. "You say it's fifty-fifty?"

"Not that clear, Cap'n," Grek said. He ran a hand over his green-skinned forehead and flung sweat onto the deck. "More like the gods ain't talkin'."

"Going in blind isn't ever any good," Big Rig said.

"What are you worried about, dwarf?" Lana cracked her knuckles. "I'll take half them sons of biscuits on myself!"

"Your hastiness and bloodlust are what I'm worried about!" the dwarf growled. "Shall I remind you how many times my wits and prudence saved your pimpled green arse, and this ship, from disaster?"

"Pimpled green arse?" Lana rose, eyes afire. Like a fast-moving storm, the half-orc's massive belly eclipsed the noonday sun. "I'll shove this fist right up your—"

"Steady on, both of you!" Jack held up a hand to cool the half-orc's temper. "And sit back down, Lana. You're blocking the light."

Big Rig's caution was appreciated. As second-in-command, the dwarf focused on navigation, inventory, and risk vs. reward for the ship and crew, leaving the former monk to manage the deckhands and discipline as first mate. The division of ranks was unorthodox, but then again, so were the Salty Scoundrels. From Jack's point of view, it allowed his companions to represent all parties on board fairly and to work to their strengths... most of the time. Big Rig, being the eldest, brought a nautical wisdom to council. Lana's personality was like a lit fuse. The half-orc thrived on the chaos and mayhem of combat. Her thirst for violence had been her downfall as a devout, leading to her expulsion from the order. And yet, as a former monk-turned-pirate her confidence and gusto managed to keep the crew's spirits high, especially under duress. In a strange irony, the half-orc managed to be an inspiration.

"This is right, lads, I can feel it." Trusty Jack took a deep pull of salty air, as if it confirmed his intuition. "That ship is full of booty... enough to keep us belly-full and hammocked in Benevolence through the storm season." He stole a glance at the deck crew. They milled about swinging sabers and prepping for the assault. "We can make repairs to *Lady Luck* and refill the stores. Then, we'll ride the trade winds and have us a time of it piratin' through the long summer."

"Can't deny it," Big Rig said, stroking his beard. "Would be nice to have a spate on dry land. My dwarven blood is missing sand and stone."

"Lana?" Jack turned his attention to the first mate. "I'll not go on this without your blessing."

"Surely you jest!" The half-orc grinned, stretching her grog-blossom cheeks. She ran a tongue over a tusk and swallowed. "'No prey, no pay.' That's been my motto since I joined the Salty Scoundrels." She aimed a massive green hand at the frigate. "There's barrels of rum on that ship that belong in my belly. Let's take her!"

"Aye," Grek said, retrieving the gems and chicken bones from the deck. "We'll all get loaded to the gunwales tonight!"

Trusty Jack slapped Big Rig on the back. "And a parrot's rest at Benevolence when we make port."

Nods all around.

"Right, lads!" Jack shouted to the crew as he rose. "This frigate needs a show." He drew his cutlass and raised it in the air. "Let's make a mockery of 'em'!"

The deck crew ran to the starboard rail. A handful of others scurried up nets with bows strapped on their backs. From the edge of the main deck, a mix of salty humans, dwarves, and half-orcs shouted curses and gestured lewdly at their prize.

"Mr. Jack, sir."

Trusty Jack turned, the precocious voice unmistakable. He knelt and met the young girl's gaze. "What is it Precious?"

"May I be in the battle?" She swung a crudely carved toy sword from side to side as if striking down imaginary foes.

"Nay, lass. Why, they'd never stand a chance if you were with us."

"But I want to be a pirate." She pouted, the wooden sword lowering in defeat.

Trusty Jack took her free hand and squeezed it. "Pirate's life ain't the way, Precious." He removed his tricorne hat and placed it on her head. The girl's face vanished underneath the black fabric. "See?" He lifted the brim with a finger and her eyes returned. "Doesn't suit you."

"You don't like being a pirate, Mr. Jack?"

"Life takes us in strange directions, lass. Wasn't my first choice, but I'm making the best of it." He hoisted her up and held her secure with an arm against his chest. His free hand took back the hat. "See that lighthouse?" He pointed towards the white speck at the horizon.

She ran a hand over the scruff on his chin, half-interested.

"That there's Benevolence Bay. There's an orphanage in the cove run by some nice folks who look out for adventurous seafarers like yourself. One's who end up without a home or..." he hesitated, "family."

The girl, who had yet to share her proper name, had earned the crew's salty badge of approval for her courage and resilience. Two weeks earlier she had been picked up on a floating piece of debris from a shipwreck, surviving a night alone at sea.

"But I want to stay with you." She clung tightly to him.

"*Lady Luck* ain't the safest place, lass. Do you know what 'benevolence' means?"

She shook her head, pinching his chin and rubbing his blonde bristles.

"Kind. Nice and welcoming. That's what it'll be like there. 'Tis a wee lonely isle, Benevolence is. And..." Jack aimed her chin so she faced the frigate. "That ship's full of gold from taxes, Precious. We're going to use it to fix *Lady Luck* up nice and shiny. I'll be in Benevolence and can visit whenever you like."

"Every day?"

"I don't see why not. At least through the storm season. But here's the thing, lass. We're going to take that tax money and give it back to folks who need it. Including a big ol' pile to the orphanage. Enough to buy feather beds and food for all the children." He turned so their gazes met. "Even enough to buy books."

"I can read."

"Can you now?"

She nodded. "Miss Parker was teaching me back home. She's my nanny."

So, it was as he thought. Precious came from privilege. Maybe someone in Benevolence could locate a distant relative or contact her extended family through this 'Miss Parker.'

"Now." Trusty Jack lowered her to the deck and took the wooden sword from her grip. He caught the eye of Myron, *Lady Luck's* human cook, who wiped floury hands on his apron and approached.

"You remember that secret spot I showed you below decks... the one in the galley?"

Precious nodded.

"Go with Mr. Myron and get yourself in there." He reached into his pocket. "Take this." Jack handed her a small tube. "You hold onto this for me, okay?"

"What is it?"

"It's a map." He made as if looking around to check for eavesdroppers. "Our little secret."

"Okay, Mr. Jack."

"And don't come out until you hear the bell." Jack passed her off to the man who heaved her up in his arms. "Promise me, lass?"

"I promise," Precious said, gazing back over the departing cook's shoulder.

"Remember, your word is your reputation. Savvy?" Jack spoke in earnest. "Honest folk always keep their promise."

"Even pirates?"

"Even pirates."

"Coming up a' broadside!" Big Rig said.

Trusty Jack locked eyes with Master Rin, who had positioned herself at the ship's stern. The glint of a large gemstone dangling from a chain flashed in the sunlight.

"Almost in archer's range," Big Rig said, holding out a bow and quiver.

Jack accepted his weapon, his left hand coming to rest in the familiar curves of its wooden handle. Though crafted from the rarest yew in the islands, it would remain unremarkable among others of its kind save for a crudely carved "J" on one of its limbs.

He reached for his quiver and paused. A single golden shaft glinted amidst a dozen cedar arrows.

"I don't know why you don't lock that thing away, lad," Big Rig said. "It sours your expression every time."

A familiar twist of regret tightened his gut. "Someday, maybe."

"Well, clear your mind of it," Big Rig said and drew his twin axes. The noonday sun shimmered off his onyx skin, highlighting muscular forearms like tree trunks. "We've got piratin' to do. And I need you in top form to cover me so I can show that drunken half-orc how to take down sea elves the dwarven way." He swung his axes in a combination and bobbed his neck back and forth, loosening up.

Trusty Jack smiled at his old friend.

"Ahoy!" Big Rig shouted to the crew. "Show a leg! Captain's got words!"

"Wait on my orders, hearties!" Jack said. "Going to be a bit of magic mischief as we near that frigate. Worry not, Salty Scoundrels! Trusty Jack's got a scheme up his sleeve. Their white flag will be flying before long." He jumped up onto a nearby crate. "By nightfall, we'll be belly-up in rum in Benevolence. How's that sound, lads?"

"Ho!" A chorus of shouts erupted across *Lady Luck*'s deck.

Jack swung to stern. He waved for Master Rin to cast the spell.

No sooner had he turned back to check on the frigate then a chill breeze swirled about the ship. Misty serpents rose off the ocean's surface as temperatures clashed.

The frigate vanished in thick fog.

"We've lost her!" Big Rig shouted. "What kind of—"

"There!" Jack pointed at a glowing outline. It was as if his eyes penetrated the opaque spell.

"Aye," Big Rig gasped. "We've got her track."

"Set a course to intercept," Jack said. "Cross the T."

"With pleasure!" The dwarf ran off through the mist.

Jack followed the spectral ship. He calculated no more than two minutes until they came up on it unawares. If he ordered Master Rin to drop the spell at the last moment the vessel wouldn't stand a chance. Not with his crew at the ready. Full out surrender would be the only option. Unless that captain was pig-headed and dumb enough to try and fight. But when *Lady Luck's* ramming prow stared them down, there would be no other choice.

"Satisfied?"

Jack turned at the sound of the mage's voice. "Quite, Master Rin. How quickly can you dissipate the fog?"

"Faster than an arrow can hit its mark at fifty paces."

Trusty Jack smiled. A long rest in Benevolence. He could feel the sweet swinging of the hammock and hear the rustle of palm leaves lulling him to sleep.

"Right in line," Big Rig said, returning. "Call it when you're ready."

"On my word, Master Rin." Trusty Jack followed the frigate's outline, leaning over the railing.

Three... two... one.

"Now!"

Nothing.

"Do it!"

Jack turned. Master Rin was nowhere to be found.

"Where is she?" He looked at Big Rig, who shrugged.

The air stirred. A whirlwind rose, lifting the fog. Benevolence appeared in the distance across the open sea. "The bloody ship's gone," he muttered.

"Jack!"

He turned at the sound of Big Rig's voice and followed the dwarf's widened eye.

Across *Lady Luck's* deck to port, the frigate barreled down on them in a T formation.

"The mage!" The dwarf pointed.

Master Rin stood on the frigate's deck, next to the warty-faced captain, her hands glowing with flaming fireballs. Sea elves with bows drawn homed in on *Lady Luck's* crew. Worst of all, the frigate's prow was a three-pronged rammer that looked like it would take out half of their sloop.

"Sink me." Jack growled. "She set us up." His eyes darted about, assessing their course and the frigate's path.

"They've got us, mate..." The desperation in Big Rig's voice was unmistakable. His old friend's eyes softened. "Your call, Jack. I'll stand with you to the last... you can count on that."

Trusty Jack scanned *Lady Luck's* deck, taking in the faces of his crew. They were loyal, and they were pirates. They'd fight if he ordered it.

A volley of arrows left the frigate.

"Brace!" Big Rig shouted.

The pitter patter of projectiles hitting home was accompanied by screams of pain.

Jack dodged an arrow that twanged into the deck. He stared at it as the shaft's vibrations settled.

Useless death. Where was the honor in that?

"Throw down, lads!" He tossed his bow and quiver at his feet. A glint of sunlight made him squint. The golden arrow stared up at him.

I should have listened to Rig, he thought.

Clangs of cutlasses hitting the deck bounced across the ship. Jack nodded to the flag master, who began lowering *Lady Luck's* skull and crossbones.

"Damn your traitorous spells!" Lana shouted amidships. "How dare you deny me my rum!" She charged forward as the frigate slowed to throw ropes and secure the sloop.

"Lana, no!"

The half-orc leapt. Light as a feather, her bare green foot touched down on *Lady Luck's* railing and she sprung, crossing the distance to the enemy ship.

Whack!

The frigate's boom collided with her head and she crashed down onto the deck.

A sea elf working the sails cackled at their quick-thinking.

"Board and take the ship!" the captain shouted, waving sea elves forward. "Bring them to me alive."

"Make way!" a burly sea elf with an eye patch barked, pushing aside his companions. "Make way for the captain!"

The crowd, who had been taunting Jack, parted and the wart-stricken man strode forward.

"I think it's time, Master Rin," he said. "Do me the honor, if you would."

The mage muttered an incantation, her hands dancing in a pattern that left a trail of sparkling light hanging in the air.

Jack's eyes deceived him, or so he thought. The captain's body and attire shimmered, as if distorted in a convex mirror. It settled and a half-elf woman in a royal naval uniform replaced the pock-marked, spell-suffering man.

"That's topaz magic, that is," Big Rig said through gritted teeth, fighting the sea elves holding him.

Master Rin smirked.

Shock and anger clashed in Jack's belly. She was no red mage. The elf had played him like a fiddle!

The naval officer's boots echoed off the frigate's deck as she approached.

Jack followed her movements. "Shiver me timbers," he muttered, recognizing the uneven gait.

"Well, well, well..." The officer strode forward with the arrogance of a new-crowned king. "Now here's a sight for sore eyes." She eyed Jack up and down. "How long has it been?"

"Don't say nuthin' Jack," Big Rig said.

"I see you still have poor taste in companions." She cocked her head towards the dwarf.

Jack eyed the uniform and plumed hat. "A commodore now... impressive."

The officer strode to a nearby sea elf, who held out his pilfered quiver.

"It'll be rear admiral after I deliver this prize to the authorities." She removed the golden arrow.

"That's not yours to take." Jack gritted his teeth.

"A welcome trophy for the palace walls. I imagine it will hold a place of honor." The commodore smirked, stroking the gleaming shaft. "My father will, no doubt, be pleased."

"Ah yes, the kind and generous regent. How is His Grace, Markus Fitzwater?" Jack's eyes narrowed. "Still surrounding himself with ass-kissers who do his bidding, dubious as it is?"

"Not this 'I was framed' nonsense again?" The commodore walked to the railing, gazing out to sea.

"Regent Fitzwater does know how to abuse power in his half-sister's absence," Jack said. "In case you've forgotten, until proven otherwise, Lady Ricarda is still the legitimate ruler of the islands."

"You really are a 'picaroon,'" She turned to face him. "Did I get that right?"

"I believe you did, Commodore," her quartermaster said, answering for him. "Scoundrels... all of them." The sea elf's one eye burned into him.

The captain's boots clicked and clacked as she crossed the deck. "You pirates love your lingo. But then you've always had a way of saying one thing and meaning another, haven't you, Jack?" Her gaze darted left and right, examining his captured crew. "'Trusty Jack'... I'm surprised no one's called your bluff."

"Them's dueling words!" Big Rig shouted, struggling against the sea elves holding him tight. "I'll not let you speak to the captain that way, you bilge rat!"

She waved a hand, dismissing him. The dwarf's curses echoed across the frigate's deck, fading as he was dragged away.

"What will happen to my ship and crew?" Jack asked.

"Correction, it's not your ship."

"I won her, fair and square."

"So I've heard. Another one of your archery feats... against a drunken pirate."

"*Lady Luck's* mine. Pirate code states—"

"Hah!" The commodore nodded mockingly. "Rules among the lawless. Illusions of morality veiling criminal and thuggish camaraderie. Official law in the Jeweled Islands recognizes no such code. Your ship will be returned to its rightful owner... the one who bought it with money legitimately earned."

"Earned?" Jack said. "On whose backs? More like a rich noble whose never had their hands on a rope or in the dirt."

"Moving on," the commodore said, ignoring his protest, "as for your... '*crew*'." She spat the word as if it were a mealy apple. "The deckhands will be pressed into service in the Royal Navy."

Five years. Jack, like all pirates, knew that was the standard term under impressment.

The commodore strolled over to a sea elf and examined Big Rig's confiscated axes. "Regarding your so-called 'Salty Scoundrels,' that foul-mouthed dwarf will feel right at home back at Longshore Prison. I believe he was serving a ten-year sentence. It's life in prison now... lots of time to commune with stone walls where his kind belongs."

"That ain't the rules and you know it." Jack struggled against the forceful grips holding him.

The commodore's head rose, examining the Ruby Island's flag atop the frigate's mast. "Indeed, but here's the thing, Captain Hawk. My father and the warden are on good terms. Did you know they share a love of harpy oysters? Rare, though they are, in the Jewels. Every month a bushel arrives at Longshore as a gesture of appreciation for keeping threats such as your band of thieves inside those thick stone walls." She locked eyes with him. "I hear an occasional pearl, or twenty, surprises the warden as she shucks them sipping a glass of port."

Jack shook his head in defeat.

"And as for that monstrosity..." The commodore pointed at Lana who lay unconscious, splayed out on the deck. A welt like a cannonball protruded from her shaved head where the boom collided with her thick skull. "That drunken savage is a danger to herself and others. Deluded by the constant grog into believing she's a devout." The commodore shook her head. "It's too bad she's so uncontrollable. With her skills she'd make a great enforcer for the peasants who skimp on their taxes. Alas, I think a ten-year stint in Longshore should lower her boiling temper to a simmer. Either that or get her killed."

Knowing Lana, she'd probably have an entire cell block to herself by the end of her first year.

"Let's see, that leaves your infamous cook. Myron, is it?" She pointed to a body on *Lady Luck's* deck. A bright red stain covered the dusty flour on the dead man's apron. "Oh dear, I'd say his last goose is cooked."

Snickers rose from the surrounding sea elves.

"And to think," she added, "if not for that bad weather this all could have gone differently."

"Aye," Jack growled out, heart burning with rage at the loss of his longtime companion. "Maybe it'd be you on that deck."

"You put Master Rin through quite the trial," she said, ignoring the jab. The commodore approached the elf, hands clasped behind her back as if strolling through a park on holiday.

Jack caught the mage's eye. The wizard's gaze was cold as ice.

"Quite the storm," the commodore said. "Sent us off course and pushed back our trap by almost two weeks." She put a hand on the mage's shoulder. "I can't imagine what you endured with these uncivilized rogues."

"I kept to myself, mostly," Master Rin said, a faint smile cracking her icy expression. "But the stars weren't the same without you by my side."

Jack followed the commodore's hand as it slid down the elf's arm.

"If not for the weather, I'd have taken *Lady Luck* before the Strait of Serpents." She swung to face him, the long brim of her plumed hat shading her features.

"What can I say?" Trusty Jack said. "The gods favor those on the side of justice."

"Indeed." The commodore fidgeted with a nail. "News reached us by crow's flight that the flagship, *Endurance,* was lost in the tempest, along with all its passengers."

Jack's eyes darted to the ropes that connected *Lady Luck* to the naval frigate. *Precious...* he thought. *Is she still hidden in the galley?* There was no sign or word from the sea elves about a child.

"Justice was indeed served," the commodore added. "The Chen family was on board."

So, Precious might be a Chen? A noble line of lawyers and judges in the Jeweled Isles who had chosen judicial oversight as their focus within the islands' government.

The commodore sighed. "I'm afraid the gods grew tired of their endless barking about leniency and compassion for the lower classes."

"Not to worry." Jack's eyes narrowed. "We'll soon cleanse the Jewels of corruption." He paused for effect. "And your father's avarice with it."

"You think you're so righteous? Stealing and giving handouts to those dirty peasants. Quite the guilt issue you have, Jack."

"Ain't about that Bonnie, and you know it."

Crack!

17

Stinging pain radiated through his cheek as the frigate's quartermaster slapped him. "It's 'Commodore,' to you... *pirate*."

"It's alright," she said, waving off the sea elf. "He and I have a long history and this..." Jack followed the corners of her lips as they rose into a smile, "is personal."

That was putting it mildly. His eyes went to her injured leg.

"Oh, I haven't forgotten about our little tiff," she said. "But this is bigger than you and me. Your Salty Scoundrels have been a thorn in my father's side for years."

"Aye, quite a pesky one," Trusty Jack said, puffing his chest. "Had some laughs at his expense on top of taking back what wasn't his to steal."

The commodore remained silent, her expression earnest.

"Not much of a sense of humor between the lot of you," he added, looking around at her crew. "I guess that makes sense when you're the butt of the joke again and again."

"You should start focusing less on humor and more on what remains of your future."

"Longshore Prison can't hold me. I broke out once and I'll do it again. I'll be back on the high seas before the trades blow come springtime. The regent will look the fool like he always has." Jack felt his pride swelling. "You as well."

"Oh, there'll be no Longshore Prison. This time, dear Jack, the joke's on you." The commodore gestured at her crew. "These sea elves are hired mercenaries from the South Seas. They're far away from home and have no care about local politics. Gold in their gills is all they're after."

A pit opened in his stomach.

She stepped close. "Just you and me out here, Jack. And now I'm going to get revenge for the pain you've caused my sister."

Jack's mind was shifting pieces on the board, but he had lost all direction. *What ruse is she playin' at?*

"I don't even want the bounty on your head." She went to the railing and looked out at the sea. "It'll be worth it just to tell my father you've been disposed of. Killed by my blade and fallen overboard." She peered over the side of the ship. "Torn to shreds by sea asps before our eyes... isn't that right, lads?"

A mixture of "ayes" and sinister laughing rose amidst the frigate's crew.

"That should sate his thirst for revenge," she said. "A lie though it will be."

Jack surveyed the crowd. Sea elves grinned and chuckled. "Who's the dishonest one now, Bonnie?"

Whack! The commodore closed the distance and sent a crashing blow against his jaw.

Warm, metallic-tasting liquid filled his mouth as his knees buckled. Strong sea elven hands kept him standing.

"Don't you talk to me about honesty."

The commodore's blurry face returned to focus.

Her eyes narrowed. "Plus, I'll be hailed a hero by the nobility." She spread her arms as if accepting applause. "Bonnie Fitzwater, the naval officer who took down the troublesome pirate, Captain Hawk."

Cornered... and out of options. There was only one move left to play. His gut wrenched with the thought of it, but he had no other choice.

"And Marian?" The words came out in a whisper. He hadn't uttered her name in... how long had it been?

"Your death will lift a burden my sister has carried far too long. Even her powers of healing can't match what will come with your passing."

"Am I to walk the plank?"

"Oh no, Captain Hawk." The Commodore stepped close and their eyes met.

Just like Marian's. Mahogany with flecks of gold that he'd lost himself in all those years ago.

"That would be too merciful." She patted his cheek, snapping him out of the dream. "The sea asps would make quick work of you." Her eyes ignited with a fiery vengeance. "I want you to suffer." She went to the railing and gazed out at sea. "And therefore, I intend to let you go."

"What are you playin' at, Bonnie?" he asked, struggling against the sea elves holding him fast.

The commodore wet a finger and held it up in the air.

Jack's sweaty cheek tingled from the caress of a southwesterly breeze. He followed the naval officer's eyes to port and his own went wide.

Storm clouds edged the horizon.

"The open sea beckons," she said. "Freedom on the swells. That's the pirate's dream, isn't it? No ties and no hitches. Just galivanting through the Jeweled Isles. And Captain Hawk, the exception to the immoral rule," the commodore held out her hands in a gesture of introduction, "the savior of the common folk."

"If it wasn't for you and your Navy bilge rats enforcing unfair taxes, no one would need savin'."

"And that's where you come in, is it? Captain James R. Hawk, the good pirate." The Commodore made as if giving a soliloquy to her crew. "Trusty Jack's his name, the man who chose freedom over commitment. Personal well-being over his pledge of honor. Who chose to leave his betrothed at the altar and—"

"That's not what happened!"

Bonnie pounced, halting centimeters from his face. Waves of hot air bounced off his chin, her nostrils flaring like a bull ready to charge. "That's what they all say."

A splash broke the silence on deck.

Trusty Jack stole a glance overboard. Five sailors had heaved a makeshift raft of crude timbers over the side. The leather-strapped logs righted themselves and drifted away from the hull. The square platform looked barely large enough to lay down on.

"Your new command." A smirk grew on the commodore's face. She removed her hat and fiddled with the plumage. "A significant downgrade, regrettably."

Jack's heart skipped a beat. "You wouldn't!"

She accepted a ceramic jug from a sailor and shoved it into his stomach.

"Dead men tell no tales. Isn't that what you pirates say?" A wide grin usurped her angry expression. "I hope yours will be long and filled with suffering and regret."

Cool air swept over the deck, flapping the sails.

"Off you go." The commodore nodded in the direction of the railing.

Jack felt the suctioned grips of sea elf fingers tighten on his arms and legs.

"A pox on you, Bonnie!" he shouted as they lifted and dragged him to the railing. "And you!" Jack eyed the mage. "I'll crush ye barnacles when I—"

He was over the side and in the drink before he could finish.

SCURVY DOG

FOURTEEN YEARS LATER...

T he macaw had been silent for an hour. It shuffled back and forth on its perch, attention focused on the bartender counting pence. With each clink of coin, the parrot's head bobbed up and down, casting shadows across the rum shack's palm timbers. Out at sea, distant thunder rumbled. Like a snoring dragon, the gentle cadence added a percussive accompaniment to the bird's monotonous shadow play.

On any other island one would claim an unidentifiable eeriness was about, but here at the furthest tip of the Jewel Archipelago, the isolated cove with its single dock and meager outpost lay close to the map's edge... so close that a terror in uncharted waters made its presence known. A venomous magic leeched into the island's bones from over the eastern horizon. It crossed nautical miles like a spectral serpent, snaking its way through the aquatic shadows. To name it was to call it closer. Pirates and sailors alike kept the words from their tongues. None knew the extent of its trace and influence. How the toxins altered the island's flora and fauna was best left to the imagination where its horrors worked in nightmares alone.

On the leeward coast, a crude fence like misaligned teeth hugged the village of Entèdi. Its spikes offered scant protection from the strange and deadly creatures lurking in the jungle, for the haunting echo of dark magic couldn't be kept at bay. Residents and passing traders spoke of an invisible offshore breeze, a palpable nudging from the island to be off and away. As for the occasional foolhardy adventurer who dared step foot in the interior, their dreams of uncovering lost treasure and forgotten ruins made for embellished tales over bottles of rum. Those safe within the outpost's walls were their storytellers, for none returned to tell their own tales.

You didn't end up on Mayrotten Island by choice. It drew those with bad fortune. "Tar luck," the pirates called it. Most did not stay long. If they did, they died. Except for the rare few. Whatever the reason, the island spared them. And it was those scurvy dogs who gathered nightly in The Dreg. Their pasts shared a common yet tragic pairing: a strange gift of fortitude and nothing to lose.

Scarlett Tanash, newly arrived on a private charter, pushed through the dangling bones and beads and entered the dilapidated shanty. As if on cue, thunder clapped.

Squawk! An unblinking avian eye burned into her from a perch behind the bar.

Over the counter's edge, barely visible from her height, a bald green crown spun towards the entrance.

"Ghosts be at it again," a gruff voice said. The clink of a coin dropping into a pile followed.

"Good evening." Scarlett's melodic voice cut through the heavy air and humidity like a cool breeze.

A creak of a stool followed and the weathered face of a half-orc, their one remaining muscular arm planted on the counter, peered over the bar.

"A gnome," he said. "That's a first."

Scarlett bowed, arms spread like wings. It was too proper a gesture in this establishment, but she'd been raised with impeccable manners. At times, they'd served her well, offering charm and, most importantly, distraction. Other times, they were a barrier to progress, whether conversational or otherwise.

She scrutinized the half-orc's face, reading his response: indifference.

"Storm's brewing," she said and pulled back her hood. Thick crimson locks fell to her shoulders. Delicate pointy ears, like barren islands in a blood-red sea, protruded from the sides of her head.

"Genius observation, that is," the bartender grumbled and went back to counting coins.

"I'm certainly glad to be in port."

Another grumble and clink.

Scarlett scanned the room: five patrons. Two elderly men, twins by the look of them, and a scarred and fierce looking dwarven woman, occupied the center table playing bones. To the left, a shirtless middle-aged half-orc, legs open wide and head slumped in a chair, clutched a rum bottle like a newborn baby. Whether asleep, dead, or petrified by a stillness spell, he had that rare look of contentment that comes from a tragic love affair with the grog.

She swept back past the trio to the opposite corner. A shadowy form sat in near darkness, facing away from the candlelight.

"Tingle," she said, her voice a whisper.

No response.

"Tingle, wake up." She reached into a vest pocket. A familiar warmth radiated against her palm. Her tiny gnomish fingers cupped its source. She withdrew her hand.

The macaw fidgeted on its perch.

Scarlett eyed the parrot. Being of the avian variety, it would be privy to the sprite's spell, but no one else would mark its effect.

Scarlett held out her hand and opened it, nodding toward the indistinct patron occupying the corner table. "Tingle, give me a little light."

Squawk!

"Go ahead," she whispered, encouraging the sprite. "It's alright."

The sparkling entity swirled in the air. A human man grew into focus as the corner magically brightened.

Scarlett's blue eyes shone with relief. A week at sea. Two storms, one that put the fright of death through her, and a perpetual unhappy belly as the ship pitched about on rough seas. Not to mention the even longer journey from the mainland to reach the Jewels before—

Squawk!

"You can't have that in here." The half-orc was back, leaning over the counter. He pointed at the sprite hovering next to her. "It's spooking Mr. Bentworth."

Again, Scarlett bowed, this time hiding a smile. A perfect gesture to gloss over the tension—an ignorant, high-class mainlander with no clue of the ways and goings-on in the Jewels, and especially not in a scurvy-ridden rum shack at the end of the known world.

"My apologies, good sir." Her tiny gnomish hand added flair, gesturing in a circle. "Wait outside, Tingle."

The glowing orb bounced up and down, defiant.

"Out!" Scarlett pointed at the entrance.

The sprite shot off through the dangling beads and bones into the darkness.

"And stay inside the fence!"

The bartender vanished once more.

Scarlett made for the man in the corner and—

"Hold it."

She turned, the proprietor in view around the bar's corner. The half-orc sat at his stool, a hulking beast of a creature, littered with tattoos. Scarlett's feet shuffled backward at the sight of him. A former pirate without question... one who had left an arm somewhere along his adventures at sea.

"Seats are for drinkin' customers only." He flipped a nut over his shoulder. With expert dexterity, Mr. Bentworth snatched it out of the air and cracked it open with his beak.

"Well then," she stepped closer, "a bottle of your finest rum, please."

"Finest rum..." The half-orc scoffed. "Right." He swiveled his stool and reached for one of a dozen jugs with a skull and bones stamped on it.

As if floating on a breeze, Scarlett's arm rose. Lithe fingers removed a stack of pence from the counter.

Squawk!

"What are you on about?" The half-orc eyed the parrot. "I sent it off." He shook his head and turned as Scarlett's hand fell into her vest pocket.

It came right back out, as natural as the eeriness on the island.

Squawk!

"Shut it, you!" The half-orc bared his sharpened teeth. "Damn bird's out of its mind."

"It does seem a bit on edge." Scarlett handed him the pilfered coins and glanced at the corner table. "And two glasses."

A thick green hand took two coconut halves off the shelf.

"Interesting." Scarlett examined the rustic containers. "Fitting for the ambience."

The half-orc shook his head and went back to counting pence.

Scarlett made for the shadowy figure. As if summoned by fate, an invisible tide rose to challenge her progress. Each footfall grew more difficult, like fighting through molasses. The hesitation and doubt that she'd kept at bay for almost a year had reared their ugly faces.

Was it the island? Or was her mind playing tricks?

Staring at the man's back, the road to the lonely outpost ran as a traumatic stream of memories. To turn back now, after all it took to get here? That would be worse than the looming and dubious future that might come to pass if she failed.

"You're a mainlander by the look of you." The man's voice was soft and yet spirited, as if a potent soul sat corked under pressure.

Scarlett caught sight of her reflection in an empty bottle on the table. Surrounding her shimmering doppelgänger, a stretched and distorted view of the tavern flickered in the candlelight.

"Eyes in the back of me head," he said, without turning. "Seen you since you came in. Clever one, you are."

"I hope you'll excuse my form of payment for the rum." She stepped forward, taking in the man's profile. The age was right, but something about his features didn't align with the descriptions. He looked less intimidating and defiant than the accounts she'd heard and read. *To be expected,* she thought. Tales have a way of growing in embellishment with each ear and tongue.

"You going to sit and open that?" His boot pushed the empty seat out from under the table.

Scarlett heaved the bottle overhead and slid it onto the tabletop. She climbed the chair's support bars and made herself comfortable.

"So, mainlander..." He popped the cork with his teeth and filled both coconut shells.

Scarlett's eyes widened. Faded and blurry inked letters peeked out from under his fraying cotton sleeve.

Three of them. The start of a word. The first of two, if she guessed right. Before the anticipation of potential victory soaked in, a swell of anxiety and danger crashed over it.

This had to be done delicately and with the utmost discretion. Otherwise, a journey of a thousand miles lasting over a year might be for naught.

"Either I'm a troll's uncle," he said, "or you've got the look of one who has travelled far and wide in search of treasure."

And I think I've found it. She chose a coy smile as her response.

"Ain't nothing on Mayrotten Island but empty chests," he said. "This here's a dead end. Slack tide day and night."

Weariness. That's what she saw painted on his face. Was it a veneer, a disguise made of circumstance, or had the man been worn through to his soul?

Scarlett scanned the room before making her move. The bartender was counting pence. Curses and cards consumed the trio at the table. The half-orc had somehow gotten even more cozy with his newborn bottle of rum. The macaw, however, eyed her with an uncanny knowing.

Damn that bird, she thought.

The man caught her taking in the scene and nodded. "As I said, dead water."

"Well then." Scarlett reached into her pocket. She withdrew a small metal object, placing it on the table. "This might turn the tide."

Squawk!

The man's hand covered the artifact with lightning-quick reflexes. Scarlett caught the bartender peering over. Even the card players halted, their veteran instincts responding to the macaw's alarm. All eyes except those of the comatose and grog-smitten half-orc homed in on their table.

Scarlett raised her coconut shell, clasping it in her tiny hands like a soup bowl, and downed the fiery liquid. She gave a nod of approval, though her face couldn't hide the elixir's bite.

"We're good, Cutty," the man said to the bartender. "Just showing this landlubber some Mayrotten hospitality." He waved off the other patrons with his coconut shell.

Grumbles and adjustments to chairs followed.

The man's gaze burned into her across the table. Weariness had been replaced by a newly ignited flame. "Who are ye?" He leaned closer, voice low. "And what in the name of the Jeweled Deeps is bringing you after me with this?"

Scarlett placed the coconut shell down in front of her. "My name is Scarlett Tanash. And I'm here," she nodded at his tattooed hand covering the object, "because I need a captain."

The man's angular jaw turned ever so slightly, his earnest green eyes checking the attention of the patrons and bartender. "No denying someone like yourself can feel the dark magic here." He slid the object back to her side, keeping it covered. "And you want to sail closer?"

"I do," she said, her tiny hand taking back the object, "but let's not get ahead of ourselves. There're other matters to attend to before that step."

"Ain't taking no steps, Ms. Tanash." He slugged his rum and poured them another round. "Now, I'll toast you once for your heart and bravery, and then off with you."

Scarlett leaned in so they were inches from one another. "I *need* a captain. A very special one..."

"Aye, one with nothing to lose."

She raised a crimson eyebrow. "I'm on Mayrotten Island. Seems the best place to recruit one."

He smiled, the crow's feet around his eyes stretching. Again, the weariness broke, revealing cracks in his outer shell. Deny it as he might, the charisma peeking through left no doubt in her mind. It was him. A legend of the dead sat across from her in living, breathing flesh.

Scarlett felt the macaw's stare from the perch. *Damn that bird.*

"Cheers, Ms. Tanash." He raised the shell and gestured to her. "I wish you luck."

"Ah yes," Scarlett picked up her bowl. "Let's toast to that." Her eyes went to the letters on his wrist. "To lady luck."

He paused, the rum inches from his mouth.

It was now or never.

"And to you, Captain Hawk."

❧ 2 ❧

SHOW A LEG

❦

Years of peaceful misery. Hard won, after a desperate struggle to survive the unsurvivable.

Trusty Jack examined the gnome across the table. How in the blazes had she found him?

Bah, he thought, *don't matter a pence.*

What had him stumped was why anyone would bother.

"That man's dead and gone, Ms. Tanash."

A lie and a truth, depending on which side of the table you sat.

"Indeed," the gnome said. "A fortuitous position to be in, if I may say so." She reached for the rum bottle.

Trusty Jack held out his cup. The firebrew swirled like a dark and foreboding whirlpool as she poured.

"You'll be happy to hear that the circumstances of Captain Hawk's death are somewhat legendary."

"Is that so?" Trusty Jack raised the shell and sipped. The low-grade rum stung, sending a much-needed jolt through his system. Behind his half-drunken haze, the inner strategist and tactician sparked. He was tacking, crossing the conversational current to buy time while closing the distance.

Ms. Tanash nodded, taking a sip and wincing. "Thirty-odd sea elves run through with his cutlass before the arrogant commodore challenged him to a duel."

"Thirty, eh?" He shot his rum. "If he'd had his bow, it'd have been triple that, by all accounts."

"Either way," she said, "the tale's punctuated by a tragic conclusion."

"How's that, lass?" Trusty Jack checked the room in the bottle's reflection. His legs could get him out of the tavern as fast as a downwind run, even sailing on a middle-aged breeze. Still, a gnome couldn't catch him, fast as they were with their small but stout legs. Now, if that sprite was waiting outside...

Lightning flashed through the window, conjuring an image of the island.

There was always the jungle. They'd never follow him over the fence.

Was he that desperate? And for what? To stay dead and gone in the eyes of the outside world until he'd drunk himself to a true death on Mayrotten Island?

"The official story tells it differently, of course," Ms. Tanash said, "but according to common folk you bested Commodore Fitzwater with blades. That is, until a mage intervened, saving the officer from the killing blow and allowing her to run you through."

Rusted, aged irony rang in his ears.

Bonnie, he thought. *And that damn Topaz mage.* He filled his cup. "'Tis a good way to be remembered." Fiery liquid shot down his throat.

"Your body was dumped over the side. Torn to shreds and devoured by sea asps."

"Like I said, 'dead and gone.'"

"Last call, lads." The bartender's words rang like a buoy's bell over the tavern's drunken sea.

"I'll stay a bit, Cutty," Jack said, eyes locked on the gnome. "Bit of business to finish up over here."

"Don't forget to cover Mr. Bentworth when you lock up," the half-orc said. "Otherwise, he'll be at loggerheads come morn. Unbearable and cranky, that bird is..."

"Aye," Trusty Jack said.

Coins clanked as winnings were distributed amongst the three playing bones.

"Come on now, Hardy." The bartender approached his drunken kinsman and kicked the stool's leg. "Closing time."

Hardy stirred and muttered inebriated nonsense until Cutty acquiesced and heaved him up over his shoulder.

Boots shuffled across rustic planks. Beads and bones rustled and then, stillness and silence filled The Dreg.

Jack poured another round from the half-empty bottle. Rain pitter-pattered on palm timbers, adding a steady rhythm to the intermittent rumbles of thunder. He scrutinized the gnome, expecting to read concern on her face now that they were alone. Instead, it radiated eagerness.

As if spinning the conversational helm to port, Jack came about. *Time to engage*, he thought.

"Mind telling me where you got that?" He nodded at the object hidden beneath her hand.

"It matters not, Captain Hawk. What's important is that—"

"Oh, it matters, lass. That object's pure evil. Got the ghost mark on it."

Her hand slid away, revealing it a second time.

Squawk!

Trusty Jack shivered. He took in the intricate ornamentation on the bulbous exterior. A dragon encircled the edges and a symbol that no one, not even the foolhardiest and treasure-hungry pirate, hoped to set eyes on gleamed from the center. "You know what that is, Ms. Tanash?" He pointed at the icon.

"I wouldn't be here if I didn't."

The gnome was proving tenacious. A formidable sailor of the tongue.

"Open it," she said, "and then I'll explain."

Jack hesitated, the sigil both repulsive and disturbing. He lowered his hand. "Meaning all respect, Ms. Tanash, I'd rather not."

With uncanny confidence, the gnome reached forward and unclasped the latch. Like a pocket watch, it flipped open.

Jack leaned in and furrowed his brow.

"It's never done that before." She joined him, bent over the device.

Like a spinning top losing momentum, the post at the compass's center rattled.

"Shiver me timbers." The phrase left Jack's lips as a whisper. "It's the island doing that."

Lightning flashed. Out the seaward window, beyond the dock and anchored ship, ominous storm clouds towered like fell beasts in the dark and stormy night. Somewhere over the eastern horizon, hidden in the mists, lay the source of what pulled at the compass.

"Now you can see my dilemma," Ms. Tanash said. "It's got no needle."

"And a good thing, too," Jack said, relief washing over him. "It's useless." He leaned back and lifted his shell of rum. "No needle, no bearing. And I don't need to tell you that there's no more blood iron left in the world."

The gnome raised an eyebrow.

"Ah," Jack said, realization dawning like the morning sun. He leaned back and folded his arms. "That's a fool's errand, Ms. Tanash. Even for a thief of the highest caliber. Ain't like taking a stack of pence when someone's head is turned." He held up a hand. "Meaning no offense, but that's folly, that is."

"I've come a long way to find you," she said. "Won't you at least do me the courtesy of hearing my offer?"

"About that, Ms. Tanash... finding me, I mean."

"Heroes never die, Captain Hawk. Some live on in legend alone. Others..." The corners of her mouth curved into a smile. "Let's just say that my profession benefits from a clandestine network." She traced a finger around the rim of her coconut shell. "Thieves keep their eyes and ears open. It's often how the best treasures are found, at least in our line of work. In this case, your miraculous survival after being outwitted by the Royal Navy—"

"Now wait a minute there, lass." Jack balled a hand into a fist. "That was complicated."

"Do tell, Captain Hawk?"

Jack leaned over the table, the blood in his veins simmering. "You have the gift of speech, dodgin' and parryin' well and what not, Ms. Tanash. I'll give you that," he growled. "The details of that day, and what came after, aren't important."

"Indeed." An amused expression peeked out from behind the coconut shell at her lips.

"The journey that led me to this godforsaken island is no one's business but mine."

"Fair enough." She nodded as a peace offering. "What about your old life? Wouldn't you like it back?"

"I'm twice sunk, Ms. Tanash. The curse of three is hanging over my shoulder. I won't roll dice in that game again. And certainly not with an offer involving that." He pointed at the broken compass.

"There will be risks and danger, no doubt. But that's nothing new for a legendary pirate."

"You're talking about sailing to Dragon Tail Island. Need I remind you of the curse?"

"You need not. I am sure, Captain Hawk, that by now it's clear from my manners and speech that I'm well educated."

Jack scoffed and drank some rum. "Educated, aye. With books and theories." He narrowed one eye as if sighting his bow. "There's a reason why that island's been hidden for a thousand years."

"I thought you more daring, Captain Hawk."

"I've been into the mists, Ms. Tanash. Nippin' the edge like a wee sip of grog. What I saw and heard was more horrifying than all your fancy words."

And we barely made it out alive, he thought. A shiver ran through him recalling the chase. *Lady Luck* had been on the run from the Royal Navy. Three days. Fast as the sloop was, they'd forced her around the south-eastern end of Topaz Island between bad weather and the coast. It had cost them time and distance, and they were forced to engage the enemy ships. As captain, he'd made the call to flee into the mists, against even Big Rig's vociferous objections. *Lady Luck*, like most pirate vessels, ran a hierarchical democracy. Unless engaged in active combat a vote cast by the three representatives overseeing the ship—the captain, the quartermaster, and the first mate - decided matters. As captain, Jack's perspective was driven by overall goals and tactical concerns, Big Rig concentrated on the ship's physical condition, its stores, and the seafaring circumstances in play, while Lana spoke on behalf of the crew, sharing their overall sentiment about the intended action or prize versus the risks. As they were already engaged by the Royal Navy, it technically fell to him in that instance to decide.

Bonnie's lead ship and a fleet of five frigates would have had them that day if he hadn't steered them into the spectral fog. Even now, he regretted the decision. Longshore Prison would have been better than the dreams that haunted him from that terrifying night at sea.

"I am aware of the concerns with crossing into the mist," the gnome said. "The Golden Elves banished a great power on that island and protected it with an ancient magic," she said. "Prudence dictated their actions."

"It was more than prudence, Ms. Tanash," Jack said, shaking his head. "What they locked away hides a foreboding and corrupt spirit, one whose forces nay but those with the elf sight of yore can truly see and understand. I'm tellin' you, 'tis of a kind best left to legend."

The gnome leaned forward and lowered her voice. "All I want is the dragon's blood. Whatever jewels and treasure lie piled high around it are yours. Think of what you could do with that amount of wealth for the common folk..."

"I told you, that man is dead and gone." He poured the last of the rum. "I'm sorry Ms. Tanash, but you need someone with fool's gold in their eyes." He stood and wobbled, placing an arm on the chair to counter the drink. "Now, I'll be closing up shop for Cutty, so if you don't mind—"

"Wait." The gnome reached in her vest pocket and withdrew a scroll. "Let me sweeten the pot." She held out the parchment.

"Nothing you could offer me will change my mind."

"Not even your ship?" Coyness glimmered in her eyes.

Jack's stomach fluttered. *What is she on about?*

The gnome waved the scroll in the air, gesturing for him to take it. "Go on, *Captain*."

Jack reached for the parchment. Tattooed fingers pinched the tube of paper and untied its red ribbon. The strip of silk floated to the floor with slow and graceful ease. He unrolled the document:

Bill of Sale:

In consideration of the mutual covenants and agreements of Transferor and Transferee, in accordance with the laws of the Jeweled Isles, and under the auspices of the Regent, the following vessel is hereby transferred in ownership as of Midweek, Month: Halish, Year: 3182.

Ship: Lady Luck
Class: Sloop
Harbor: Lexton Bay, Ruby Islands
Hereby Sold: Sir Renald Halton, Esq., Earl of Garington.
Hereby Purchased: Ms. Scarlett Tanash.

Notary: Carlton Properties & Trading, Redtown, Ruby Island

The gnome grinned. "It's in my name... for now."

Trusty Jack sat back down. "She's still on the water?"

"*Lady Luck?* Oh yes, and quite the beauty. Refitted two years past. One of the finest older sloops sailing the Jewels, that's what they say. I've no idea about ships." The gnome shrugged. "She looks quite nice anchored in Benevolence Bay."

Benevolence? It was as if the space between the bookends in his life, a span of fourteen years, vanished. Long tomes, filled with blank pages straddled by a past of adventure and a future where he could have it back, fell from the shelf.

"I'll bet she'd look even better at sea," she added.

Jack stared at the deed.

"Sail me to Dragon Tail Island, Captain Hawk, and get me back safely, and *Lady Luck* is yours. Along with whatever treasure we find... other than the dragon's blood, of course."

The words reached Jack's ears, but he was a thousand nautical miles away. Hands gripping the wooden helm, a salty breeze caressing his cheek, the skull and crossbones flying proudly from the mast, the flap of the sails like music, and the shouts of the crew—

He looked up from the deed. His crew. And those closest to him—his irreplaceable longtime companions, the Salty Scoundrels. *Lady Luck* would be like a ghost ship, hollow and soulless without them.

What of their fates? he thought.

Like a guilt-laden treasure chest falling into the sea, his heart sank.

Big Rig was rotting in a cell. And what about Lana? She'd be out going on four years now if she'd survived her time inside. And poor Myron... the memory of his body lying on the deck, an arrow soaking the flour on his apron after Bonnie played her ruse off the coast of Benevolence Bay...

Nay, it wouldn't be the same without me hearties. He sighed.

"You're concerned about your old crew, I assume?" The gnome closed the compass and held it in front of her, examining the dragon ornamentation.

Jack rolled up the deed and stooped, grasping the ribbon off the floor. He tied it around the parchment.

The gnome gestured, halting him from offering it back.

"I've done some preliminary scouting," she said. "Your former quartermaster, Mr. Riggins, is locked in a cell at Longshore Prison."

"Aye, life sentence," Jack said and sat. He couldn't imagine what it'd been like for the dwarf to be back inside all these years.

"And your first mate... well, she proved a bit more difficult to track down."

"Lana?"

The gnome nodded. "She's on Emerald Island. In a small town a few miles inland. Liddleton, I believe it's called."

What in the blazes is that scallywag doing there? he thought. The cantankerous and ornery half-orc was living in a quiet little hamlet?

"I won't lie," the gnome said, "breaking out Mr. Riggins will be difficult, but not impossible."

"You can't be serious?"

"We are now in my area of expertise, Captain. As I said, difficult but not impossible. Your first mate, however." She rolled her eyes.

"What?"

"That may prove to be a bit more... complicated." The gnome placed her hands on the table. "I propose a secondary, related deal."

Jack scoffed. "I'm all ears, Ms. Tanash. Can't run a rig to match this nonsense."

"Good. Here it is, Jack. May I call you by your first name?"

"I prefer it, lass. Especially when my legs are on dry ground." He bumped his fist on the table like a gavel. "Of course, pirates be expecting reciprocity. You may not know it, Ms. Tanash, but our social rules work a bit differently aboard our ships. You landlubbers stick to your classes. But at sea people are voted into roles based on ability and respect, not birthright tosh or status nonsense."

The surprise on her face rose like a morning tide. "In that case, please call me Scarlett."

He gestured to proceed. "Mind you, Scarlett, I haven't agreed to your initial proposal."

"Here it is, Jack. Plain and straight. I'll assist with the recovery of your companions, and in exchange, you and your team accompany me to the Regent's Palace in Redtown to..." she hesitated, "steal the last of the blood iron from the treasury."

"Blow me down! Are you mad?"

"Not in the least," Scarlett said. "In fact, I believe it will prove easier to abscond with the legendary blood iron blade than recruit your former first mate in Liddleton."

"If you don't mind me askin', how are you going to forge a compass needle from that dagger? It would take someone with specialized smithy knowledge of—" Jack paused.

Blimey, she's good, he thought.

He pointed at her, grinning. "Not bad, Ms. Tanash. You got a schemer working."

Scarlett lowered her chin ever so slightly.

With a screech of chair legs, Jack stood, walked to the bar, and pulled another bottle from the shelf. He popped the cork with his teeth and spat it onto the counter.

Squawk!

"Alright, alright..." Trusty Jack picked up the cork and threw it in the basket. "Damn bird... shuteye time, Mr. Bentworth." He tossed the blanket over the macaw's cage and strode back to the table, filling both cups.

"Give me the gist," he said and sat. "Start to finish."

"First the mountain dwarf from Longshore," Scarlett said. "For obvious reasons. And then your half-orc first mate. From what I hear, she's handy should there be trouble."

If you can keep her powder keg from lighting.

"With your and their aid," Scarlett continued, "we'll sail to Redtown and get the dagger. Mr. Riggins forges the needle. Then, we make for Benevolence and sail *Lady Luck* to Dragon Tail Island. I get the dragon blood. You take the treasure." She raised a crimson eyebrow. "And I sign over the ship to you."

"You failed to mention the island's curse and the danger that's kept at bay along with it."

"Between *Lady Luck* and the legendary chest of gems and gold, I would think it's a fair exchange between risk and reward?"

She was sounding like a pirate.

"Dangerous business, this is." Jack shook his head. "And if something should happen to you before we make it back?"

"We've entered negotiations, have we?" She brushed a speck of lint from her vest. "Very well. Would an amended deed to the ship ease your concern?"

"Such as?"

"A clause that *Lady Luck* passes to you should unforeseen events cause my..." she hesitated, "failure to return."

"That sweetens the cauldron. But the stew's still tastin' short." Jack's pirate eyes scanned her face like a spyglass. "One thing troubles me still."

"Oh?"

"What's so important that it'll take you to thieving blood iron from the palace and sailing into the mists?"

"I've taken an interest in local politics."

"With respect, you're not even from the islands."

"I'm a change agent for hire, Jack. Albeit one with light fingers..."

He shook his head. "Not even getting my crew back, and my hands on the helm of *Lady Luck*, would make me accept an offer through that morning fog."

"It's time to shake things up in the Jewels." Scarlett leaned close and whispered, "You wouldn't mind some new leadership at the palace, would you, Jack?"

"I don't care about government, lass... past or present." He eased back in his chair. "All I care about now is me."

"Oh come Jack, I find that hard to believe. If I may be so bold... even with fourteen years gone past, I think your passion for fairness and equity in the Jewels is still as potent as this rum." She held up the bottle and shook it. "Here's a chance to help make it happen."

"And you need the dragon blood to do it?"

"This is not an assassination, if that's what you're thinking," she said. "The dragon's blood heals; it doesn't kill. If I wanted to take out the regent, I know the right people. But that doesn't solve the larger problem."

"And what problem be that, lass?"

"Politics." Her small arms spread wide like wings. "It trickles down from the palace in Redtown to the masses at the docks and villages across the Jeweled Isles. Look here Jack, we both have our reasons. Mine lean towards justice, I assure you... albeit through a rather cunning backdoor." A blue eye winked. "I won't even be breaking the law... well, with my end game. Sure, we free a prisoner and abscond with a priceless artifact, but beyond those violations once we complete the actual contract, my use of the dragon blood is more like working outside the boundaries of the law." She put a finger to her lip. "In fact, I do believe it's not so different from your pirating ways."

"I can't say I fancy any king or queen ruling from the palace."

"True to your reputation." She raised her glass. "Need I remind you that the longtime regent, who I understand you are quite fond of..." She smirked. "...will soon, by decree, complete his interim council monarchy to become the permanent and absolute ruler over the islands?"

How the time had passed. He had been a mere lad when Marian and Bonnie's father had stepped in for the absent queen. Jack had seen Lady Ricarda once when he was a child. Her royal galleon had sailed past Pelton Point en route to Emerald Island. The entire village had gone out on the peninsula to view it.

"There she is lad," his father had said in his ear, "in the fancy blue dress to aft... on the upper deck."

Jack, peering through his newly gifted spyglass, swept the circular lens to the rear of the ship. The queen sat in a regal chair, one hand on a bulge in her belly.

"That be the future king cooking in her oven," his father had said.

"How do you know it's a boy, pa?"

"We ain't sure, lad. But word is the arch mage done an augury that said so."

And then the queen and her ship had vanished. According to reports, they never made port after breaking into open water. With no one of direct royal lineage left, the seat passed to Markus Fitzwater, her half-brother. Born of a mistress and their father, the previous king, he had ruled as a regent with limited authority ever since.

"Jack?"

The pirate came back to the present, passing over the lost dream taken from him by the regent, and his life's course through a career of buccaneering up to Mayrotten Island.

Trusty Jack knocked back his rum. In less than a month, it would be forty years to the day since the queen vanished. According to the long-held succession laws, that was the span of time a regent, under the watchful eye of a temporary council made up of lesser nobles and high-ranking mages, had to preside as interim head of state before a new royal family was officially recognized as the rightful monarchs. Jack had no doubts about the exact date. The birthday present from his father two days prior to sighting the queen's ship made that certain. His heart sank at the loss of that spyglass. Another reason to damn fate that day when Bonnie Fitzwater took *Lady Luck* near Benevolence Bay.

But the gnome was right. The dissolution of the interim council, and Markus Fitzwater becoming the undisputed and absolute ruler of the isles, didn't bode well for anyone except the nobility and gentry. His track record was a rap sheet of heavy taxes, impressment gangs, species displacement, and ignorance of environmental protection in the Jewel Islands. And that didn't even address his dubious political agendas. Even so, there were limits to what a regent could do under the council monarchy and though Markus Fitzwater had found many a loophole for his political corruption, the new unbridled powers as king would unleash a potentially irreversible and permanent abuse of power.

Bollocks to all it, he thought and scoffed. *Useless to fight this flotsam and jetsam at my age. I'll have* Lady Luck *and me mates. That's good enough for me.*

He lifted his rum and gestured toward the gnome. "You do what you need to do, Scarlett. Frankly, I don't give a damn."

"Indeed…"

He held her stare.

"Well, I doubt that seeing the current regent replaced would upset your conscience," she said. "Add it as a bonus to the treasure and your ship… and I expect the scales are tipping towards conspiratorial justice?"

"I'm still here, aren't I?"

A thought had flickered as the gnome nudged him with baited words. Hidden behind his hard and experienced exterior, he wouldn't yet acknowledge the hope it could shine on his past. If the regent was indeed ousted, he might be able to expose what that bastard had done to him. Did he care about his official record? Not for a pence. He was a pirate. That reputation was a boost of salty clout among his hearties. One that he'd dressed in authentic and sordid evidence in the years that followed on the high seas. But try as he might to deny it, ousting the regent might clear his name with Marian… *Bah, you're dreamin', Jacky boy. That ship's long sailed. Far as she's concerned you've been sea asp bait for ten and four years.*

"Well," Scarlett said, "seems like we have an understanding?"

The anger he'd kept at bay with rum and hiding on Mayrotten Island got the better of him. "Understanding? That's pushing the barrel to the railing, Ms. Tanash." He leaned in. "Don't mistake it. You're playing bones with a fool if you think I don't know this don't all add up straight." Jack balled a hand into a fist, blood rushing through his veins. "I don't put my neck or those with me on a plank unless I know the score." He aimed a finger like an arrow. "If you send me sailin' to that island under false pretenses and hornswaggle me, I assure you that the kind-hearted pirate they speak of in my so-called legends will show you quite a different side of buccaneer practices. Let my name be a reminder... trust among thieves on an endeavor like this is the only way you survive."

"Indeed." Her blue eyes glimmered. "Thief's honor." She placed a tiny hand over her heart.

Jack grumbled, memories of pirate parlays gone wrong rising from the ashes of his former life.

"Now that I've sworn in," she said, "do you have any more questions for the witness?"

Jack remained earnest, the gnome's attempt at levity deflecting off his stoic armor. "How loose are the particulars?"

She examined one of her manicured nails. "There are some minor details that still need arranging."

"What be these 'minor details'?"

"Well, we'll need to locate a forge and whatnot." She waved a hand. "That kind of thing."

"Transportation?"

"I cover our fees over land and sea until we rendezvous with *Lady Luck* in Benevolence."

"What about a crew?"

"That's your purview, Jack. Funds aren't a problem. It's the tangibles."

It could be done. Big Rig mustered a pirate crew better than any seadog.

"It may be difficult convincing them of our destination," Jack said, "even if we fill their pockets."

"Do they need to know?"

"You've got a lot to learn about pirates, Scarlett. We ain't impressed sailors in the Royal Navy. They'll need to be privy to the ruse. It'll be 'no prey, no pay' after an initial compensation to join the crew of *Lady Luck*."

The gnome cocked her head.

"A share of the booty if we're successful."

"And if we're not?"

"Empty pockets, same as you and me."

"Fair enough. I'm starting to gain a new appreciation for pirates." She reached for the rum.

"Don't get overzealous," Jack said. "There's a wide range sailing the Jeweled Sea. Some of us be better than others when it comes to manners and interactions, especially with upper class folk."

Thunder clapped. The muffled scraping of taloned feet on wood emerged from under Mr. Bentworth's blanket.

"Some can be downright sinister and violent." He narrowed his eyes. "I don't need to mention the captain I'm referring to, savvy?"

"Oh yes, I 'savvy.'" Scarlett lifted her cup. "That infamous pirate came up more than once as we crossed the open water between Emerald and Topaz Islands ... and not in a good way."

It didn't surprise him to hear it. Being a rare and unique species, that scurvy dog had a lifespan of over two hundred years. She and her legendary ship were still marauding, and he suspected, leaving a trail of blood and death in their wake.

"So," Scarlett said, "are we agreed?"

Trusty Jack stared at his rum. A chance at gaining back *Lady Luck* and reuniting with the remaining Salty Scoundrels? There was an abundance of risk. It was plain to see in the destination and hear in the plans before they even got there.

Jack ran his eyes over the gnome. *You're holding a strong hand*, he thought. And yet, he still felt like they were playing with a stacked deck. It was all too easy and at the ready. Each question he asked had an answer. Each concern had a solution. *'Minor details that still need arranging.'* Those words were like a hazard buoy's bell ringing in the fog. *And after that?* he thought and shivered.

Setting course for Dragon Tail Island. Was he mad?

The Dreg's comforts stared him down. *What is left for you here, Jack? Twenty, maybe thirty-odd years of half-drunken boredom?*

At least with Ms. Tanash he'd be on the sea, *Lady Luck's* planks under his boots. That ship was the closest thing he had left to a companion. He'd lost the other one so long ago the memories were fading into a dream.

The compass, with its ghostly icon, eyed him from the table.

Where and how had the thief gotten her tiny hands on it?

Whoever removed that needle did the Jewels a service worthy of a statue and song. He knew exactly what was on that island. The ancient map detailing the tomb, which he'd put into the little girl's protection when the commodore commandeered *Lady Luck,* told a horrifying and dangerous tale of obstacles and unspoken terrors. Had Precious survived? Was the tube now buried somewhere in the Jewels under lock and key? *Oh, the irony,* he thought. He'd sworn to himself he'd never set shovel to the sand that he intended to bury it in had they reached Benevolence and not been caught that day. And here was fate, bringing the Dragon Tail Compass to him in the hands of a resourceful and cunning thief.

Risk and danger. Ain't that a pirate's life?

If they survived, he'd be free. Back on the high seas with his ship and his best mates. And if not? *Well, then it's Davy Jones Locker.*

An old fire sparked like hoisting a sail. Trusty Jack raised his cup. "Here's to piratin', Ms. Tanash." He swigged the rum. "You've got yourself a deal."

"Excellent!" Scarlett knocked back her drink.

"Now," he said, "you came in on that charter out there, aye?" He aimed a finger at the window facing the dock. "When are they fitting to depart? Will it be with the morning tide or—"

"Tingle!"

Jack followed Scarlett's gaze. The luminous sprite collided with the windowpane, trails of sparks bursting forth with each impact.

The gnome dashed over and threw it open. "What is it, Tingle?"

The sprite swirled and danced about.

"We need to move up our departure," Scarlett said, eyes wide with fear.

Jack hastened over and peered out. Beyond the sawtooth fence, the dark shadow of land rose toward the island's volcanic peak. Blood-red eyes by the dozen glowed like molten fireflies in the night.

A fierce roar echoed in the distance. Another answered, closer.

"Jungle orcs!" he said.

"What's happening? Why—"

"It's the compass. Drawing the beasts to the magic."

Squawk!

Scarlett tucked Tingle into her pocket.

"Show a leg!" Jack dragged her towards the entrance.

"This is terrible!" she said. "We need to get to the ship!"

Crash! The unmistakable sound of a section of fence smashing to the ground reached his ears.

"Too late," Jack said.

3

WEIGH ANCHOR

Trusty Jack dashed to the entrance and slammed a fist into the wall. The cutlass hanging over the doorway dropped into his hand and he thrust it into the gut of an orc bursting into The Dreg.

The beast's red eyes widened, a growl drowning in blood rising from its throat. Jack lifted a leg and kicked the brute back, freeing his blade. He swung the cutlass a second time, slicing through its neck. The orc crumpled to the floor.

"Come on!" He pushed through the beads.

Rain pelted down, turning the dirt lanes to mud. A scream rang out from a side alley. In the darkened street, Jack caught sight of the dwarf from The Dreg heaving her axe to and fro, warding off three fury-filled orcs.

"Make for the ship!" he told Scarlett. "I'll be right—"

Before he could finish, two of the orcs surrounding the dwarf fell, daggers in their throats. The gnome winked and dashed toward the dock.

Blood-thirsty beasts ran to and fro, wreaking destruction. Jungle orcs were feral and relied on brute strength for dominance. Driven to madness by the compass's eerie magic, their fists and shoulders crashed down doors and ripped planks off shacks with no quarter.

"This is madness!" It was Berilda, the dwarf. She released a severed orc head from her grip and kicked it down the street. "Filthy creatures."

"Where's Cutty?" Jack asked, looking about.

"He went for the skiff," she said. "The old twins are roundin' up who they can."

"The orcs should retreat once I—"

"Look out!" The dwarf thrust him aside.

Pain ripped through Jack's arm as Berilda's axe whirred by his ear. An orc fell next to him, splashing in the mud. The thick curved steel of the dwarf's weapon lay embedded in its chest.

Jack checked his shoulder. Thankfully, he'd only been scratched by the beast's claws. If it were the tusk, a deadly toxin in the creature's saliva would be running through his system.

"Jack!"

Scarlett waved from down the street and pointed at the dock.

Two orcs barreled around a corner, making straight for her. The gnome ducked against a wall. With the grace of a dancer, she swung her cloak up and wrapped it about her. Like sugar stirred into tea, her form dissolved. The orcs halted, grunting and breathing in heavy gasps, confused. One roared in frustration and they ran on.

Full of surprises, she is, Jack thought.

"Make for the skiff, Berilda," the pirate said. "Get on the water. Once I'm away on that there ship," he pointed at the sloop, "it should pass."

"What should pass?"

"This madness!" Now it was Jack's turn. He lunged over the dwarf, crashing into an approaching orc. They fell to the ground. He raised his cutlass, aiming the handle at the beast's face. Hairy, vise-like fingers gripped his throat, halting his blow before it could land. Jack's face flushed and swelled. His ribs froze, stomach muscles wrenching against his tightened windpipe. He needed air! Where was Berilda?

With pirate instinct, Jack sent a knee crashing into the orc's groin.

Its grip on his throat loosened and he heaved in a breath. "Bloody beast!" He slammed the handle into the creature's face and it went limp.

"Berilda!"

Jack turned as the dwarf's axe splashed into the mud. Her legs kicked wildly, struggling against the orc that had her off the ground, its thick hand on her throat.

Jack lunged. Before he reached her, a bolt of lightning shot up through the orc's legs. Its hand released the dwarf and the beast exploded into black ash. Tingle hovered in the void where the orc had been.

"Jack!" Scarlett was back, pulling on him. "We have to go."

"Get to the skiff," he told a bewildered Berilda. "Trust me, lass." He shook her out of the daze. "As soon as that sloop gets out of the harbor, this will pass and the orcs will retreat."

"You're leaving?"

"Aye." There was no time to explain. "You want to sail with me? For adventure and death?"

Berilda smirked. "Tempting as it is, someone's got to stay and keep these drunkards safe."

Jack slapped her on the shoulder. "Get to the skiff. No heroics."

She heaved her axe up and over a shoulder. "Farewell, Jack." The dwarf bowed her chin. "It's good to see your spirit again."

He always sensed she knew more than she let on. The dwarf was good folk.

Roar!

A dozen red-eyed figures crashed like a wave through the broken fence.

"Move! All of you!" Jack shouted and darted for the dock.

"Tingle!"

In the corner of his eye, Jack caught the sprite darting back into The Dreg.

"Tingle! No!" Scarlett shouted.

Jack yanked the gnome along. "To the boat!"

Stride after stride they ran through the muck and mud. Without halting, Scarlett flung a dart underhanded at an approaching orc, placing the shot squarely between its eyes. It fell like a giant oak as they passed. The way the beast lost control of its limbs, Jack guessed the blade was doused with a potent toxin.

Squawk!

Mr. Bentworth flew over his shoulder, heading for the beach.

"Tingle, hurry!" Scarlett shouted.

Jack risked a glance back and wished he hadn't. At least two dozen orcs were rushing down the street, mere steps behind the tiny sprite who had freed the macaw from its cage.

Planks creaked as he and Scarlett leapt onto the rickety dock.

"Push off!" a sea elf shouted from the ship's railing. "Ship away!"

Whoever captained the chartered sloop could share a rum bottle with him anytime. They'd brought the boat about and it sat, sails half out, ready to run.

Without asking permission, Jack reached down and grabbed Scarlett. He leapt. They crossed the gap and tumbled down on deck, crashing into a crate.

"Away! Away!" another sailor shouted.

Jack stood and scanned the beach. In the shadowy darkness, he made out the old twins from the bar holding the skiff in knee-deep water. Berilda was on board, her small shadow unmistakable.

"Sink me!" Jack said, following the shoreline.

Cutty, the Dreg's one-armed bartender, ran at a clip towards the skiff with a drunken Hardy slumped over his shoulder. An orc pursued them, gaining with every stride. Berilda and the others shouted encouragement from the boat.

"Bow! Give me a bloody bow!" Jack shouted, throwing aside crates.

"Sir!" A sea elf handed him an elegant longbow. "You'll not make that shot from here. Not in this dark."

"Bollocks I won't!" Jack spat over the side for luck and nocked the arrow. He drew back the bowstring. It had been fourteen years since his fingers touched a hempen line but it felt like no more than a day. He gauged the distance—the ship's movement, the wind swirling the rain... He held his breath and aimed between Cutty and the orc.

Twang!

The arrow vanished in the darkness.

Miss!

The orc swiped, its claws cracking Hardy's dangling jug of rum. The drunkard kept his grip on what was left of the handle.

"Tingle, hurry!" Scarlett shouted somewhere to aft.

"Give me another!" Jack demanded, hand out.

A cedar shaft landed in his palm and he nocked the second arrow. As he sighted, he thought he saw Hardy mouth a curse at the orc as he dangled over Cutty's shoulder.

"The orc's got them, sir," the sea elf said.

'Just you and the arrow, boy.' His father's words rang in his ear.

Jack exhaled and released the shot.

The orc sprung.

As if hit by an invisible wave, the beast twisted in the air and rolled away.

"Blarney's Britches, but that was a shot!" the sailor said.

Through the chaos, the sound of Cutty splashing in the shallows and the shouts of the twins crossed the harbor.

The ship pitched. Jack caught himself on the railing. He reached out too late and the sea elf next to him tumbled overboard.

Gurgles and bubbling filled the pirate's ears as a dark shape broke the water's surface. Long fleshy fangs opened at the center of a bulbous head and swallowed the sailor alive.

"What is that?" Scarlett peered over the side.

"Don't know, lass. The compass be drawing it from the deep."

"We're held fast!" a deckhand shouted.

"Look!" A sailor pointed at the dock.

Orcs were in the water, making their way to the ship.

"Tingle, hurry!" Scarlett waved, encouraging her companion.

The sprite shot forward across the open water.

Again, the monster rose. It lashed out with tentacles for the mast.

Jack eyed the massive limbs. "We're done for..."

The creature's head broke the surface. Fleshy fangs opened wide, emitting an eerie groan of triumph.

The sprite halted halfway to the sloop. It bounced up and down, communicating with its longtime companion.

"No!" Scarlett shook her head and dashed to stern. "No, Tingle. Don't!"

Jack caught himself on the railing as the ship tilted from the pull of the monster.

Scarlett crashed down on deck, tumbling to the rail.

Like a falling star, Tingle plunged into the creature's gaping mouth.

Boom!

A burst of light sent a luminous shock wave over the harbor. The beast's grip on the mast fell away.

Nothing of the mouth or head remained, only ripples of darkened water swirling with viscous liquid and scraps of strange and eerie sea flesh.

"Sail! Away!" the captain shouted.

Jack ran to Scarlett, lifting her up and on her feet. Through the rail's openings, he watched as the distance grew between the ship and the orcs thrashing in the water.

"Sailor!" Jack waved over a sea elf. "Give me eyes o'er there." He pointed to where the skiff had pushed off the shore.

The sea elf squinted. "Aye, the skiff's away. I see two men, a dwarf, and two half-orcs... sorry sir, but one of them half-orcs don't look like he made it. Slumped over the side he is..."

"Nay, lad." Jack slapped the sailor on the back. "That's just Hardy being Hardy. Lad's three sheets and footloose."

"Looks like a macaw landed on the bow."

"Aye, that would be Mr. Bentworth."

The sea elf's spiky-ridged ears twitched. "That shot you made, sir. Had a bit of magic on it, didn't it?"

Trusty Jack shook his head. "Desperation, lad. And a bit of family legacy."

"Jack, are we ..." Scarlett's voice cracked and she wiped her eyes. "... are we still in danger?"

The pirate waited until the sea elf moved out of earshot.

"The sooner we head west," he said, voice low, "the sooner the compass's power lessens." As he spoke, the edges of shadowy jungle passed as the ship exited the cove. Rain fell, but already it was starting to lessen. Jack examined the sky. The storm was moving on, heading east.

He wiped rain and sweat from his face. "We'll be turning to starboard in a moment, lass. Soon as we do the safer we get."

"Mind my pardon," a sea elf said, approaching, "but if you need that shoulder patched head down to the galley. The old healer can get you mended. He's blind as a bat but works the herbs well on touch."

Jack nodded his thanks. He took a moment to assess the sloop. As far as his seafaring eyes could tell, no serious damage from the sea monster would hinder their progress.

"Lass," he said, kneeling next to her, "I'm sorry about yer sprite."

"Come on." Scarlett turned away quickly from him and made for the helm.

Aye, Jack thought. *I understand.* He followed the gnome across the deck.

"Set a course for Ruby Island," Scarlett said, approaching the captain.

"Aye, Miss."

Trusty Jack followed the back and forth of the helm as the sea elf sought the sweet spot on their tack. Her amber eyes focused on the sail overhead, reading the tautness of the canvas. The ship pulled against its course, rudder fighting the passing storm's lingering crosswinds.

As if falling into a feather bed, Jack's body eased.

Back at sea, he thought and grinned.

The chaos and danger he'd left behind on Mayrotten Island a moment earlier paled next to the simple love for the open water and a steady breeze. He might live to regret his decision, but no price could match the salty satisfaction of nautical life. The pitch of the hull, the splashing of swells as the bow cut the sea... all he needed were his companions back and the grip of a helm. Would *Lady Luck* really be his if they pulled this off?

"Take us around the eastern shores of Ruby Island," the gnome said. "I would like to avoid drawing attention."

Jack caught an all-too familiar edge to Scarlett's voice. Tingle's demise may have saved them, but the cost was plain to hear in the thief's tone.

"We're not heading to the capital, then?" The captain looped the steering rope on a wheel pin to lock the ship's rudder.

Jack stepped forward, joining them. To the northwest, the storm's edge gave way to familiar constellations. The captain would use the stars to steer them. Jack too preferred celestial navigation over a compass. On his first sea adventure, he had sailed on a pirate vessel under the command of Lady Lash. Also a sea elf, and quite a nasty one, she had taught him the navigational art and a great many other valuable seafaring lessons besides.

"No," Scarlett said, "make for Longshore."

"Longshore? All respect, Miss. Nothin' there but a small village... and the prison on the point."

"Indeed, I'm meeting a colleague at the inn."

The captain's ears twitched in the sea elven response of approval. "'Tis a safe passage along that coast," she said. "Easy pay. I'll chart a course."

With the sails full and the ship breaking into open water, the hull settled. The three stood silent as moonlight broke through the clouds. Cool and stoic, it shimmered on the surface of the sea. As if reflecting a majestic starry sky, an array of glimmering colors dappled the gentle swells as schools of jellyfish caught the light.

"All or nothing now, Jack." Scarlett looked up at him.

"Aye, lass," he said, and put a hand on her shoulder. "Let it be fair winds and following seas."

"I'll drink to that," the captain said, and reached for a jug of rum. "And to seein' us put distance from that island."

Jack glanced back at the shadowy contours of Mayrotten's shores. He too felt a renewed vigor with every swell they crested heading west. A mixed blessing, for he knew that the diminishing sight of the haunting isle wouldn't be his last. If they were sailing to Dragon Tail Island, they'd pass this way again.

He accepted the jug from the captain and swigged.

And through that bloody mist.

❧ 4 ❧

GROUNDSWELL

❦

Marian Fitzwater sat beside the straw bed and waited for the child's breathing to ease. Morning light beamed through the open window, illuminating motes of dust in the humid air. She dunked a rag in her bucket, wringing it out and dabbing the half-elf's forehead. The girl stirred, mumbling inaudible words.

"Rest," Marian whispered, and tucked a loose curl of blonde hair behind the child's pointed ear. "The spell will soon ease the—"

"Pardon the intrusion, my lady."

"You're not intruding, Sargeant. You know that." Marian repeated the action, soaking the rag and dabbing the girl's cheeks.

"Yes, quite right, my lady." The man ducked to pass through the doorway.

"And I've told you about that title." Marian eyed her personal guard.

Sir Roderick had been like the returning tide through the passing years. Never once during three decades of service had he faltered from protocol. Honor and duty, as the soldier often reminded her, were of the utmost importance for a Knight of the Red Order.

"Another with the fever?" Sir Roderick's plate armor clanked as he crossed the bedroom.

Marian nodded, adjusting her blue robe. "And it's going to be hot today."

The mage ran her eyes over the rash flushing the girl's skin. Prickly specks on her tan forearms, bright red minutes earlier, were fading to a softer pink. At least the spell would stave off the worst of it.

An arrival horn sounded from the harbor, echoing through the alleyways and bouncing off the district's haphazardly stacked, multi-colored buildings. As usual for mid-morning, Redtown's eastern port was alive with activity, the urban music of its seaside in full swing. Creaks of pulleys bounced along side streets as cargo was offloaded from supply-laden ships. Merchants called from dockside stalls, announcing the daily catch and competitive prices. A chorus of gulls, their white specks like daylight stars against the cloudless blue sky, sang in a steady rhythm.

"Raaak!"

Marian followed a greka's flight as it bullied the gulls over the docks. The large and solitary bird, native to the Jewel Islands, was a common sight along the coast. Its red and white coloring, with feather-less web-skinned wings and a bone-white beak like a lance had earned the species its nickname: little dragon.

The greka shot back and forth, arcing over an arriving galleon's royal colors. To think that there was a time when golden dragons, a hundred times a greka's size, did much the same thing in this very harbor.

That was another age, Marian thought, *and a better time for our city.*

"The regent wishes to see you, my lady. Lunch at the palace," the Red Knight said.

She sighed. *Of all the days.*

"Your sister will also be in attendance." The knight crossed the morning light to the window, the famous fire-enchanted greatsword strapped at the center of his back. Reflections bounced off his plate armor, dancing over worn timbers and peasant furnishings—knick-knacks, a crude portrait of a long dead relative, and a stack of dried flowers bundled atop a clothes dresser.

"Then we better get a start." Marian tucked the blanket around the half-elf's chest. If Bonnie was attending, then this was an official family gathering and not one of her father's whimsical annoyances. She had little doubt that it pertained to his upcoming inauguration. Not that any of it mattered or affected her, not after the unforgivable decision she'd made two decades earlier.

Sir Roderick turned from the window. "My lady, seeing how the heat is up, I sent the page to fetch your horse."

Marian ignored the use of her title. "Well then the mare will have an easy walk uphill to the palace with the rest of us," she said and stood. "I'm not riding past a thousand Redtowners who are using their feet."

"I thought you'd say that," Sir Roderick grumbled.

"You *knew* I'd say that, old friend." She patted his plate-armored shoulder. "And yet you brought it anyway."

The Red Knight mumbled something about "standard protocol and maybe this time I thought you'd reconsider..."

Marian examined Sir Roderick in the window's light. Like sparking embers, the tight gray curls running around his onyx forehead caught the sun's rays. He removed a red glove, adjusted his eye patch, and wiped the sweat from his burned and scarred flesh.

A flash of the man's younger face, before he'd been disfigured defending her father's caravan, crossed Marian's memory. The knight had a full head of hair then, ash brown and textured, and two working eyes. His proud and earnest expression had been the spitting image of knighthood, but whatever youthful optimism ran in his veins died that day along with the Magma Giant that left him the sole surviving defender from the lance company assigned as the regent's travel protection.

That incident grew to infamy among his order as both a tragedy and a heroic demonstration of the order's dedication as public servants. Three days into the journey, at Roundhorn Pass, they were forced to turn back after the horrifying attack. A badly wounded Sir Roderick was transported to the capital—a long recovery followed. One that Marian's mentor oversaw and that she cut her healing teeth on. As for the cause of the attack, whatever had drawn the solitary and aloof creature out from the volcanic caves above the mountain pass was never discovered.

After that near fatal incident, Sir Roderick had been assigned as her personal guard. An honor worthy of his dedication and bravery, and one that had proved impotent with the life decision she had made shortly thereafter.

"Something amiss, my lady?"

Marian shook off the memory. "No, Sargeant. Just lost in thought." She gathered her things and stopped before the dresser mirror. Her own face stared back at her. *How the years have changed you as well,* she thought. The black hair that had been as pitch as a jungle panther was now streaked with strands of white, as if the salt of the sea ran through her veins. Her brown eyes, with their signature sleek and narrow design from her half-elven blood, pulled to angular points toward her ears. Creases and wrinkles punctuated what had been a porcelain-like surface in her youth. It wasn't that she was old, but middle age had moved in and unpacked its bags, with no intention of leaving.

Marian tied her waist-length hair up into a bun. As she lowered her arms, sunlight crossed her neck and sent a flash back from the mirror. She paused, staring at the pendant of Telathia that lay between the blue-trimmed edges of her mage's robe.

Would you even recognize me now? she thought, surveying her appearance.

"My lady... we really should get—"

"Of course." She turned to face her escort. "Duty calls."

The Red Knight led the way through to the main room.

"How's my sweet Irina?" The girl's mother wrung her hands.

"Your daughter's got the fever," Marian said, stepping into the main room of the humble abode. "It's early and that's good." She put a hand on the woman's shoulder. Even a simple touch, she had learned from her mentor, could soothe as much as an herbal remedy. "I cast a mild water elemental spell to counter the rash's fire." She released her hand from the woman's arm and smiled. "It's already going down."

"I can't thank you enough, Mage Marian. We can't, I mean my husband and me... Irina's always running about the docks to try and help with our earnings. This and that she does, but you know what passes around down there." The woman shook her head. "Well, you probably don't frequent that part of town... seeing your status and all."

"The healers of my order are there as much as any other citizen of Redtown, especially when treating the sick and wounded."

The woman lowered her head. "My apologies, I didn't mean to bring up—"

"You're fine." Marian smiled and gestured for Sir Roderick to wait outside. "The Order of Telathia serves all in need regardless of status. We're *all* citizens of this city."

The woman nodded and hastened to a chest along the wall. "I want to give something as a donation... we've got a bit saved from—"

"Keep it." Marian held up a hand. "Use it to get these herbs." She pulled out a small notebook and stick of charcoal and scribbled down a list of items. "Do you know your letters, Miss?"

The mother shook her head. "My husband does. The sea elves take pride in passing it down, but he's at sea."

"No matter. I'm putting my personal mark on this." She tore out the piece of parchment and placed it on the supper table. "The alchemist will recognize it. You'll get the best price and need not have to worry about quality. I want you to divide the ravensfiddle, yester blooms, and rosemary into three equal piles. Mix one of each so you have three of the same. Then steep a tea each day until it turns the color of red velvet. Give it to Irina first thing every morning."

"One a day at sunup for three days. Thank you."

"If, as I suspect, she's on the mend when you finish the treatment then you can start her back on simple foods."

"Oh, thank you, Mage Marian." The woman clasped her hands.

"And keep her hydrated. She'll resist due to the tea's effect but use a mother's touch." It still felt strange saying that after all these years of service, seeing how she'd neither married nor bore a child. "Let her move about that room if she likes but don't allow her to leave the house. Both for her sake and that of other children."

"'Tis a shame they don't be giving the remedies out to the young'uns anymore." The peasant shook her head. "But hard times are hard times. It's enough for your father—" Her eyes widened. "Pardon my words, Mage Marian! I mean the regent... he has it hard enough even with the amount of taxes we can give."

Indeed, Marian thought, hiding her frustration with a compassionate nod. The head of her order had told her father, and the council, that it was a mistake to stop the distribution of preventatives, but they were convinced it was no longer needed. That, and their priorities were elsewhere.

They always are, she thought.

Clang! Clang! Clang!

"Is that three bells already?" Marian asked, the neighboring district's temple sounding in the distance. "I must be on my way." She adjusted her robe and stepped out onto the street.

The heat was indeed up. The late morning sun, close to its noon zenith, blazed down on the colorful wooden exteriors in Eel Town. She held up a hand to shield the light and gazed north. Beyond the district's residential neighborhoods, past the ornate buildings dominating the Guild Square, a ring of greenery rose like a verdant collar to mark a boundary both literal and symbolic.

Marian tilted her head back, her eyes passing over the gardens to the walls of the palace. The ostentatious architecture rose behind it in overstated majesty.

"A fading jewel presiding over an endless sea," she whispered.

"My lady?"

"Nothing, Sargeant," Marian said and started off. "Just admiring the view."

5

A CRACKED EGG

The ruggedness of Ruby Island's northern coast appealed to Scarlett's taste for defiance. Bone white cliffs, obstinate in the face of a pounding sea, ran in endless succession northward to the cape. Two currents met in the nearby waters and the result was a region defined by a hard, wind-driven topography. Rocky peninsulas speckled with bent and withered cypresses added to its spartan elegance. Nestled in the sheltered coves between the weather-beaten promontories, the familiar tropical ecosystem endured. Palms persisted along the shorelines, but the mangroves and abundant plant life of the island's central and southern regions were absent, replaced by sandy stretches of grasslands and flowering fruit trees tucked between towering cliffs.

"Bring back memories?" Scarlett joined Trusty Jack at the ship's bow.

The pirate gazed at the stone fortress looming ahead on the nearest peninsula. It rose as if pushed upward from the rock itself on the farthest tip, overlooking the sea.

"Nay, lass. My mind was a thousand leagues from here. 'Fore I ever set eyes on that bloody prison."

"What is that?" She pointed at a contraption extending from the ramparts.

"That be a Hempen Halter."

"A what?"

"A gallows, lass. For Jack Ketch."

"Who's Jack Ketch?"

Trusty Jack raised an eyebrow. "The hangman. If you go dancin' with him, well..."

Scarlett narrowed her eyes. A thin, indistinct noose dangling from the gallows grew legible. "How do they retrieve the body? I mean, afterwards..."

Trusty Jack pulled a cheroot out of his shirt pocket and walked to the coal bucket. Taking the tongs, he pinched a smoldering cube and touched it to the tip of the rolled tobacco, puffing away until it glowed red. Smoke as dark as rum belched from the sides of his mouth and vanished to stern.

It fits him, she thought. *A very pirate look.*

"Trades blow onshore in the north," Jack said, returning to the rail. "Sea's pungent, lass, but a rotting corpse... well. It keeps you up at night." He took a drag and stared up at the prison. "Guards always got a rise out of it. Takes about four days for the gulls to pick it clean."

An uneasy tide rose in her belly. Looking up at his chiseled profile against the backdrop of ropes and sails, she was reminded that the man had been through a lifetime of hardships. She'd been briefed on his biography by the Thieves Guild, covering the most important events that made him a pirate and a lone wolf who'd run away from the world, but omission of personal details kept his role as an asset straightforward and uncomplicated. These small moments of life experience punctured a hole in the professional waterskin.

"Bah," he said and puffed. "Most of them who hanged were filthy bilge rats. The Jewels are better off without them." He examined his cheroot. "These elvish smokers meet my approval. Right nice of the captain to offer."

Scarlett steadied herself with a hand on the rail as they turned to port. Sea spray shot over the side as the hull rose and fell, crossing the southward swells.

She let the mist relieve the afternoon heat on her cheeks.

"Lower sails!"

The quartermaster's voice set off a nautical call and answer as the crew transitioned for the glide into Longshore's harbor. Two sea elves passed, each holding an end of a long plank. An intricately carved and brightly painted ship's name ran on its side.

Clever, she thought, watching as a third sailor lowered herself over the side and hammered the plank over the ship's actual name.

"Got us an extra set of sails too," one of the sea elves who carried the lumber said. He wiped his hands and approached Trusty Jack.

"Lad, in all my years at sea, I never thought of doing that." The pirate took a puff on his cheroot. "Right prudent of the captain, that is."

"Aye, different thread count and stained the color of wine. When we're back at sea we'll take an afternoon and switch these back out."

Scarlett followed his thumb as the sea elf pointed at the lowered white sails. "And unmask *Felicity's Favor* so she can sail under her rightful name... innocent and carefree."

The sailor moved on to tasks related to their arrival.

After they dropped anchor, she and Trusty Jack would row in on a dinghy and meet her contact. Unfortunately, her update would be a mix of success and failure. Already, there were complications to her plans from the debacle escape at Mayrotten Island.

Scarlett shrugged. *One step at a time.*

Cool air tickled her exposed skin as the cliffs hugging the cove blocked the sun. She closed her eyes, embracing the blanket of calm as the noise of the open sea faded.

She'd been gaining an appreciation for arrivals in port. They brought a strange relief and yet were countered by regret at the loss of nautical freedom. Sailing out of sight of land had quite taken hold of her. It had become thrilling and liberating in a way foreign to her before she'd set off to the Jewels; she found herself attracted to the call of the sea. It hadn't passed her notice that Trusty Jack's spirits had risen when they'd broken into open water after fleeing Mayrotten Island.

"Drop anchor!" The shout of the quartermaster echoed over the placid water, bouncing back off the rocky cliffs.

Scarlett opened her eyes to a view of a quaint seaside hamlet. A dozen fishing boats lay anchored close to shore. Beyond, a line of seafront homes in bold colors, fronted by market stalls, ran along the wharf. Residents milled about, complimented by pockets of gulls circling where food and fishing scraps offered easy pickings.

She spotted the inn's sign on a street leading away from the harbor.

"Can't say I'm looking forward to dry land," Jack said.

"Think if it as one step closer to *Lady Luck*."

"Aye." The pirate spat on his palm and snubbed out the cheroot.

"Plus, I hear the inn is rather cozy," Scarlett said. "More so than the accommodations on the cliff."

"Truth to that, lass," Trusty Jack said. "Now, what be the plan?"

"Meeting a colleague."

"Right. And then?"

"Not here," she said. "Wait until we're ashore and away from others' ears."

The pirate gave her a knowing nod and tapped his nose. "Ashore it is."

Scarlett made her way to the dinghy, following Jack's earnest strides.

If my contact's here to meet us, she thought. If not, things were going to hit a roadblock and fast. The only way to find out was to check for a marker outside the inn.

۞

THE CRYING GULL INN HAD THE LOOK OF ANY STANDARD VILLAGE accommodation catering to a traveling clientele. Close enough to the harbor for traders and merchants to access the wharf, as well as host the infrequent family member visiting loved ones at the prison, and yet far enough back from the docks to be free of the potent aromas that saturated the seaside streets of any fishing town.

Below the hanging wooden sign with its crudely carved seagull, the door to the tavern lay open. Scarlett's gnomish ears twitched at the clanking of dishes that accented the inn's steady stream of afternoon banter. Without stopping, she strode up to the building's corner.

"This is north?" she asked, peering about.

Jack nodded.

Her eyes roamed the teak siding.

"What are you seekin', lass?"

Scarlett checked the passersby and waited until a human woman with a bucket of fish rounded a corner. She pushed aside a clump of daisies.

"You've got to be kidding," she muttered, reading the thieves' cant scratched on the siding.

"What's the matter?" Jack bent down at her side.

"Oh, I found it!" she exclaimed and knelt as if picking something up. "Look at that, aren't we lucky." She smiled so the half-orc passing with a cartload of shellfish would observe her relief.

As she had hoped, the cunning pirate picked up on her cue.

"You're right lucky there, miss. Could have been lost forever." Trusty Jack leaned down and spoke in her ear. "What's wrong?"

"It's not worth explaining. We're fine."

"Fine tends to lean into the wind..."

"My colleague isn't here."

"Isn't here?" Jack's face shifted. He pulled aside the flowers. "That be thieves' cant, that is. Seen it used in Longshore. You said your colleague—"

She held out a tiny hand. Surprisingly, the pirate halted. "It's fine, Jack. Someone from the guild is here to meet us this evening, but not who I requested."

"Is that a problem?"

"Not for you." She sighed. "Just for me."

"That morning fog in your words is rolling in again..."

"You'll see soon enough. Come on." She clasped his shirt sleeve and pulled him back towards the harbor. "Let's kill some time. We'll take a walk around the wharf. Afterwards we can head to the inn and get our rooms before the meetup."

"Don't believe in killin' time," Jack said as they walked down the cobblestones. "That's for those who don't cherish life's ticking clock."

She jumped in front of him, walking backwards. "This from someone who spent how many years at The Dreg on Mayrotten Island?"

Trusty Jack grumbled something about fancy words and books.

6

SCALLYWAG

꧁꧂

S carlett descended the steps from the inn's second floor, steadying herself with a stretched hand on the railing overhead. She'd concluded that Longshore didn't see many smaller folk. Not only were the rooms designed with taller guests in mind, but the common areas such as this one lacked the usual accommodations—two-tier railings on stairs for a start. So far, from her observation around town, Longshore was comprised mostly of humans and half-orcs. Sea elves were about on the docks, but their anchored ships provided hammocks and cabins for rest. Not a dwarf to be seen since their arrival. That would hopefully change soon.

She halted at the bottom step and ran her gaze over the tavern's patrons.

"Left corner, Jack," she said and made for a table lit by a candle sitting low in a bowl.

"Good evening," a gnome said, his hood still up and his face in shadow.

"What are you doing here, Doni?" Scarlett climbed up and into a chair.

Jack took the one across from her, giving them both a line of sight through the room. It was good to have a pirate alongside her when out and about. They understood tactical advantages in social settings without having to be schooled on the basics.

"Took you long enough." The gnome lowered his hood. A neatly trimmed beard and hair the color of a ruddy sunset framed a face full of enthusiasm.

Too much enthusiasm, Scarlett thought.

"I've been going out of my mind in this one-dinghy town." The gnome twisted the curl of his waxed mustache, grinning like a cheshire cat. "You were supposed to be here two days—"

"Why are *you* here?" Scarlett leaned in.

"What'll it be?" The Crying Gull's human owner wiped his hands on the apron at his belly.

"Rums all around, Samath," Jack said.

At hearing the proprietor's name, Scarlett recalled the pirate's outgoing and friendly demeanor when they'd booked their rooms. He'd wisely employed a cover name to avoid identification, even if it'd been fourteen years since his so-called death at sea. Nevertheless, even as "Mr. Morgan," Trusty Jack's friendly and laidback personality had quickly won over the innkeeper.

"Stew's fresh today," Samath said. "Three bowls?"

"By luck of eights, it wouldn't be fish stew, Samath, would it?" Trusty Jack raised an eyebrow.

"How did you ever guess, Mr. Morgan!" The proprietor's barrel-sized belly bounced as he bellowed a hearty laugh. "We decided to do something special for a change. In fact," he eyed the chalkboard behind the bar, "perhaps I better replace 'stew' with 'fish stew' on the board."

Now it was Jack's turn to laugh. "Aye, three stews, mate." The pirate looked to the two of them for confirmation. Scarlett nodded, as did Doni.

"Samath, lad," Jack asked, "Is that there half-orc at the bar drinking a Longshore Porter?"

"Indeed."

"Gimme a pint on the side, if you would be so kind." Jack's eyes brightened. "Anyone else?"

Scarlett shook her head and spoke for her colleague as well. "We're both fine."

"Coming right up." Samath crossed to the bar like a buoy heaving back and forth on the sea.

"What were you asking me?" Doni said to her. "A pleasure to meet you, by the way." He nodded at Trusty Jack. "We haven't been properly introduced... Doni Tarnackle."

"James Hawk. Call me Jack, lad."

Doni nodded. Scarlett picked up on the nervousness in the gnome's tone. She'd be intimidated too if she were in his shoes.

"They had to re-route Renato to a botched job in the Raison Quarter," Doni said, meeting her gaze. "I was in the den when they were discussing it." The thief grew an inch taller in his seat with the brag. "The *main* den under the market, mind you. Not the sewers." He nodded as if waiting for her to be impressed.

Scarlett gestured as if to say, "and?"

"Anyway, I cashed out the loot on a small job I pulled with the fence... you know, putting in my time to bump rank." Doni winked.

The gnome still had a good way to go. For five years he'd been treading water in the mid-level guild tiers due to several factors, most notably a personal problem that he carried as a constant burden.

"When I heard it was you out here, and seeing I'd never been off the mainland, I offered to step in. And what do you know, they let me!" He pounded the table with glee.

Scarlett covered his hand with hers. "You idiot!" she whispered, looking around. "Keep it down."

Doni eyed her hand on his, a wide smile turning his cheeks round and ruddy.

She yanked it back.

"Jack, did she tell you we were to be married?"

Scarlett rolled her eyes.

"Is that so?"

"Oh yes," the gnome said. "We pledged ourselves to one another, true as true."

"We were twelve years old." Scarlett did her best to hide the tired exasperation of hearing this again. "Can we please move on?"

"Rums around," Samath said, returning with their drinks. He placed the three shot glasses down and with a well-practiced motion, eased the glass of porter onto the table without spilling its frothy head.

"Aye, now that's a sight," Jack said. "As foamy as a stormy sea."

"On the house, Mr. Morgan," Samath said, his voice proud. "I appreciate a man who has his manners and knows his porters."

"Too kind, Samath," Jack said and raised the glass to his mouth.

The owner waited.

Scarlett found herself eager for the response. "How is it?"

Jack set the glass down and licked his lips. "That's top shelf, that is. Your brewer's got a trick up his sleeve."

"Oh?" the proprietor asked, feigning innocence.

"Aye. I'd put a copper down that there's a twist of oyster in that brew."

Samath leaned down so he could whisper to the three of them. "Brewer's secret." He winked.

A small green arm appeared over Scarlett's shoulder. "Mind my reach, miss." A bowl of fish stew plopped down in front of her. She followed the half-orc, a girl in her early teens, who placed the other two bowls down for Doni and Jack.

"My daughter," Samath said, indicating the child. "Adopted her five years back. This will all be hers someday." He indicated the tavern around them.

"You make sure you learn the recipes, lass," Jack said. "Including this here porter." He held up the glass and sipped.

"Yes, sir." The half-orc bowed and scurried off.

"She's a bit bashful," Samath said. "I just started her on the floor. Now, I've got to tend to the regulars. Enjoy."

Scarlett bowed her head in thanks as the owner moved on to his other guests.

"Raise them up," Jack said, switching to the shot of rum. "One sip for three..." He extended his hand within reach. Scarlett, along with Doni, clinked glasses with the pirate.

She tilted the shot glass back and sipped, toasting with the others, biting down to fight the sting.

"And one more for the sea," Trusty Jack said, and knocked back his remaining shot.

Scarlett took another small sip.

"Woo." Doni's face went beet red. "That's one heck of a sting." He put down the empty shot glass.

"There's a lad!" Jack nodded approvingly.

"I brought it with me, you know." Doni smirked and examined his empty glass.

"Brought what?" Jack asked.

"The marital pledge... knowing I would see Scarlett." The gnome dropped a hand into his cloak and produced a fraying scrap of burlap. Scarlett reached out to intercept the handoff but her fellow thief was too fast and pulled back.

"I believe you gave this to *me*," he said, stroking his russet beard. "I'm sharing it with an interested party."

She grumbled.

Jack accepted the burlap from the gnome and held it close to the candlelight. "Now let's see here..."

Scarlett felt her cheeks flush.

"Looks official," Jack said. "You know," the pirate looked her way. "As a captain, I have the authority to marry."

"Yes, well," she whisked the scrap from his hand, "you need a ship first. And as of now, you don't have one. So, oh well. And by the time you do, Doni will be back on the mainland." She flung the pledge back at her colleague.

A snort followed.

"Something to say, Jack?" She narrowed her eyes at him.

"Nay, lass." He sipped his porter. "Enjoying the evening's entertainment is all."

"Let me remind you both, we're here on business." She tapped her index finger onto the table three times, one for each syllable of "business." Leaning forward to keep her next words private, she said, "I assume you have my supplies?"

Doni nodded. "Of course. They're out back near the stables."

"Excellent." She tucked her napkin into her collar and spread it over her chest. "Let's eat."

৩৯৩

THREE FULL BELLIES AND TWO MORE ROUNDS OF RUM HAD PUT THE trio into a state of lulled satisfaction. Even an hour of listening to Doni talk about everything from their "engagement" to the weather hadn't dampened Scarlett's contentedness with the inn's hospitality and comfort. Whether Trusty Jack's "ayes," and "ain't sayin's?" through Doni's endless chatter had been courteous and a demonstration of good sportsmanship, or a genuine expression of interest, remained uncertain. Watching the two of them banter on through a mild daze of rum, she had lost track of time. It was only when a raucous eruption of laughter at a nearby table overrode the hum of tavern talk that she snapped out of the weary, oddly delightful, lull.

"Pay the bill, would you please Jack?" Scarlett took advantage of a rare moment of silence from Doni and handed the pirate a pouch of coins. "And then meet us out behind the inn."

"I'd rather he pays." Trusty Jack slid the purse to Doni. "And catches up after."

"Fine." She did her best to keep her tone neutral. "Don't go skimming off the top," she told the thief. "That's guild funds. Every pence is accounted for."

Doni rolled his eyes. "As if I need it." He hunched forward and spoke in a low voice. "My pockets are full on account of those traders." He nodded to a corner table. "They sleep like cows with a belly full of ale."

Idiot, she thought. He was risking getting caught and thrown in the very prison they were trying to break someone out of... all for a few measly gold pieces. *That's why he's still a Three-Finger.* She, along with her Four-Finger colleagues in the Thieves Guild, understood that it took prudence and restraint, as much as skill, to advance to the coveted higher ranks.

Scarlett stood and led the way out of the tavern and around back to the stables. She checked the surroundings. A human stablehand was bedding down a pair of elegant horses, most likely the steeds ridden by the traders whose pockets were now lighter from Doni's larceny.

"It does smell pungent," she said, taking in the air and looking up at the starry night.

"Aye," Jack said, inhaling. "Onshore breeze, like I said. Brings back memories I'd rather do without."

An angular shadow cut across the stellar blanket. Scarlett recognized the shape as a common nighthawk. "I like it here," she said. "Not the prison, I mean, but the land and sea. It's..."

"Gritty."

She smiled. "Yes, that's a good word for it."

"Your purse," Doni said, joining them and handing it back with a bow. "I complimented the cook who was at the bar. Don't see too many dwarves in the islands."

"Well, if all goes well, you'll see another tomorrow night," Scarlett said. She gestured for him to get on with it.

Her fellow guild member approached a shadowy corner and heaved a burlap sack out of the bushes, rummaging through its contents.

"For the captain." He handed Trusty Jack a cutlass.

Grasping the hilt, the pirate checked the weight and balance and set his sights down the blade. He turned the weapon over and then back. With a whoosh, the curved edge cut the air in a back-and-forth motion. "Aye, this will do."

"What about the bow?" Scarlett asked.

Doni raised a finger. "Right!" Another moment of rummaging and he produced a mid-sized bow with an ornate leaf motif.

Jack looked it over, testing its balance and draw. "Either I'm a troll's uncle or this has an elvish hand to it."

"Indeed," Doni said. "Part of a recent score in the province of Karlanda. From the horde of a goblin king. Our guild appraiser thinks its origin is Second Kingdom."

"Something odd about it." Trusty Jack pulled back the string and sighted an imaginary arrow.

"How so?" Scarlett stepped closer. "Is it flawed or..." she eyed her colleague, "damaged?"

"Nay." Jack's voice was a whisper. His eyes ran over the weapon's limbs, finger trailing along the carved leaves. "I think it's got a bit of magic in it." His eyes brightened. "Only one way to find out." He set it down.

"All the other equipment you had on the list is in there." Doni indicted the sack.

"And the potions?"

"About that..."

Scarlett's eyes narrowed. She was all too familiar with that phrase. "About what, Doni?"

"Well, it was a rough crossing and there was a storm. Everything was pitching about. I had the flasks on my bunk and—"

"They broke?"

His head went up and down in rapid succession.

"Damn it, Doni!"

"What were they, lass?" Jack asked.

"Invisibility potions. Our means of bypassing the guards. Between those, my cloak, and Tingle, this was going to be a breeze."

"Hold it..." Doni cocked his head. "Where's Tingle?"

Scarlett opened her mouth, but no words came out.

"She's not with you?"

"Let it go, lad," Jack said, shaking his head.

Scarlett pushed back the tears in her eyes.

"Oh," Doni's voice softened. "I'm so sorry, Scarlett."

"Thanks," she said, and meant it. If anyone knew how much the sprite meant to her, it was Doni. He'd been there when she'd discovered the magical creature in the woods near their childhood home. When she and Tingle had bonded in the enchanted pact, Doni had been witness to the ritual at the fairy circle.

Scarlett sighed. The sprite's loss only added to her determination to see this mission through.

"Longshore's no eggshell," Jack said. "Walls are thick, the gates are guarded... even got them some magic wards and right-nasty traps." He shook his head. "I've seen the leftovers from breakout attempts. Let me tell you... looked like a butcher's table at market."

"We can't pull this off now." Scarlett did her best to keep her voice steady. "Not without time and a new strategy. And we have no time to spare." She paced in a circle. "I can't believe you, Doni!" Her hands tightened into fists.

The guild was going to be furious and she—

What am I going to do? There must be a way...

"We're coming about?" Jack's forearm flexed as his grip tightened on the cutlass. "What about my ship?" He poked a thumb in his chest. "And the bloody regent?"

"Oh, so now you care about the regent?"

"I care about *Lady Luck* and me mates!" The pirate towered over her.

"I know, Jack." She held out a hand to lower the temperature. "But I don't see a way forward."

"Scupper that!"

"Look, without your mountain dwarf, we've got no smithy," she said. "And no quartermaster to help muster a crew and sail us through the mists." Scarlett veered towards Doni, eyes burning into her childhood companion. "This is a disastrous setback."

"And we're two days behind schedule to boot?"

Unfortunately, Jack hadn't missed Doni's passing comment inside the inn.

"If it's any consolation... meaning the potions, mind you," the gnome fidgeted and put his hands in his pockets. "I did find a replacement when I made port in Redtown... before the boat ride down here." He held up a small vial.

"Invisibility?" That was a near impossible feat. They were rare and exceedingly difficult to produce alchemically.

"No, a sleep concoction."

"Are you kidding me?" She flapped her arms in exasperation. "We'll be screwed but well rested? Great!"

"No, don't you see? I was thinking... what if we got—"

"We?" She took a step toward him and pointed a finger like a spear. "You're not coming with us, errand boy. You're too much of a liability."

Doni lowered his gaze.

"Now wait a moment, lass. Hear him out." Jack stepped up while performing a bit of shadow play with his new cutlass. "What's your schemer, lad?"

"My what?"

Scarlett was ready to blow her top. "Your idea, idiot! Your scheme."

"Oh well..." Doni rubbed his hands together. "I was thinking what if we were able to get that sleeping potion into the guard's food?"

Scarlett's temper simmered. It wasn't a half bad idea. "Go on," she said.

"I had thought we might be able to work something out by having Tingle—" He stopped. "Oh..."

"Dead end," she said to Jack. "I told you. Waste of time."

"I could always shift and—"

"Hold on a minute, lad." Jack pointed the cutlass at the gnome. "Did you say 'shift'?"

Scarlett met Jack's gaze. *Damn it,* she thought. *This is a bad idea.*

"I did," Doni said.

Then again, there was nothing else for it. She nodded to Doni. "You can tell him."

"I've got a bit of Asan blood in me. Not sure how far back, but I can shapeshift."

"At will?" Jack asked.

Scarlett raised an eyebrow at the pirate's knowledge of the rare gift.

"For the most part, yes. If I can concentrate without too much distraction."

"'Too much distraction' being the—"

"Shiver me timbers, lad," Jack said, cutting her off. "That there's a rare gift. I seen it once in a sailor. Far from home she was, and mostly human but the Asan was right noticeable in her features. A bit fox-like... turned into a seahawk 'fore me very eyes and took off from the deck to a ship a mile distant." Jack slid the cutlass into its scabbard. "What's your shape?"

Doni looked at the ground.

"Mouse," Scarlett said, meeting Jack's eye.

"Stroke of luck!" The pirate slapped the gnome on the back. "Quiet as one, aye Doni?" The pirate winked.

The gnome grinned. "If you strap that vial to my back when I'm shifted, I can scurry in and sour the stew."

"Guard changes are at sunrise and sunset," Jack said, meeting her eye. "They feed them before and after work."

Scarlett bit her lip. *Maybe this can work after all.*

"How potent is that there potion, lad?"

"Our guild alchemist in Redtown told me one drop in a pot will do the whole lot."

"How long?" Scarlett asked.

"Until it works?"

"Well, that too," she said. "But I was asking how long it lasts."

"Thirty minutes to take effect. Hour duration."

"Going to have to be fleet-footed with that timeframe," Jack said.

"We'll need to be inside and in position, waiting for it to take effect," she said. "That way we can move in with as much time as possible to get to the cells and back out again."

"Speaking of that," the pirate said. "How are you fancying getting inside Longshore?"

"What about the watchtower guards? Can you take them out with that?" She indicated the bow.

Jack shook his head. "They've got redundancies, lass. All three tiers have a watcher lookin' out. All four cardinals."

"Then we wait until they all fall asleep from the stew and move at speed," she said, a renewed optimism in her tone. "And hope for the best." She turned to Doni. "Alright, you're in."

"I'll make Four-Fingers with the guild if we pull this off!"

"Just focus on staying calm so you can do your part," she said. "Otherwise," Scarlett looked at the pirate, "we'll all be dancing with Jack Ketch."

"Not sure who Mr. Ketch is," the gnome said, "but with all respect, Scarlett, you're a terrible dancer. Never had legs for it. Remember midsummer festival, that year when you tried—"

"Doni!" Her eyes burned into him.

"Right, focus..." A meek smile stretched his mouth and pulled at his beard.

I'm going to regret this. Scarlett knelt and began dividing up the necessary equipment. "We should get some rest," she said. "In the morning we'll hike the peninsula and assess the approach and target.

We'll use the afternoon to go over the plan and eat an early supper before we make for Longshore at sunset."

The two nodded.

"Let's get these things packed up and head back inside." Scarlett knelt and stuffed a pile of equipment into her leather backpack. Her eyes went to the night sky. She inhaled the salty air, her nostrils twitching.

"You coming?" Doni said, heading to the inn with Trusty Jack.

"I'll be there in a moment. I need..." She sighed.

"Come on, lad." Jack led the gnome away. "I'll get us a bottle of rum for the room. You can tell me more about your engagement to Scarlett... she's been talking about you all afternoon."

"Has she?"

"No." The slap of Jack's palm on the gnome's back reached her ears. "I'm hanging your jib, is all."

"What's a jib?"

"Come on, ya scallywag."

She couldn't hold back a smile. It stayed the sadness rising at the thought of Tingle's demise. But that wasn't the only thing troubling her tonight. The revised plan added new concerns. With a weary strength, she pushed herself up and flung the pack over a shoulder. Passing by the stable, she cut across a grassy rise leading up towards an outcropping pushing into the sea. When she'd walked far enough to gain a panoramic view of the surrounding land and sea she halted and took in the majestic quiet and beauty of the night.

She reached her tiny fingers into her vest pocket where Tingle would have been. This time, instead of the glowing warmth of her longtime companion, she grasped the prickly stems of a dried rosemary plant and withdrew it. Holding it up, she whispered memorized words.

Thin, needly leaves fluttered. With a sudden jolt, the stem glowed blue and rushed through her fingers into the sky.

A voice reached her ears from below at the inn. She squinted in the dark, relieved to see the stable boy speaking with someone as he closed up for the night.

Whoosh.

Something passed her ear with stealth and speed.

A dark shape circled her thrice. With a flap of its wings, a nighthawk landed in the grass at her feet.

She knelt and took a small scroll from her other pocket, fastening it to the bird's leg above its talons. The hawk stared at her, its gaze more piercing than the macaw from The Dreg.

Unlike the parrot, this one was an ally and not a victim of circumstance.

"Fly swiftly," she whispered.

The nighthawk spread its wings and took flight.

Scarlett tracked its course over the peninsula until it arced southward and vanished in the night.

7

CLOSE QUARTERS

❧❧❧

Despite loathing everything the palace stood for, Marian loved the royal gardens. Leaning on the veranda's polished marble, she gave herself over to the sweet scent of native flowers and the music of songbirds that darted to and fro. Cascading in a gentle slope, the verdant boundary ran for a half mile to the city's upper limits. From there, Redtown's five districts spread like cooled lava from the island's volcanic peaks. The ocean beyond was a blanket of blue, dotted by the occasional merchant ship or navy frigate making use of the abundant sea breezes blowing from the southeast.

Marian dragged a finger over the band of black quartz that interrupted the royal balcony's white marble. The compacted minerals ran like a winding river through the polished slab, unique among the stones lining the veranda. If one stood in the right spot, the passageways, multi-level floors, and towers of the palace all vanished from view. The architects of old had mastered their art, understanding how to cast a spell over those lucky enough to visit or inhabit the premiere seat of government in the Jewels. The care the golden elves had taken to keep the island's natural spirit undisturbed spoke of their deep connection to the archipelago. Careful orientation of its forty-rooms and three grand halls ensured that not even the fortress's shadow passed over the gardens. Despite what the palace came to represent in the hands of her father, to Marian, the half-mile-wide collar remained more beautiful than any gem-encrusted necklace by a master artisan.

It was more than beauty that drove her passion for the sanctuary. The preserve had been the site of her most profound and influential rites of passage. Strolling the gardens alongside her tutors, she'd grown enthralled by both the natural fecundity of the island and the philosophical treatises introduced by scholars for debate and analysis. Her pride in learning the names and uses of the rich variety of tropical plants and trees did not go unnoticed by the alchemical mages. Nor the naturalists, who marveled at her ability to identify each bird by sight or song alone by the age of twelve.

A pair of rainbow macaws soared over the canopy. Marian followed their wings as they rose and fell in elegant synchronicity. To see two creatures so perfectly paired was—

"Good day, Sister."

Bonnie, in her admiral's uniform with its signature blue and white flamboyantly plumed hat, joined her at the ledge. "It's still here, I see." She traced a finger along the black minerals meandering through the marble.

"And it will be long after we're gone," Marian said. "When did you arrive?"

"This morning. I brought a new ship into port for the festivities."

Marian nodded. "I saw it... a galleon?"

"Look at you, well done, sailor." Bonnie removed her hat and placed it on the ledge.

Her sister, two years younger and in her late forties, had taken on a stately appearance over the last few seasons. Her brown hair, now short and cropped, framed a half-elven face once narrow and lean that had filled in, adding strength to her jawline and cheekbones. It was as if her body responded to the role of admiral like working muscles through heavy lifting. Her newfound authority showed in the calm and distant stare of what was now a master tactician who acted not out of haste, but with forethought and prudence, commanding power through orders carried out by her lessers. Marian hadn't considered it before, but presiding over the royal fleet was not all that different from ruling the population from the palace. Both required strict adherence to rank and file with, unfortunately, a common prejudice against the lowest classes as somehow unworthy of a measure of respect.

"I assume this is an official family meeting?" Marian asked.

"Indeed. Father wants to go over the inauguration and our roles in the proceedings."

"Our roles?" Marian turned from the view.

Her sister nodded in earnest. "No hiding in the gardens like the old days." She paused. "Our spot was somewhere there, wasn't it?" Bonnie pointed at a cluster of stout trees teeming with yellow spiraling fruit. "The tee-tee trees, if I remember?"

"Those are Ponangs," Marian said, correcting her.

"Yes, well, the gardens were always your haven, mine was on the palace's backside."

Luckily the clash of blades and the spirited shouts of the elite guards that dominated her sister's youth in the training yard had gone unheard on this side of the palace.

Two sisters. Two very different childhoods, Marian thought.

"Seems like another lifetime now," Bonnie said, and gazed out at the gardens.

"Who's that?" Marian indicated a woman in her late-twenties dressed in pristine naval colors standing at attention near Sir Roderick.

"My new protégé." Her sister rolled her eyes. "Pleasing to the eyes but leaves much to be desired in the areas of logic and reason. And before you ask, no."

Marian smiled. Keeping up with her sister's romantic escapades was something she'd given up on decades ago. Nothing had stuck since the elven mage, Master Rin, had broken off a relationship that lasted over a year. Bonnie's longest on record, in fact. Since then, the naval officer had plundered many a woman across the Jewel Islands, none lasting more than a few months. If that worked for her, then so be it. Like all siblings, Marian and Bonnie had their differences. Most stemmed from familial obligations and attitudes regarding the classes, but a sister was a sister. If she was happy with the course of her personal life, then so be it.

"Is that a new galleon in port?" a familiar voice asked behind them.

Marian rolled her eyes.

"Indeed, Father." Bonnie disappeared from her side. "A beauty, isn't she? I sailed in on her this morning. Maiden voyage from the docks in Dar Harbor."

"Dar Harbor?" Her father's voice grew in volume as he approached. "I didn't know we were building ships on Sapphire Island?"

"First one. The yard's been up and running for nine months."

"She is a sight," her father said. "Bigger than the others."

"Largest in the fleet. A new boom extension on its rear mast... designed by an up-and-coming builder. Would you believe she made the crossing in five days?"

"Well, 'blow me down,' as they say."

Marian shook her head at the banal attempt at sailor speak.

"Name?"

"*Royal Patriarch*," Bonnie said.

"You shouldn't have. I'm flattered."

"The timing was perfect, and the Admiral's Council all agreed."

"Thank you, Daughter."

I have to endure an hour of this? Marian held in a groan.

"And I see my eldest is here as well..."

"Hello, Father," Marian turned and bowed in the formal greeting of a subject of the realm. No hug or touch had passed between them in over two decades, and that was fine by her.

A nod of acknowledgement was all she received in return. Regent Markus Fitzwater's expression held its usual combination of arrogance and condescension. He raised one eyebrow from below dark thinning hair, his widow's peak accented on either side by white tufts. Her father's face had often been described as sleek and sharp, especially since he'd added a goatee to his chin.

Per standard palace fashion, the regent was dressed in a finely tailored linen top and pants accented with a vest and ascot. The top and tails were of a rich crimson, dyed with Radani, the root of an indigenous cacti plant scattered about the arid cliffs at the feet of the island's volcano. The silk ascot and vest were the signature green of the Fitzwater family, made from crushed emerald dust pounded to a fine powder and boiled until it leeched into a brew used to stain fabric. She'd lost count of how many times the man had boasted that the combination of the ruby outfit with the Fitzwater compliment of green was a sign of their destiny as rulers over the island.

"Lunch is served, Your Grace." Frianté, the elderly human butler, said as he bowed and then gestured to the finely set table under the canvas awning.

"Come," her father said to his daughters. "Let us dine. There is much to discuss."

Marian followed her sister to the table and took her usual seat facing the gardens. Her father presided from the head to her left, an empty seat between them. She'd long grown accustomed to the void where her elven mother had once sat. Hildara Fitzwater had passed on eighteen years back, but that didn't mean she'd been forgotten. Unlike the lost love of Marian's youth, the handsome archer-turned-pirate, her mother's spirit remained close and palpable. James Hawk, on the other hand, who had captured her heart before turning to criminality, was no more than a fading ghost—dead by her sister's hand going on fourteen years. He'd sat at this table once, after winning the annual competition and the coveted golden arrow as his prize. Through a potent irony, that talisman now lay in a locked case in the palace's halls. She could still see the restrained anger on her father's face when the young man, a peasant from the village of Pelton on the southern coast, had offered it to his eldest daughter. Despite Markus Fitzwater's prohibition, taking much offense at a lowly peasant courting his eldest and heir to the regency, it ended up here years later—a trophy of her sister's rout of the traitorous man's ship and her murderous revenge. All to ease a sister's burden, or so Bonnie had said. Marian never told her, but it did nothing of the sort. Conflicted pain lingered, despite her attempt to deny it. The rebellious decision to exit the family's royal line, and leave the palace for the order of healers, was made more cathartic by not having to see that arrow and its reminder of a past that turned a romantic dream into a tragic nightmare.

"I can't remember the last time we were all here," Bonnie, on her father's immediate left, said. The seat spoke of the government's symbolic hierarchy emphasizing the ranking of family inheritance. With her choice to sign away her right as the next in line to the regency, Marian passed the familial torch to her younger sister. Bonnie fit the post like a glove. Unfortunately, Marian doubted all that much would change in the islands when her father passed on and that power was transferred to the military leader.

"Well," her father said, "it looks all but certain that in twenty days' time, we as Fitzwaters will no longer be regents under the watchful and controlling eyes of the council, but the rightful rulers of this most glorious island kingdom." Markus Fitzwater grinned proudly, raising his glass.

"Congratulations, Father," Bonnie said. "You must be relieved."

"This is not about me, dear daughter." He shook his head with practiced modesty. "It's about recognizing the needs of the people."

Marian's blood rose, matching the heat of the day.

"And," the regent continued, "we can finally make the economic changes to build more of those glorious ships of yours and protect our merchant fleet as we expand our trade routes. Not to mention, roll back the remaining regulations those stubborn council members keep blocking. The laborers in the lower districts aren't working like they should."

"How long has it been since you've visited the Eel District, Father?" Marian forked her food but didn't eat it. "Or the streets of Barnacle Town on the west end?"

"I have no need," he said with a dismissive sniff. "My advisors keep me well informed."

"Right." Marian nodded. "I'm sure they report nothing but teeming prosperity."

"On the contrary, I hear concerns with laziness and lack of appreciation of *our* efforts on their behalf."

"Did you know the fever's back?"

He glared at her.

"I take it by your silence that you've been informed." Marian took a bite of her lunch. She caught Bonnie's poker face break at her aggressive retort.

"You seem to forget, Daughter, that you signed away your family. Therefore, you have no business interfering with what concerns we have over our subjects."

"They are not subjects!" Marian slammed her fork down. "They are *citizens* of this island."

"Let's not do this," Bonnie said, holding her hands up in a gesture of reconciliation. "Father, why don't you tell us what is planned for the ceremonies."

"Quite right." The regent gestured to his butler. "Send for Joran, if you would."

The butler bowed and hastened off.

"The social minister will go over the details. Suffice it to say that you, Marian, *will* attend. You will be seated with the family behind your sister. I will speak of your sacrifice to the order in my inauguration speech, and how it casts a gesture of humility over our family's rule."

Marian had nothing to say, and so she said nothing.

"Ah, Master Rin," the regent said. "Do join us."

"Thank you, Your Grace." The elf nodded to Marian, making the clasped-hand gesture to a fellow mage, before taking a seat next to Bonnie. "You look well, Admiral." Master Rin gave a polite nod.

"And you as well." Bonnie smiled.

Marian, knowing her sister better than anyone, caught the tinge of resentment behind her professional exterior.

"Your Grace," the arch mage said, "I have an update on our efforts to push out the Nocsi from the kelp forests off Emerald Island."

"Good news, I hope?"

The elf smirked. "Those extra taxes went to good use. We've lined enough council members' pockets for them to look the other way on the Nocsi's claims of first rights over the natural habitat."

"Excellent, that species is a nuisance," the regent muttered, mouth full of food. "Tell me, as for..."

Marian pulled away from the conversation, her mind drifting as she stared at the gardens. Thirty minutes of discussion about everything from trade, to negotiations with the governors of the surrounding islands, to political dealings with the mage's guilds, passed as if on an empty breeze. By the time Joran, the portly gnome who ran social events for the royal family, arrived and reviewed the inauguration ceremonies, Marian was no more than a forgotten table ornament.

After a dessert of fresh fruit and coconut pudding, she drifted off to the ledge relishing in the solitude of the garden's flora and fauna. Her father rose and exited shortly thereafter, exchanging a brief performative nod with her before she once again lost herself in the childhood game of naming various trees and flowering plants.

Fire Rudekia, Gildenwort, Ironia Lace, and that's Trianti Leaf—

"Pence for your thoughts?" The bold colors of Bonnie's Royal Navy uniform entered her peripheral vision. "And don't say something about the needs of the poor."

"Then don't ask."

"This is an opportunity, Sister."

"For you," Marian said, eyes on the urban districts spread like fingers into the azure sea.

Bonnie tugged her arm. "Hey."

Marian faced her sibling. The officer's garb had always suited her. Bonnie had more muscle in her legs and shoulders than she ever had, even as teens before joining the Navy. Her sister's taut and defined thighs in the leggings exuded a commanding presence worthy of her post. And that subtle limp... it added salt to the meat of her nautical reputation.

To think of the irony of who gave it to her, Marian thought.

"It won't always be like this, you know." Bonnie checked to make sure they were out of earshot of Sir Roderick and her protégé. "Once I'm in charge, I mean..."

Marian tilted her head as if to tip a scale.

"I don't agree with everything Father says," Bonnie whispered. "And when the time comes, I'll listen. Okay?" Her sister clasped her hand, the callouses from years of running ropes rough on Marian's fingers.

"*He* should listen now," Marian said. "Do you know what I did this morning? I treated a child for fever. Her body showed signs of the ancient plague. I got to her early, so her chances of surviving are better than the others." She gazed at the colorful houses and wharf in the distance. "And believe me, there will be others. Too lightly has the council brushed off that lingering and malignant magic. That sickness needn't be in the city, Bonnie. Nor anywhere in the Jewels. But because of father's endless obsession with saving money and indulging in—"

Her sister squeezed her hand. "I've heard this, Marian."

"These are children, Bonnie. They're the future of this city."

"This is a little picture issue," Bonnie said, "focused on the least important people in the—"

"The most important!" Marian ripped her hand free. "Damn it, Bonnie, I am not getting into this again."

Her sister held up her hands. "You do your thing, Marian. I'll do mine."

"You always have."

"What is that supposed to mean?" Bonnie's cheeks flushed. The face of a hard and stern naval commander rose to usurp her more personable demeanor.

"It means that ambition is a virtue, when balanced with empathy."

"Oh, so this is a spiritual conversation. Are you trying to convert me?"

Marian sighed. "I'm leaving."

"Wait." The sailor's iron grip tightened on her wrist.

"Let go of me."

Bonnie's fingers fell from her arm. "I just want you to be happy is all."

"What is it with you two? You think you know what makes me happy?" Marian leaned in, the older sister in her growing bold. "The moment I disavowed myself from the royal line was the moment my life turned around. I get up each day with a purpose and go to sleep knowing I've done what I can, yet I'm always hungry for more. You have no idea about healing arts, Bonnie. All you know is how to dominate and destroy."

"I guess that's a compliment?" Bonnie fiddled with the plume on her hat.

"Keep me out of all of it." Marian spoke through gritted teeth. "You and Father have yourself a time of it stomping on the poor and taking all that you can get your hands on from the islands. It's no better than piracy."

"That's stretching it a bit."

"Is it?"

"We have the law on our side."

"You *make* the laws."

"True." Bonnie put the bicorn on her head.

"This is all moot." Marian did her best to keep her tone steady. "You heard Father. I'm a nobody now. I'm only important for appearances. 'Marian the martyr.' The eldest daughter who sacrificed the throne for a noble cause. It's a great line. But it's nothing more than political spin to cover his embarrassment. I sacrificed nothing." She sliced her hand through the air. "What did I get from my decision? Freedom. From him. From the palace. From the corruption—"

Bonnie made a face.

"Don't even, Bonnie..."

Her sister frowned.

"I want nothing to do with any of it. And guess what?" Marian held up her hands. "I can't now anyway. I signed it all away. I've let it all go."

"All of it?" Her sister's eyes dropped to her left hand.

Marian's feet faltered. "How dare you..." She steadied herself on the ledge.

"I'm sorry, Marian. I didn't mean.... It's just—"

"Sargeant!"

"My lady." The thud of Sir Roderick's feet stomping with ceremonial pomp echoed across the veranda.

"We're leaving."

"Yes, my lady."

Marian stormed past her sister and made for the exit.

"Shall I have the page bring your—"

"On foot!" she said.

8

JURY RIG

Longshore loomed large in the growing night. Jack knelt with Scarlett atop the treeless peninsula, sheltered in a small gulley. From their position a few hundred feet from the main gate, the white stone structure was like a solitary fang jutting into the sea. Torches flickered on its ramparts, their warm light bouncing off the prison's sturdy towers. Beyond the cliffs, the ocean was a blanket of darkness. Only a sliver of orange glowed at the horizon, the last trace of the passing day.

"He should be back by now," Scarlett said.

"Give it time, lass," Jack said. "He's being cautious is all."

An hour earlier at sunset, they had sent Doni off with the vial. That had been a sight Jack wouldn't soon forget. Not just the brown mouse with a sleep potion strapped on its back, but the shift that turned a gnome into a rodent. He'd seen some uncanny magic in his days, but this gave new meaning to strange. It was as if Doni buckled and folded in on himself, like too much clothing stuffed into a chest. Once the thief was fully transformed, he looked no different than any other vermin stowaway below decks—one more tiny freeloader scurrying back and forth, twitching his nose, and standing on his hind legs to peer about.

Scarlett's nostrils flared as the breeze picked up.

"You smell it, don't you, lass?"

She nodded.

"Onshore winds." Jack took a deep inhalation. "Smells like this one's been hangin' for three suns."

"Wind isn't good," Scarlett said. "Not for our plans."

Jack licked a finger and popped it in the air. "Going to pick up in knots." He craned his neck. Cumulous clouds like shadowy cotton balls drifted across the stars. Jack counted the seconds as they passed. "I'd say double what it's blowin' now within the hour."

"Double?" Scarlett checked her gear. "Everything is going wrong," she muttered.

"What's the wind got to do with it? We're not going over the walls to get in?"

"We *are* going over the walls to get out."

"Bah... I've been hanging on ropes me whole life." Jack reached in his shirt pocket and removed an unsmoked cheroot. He ran it under his nose, taking in the savory aroma of burnt leather and molasses. "I've been up the yardarms in storms that would make a navy rat piss a pot." He winked. Softening this kind of nervous anticipation was nothing new to a ship's captain. Landlubbers often needed a bit of reassurance. "See this here cheroot?" He stuck it in his mouth and feigned a hearty puff. "Going to taste even better if that onshore's blowing hard when we drop into the drink. Make the reward after sticking it to the warden and her bilge rat guards that much sweeter. And I got another of these elvish smokers waitin' for me old mate, Big Rig." He patted his shirt pocket.

"It's not the—" A gust whipped her cloak. Scarlett slapped a hand on the fabric before it covered her face. "... it's not the ropes that have me—"

Eek!

The gnome jumped.

"Doni, lad!" Jack said, keeping his voice low. "See, lass." He nodded reassuringly at the thief. "Quiet as a mouse. Snuck up on us, he did."

"He *is* a mouse," she said.

Doni's rodent form stretched and pulled. Jack watched with disturbing fascination as the gnome regained his usual form.

"Shiver me timbers, but that's a sight, that is..." He put the unsmoked cheroot back in his pocket.

"You're late." Scarlett's tone was that of a scolding headmistress.

Jack examined her expression. Her blue eyes shone through narrowed eyelids, and the soft purse of her lips didn't quite match her tone. *Well, sink me,* he thought. *There be affection hiding under that mask. I'd put five gold in the pot that her heart ain't so cold to him.*

"I didn't want to take any chances, so I stayed shifted all the way back." Doni huffed, catching his breath. "Mouse feet are tiny, Scarlett!"

"Keep your voice down," she said.

"Are we all set, lad?"

Doni nodded and ran a hand down his russet beard. "I got into the kitchen and spoiled the stew." He wiped sweat from his brow. "That cook's a nasty one!"

"Aye, that be Bloomie," Jack said. "Cranky half-orc, she is. Seen her scold the warden once in the yard for low quality cabbage and parsnips... chased her with a frying pan, she did. The elf scurried off with her tail between her legs. Had all of us in stitches."

"So, everything went to plan?" Scarlett asked.

"Well, about that..."

"Doni..." Scarlett's cheeks burst into flames.

"There's a problem. But it has nothing to do with me!" He held up his tiny hands as if to hold back a flood. "That Bloomie was going on about a special dinner tonight. She said the warden and the tower guards aren't eating with the others."

"Why not?"

"Something about a bushel of harpy oysters from the regent. Going to dine separately in her quarters."

"Damn!" Scarlett balled her fists. "Crossing to the barracks unseen will be impossible."

"Hold on, lass." Jack's mind was racing, the layout of the prison unfolding in his mind. "The west tower is close, right inside the gate. It's got a door leading down to the blocks."

"That's something, at least," Scarlett said.

"The problem is—"

"Getting back out," Scarlett finished for him. "Those tower guards will be wide awake with eyes open when we make for the seaside wall."

"This blade may get some use." He tapped the cutlass handle at his waist.

"Jack, if we go into the cells from that tower, I'll need your memory of the prison's layout to get to Mr. Riggins," Scarlett said. "According to the guild's spy network, they have him in Cell Block Four."

Poor lad, Jack thought. *I don't want to think about what kind of shape he's in down there.* "Aye, I know Block Four. It's on the southwest side. Not far from that there tower."

"That's good, right?" Doni asked.

"It is." Scarlett's tone carried more ease. "The quicker the better at this point."

Jack's eyes were on the ramparts. "Look." He pointed. "See that?"

Two shadowy figures met in the torchlight. The one that arrived stayed and the other vanished. "That's the shift change."

"They've eaten?" she asked.

"Aye. They're belly full of oysters, lucky lot," he said. "And that means the lowly blokes down in the blocks have had their stew."

"Thirty minutes to take effect, right Doni?" Scarlett asked.

The gnome nodded.

"I say we move in five," Jack said. "That'll put us inside by the time it hits 'em. Give us almost an hour so long as we get past the watchers. Sooner we're in and out the better. We don't want the warden or a tower guard wandering about and finding someone asleep."

"Or Bloomie," Doni added. "Don't know if she ate the stew."

Blimey, Jack thought. *I forgot about that blasted cook.* "Aye, lad," he muttered. "Nor her."

Jack's eyes were on Scarlett, who stared out to sea lost in thought.

"What is it, lass?"

"We need a distraction to get inside and past the tower guards," Scarlett said. "How did you escape last time?"

"Lucky break." Jack grinned. "Aye, that's a punner, that is!"

"Oh wait," Doni said. "I get it. Like a 'schemer' but with a pun."

"Thank you, Doni. That wasn't obvious." Scarlett rolled her eyes.

"Anyway, lass, the Hardy Gang were on my cell block... regent was going after them hard in Redtown. More members kept gettin' locked up. Their leader, a forest dwarf by the name of Pounce McHardy, got himself a schemer." Jack winked at Doni. "He started having his gang get themselves caught. Pretty soon they had enough blokes inside."

"For what?" Doni asked.

"Mutiny," Scarlett said. "A riot."

Jack nodded. *She's quick.* He didn't want to tell her, but he'd uncovered her secret: Scarlett had street smarts as much as book smarts. What he wanted to know was the origin story of that grit. If she was from privilege, book smarts made sense. But what had led her to the gutters? Was it a choice? Or was she forced on the run?

"Big Rig and I were cellmates," Jack said, continuing, "and we'd lent our knuckles to the Hardy gang on a few occasions when the Flounder Clan took them on in the yard." He spat. "Never liked them Flounders. No morals and untrustworthy." He held up a hand. "Not that a McHardy wouldn't stick a blade in yer back given the chance, but they'd do it for reasons. You get my tidal drift, don't you, lad?"

Doni nodded, but somehow Jack got the sense he didn't fully understand.

"Big Rig and I got out in the mayhem. Hitched a ride around the cape with the McHardy's on the clan's ship they had waiting a wee bit north." He pointed up the coast. "That was a sea tale for you. Right close to feeding the fish we were going round the Ruby's horn."

"And from there?" Scarlett asked.

"Another time, lass. That's a long one. Better Big Rig give you that tale." Jack gazed upwards and checked the position of the stars. "All the more reason to get this started, aye? I'd say that's a solid five minutes."

"Wait here a moment." Scarlett withdrew a small object from her pack and threw her cloak about her. Like during their escape from Mayrotten Island, she dematerialized.

"Where's she going, lad?"

"Signaling the ship." Doni pointed in the direction of the cliff's edge. "Focus on the grass."

Jack's eyes swept over the blowing blades. In the near darkness he caught a disturbance to the wavy rhythm leading to the edge. If Doni hadn't pointed it out, he would have never noticed.

"Keep your eye out to sea," Doni said. "A bit to the left."

"Port, lad."

"Sorry?"

"To port. That's left in boat terms."

"Right."

Jack eyed the gnome. "If that's meant to be a punner..."

The gnome smirked.

Jack looked to sea. Sure enough, a faint light shone three times from the ocean's pitch.

A moment later Scarlett reappeared before them.

"Now how you be linking with that ship, lass?"

"Come close," she said and knelt.

Jack joined her. Underneath the shelter of their bodies, she cracked open a space between her fingers. A green light shot through the empty spaces.

"Glow stone," she whispered. "From the far northern caves at the Fjords of Raukulnen."

"Now that's a wonder, that is..." The pirate met her eyes in the faint illuminating light. "Never been that far north."

"Well, if we get through this maybe you should sail *Lady Luck* up the Drakeland Coast. Raulkulnen's the edge of the world, Jack." Her blue eyes went wide with wonder. "A land wild and untamed. Beautiful... blankets of pristine snow and tall firs, with stones of black and ice like javelins for giants."

A rush of excitement filled his veins at the freedom inspired by her elegant words. "Aye, that would be a tale to tell."

She tucked the stone away and threw back her cloak. "We still need a distraction or we'll never get inside," she said, scanning the ramparts.

"Aye, long enough to get us to the tower door."

A gust of wind passed over the grass. The motion was like an invisible wave rolling on to a distant shore.

"Jack, what's behind that wall?" The thief pointed at a section of the ramparts a third of the way from the front entrance.

Jack imagined a bird's eye view of the interior. "Stables. If you cut a line straight in from that torch there," he pointed at one of the orange flames lining the wall, "mostly piles of straw and feed for the horses."

Doni edged up next to his fellow thief. "Are you thinking what I'm thinking?"

"I am," she said.

"Think he can do it?" Doni asked.

"Well, we're going to have to try," she said. "We can't lose any more time or we'll never get to Dragon Tail Island and back before the inauguration."

"What in blazes are you two on about?" Jack said. "Me ears be burning and I'm right next to you scallywags."

Scarlett rose and wiped her hands. "Your distraction."

"*My* distraction?"

She motioned them to follow her, keeping low.

Jack scurried behind her, with Doni pulling up the rear.

They halted about a hundred and fifty feet from the wall.

"I want you to shoot that."

Jack followed the line of sight from the gnome's tiny finger. "Are you mad, lass? At this range... and with this wind?" He gauged the distance. It had to be edging on three hundred yards between length and height. The amount of compensation to calculate was just...

"It's really a simple sequence of events," she said. "You hit the torch... from this angle, it will send embers up and back, over the ramparts. They fall three floors and, gods willing, land in the hay pile next to the stables, igniting it. As soon as it's noticed, a guard will sound the alarm bell. With the guards distracted by the fire, you and I get to the front gate. Doni will be inside." She turned to her colleague. "You have to shift again for this to work. Do you have the strength left to do it?"

He put a hand over his heart. "For you, anything."

"Seriously, Doni."

"I think so."

"You have to."

He nodded.

"Slip in under the portcullis like you did for the stew," she said.

"Shift back to open it for us. Crank the mechanism up enough for us to slip under. We'll make for the nearest tower. If the door down to the cells is locked, I'll pick it and—"

"Oh, let me pick it!"

Scarlett flashed her guild companion a look of death. Jack couldn't tell if it was for the suggestion of performing the rogue action or for interrupting her.

"Sorry... of course, you can do it." He threw a blade of grass he'd been fraying down onto the ground in defeat.

"You're not coming with us," she said. "I need you to make your way up to the gallows over the sea and prep our escape. Haul up the equipment we left on the cliffs and set everything up. I'll give you my cloak. That will make sure you can move unseen."

His eyes went wide.

"I'm loaning it to you, Doni. You'll get your own one day." She smiled at him.

There's that twinkle again, Jack thought.

Doni nodded, excitement in his eyes.

"Why not give it to the lad now?" Jack said. "He could take it with him and do everything to get us in like a ghost in the night?"

Doni shook his head. "Magic items don't reduce when you shift."

"Bollocks," Jack muttered.

"Plus, from what my spies tell me, Longshore upgraded its locks last summer," Scarlett said. "They're master level systems from Harnick & Rattison... brought them in from Drakeland." She put a hand on Doni's shoulder. "No offense, but you'd never be able to pick them. And even if you could it would take far too much time."

"Can you?" Jack asked.

"I spent a week practicing on one. It should only be a single lock if we go down through the tower. The original route would have required two. Once I open that door leading to the dungeons, we can pilfer the keys from the sleeping guard in Cell Block Four."

"Alright, lass. And the magic ward? You know there's one at each cell block's entrance?"

"We dispel the magic ward with this." She held up a scroll.

"Now where'd you get that?" Jack said. He had to hand it to her; she was full of surprises.

"You think I don't come prepared? I'm a master thief, Jack. I do my homework. Research and reading and whatnot... you know, educated." She tapped her tiny skull, a smug grin on her face.

He snorted. "Aye, but you ain't a gambler. That's for sure. You'd be broke in a game of bones after three hands if you think this plan's odds are sound."

"It's the only one we've got. Now, once we are through and in the block, you'll take the lead with Mr. Riggins. We'll free him from his cell and meet at the gallows."

"I don't like the way you phrased that last part," Doni said.

"Me neither, lad." Jack reached into a pocket and withdrew a copper piece. He placed it on his thumb tail-side up and flung it into the darkness. He leaned over to Doni. "Pirate superstition, lad. I reversed the jinx. Smooth sailing now."

"Then that's that," Scarlett said. "A simple sequence of events. Not a bad improvised plan if I do say so myself." She blew a kiss in the air.

Doni made as if catching it and smiled.

"You wish." She rolled her eyes.

"Aye," Jack grumbled. "'A simple sequence of events'... hit a torch head at three hundred yards. At night, in this bloody wind, at an angle like cresting a rogue wave, with a bow you've never shot before... that's hornswaggle if I've ever heard it."

"I saw you make an equally difficult shot on Mayrotten Island." She raised a crimson eyebrow.

"You're supposed to be a legend with a bow," Doni whispered.

Legend or no legend, this was a near impossible shot. Plus, that arrow he put in the jungle orc from the ship in Mayrotten's harbor was made from desperation... to save a life in immediate peril. There was no time to think, and that was half the reason he'd hit the target.

"You can do this, Jack." Scarlett said.

"If I miss, lass..."

"If you miss, chances are the whole thing is lost. We'll have to scramble away if we don't want to end up behind bars. They'll double-down all the watches for a month. That means no breaking out Mr.

Riggins, which means no way to smith the blood iron needle, which means no—"

"I get it," Jack grumbled and shook his head. *Bollocks,* he thought. *All on you, Jacky boy.*

"I don't want to push you, Jack," Scarlett said. "But Mr. Riggins is sitting in a dark and dank cell over that wall. And I would bet if he were here, he'd say you could make it, if anyone could."

Jack sighed.

"We've heard the tale of the golden arrow," Doni said. "It's true, isn't it?"

Jack's blood rose. "Who's saying it's not?"

Doni held up his hands. "I just—"

"That shot was far harder than this," Scarlett said. "And I imagine under more pressure..."

"I know what you're doing," Jack said, eyeing her. "Sweet talkin' me in reverse. Scarlett's fancy words..."

She gestured innocently at herself as if to say, "Who me?"

Jack picked up the bow and ran his hand down the leaf pattern on its limbs. His finger tingled with a warm sensation.

"Those cheroots are itching to be smoked," she said.

Madness, that's what this is, he thought. "Ever been in prison, lass?"

Scarlett shook her head.

"I have." Doni raised his chin proudly.

"Have you now, lad?"

"Well..." The gnome flicked a pebble with a finger, the confidence in his tone dropping. "For a few hours... once. In a village holding cell. They gave me wine and porridge."

"Oh, you'll both have a grand time," Jack said. "Doni, you can get to know Bloomie. And you," he eyed Scarlett, "will enjoy the prison library."

"There's a library?"

Jack chortled. He knelt and nocked an arrow.

"Go, Doni," Scarlett said. "And good luck."

Her colleague took a deep breath. Jack could see he was mustering whatever magical energy he had left. Eyes squeezed tight, the gnome's cheeks flushed. It took longer this time, but eventually he folded inward and transformed into the now familiar furry rodent.

Jack waited until the creature vanished in the grass and then he took aim.

He focused on the breeze, familiarizing himself with its ebb and flow. The arrow needed to release at the end of a passing gust. Hopefully, in the slack between currents, it would fly true to its target.

The problem was the guard. An armored half-orc patrolled back and forth along the rampart. Like an eclipse, Jack needed the timing and alignment just right, with the guard walking away from the torch at the same time the wind ebbed.

"Come on," Jack whispered, bow drawn. "Bloody move it..."

The tropical breeze caressed his cheeks.

The half-orc passed the torch.

"Only a few more steps..."

The wind eased.

Twang!

The arrow arced up and towards the ramparts.

A sudden gust blew the hat off Jack's head. "No!"

Scarlett appeared next to him, the two watching in earnest.

"It's going wide to port!" he said.

A sensation, like easing into a warm bath, ran through his fingers gripping the bow.

Jack's eyes went wide.

Poof!

Sparks flew off the torch's head. The arrow had veered back an inch through the wind!

"Blow me down!" Jack whispered, eyeing the bow with wonder.

"Come on!" Scarlett pulled him towards the gate.

9

ANY PORT IN A STORM

※

Sure enough, shouts rose from inside Longshore's walls. Through the portcullis, an orange glow shone across the prison yard. Shadows of rising flames danced on the dirt.

The fire bell rang.

"You two!" a half-orc shouted. "Grab some buckets and help put this out."

The two guards posted at the entrance dashed off.

"It's working," Scarlett whispered from the shadows near the entrance. "Come on."

Jack stayed low and followed her to the portcullis.

"Good evening." Doni spoke through the iron grid. "Fancy a tour of the prison?"

The portcullis creaked up and they rolled underneath.

The yard was alive with activity. A bucket chain had formed, with a line of guards feeding water to those at the stables who doused the flames.

The three intruders kept to the shadows, hugging the curving stone of the west tower. With the fire's distraction and the dark of night for cover, they made it to the archway without incident.

"So far so good," Scarlett said, ducking inside.

"Alright Doni." She took off her cloak and handed it to the thief. "Good luck."

"See you both at the—"

"Don't say it lad, just go," Jack said.

The gnome fastened the cloak at his neck and threw it about him, whispering words in a strange tongue.

A brief glitter of light passed over his form and he vanished.

"Now to pick this lock." Scarlett pulled out a small leather pouch. She removed a steel needle and a long tool like a row of shark's teeth and began fiddling with the mechanism.

Jack read the letters on the plate: Harnick & Rattison.

Scarlett's ears twitched.

A moment later, Jack caught voices bouncing down the tower's outdoor curving stairs.

"On it," Scarlett said, concentrating like a surgeon working on an open chest. "I heard it before you did."

Jack loosened the cutlass in its scabbard.

"Come on..." Scarlett said, jiggling the lock.

The shuffling of feet on the stairs grew louder.

"Bloody hay piles gone up," a gruff voice said.

"It's this wind," another added.

A long shadow stretched across the curving stones in the torchlight.

"Lass..."

Click!

"Got it!"

They were through with the door shut behind them just as the two guards passed. Scarlett leaned against its thick wooden planks, exhaling a sigh of relief.

Jack loosened the grip on his cutlass as the voices faded.

"Thrill of the job, Jack." She winked and made for the corner.

He was starting to think that thieves were simply pirates on land.

"Are you coming?" she whispered from down the corridor.

"Aye."

They travelled two sets of stairs down into the dungeons and then reached the first checkpoint.

This was it. Either Doni's potion had worked, or they were in for a world of trouble.

Scarlett signaled for Jack to wait and snuck ahead. Balancing on her tippy toes, she peered through a leaden window into the guard station.

Jack waited in earnest.

Scarlett clasped her hands together and placed them on the side of her head like she was asleep.

"I'll drink to that," Jack said and caught up with her.

Another two minutes and they'd passed Cell Blocks One, Two, and Three with their glowing purple wards barring the entrances.

"Cell Block Four is ahead," Jack said. Was his old shipmate really in there? He was trying to think of how to approach the dwarf. The quartermaster, like everyone else, assumed Jack had been dead going on fourteen years.

Scarlett halted at the entrance to the cell block. A faint and eerie violet light radiated on the wooden surface. She pulled out the scroll.

"Caramun il treanto."

The paper disintegrated in her hands and with it went the purple glow on the door.

Trusty Jack grinned. "Now that there's a fancy trick, lass."

"Expensive too."

"Having those on hand is a right boon, for sure."

"I agree. And unlike Doni, I always bring extras in case of mishaps." She turned around. "Ready for this, Jack?"

"Aye, for fourteen summers."

The gnome pushed on the door and peeked inside. She edged forward and Jack followed her through. A burly half-orc sat slumped on a stool, snoring. The image brought back memories of Hardy in The Dreg.

You're a long way from that drinking hole.

Scarlett grabbed the ring of keys off the wall. Without speaking, she handed them off and indicated for Jack to take the lead.

The pirate crept down the row of cells, haunting memories of his time inside returning with every step. He peered into the first cell on the left.

Empty.

Across, on the right, a darkened form sat hunched in the corner. He took a step closer and—

"Fresh meat! Fresh meat!" A wild-eyed elf with deep purple skin and white hair to her knees lunged at the bars. Mouth open and fangs dripping, her lean and muscular arms reached through trying to grab hold of him.

"Quiet, you!" a deep voice shouted from down the block.

Jack turned his head. *I'd know that voice anywhere.*

"Fresh meat! Fresh meat!" the night elf shouted ravenously, ignoring her fellow prisoner's demand.

Jack motioned Scarlett to hang back and proceeded down the rows to the voice's source.

He halted before the cell in question and mustered his nerve.

"*I crossed from Emerald to Ruby, one spring to seek me lass.*" Jack's singing voice, rich and vibrato, echoed off the stone walls.

A shuffling of feet from inside the cell followed. "I be hearin' things," a voice whispered.

Jack hung back from view. "*I hoisted the main, and tightened the jib, with money and haste to marry.*"

Silence.

And then, a baritone voice rose, "*No port did I see, no shore with a lee...*"

Jack grinned. He took a breath and finished the line: "*...it was then that my heart sank deep.*"

"*The first mate did pout. The crew they did shout...*"

Jack stepped in front of the cell. "*You're a fool, Jeb Hardy, a fool!*"

Holding the bars, his one eye wide, stood Dûr Riggins. His old friend was a sight for sore eyes. He'd aged, even for a dwarf. The beard that was once brown and rusty was now a sea of white and grey against onyx skin. The former quartermaster of *Lady Luck* wore mere rags and no shoes. But it was his expression that hit hardest.

"Lest my eye be deceiving me, that be the ghost of Captain Hawk," he whispered. "It's my time, it is. This be the spell of stone cast on me.

My forefolk spirits are coming to take me home to the mountain halls..."

"Scupper that," Jack said. "'Tis I, your old mate in the flesh and bone!"

Big Rig shook his head. "It's so real... be ye the spirit of Trusty Jack here to guide me?"

"Bollocks!" Jack knelt and looked his old friend in the eye. "It's me, your old mate, true as true."

"Jack, lad? The spirits are deceiving me..."

"No, no..." He held up a hand to calm the dwarf. "Look here." He rolled up his sleeve and showed him his tattoos. "We got this here one together." He pointed at a tattoo of crude letters that read, "Wahoo."

Big Rig gasped and looked at his skin where gray letters, faded and blurry, matched the ones on Jack's arm.

"At the *Pelican's Poop* in Port Maverick," Jack added. "Sloppy Tom done give us these... after far too much rum."

"Shiver me timbers! It's really you?"

"Aye." He stood and spread his arms. "I'm here to break you out."

"Ha!" The dwarf placed a hand over his heart. "You're alive! But how, lad? Bonnie... and that damn Topaz mage that duped us ..."

"It's a long tale, that. Worthy of a jug of rum." Jack leaned forward. "How about we get out of here and I tell you all about it?" He jingled the keyring.

"Aye, open the bloody lock! I can't believe me eye." Big Rig smacked his bald head and shook it. "Okay. Okay. This is real.... so, you've got a way out of here?"

"Yes, but not much time, lad. We have to move right fast. We're going down the next hall to the cross leading to the kitchen. We'll follow the guard hall right up to the gallows."

"Not anymore you won't," a voice said.

Jack swung around and drew his cutlass.

Green eyes like emeralds appeared from the darkness in the cell across the hall. As the prisoner reached the bars, their form took shape.

A Nocsi, he thought. *Now that's a rare sight.*

An otter-like species with a humanoid frame, the Nocsi were able to move on land and sea. Cunning and witty, even rambunctious, they thrived in the kelp forests along the edges of the Jewel Islands. The creatures were imbued with a unique magic fueled by the food of their underwater habitat.

"Shut yer trap you lousy bard!" Big Rig shouted.

"You're wasting your time going that way," the nocsi said, ignoring the dwarf. "You'll end up in here with the rest of us. It's a dead end."

Jack examined the prisoner's features. Coffee-colored fur from head to toe with claws, and a white patch on her belly, with two prominent upper teeth and whiskers.

"You're saying that don't lead out?" he asked.

She nodded.

"Well guess what, lass? I spent eight years inside these here walls. And I know that way's sound."

"*Was* sound."

"She's right, Jack."

He turned back to the dwarf and returned the cutlass to its scabbard.

"They closed that off, lad."

Jack opened the cell, freeing his old friend.

Big Rig touched his arm hesitantly. "Flesh and bone..."

Jack knelt and gave his mate a hearty hug.

"Oh lad, I thought you were in Davy Jones Locker," the dwarf said.

Jack pulled back and took in his old mate's face. He wore a different eyepatch but other than that and some age, Big Rig looked like Big Rig.

"Felt like it at times," Jack said.

"I know how to get out," the nocsi said.

Big Rig grumbled.

"Alright, lass. I'll hear you out."

"Jack, no." Big Rig's white beard went back and forth like a maid sweeping a floor in haste. "We don't need her help. We'll get out. Back through the yard. Nice and quiet."

"About that, lad. Yard's a bit topsy-turvy right now. We caused a bit of mayhem. Ain't getting out back that way."

"I've got the solution to your problem," the nocsi said, words like wine.

Alright then, he thought and swung around.

The dwarf grabbed his shirt tail. "I'm begging you, Jack... me ears be bleeding for months. Day and night she rambles on." His former quartermaster pulled him close, his one eye wide. "The poetry, lad... it's brutal."

"Steady on, Rig." Jack slapped the dwarf's muscular arm. "It can't be that bad."

"It's worse than Lana singing a shanty."

That *was* bad. Jack cringed thinking about the half-orc's off-key voice leading *Lady Luck's* crew in song.

Big Rig peered over Jack's shoulder. "She's probably working on one right now..."

Jack checked on the nocsi. She was mumbling to herself, her two large upper teeth tutting as she paced the cell.

"Well, there's nothing for it," Jack said. "We're run ashore otherwise. If you want out of here, we need to make a deal." Jack leaned in close, his voice a whisper. "What if I told you I've got a line to *Lady Luck*?" He winked. "She'll be ours again."

"*Lady Luck*? She still sails?"

"Aye, and a beauty she is, I hear. Refitted and waiting for us in Benevolence. Deed and all."

The dwarf's eyes shifted. Jack knew that look. *Hook, line, and sinker,* he thought.

"There's more, mate. We've got ourselves an opportunity to stick it to old man Fitzwater."

"The regent?"

"Aye. How's your smithy skills?"

"You trying to give offense?" The dwarf's face wrinkled with insult. "I'm a mountain dwarf, not some bloody forester. It's in me blood. I can forge a—"

"Steady on, lad!" Jack laughed. "Wasn't meaning no harm. So long as you're willing to pick up a hammer and take a wee trip into the mists to—"

"The mists?" Big Rig took a step back.

"You heard me clear as a sounding bell." Jack's face grew earnest. "We're sailing to Dragon Tail Island, lad. There and back with that there gnome." He pointed at Scarlett down the block. "Whatever treasure is in that tomb is ours. And we get to keep *Lady Luck* when we return." He winked, knowing his close friend understood the finer details involving the map. "Now," Jack puffed his chest. "You ready to sail under this captain again and do me the honor of being quartermaster? Even if that there nocsi's spewing sonnets while we make our escape?"

The dwarf's one good eye brightened. "Aye, I can do me some fleeing with that scurvy dog," he said, nodding to the other cell. Big Rig's white beard stretched, a hearty grin creasing his aged skin. "Back on the sea together!"

"That's the spirit! Show a leg, lad." Jack slapped his old friend heartily on the shoulder. "Let's parlay with this here nocsi."

"Jack!" Scarlett called, scurrying down the hall. "We have to go. The guard is starting to stir."

"Scarlett Tanash," Jack gestured at his old crew mate. "Meet Dûr Riggins."

"Pleasure," she said. "Now let's get out of—"

"Wee problem, lass," Jack said. "The corridor leading to the gallows is no longer accessible. This here nocsi says she's got a way around it." He held up a hand. "And before you ask, it's no bag of tricks. Big Rig here confirms it."

The gnome sighed and paced back and forth. "Right. I'm going to try and get to Doni back the way we came... see if I can speed up the prep for the drop. We need to get out of here as fast as possible."

"Without your cloak? You'll never get through the yard and up to—"

"I'll be fine. Remember, I'm a master—"

"Aye, understood." Jack nodded. By now he knew to not question her roguish abilities.

"Mr. Riggins, a pleasure." Scarlett nodded politely and met Jack's gaze. "See you at the gallows."

"Stop saying that!" Jack took another copper pence from his pocket and flung it into Big Rig's cell.

"One for me too, lad." The dwarf's grip on his wrist spoke of their shared superstition.

Jack tossed another coin and went to the nocsi's cell. "Time's short, lass," he said, peering through the bars. "Talk."

"A proper introduction first." The furry creature stepped into the light. "Siân Whetstone... bard and master of the spoken arts." She bowed.

"Captain James R. Hawk." Jack bowed in kind. "Pirate."

"Ah yes, the legendary Trusty Jack."

Now, how'd she know that?

"As for the route," Siân said, "I know of a hidden path that leads up to the gallows on the outer wall."

"Let's hear it."

She shook her otter-like head. "Not until I'm dealt in."

Jack furrowed his brow. "You've got another option? I seem to be holding the best hand."

"As a matter of fact, I do." The otter-like humanoid put her hands on her hips. "I'm in negotiations with the Flounders about—"

"Listen, lass. We ain't got time for no extended parlay. That guard and all the others are going to wake in mere minutes. I rotted in these cells for eight years." Jack spat. "I know the Flounders. They'll turn on you faster than a sloop coming about."

The nocsi tutted her two upper teeth.

"You're halfway out already," Big Rig said. "You just need out of that cell. And he's got the key."

"Aye, that's better than any schemer you've got working." Jack jingled the keyring.

The guard down the cell block stirred.

"'Schemer'... I like that." Siân touched a paw to her chin. "Clever. Quite piratey."

"If anyone would put a knife in your side once they had the route out," Jack said, "it'd be the Flounders. You'll end up in Davy Jones Locker to be sure."

"I know that one!" She clapped her paws. "'I'm working on a song about the death of—"

"Yes or no, you bilge rat!" Big Rig said. "This is your chance to get out of here. Then you can go your merry way and write, sing, poeti... poetize... whatever you call it!"

"What kind of deal is that?" The nocsi twitched her whiskers.

"You should be thankful you're even getting a parlay." Big Rig grumbled. "Your words are more slippery than the snakes who run this place."

"Well, if that isn't the sea turned upside down," Siân said. "A pirate isn't exactly an exemplar of—"

"Listen, lass," Jack said. "There's no time. And about us pirates... we don't respect the law because the laws and those who enforce them are unjust."

The nocsi's thick tail fluttered. "That I agree with, wholeheartedly. The regent is no friend of my people."

"Then we stand on mutual ground," Jack said.

"I have one condition," Siân said.

"Name it." Trusty Jack checked the sleep-stricken guard. The half-orc yawned, slumping on his stool.

"I sail with you on whatever this upcoming adventure is to the Dragon Island place..."

Jack's eyes narrowed. He had forgotten how good a nocsi's hearing was. She'd probably caught everything that passed between him and Big Rig.

"If this involves sticking it to Regent Fitzwater then I want in." She approached the bars. "He's out to push my people from their homes and destroy the kelp forests. As for my second condition—"

"You said one!" Big Rig whispered.

Jack grabbed the dwarf's arm as the guard stirred, mumbling and half-asleep.

"Two," Siân said, "I get to write your biography."

"Bard, if we live through all of this you can sing my tale across the Jeweled Sea," Jack said.

"Excellent!" She held a pawed hand through the bars.

Jack spat on his palm and shook it. "Agreed."

"Ew. That's a pirate thing that I am certainly not fond of." Siân withdrew her paw and wiped it on a furry leg. "That will not be going in the chronicles."

Jack matched the key number to the cell and turned the lock. "Now, lead the way."

"Oh no," the nocsi said. "I'm not coming out. You two are coming in." She gestured for them to enter.

"I don't think so," Jack said, smelling a trap.

Big Rig folded his arms and stood fast.

"Suit yourself." Siân strode to the rear of the cell. She ran a claw along a slab in the floor and lifted it up slowly and silently.

You crafty little nocsi, Jack thought and stepped inside.

"It takes us under and across the blocked corridor. We come out in the crossway... only a short distance up to the ward blocking the way out to the gallows."

And that's why you're still stuck here, he thought. *The bloody ward.* Scarlett, on the other hand, would take care of the magic barrier and be ready when they got there.

The nocsi dropped into the tunnel.

"Wait a moment," Jack said. He ran across the hall and carefully closed Big Rig's cell and locked it. Then he did the same to the nocsi's, reaching through the bars with the key.

"Clever," the bard said, her furry head sticking out of the tunnel.

"Every minute counts," Jack said.

"And all this time I thought you were scratching the stones to annoy me," Big Rig said.

"Typical dwarf. Totally self-centered." Siân vanished into the tunnel.

Jack dropped in after Big Rig. It was tight. He could barely fit along the crudely cleared passage. In the dim light from the opening behind him, he did his best to follow along.

"Is there a lute available on board?" the nocsi whispered.

"What's that?" Jack kept a hand on Big Rig's back to guide him in what was now utter darkness.

"A lute? Or perhaps a lyre? You can't expect me to sail the high seas with a famous pirate without musical accompaniment for my literary verse."

"I don't even have a ship yet, lass."

"What?"

Jack bumped into Big Rig, who stopped short.

"Just…" the dwarf grumbled, "… keep moving or we'll all be back in those cells. We'll get you a bloody harp."

"A lyre," Siân said. "There's a difference, Shorty."

"You regretting this yet, Jack?" Big Rig said.

"Keep moving, lad." Jack patted his old friend on the back. "We'll soon be free."

"I imagine your crew can teach me some sea shanties," Siân said, starting off again. "Oh, what a delight! I can even compose new—"

"No crew either," Jack said.

"No crew? Are you really *the* Trusty Jack?"

"Watch yourself, Nocsi," Big Rig grumbled "Jack's a man of his word, he is. That's why he's here breakin' me out, see?"

A pang shot through Jack's gut. He *had* kept his word. He and his former cellmate had vowed to do their best to free one another if ever either of them ended up back in Longshore. But it had taken fourteen years and a nudge from Scarlett Tanash for him to find the spirit to do it.

I should've been here years ago, he thought. The ghost of regret loomed over his shoulder as they scurried through the tunnel. Love, loss, and now his own selfishness in turning his back on the world, and a dear friend, rose.

"Okay, quiet now," Siân said.

Jack's ears recognized the familiar sound of a claw scraping stone. He shooed the specter away and readied himself.

With a creak, dim light returned.

The three crawled out of the passage.

"I know where this is," Big Rig said, looking about. "We're near the upper barracks."

The nocsi waved them forward.

Jack, getting his bearings, checked the passage in the opposite direction. All clear behind them. They were close. If he had his floor plan right, they were only two turns from—

"Hold it right there, you rats!"

In one motion, Jack swung around and drew his cutlass.

A guard closed the distance, a spiked mace in one hand and a bull's horn in the other.

"Carl, be that you?"

"Jack Hawk?" The guard stopped short. "It can't be... I'm seeing a ghost!"

"Aye it's me, lad."

"You're long dead!"

"Nay, I'm alive and well despite the warden and the regent's desires." Jack stepped forward, holding out the cutlass. "Now look here, Carl. You're a good lad. You never done me wrong while I was inside."

"Nor me," Big Rig said, behind him.

"You're breaking him out?" Carl pointed at Big Rig with the horn. "And that fur ball?"

"Carl, now I know you got sea pups at home..."

"They're all grown, they are. One just married."

"Oh, well that's mighty nice to hear," Jack said, and tightened his grip on the cutlass's handle. "Now, listen. I'm breaking these two out, see? I don't want to hurt you, Carl. So, let's make ourselves a deal, aye? You turn and walk away and we'll do the same."

Jack kept his eyes locked on the man's face. If he went for the horn, he would try and slice his arm off before it reached his mouth. If it got there first, he'd take the lips right off his face. "Otherwise, and it sorries me to say it, I'll have to stick you with this here cutlass."

The guard's expression softened. "I always liked you boys. Good prisoners, you were. Never made a fuss unless it came your way. Not like them Flounders."

"Aye," Big Rig spat. "Bilge rats all of them."

Shouts echoed down the hall.

Carl turned at the sound of more guards approaching.

"Moment of truth, lad," Jack said, dancing the blade through the air.

The man grinned. "Good luck to you, Mr. Hawk. I ain't afraid to say it. I'm glad to see you alive and kicking. Heard about your pirate exploits. And you too, Mr. Riggins. I don't want to see you back here a third time." Carl raised a thumb to his forehead, Navy style, and scurried back to the corner.

Jack smiled ruefully. *Always knew he had sailor's blood.*

"Oy!" Carl shouted. "They've gone that there way." The man pointed to the left.

Three guards ran past.

"Let's go!" Jack said.

The world was a topsy-turvy place. So many people trying to get by. *Good folk, most of them.*

"The magical ward's down!" the nocsi said, pointing ahead.

"Aye, Scarlett made it to the top. I'll go through first." Jack pushed open the thick wooden door, its hinges creaking like an old man's bones. He peered about. The outer wall, with the gallows projecting over the cliff, stood silent in the moonlight. No sign of Scarlett or Doni.

He motioned them to follow and made his way out.

"To the gallows," he said, pointing with his cutlass. "That there rope leads down to the sea."

"Where's the gnome?" Big Rig asked as he crossed the rampart.

"Well, well, well..." a fourth voice said from behind.

Jack swung around. "Blimey..."

The warden stood clutching Scarlett, a knife at her throat. "I must be dreaming because you look the spitting image of James Hawk with ten-odd years on him."

Jack took off his tricorne hat with his free hand and bowed. "Fourteen actually, Warden."

Bloomie, the half-orc cook, appeared from the stairs wielding a frying pan.

"I'd say you've got yourself in a fix," the warden said. The elf glanced over the wall to the inner yard behind her. "Come on up, lads! We got them!"

"I've got a nice cell down in solitary all made up, Mr. Hawk. Perfect place for a rat like you."

Jack caught movement on the rampart to the warden's right. A mouse scurrying closer...

"Don't think I don't know your part in framing me, Warden," he said. "You done abused your power and brought harm to me and lots of other folk in here."

"To criminals?"

He aimed his blade at her elven eyes. "I was innocent until you helped make me guilty."

The mouse edged closer.

The elf tightened her grip on Scarlett and stuck the dagger's point into the gnome's skin at her throat. "A nobody peasant trying to marry a princess? Fairy tale tosh, that is." The warden's eyes filled with fiery disgust. "It was my pleasure to help stop it. The regent and I have been fast friends ever since."

Eek!

Trusty Jack leapt as the mouse launched himself forward onto the warden's face.

The elf screamed.

Jack brought his blade down, taking her arm with the dagger clean off.

The warden's face spurted blood as Doni chomped her cheek.

Scarlett's form flashed by Jack's feet. In a blur, the gnome spun and swung something at the cook.

Bloomie halted, frying pan overhead, and gasped—the warden's dagger was stuck in her chest, the arm still gripping the blade's hilt.

Jack lifted a boot over a kneeling Scarlett and kicked the cook down the stairs. Bloomie tumbled like a rolling stone, taking out the guards on their way up. The lot of them rolled to the bottom and collapsed in a heap.

"Doni!" Scarlett leapt and reached out as the warden stumbled backward, colliding with the interior rampart. The gnome clutched the rodent off the elf's cheek just before she went over the ledge, landing with a thud in the prison yard three floors below.

"Come on, lass!" Jack grabbed Scarlett and threw her towards the gallows.

Siân and Big Rig were nowhere to be seen.

"Go!" he shouted.

Scarlett tucked Doni in her pocket and plunged down the rope.

Jack sheathed his cutlass and followed her, giving one last look back at the guards who had now reached the top of the steps.

"Trusty Jack is back, lads!" He cackled and shot down the rope. Two-thirds of the way to the sea, the line gave out and he splashed down into the water.

A head popped up next to him.

"Oh, this is wonderful! Wonderful!" Siân dove and appeared on the other side of the dinghy with amazing speed. The bard swam in circles around the boat.

"Give me your hand!" Big Rig reached over the railing, his iron grip taking hold of Jack's wrist and pulling him on board.

Splat! Splat! Splat!

A volley of arrows smacked the water around the boat.

"Go lad! Row!" the dwarf shouted to the sea elf at the oars.

Jack, drenched to the bone and dripping on the deck, bellowed a hearty laugh. "Scarlett Tanash, you're a right lass! That was a sight up there, that was!" He turned to find Doni reformed into his gnomish self. "You done good tonight, lad." He slapped the thief on the back.

The gnome grabbed the railing to save himself falling over the side.

"You really did," Scarlett said, a sparkle in her eye. "That was very brave of you."

"I lost your cloak. It was the only way to shift."

"You saved my life, Doni. The cloak doesn't matter."

"Do you think I'll make Four-Fingers for this?"

That teasing expression Jack had observed on Scarlett's face before they broke Big Rig out returned. "Maybe."

Doni's expression soured.

She pecked him on the cheek. "I'm sure of it. I was kidding."

Jack thought the gnome might fall overboard when she squeezed his hand.

"I'll never wash this cheek again," Doni said.

Scarlett slapped his arm playfully, taking a seat next to him.

"You're going about it all wrong, lad!" Big Rig stomped to where the sea elf was rowing them out to the sloop. "You need to head more to the northeast. The current's moving that-a-way." The dwarf's muscular arm aimed across the starlit sea. "You're adding minutes to the task."

Jack smirked. *That didn't take long.*

"Rig." Jack waved the dwarf to follow him to the seats at the stern.

Jack plopped down and thunked his boots up on the rail. The dwarf joined him, his bare feet coming to rest next to his own.

The dinghy swayed, the torchlight of Longshore growing more distant with every swell.

Jack reached in his pocket and held out a wet cheroot.

The dwarf leaned forward. "Oh, lad. How I've craved one of these!"

Trusty Jack glanced back over his shoulder. Scarlett met his gaze and smiled. "Soon as we're on board, we'll dry them out and spark em', Rig," he said. "Just like old times, mate."

"Ha!" In his ripped and ragged prison garb and long white beard, the dwarf looked like a hermit who had just emerged from a remote cave. "Good riddens!" He shook his fist at the prison on the cliff. "Now, Jacky boy." Big Rig stuck the cheroot into the corner of his mouth. "Where are we headed?"

"To Emerald Island, lad." Jack made as if puffing his unlit cheroot. "We're going to get Lana."

❦ 10 ❧

A SHOT ACROSS THE BOW

❦

Marian hurried through the streets of Redtown. In the crimson light of sunset, the upscale neighborhood of Kiha-Olo was aglow. Teak siding and mahogany shutters were lit up with fiery edges as the sun slid downward over the sea. The warmth of its rays was matched only by the euphoria running through her veins. She felt light as a feather, the lingering rush from the last hour of physical activity making the fifteen-minute walk from the library pass like a morning breeze.

The familiar whistling of the district's human lamplighter bounced down the cobblestones. He stood a block ahead on the curving street, his flame-tipped staff extended as he deftly lit the candle box at the entrance to The Palmetto Pub. Marian arrived at the thick wooden door, out of breath and tingling with sweat under her blue robe.

"Evening to you, Miss," said a well-dressed half-elf with an immaculately groomed white beard, as he opened the door.

A wave of raucous conversations, along with savory aromas from hearty plates of food, rolled past her and out into the street. The tavern's lively and vibrant evening crowd mixed and mingled.

"Packed to the gills as usual," the half-elf said.

With standard business hours over, and the fading light calling most of the service and labor jobs to wrap up for the day, everyone in the Kiha-Olo District had dropped by the local watering hole to relax, socialize, and celebrate another day's passing.

"Marian!"

Deep into the dense crowds and cramped tables, in the back corner, her fellow mage, Alara, waved a human hand back and forth as if she were a marooned sailor signaling to a passing ship.

Marian reciprocated and snaked her way through the rowdy patrons. Tables filled with humans, elves, half-elves, half-orcs, and a smattering of less common species like gnomes, dwarves, and nocsi were alive with chatter and drink. Even the aisles were crowded with those who opted to stand and engage in casual conversation with their fellow citizens.

"Sorry!" Marian raised a hand in apology as she bumped into a half-orc holding a long-stemmed pipe. The well-dressed patron nodded and took a pull on his smoker. He blew out a smoke ring before continuing his conversation with two humans and a half-elf.

"About time," Alara said as Marian reached her friends' table.

"Sorry, the evening got away from me."

Her fellow mage pushed out an empty chair for her to sit.

The two others at the table, elvish childhood friends of Marian's, Sinfu and Hana, smirked.

"What?" Marian slid her Palmetto Breeze, that someone had thoughtfully ordered for her, over from the center of the table and took a sip. She needed the hydration. The library had been exhausting in the best way possible.

"You think we don't know what's going on?" Hana raised an eyebrow.

Marian shook her head innocently.

"You're glowing brighter than the sunset out there, for one," Sinfu said, and thumbed in the direction of the pub's windows. "And two," the elf leaned forward across the table. "My friend who works across the street from the library saw you coming out of the director's quarters upstairs...same time, same day, the last two weeks. And interestingly enough... same day as today." The elf folded her arms in smug satisfaction.

Marian's mouth opened but no words came out.

"I knew it!" Alara pointed, a wide grin on her face.

"*Oh, I'm going to the library...*" Hana made as if strutting in her chair. "*There's so many interesting books to read.*" She pretended to pull one off an imaginary shelf and flip through it.

"I... you..." Marian's cheeks felt like they were on fire.

The group broke into laughter. She joined in, raising her glass. "A mage has needs, you know."

"Hear, hear!" Alara, also a magic user, raised her glass. "And you're still a wee sprite. Fifty's a spring chicken."

"He's what..." Sinfu said, eyes wide with curiosity, "thirty, at most?"

Marian rolled her eyes. He was thirty-three but she wasn't telling them anything. It was a perfect arrangement. Twice a week they met with no strings attached. So far, over the last two months, it had stayed that way. She'd not yet seen that puppy dog look in his eyes. When that happened, it was time to cut the cord and move on. She didn't need anyone following her around or wanting to tie her down. A bit of fun and physical intimacy suited her fine. The rest of it? At this point in her life, that was off the table. It was out the door and on the next ship to the mainland.

"He's very handsome," Hana said. "I mean... those spectacles."

More laughter.

"I admit to being jealous," Sinfu said. "It's bone dry down in the textile district. Everyone is either in a relationship or too obsessed with work to bother."

"So how long will you keep this one around, bookworm?" Alara asked.

Marian shrugged and took another swig of her Palmetto Breeze, settling in. She scanned the tavern. The weekly meetup with her long-time friends was the best medicine. *Well,* she thought, *almost as good as going to the library*.

"I say three months," Sinfu said.

"That would be a record," Hana responded.

"Okay, enough." Marian gave in. "And how are all of you doing?"

"Don't try to change the topic. We want details!" Alara said.

"Shhhhh..." Marian made a playful gesture with a finger at her lips. "It's the library. No talking, remember."

The group waved her off.

After two more rounds and two more hours of laughter, light-hearted conversation, and loud exclamations, they were making their way out of the tavern and into the street.

"Come on," Alara said. "I'll walk with you back to the fountain." The woman winked. "We mages have to stick together."

Marian hugged the other two in turn, said her goodbyes, and took a few more jabs about Tristan the librarian before she and her friends went their separate ways through the streets of Redtown.

"How are you doing with the fever in the Eel District?" Alara asked. Being a specialist in destruction magic, and a member of a separate guild, her colleague's time was given over to a quite different set of concerns.

"It's spreading, but no one wants to acknowledge it." Marian shook her head. "If we don't address it soon, it's going to reach the other districts. And, if it hops on a boat..."

"You're paranoid," Alara said. "It will pass. It needs to run its course."

"I don't think so. Not this time," Marian said. "I treated a child the other day. I got to her early enough that she should beat it. But the symptoms..."

"What about them?"

"They came on quicker this time. And there was a rash more intense than I've seen before."

"Could be an isolated incident. Maybe she's sensitive to the fever."

"Maybe..."

Being in a safer part of Redtown, the two let their guard down and turned to gossip and politics between the various schools of magic. Fifteen minutes later, they had reached the fountain and circle of guild halls. Each mage residence ran in succession, hugging a central fountain with a statue of an ancient golden dragon. Standing proudly on its hind legs, wings spread, the drake's head rose on a serpentine neck. Water, the color of blood, shot from its mouth, arcing down and into the surrounding pool like aquatic fire. The clever touch reflected the current ruling family's colors, its source the ancient elven magic of the sculptors who crafted the fountain before taking leave of the islands. The stone dragon's noble gaze was aimed at the sea—the direction the golden elves had fled on the backs of the majestic beasts a thousand years ago.

According to the surviving records, it was a strange and sudden departure. Shortly after saving Redtown from near destruction, the elves had declared their bond with the Jewel Islands broken. They had fled east over the sea into an unknown and, to this day, unexplored region of Arsel. Though the traces of their culture and magic lingered in the isles, the justifications for their flight remained closely guarded. As such, conjecture turned to legend by those of other species, as if the very grace of the elves had laid the foundation for rich and enthralling tales to cross the centuries.

"Great to see you as always, Marian."

"Same, Alara." She hugged her fellow mage and the two went separate directions around the fountain.

Marian spotted the usual candlelight coming from the upper rooms of the guild hall. That brought relief. She'd managed to get back before everyone was asleep. Navigating the creaky stairs and avoiding the high-pitched squeaks that might reach the guild master's elven ears was no easy feat. Even with years of practice the wooden steps still surprised her. If the elf woke up, well... then it was at least an hour in the kitchen with her while the old mage boiled water and drank a tea to put herself back to sleep. Standard punishment for those who chose to be, as the guild master called it, "crazed youths."

Marian approached the massive double doors with the guild's icon of healing magic.

A shadow, too dark to be cast from the nearby street candles, shifted at the corner of the building. Marian slowed her steps and reached into a pocket. Her fingers found the pre-mixed herb pouch for her blinding spell. Her other hand gripped the ornate dagger at her waist.

"Do yourself a favor, thief," she said, "and run along. You're in the wrong part of town looking for pockets to pick. Mages don't take kindly to intruders." She squeezed the herb packet tight and opened her mouth to speak the spell.

"My lady." The figure stepped out of the alley, their shadow morphing into a familiar face.

"Lithana?"

A human girl in her mid-teens nodded, removing her hood.

"What are you doing here? Shouldn't you be at the palace?"

"I should, yes." Her kitchen staff uniform peeked through the gaps in her cloak. "We're practicing some dishes and desserts for the upcoming celebration, and I was able to sneak out."

"Why?" She put away her dagger and the spell pouch.

"I overhead something, my lady." The girl looked around. "And I thought it important enough to come and find you."

"Alright, let's get you off the street. If you're seen out here you'll be in too much trouble for me to get you out of it. Chef Molard is a force not to be reckoned with."

"Ain't that the truth."

The dwarven chef was almost as intolerable as her father. Though, Marian was willing to give Molard a pass considering his sweet potato pudding had no rival in the Jewel Islands.

"Come on." Marian led Lithana towards the steps.

"Are you taking me into the guild hall?" The palace worker halted.

"Indeed." Marian smiled. "And you better be quiet inside or else the guild master will wake up and turn you into a toad."

⚬⚬⚬

LITHANA DID NOT TURN INTO A TOAD.

After entering the guild hall, Marian allowed the girl a moment to take in what she knew had to be a fascinating and unusual sight. Rich mahogany walls alive with intricate carvings, portraits of famous mages, and tapestries as blue as the deep dark sea surrounded comfortable couches, cozy armchairs, and low-lying tables.

Lithana gasped at the sight of Marge, the guild's sprite, when she floated down the hallway. The enchanted creature had been in residence for over three hundred years, its former bond companion a long dead mage from an earlier era of the guild's history. Marian managed to keep the girl quiet, whispering to her that the glowing orb was harmless. In fact, Marge was a powerful guardian who kept the members safe from intruders and other unwanted guests.

"Is that—" Lithana pointed at a row of wooden slots over a small table.

Sitting on a ledge underneath a label reading, 'Marian Fitzwater', a tiny blue ghost waved.

Marian managed to get her hand over the girl's mouth before she screamed. "It's fine," she whispered. "It's only an illusion."

The skin around Lithana's mouth was as taut as a sail in a gale. Marian could sense that the youth's entire body had gone stiff.

"It's not a ghost, I promise," she said. "It means I have mail."

That was a mistake. The combination of the extraordinary spectacle of illusion magic and its mundane significance appeared to put the girl into a state of terrified confusion. It was easy to forget that while magic was an established part of society in the islands, its use and purpose wasn't always accessible to common folk.

Many individuals had access to magic in the archipelago. Some, like sprites and nocsi, were born with innate abilities to harness it. While sprites could conjure spells at will, the otter-like species relied on local food sources to charge its magical potency. Other creatures in the wilds on land and sea were similar, and the majority were dangerous and to be avoided.

Then there were the trained arts, abilities taught to those with an interest and a talent for mental concentration and academic studies. Those schools of magic involved various arts—spell casting, imbuing magic into scrolls, enchanting physical items, augury through ritual and materials, and alchemy where herbalists crafted potions and poisons. All species could learn these arts, none more powerful or having a predilection greater than any other. It all came down to how hard one trained their mind and body to tap into the lingering traces of magic flowing through the islands.

With a wave of her hand and a single word whispered, Marian dispelled the postal specter.

"All good now?" she asked Lithana, still covering her mouth.

The girl nodded in earnest, but her eyes told a different story.

"You sure?"

A muffled "yes" came from the palace staffer.

Marian released her hand and checked the mail slot. "Give me a moment," she said, and opened the folded note that lay inside.

Dear Mage Marian,

I had the alchemist you recommended write this note. The herbal tea eased my daughter's rash and symptoms and we were hopeful the fever was passing. Today, it returned stronger than ever and she's taken a turn for the worse. We are already in your debt, but if you can help us in any way... we don't know what to do. I fear our daughter is fading and may not see the dawn.

Ever thankful to the Order of Telathia,
Kira Renshire

It's as I feared, Marian thought.

No sleep tonight. Once she wrapped up whatever news Lithana had brought with her, she would make for the Eel District. As the guild master often reminded her healers, working within arm's reach on one life was a most admirable task. The order's deity, Telathia, was herself a wandering altruist with a belief that all lives, regardless of species, status, or place of origin, were equal and deserving of compassion and grace.

Marian checked on Lithana. The girl gazed about, a mixture of curiosity, wonder, and guarded terror passing over her features.

She touched the youth's arm.

Lithana gasped and almost jumped through the ceiling.

"Quietly," Marian whispered and motioned her to follow down the hall. The stairs to the lower level of the Healer's Guild were built of stone and, if anything, were more dangerous as a slippery surface than a creaky disturbance. With a wave of her hand, Marian cast an illumination spell. A simple and untaxing magic, it created a soft light around her to light their way down the narrow steps.

Her hunch was correct. The lower level lay in darkness save for a thin line of light peeking out from under the doorway at the end of the hall. That would be Desdianté, a night elf obsessed with potions. Ever hard at work attempting to recreate ancient remedies from scraps of texts gathered in the guild's archives, Marian was more concerned with disturbing the elderly mage than being disturbed by him. The night elf, always hooded and with skin so dark one only noticed his glowing violet eyes, was a recluse. As a member of a faraway subterranean people, he ended up in the Jewel Islands ten years prior on a quest to locate rare ingredients for his experiments. According to the guild master's account, Desdianté had located the partial page of a recipe originating with the golden elves in the archives and had remained here working to solve its missing components ever since.

Marian led them to the first room on the right, an alchemical laboratory where she had a corner station along with several other mid-tier mages. Glass tubes of various dimensions and curving designs stood on tables next to mortars and pestles, and shelves with jars of powders, liquids, and other sundry preserved objects stacked so full some teetered on the edges.

"Don't touch anything," she said and closed the door behind them. Lithana nodded vigorously, her response making it clear she understood it was for her own protection. "Now, what's this all about?" Marian motioned for the girl to take a seat on a nearby stool.

"My lady, I was—"

"Lithana, you don't need to address me like that. Marian is fine."

The girl nodded, but she could tell the palace staffer was too uncomfortable with the shift from traditional classism.

"Mage Marian also works."

"Thank you, Mage Marian."

Lithana's slow, awkward enunciation of the title lingered in the air. "I overheard words... when I was crossing from the kitchens to the gardens to fetch herbs. They had the grand hall blocked off because it's being prepared for the celebrations."

Marian perked up. She knew from her time in the palace that the alternative route meant walking through the offices where her father, Master Rin, and other high-level government officials carried out affairs of state.

"I heard voices, and mind you, My... I mean, Mage Marian, I wasn't eavesdropping."

"Of course." They both knew that was a lie. All the staff did it, mainly because it offered gossip that livened up the monotony of their daily routines. Marian was certain there were one or two who passed information on to outside sources in the city, but she doubted Lithana was one of them. The girl was the daughter of a longtime employee in the kitchens, one who had been present during most of Marian's childhood and one whom she trusted. Besides, it was clear that the girl was terrified to be here.

"They were saying there'd been an escape from Longshore Prison. And that the warden had been murdered."

That got her attention. The warden was one of her father's closest allies. A despicable elf. She didn't grieve in the least for that one leaving the world, but the timing and impact of it would certainly resonate, especially so close to the inauguration.

"Go on."

"They said that two prisoners escaped, Miss. A nocsi and the other... well, it was a dwarf. A pirate who used to sail with Trusty Jack."

Marian rolled her eyes.

So, this was related to the never-ending drama and gossip at the palace about her earlier engagement and its so-called "tragic" turn of events.

"Lithana, please tell me you didn't come all the way down here to tell me that? It has no relevance to anything other than an event in my life over thirty years ago."

"Minding your pardon, but there's more. When I was walking past the office, it was Master Rin who was speaking. I heard the regent respond with much the same as you. But then the arch mage said that the second-in-command at Longshore had reported it was a man who broke them out..." Lithana rubbed her hands together. "Well, you see..."

"Who was it? Out with it!"

"Captain James Hawk."

Marian laughed. "Right." She shook her head and approached the girl. "Lithana, that man, that pirate, has been dead for fourteen years."

"I'm sorry. But I thought you would want to know."

"And why would I want to know that?

"Well, seeing as how—"

Now I see, she thought, reading the girl's face. *The endless dream of a fairy tale romance between a royal and a commoner.*

"First," Marian knelt in front of Lithana and softened her tone, "it's clearly a ruse by someone passing this information between its source and its destination... to spread rumors and even raise spirits with a false hope." She had to admit, anything that mustered the population against her father wasn't something she would dismiss, "or," she added, "simply for entertainment."

The palace staffer lowered her head.

"More to the point..." Marian eyed the girl. "The man was a scoundrel. A liar. A criminal. A pirate. A—" She caught herself as the fire rose inside her belly. "He's dead. And the Jewels are a better place for it. Understand?"

Lithana nodded. A hand reached into her cloak and withdrew a roll of parchment.

"What's that?"

"Minding your pardon, Mage Marian." The girl undid the string. "But they mentioned a sketch of the inmates and one of..."

Marian held out her hand.

Lithana hesitated.

"It's fine." She gestured to give it to her. "You need to put this back as soon as you return to the palace."

Marian unrolled it.

Her eyes went wide.

She knew that face. The cut of that chin. The eyes...

"Did they say who made this?"

"I heard Master Rin say one of the guards at Longshore has a talent of the hands."

Impossible, she thought. Her eyes passed over the other two sketches. A nocsi, coy and young with a sparkle in their eye, and a dwarf with an eye patch and thick beard. She read the name scribbled below the image.

Dûr Riggins, aka Big Rig. Former quartermaster on the Lady Luck.

Marian stepped back as if retreating from an unknown force.

There has to be an explanation, she thought. *Someone is playing games.*

"Did my father say anything?" Marian glanced at Lithana. "Sorry... did the regent say anything?"

"He did." The palace staffer's fingers tightened their grip on her cloak. "He said it was some kind of... I think the word he used was 'prop... propa...'"

"Propaganda." For once, she agreed with him.

"Miss?"

"Yes." Marian was half-listening, her eyes back on the portrait of James Hawk.

"Master Rin then said, 'I was there when the admiral,' meaning your sister, 'captured him.'"

"Yes, that's true."

"But then the arch mage said, 'I am not sure if your daughter ever told you what happened, but it's possible Captain Hawk could have lived.'"

"What?" Marian's eyes darted to the palace staffer. "What did the elf mean by that?"

"Apologies, Miss. A guard came by on rounds and I had to move on. That's all I heard."

Marian's mind spun like a rudderless ship. *Bonnie? What did Master Rin mean by 'it's possible?'* Her sister had run a blade through the pirate's heart. And hers with it, even though she hated the man for what he'd done.

"I'm sorry. If I don't return soon—"

"Yes, you need to go." Marian rose and handed back the sketch. "Return that before someone notices it's gone missing or they'll be even more trouble."

Lithana tucked the scroll away and wrapped her cloak about her.

Marian led her to the door.

"Actually, wait a moment." She scurried to her desk and grabbed a set of vials, stuffing them into a small pouch. "Take these with you. Keep them out of sight. Store them somewhere cool, away from the light."

"What are they?"

"Treatments for the fever."

The girl's eyes widened.

"That sickness doesn't discriminate between the city and the palace. It will get there eventually." She handed them to the palace staffer. "Give them to anyone on staff with children who needs them. It won't cure it, but it will give the infected one the strength needed to fight it." *I hope.*

"Thank you, Miss." The girl curtsied.

"And obviously don't let anyone near my father know about these."

Lithana nodded.

Marian recast the light spell and led the way back up and out of the guild hall. The night had taken on its full presence, with a blanket of stars over their heads. The splashing of the dragon fountain echoed off the surrounding buildings.

Marian placed a hand on Lithana's shoulder. "I appreciate you coming down here. But that part of my life is over. Even if it were true."

The girl's eyes lit up.

"And it is *not*. The man was a criminal, remember?"

"But he and the Salty Scoundrels always helped us common folk. The stories say—"

"The stories can say whatever they want about the man. It doesn't change the fact that he, and those who followed him, were outlaws. Trust isn't something they regard as valuable, despite the nickname. All pirates care about is gold, rum, and self-preservation."

"Yes, my lady."

"And for the sake of all the jewels in the sea, stop calling me that." She patted the girl's cheek. "It's Marian now. Or, if you prefer, Mage Marian."

Lithana's cheeks bloomed like roses.

"Run along. And tell Mrs. Yarlton in the kitchen that I said hello."

"I will." Lithana scurried off.

Despite her effort to shake it free, the crude sketch of her former lover and once betrothed, James Hawk, lingered in her mind.

꧁ II ꧂

CUT AND RUN

꧂

Three days at sea had been the best medicine. Scarlett noticed the change in Trusty Jack as soon as the sun rose after they fled the Ruby coast. With his longtime companion back at his side, the pirate's mood brightened like the morning sun. Hearty slaps on the back between them and intense discussions of the ship's riggings, its course, and other nautical minutiae were sips of a potion to the sea dog's spirit. She and Jack hadn't discussed it, but the fact that he'd gotten revenge on the warden, and an admission that the elf had helped the regent frame him, appeared to lift a weary burden from his prideful shoulders.

The dwarf was quickly making it onto her list of favorite people. Big Rig took no time at all to adjust to his newfound freedom. Dressed in an extra set of sailor's clothes, the pants and sleeves ripped and folded to accommodate his short and hulking frame, the former quartermaster stomped about as if he'd been on the ship for years. She'd had a fair amount of interaction with forest dwarves and spent enough time with their rarer mountain brethren to know that the ease with which Big Rig took to the sea was extraordinary among his people.

Regardless, his spirited and gregarious personality was infectious, and she found herself smiling whenever he was about.

Doni, on the other hand, had become... well, complicated. Undeterred by her attempts to find space to reflect on her conflicted feelings, her childhood companion was there whenever she turned around, smiling with a newfound glow in his eyes. It had been brave of him to intervene with the warden during their escape. Loathe as she was to admit it, something stirred within her that had been dormant since their youth. Despite her best efforts to convince herself otherwise, the warm and fuzzy feeling lingered.

Scarlett gazed off the starboard bow, scanning the Emerald Island's lush and verdant coastline. White sandy beaches and rolling hills drew closer with every passing swell. She glanced back at Doni, who sat in animated discussion with the nocsi. Siân listened to the gnome in earnest, strumming chords on an elven lute borrowed from a sailor as if putting words to song. That wasn't a good sign. Especially with the news she had to break to her guild companion when they reached Port Biathstone.

Scarlett sighed. Had her feelings in the moment gotten the better of her on the dinghy? *Put it aside,* she thought. *You have business to attend to...*

"Ship, ho!" a sailor shouted from the crow's nest. "Starboard tack!"

Trusty Jack and Big Rig were at the rail before the sailor finished his vocal alarm.

Ashana, the sea elven captain, joined them. She peered through her spyglass and then handed it to Jack. A brief conversation ensued between all three, with Big Rig pointing to an area along the approaching coast. Nods followed and they dispersed.

"What is it?" Scarlett asked as the dwarf stomped up to the front of the ship.

"You don't want to know." He grabbed a rope and helped the sailors trim the canvas.

"We're making a run for it." Jack said as he came forward, strapping his cutlass to his waist.

"Is it a Navy vessel?"

The pirate shook his head.

By now, word of the escape and murder of the warden would be out. The only thing they had going for them was that the sloop had been veiled in darkness during the extraction. The regent's ships would be looking for a dwarf and a nocsi, and a pirate claiming to be a dead legend, but they'd have no idea of the fleeing ship's class or profile. Scarlett was betting on the fact that their pursuers would also have to consider a brief escape by sea, followed by a run over land. In short, her idea had been to have the authorities thinking they could be anywhere on Ruby Island or fleeing its surrounding waters.

"See that inlet?" Jack pointed to a narrow chasm interrupting the flowing hillsides. "We're making for that cove."

"Can we fit through there?"

"Aye." Trusty Jack put his hands on his hips and stood tall. "That's why most pirate ships be sloops, lass. We can slip into sheltered coastlines where bigger frigates and galleons can't follow. Saves many a pirate's backside, a sloop does." He patted the ship's railing affectionately.

"They're faster too, from what I've witnessed," she said.

"Well, lookie here." The pirate raised an eyebrow. "Is that a bit of salt I see dried on those pointy ears?"

She swatted his encroaching finger away and laughed.

"Need not worry about that ship yet, lass. Plus, we've got the weather gauge."

"Weather gauge?"

"Aye, advantage with the wind. It's in our favor."

Scarlett narrowed her eyes and focused on the approaching ship rounding the coast. It looked massive, with three masts, but its details were shrouded in a hazy blackness. Something about that left a sour feeling in her stomach.

"I'm trying to make out the ship but... it's strange. I can't—"

"You'll see it soon enough." Jack's crow's feet creased as he met her gaze. "And you'll wish you hadn't."

"Is it a pirate ship?"

"Aye. The worst kind." He peered up at the sails and scanned their course. "We'll make it to that cove, though. It's a matter of if they've spotted us or not." He slapped her back. "Hold fast, sea dog." The pirate strode off, making his way to the captain at the ship's wheel.

"What's going on?" Doni asked, joining her at the bow, the nocsi at his side.

"Pirate ship," she said. "Jack thinks we'll make it to that cove." She pointed ahead.

"And then what?"

"I don't know." Scarlett peered over the side. The water's hue shifted to a lighter and clearer blue as they ran past a stretch of bone-white coral at a depth of no more than thirty fathoms. "Something's wrong with the reef here."

"That," the nocsi said, peering over the side, "is what happens when you over-harvest sea kelp."

"Sea kelp? Is it that much in demand?"

"No." The otter-like creature's voice shifted, growing earnest. "It has its uses in food products and salves, but the intent is to destroy the natural habitat."

"Why would they do that?" Doni asked.

"To promote a delicacy. And, conveniently, to force my people to migrate. When that happens, the balance of aquatic life breaks down. Without sea kelp, we can't thrive." The nocsi gazed at the reef as the ship cut through the shallow water. "Remove my species and you have no way of controlling the shellfish population." A furry paw pointed at the passing coral.

"Are those oysters?" Scarlett asked. The dead coral now appeared as an endless landscape of shimmering gray and blue shells.

"Indeed. I would be lying if I said I wasn't holding back from jumping over the side and tasting one."

The ship eased. The flapping of canvases followed along with shouts from the crew. Down the coast, the black ship vanished behind the cove's sheltered hillside. Colorful birds, of a variety unknown to her, flew about and huddled in nests on the cliff's rocky sections between lush, blooming vines.

"How do you survive without the kelp?" Doni asked.

"Oh, we can eat different foods, like you. But the kelp is how we're able to reproduce, and how we access our magic."

Force waves, Scarlett thought. She'd heard about Nocsi powers—a form of psionics unique to the species. "It comes from the kelp, doesn't it?"

Siân nodded. "Without it, our magic stirs, but can't manifest. And our population is born of a mating season spurred by the late-blooming kelp blossoms that trigger a dormant desire."

"The upper classes have a keen taste for oysters," Doni said. "I witnessed that in Redtown."

"Indeed," Siân said. "Not to mention they're exported to Drakeland for a similar purpose. The regent's attitude is that nocsi are a nuisance standing in the way of massive profit. He's got a personal love for the delicacy, from what I've heard." The bard strummed the elvish lute, a tragic tone of lament drifting away over the cove's placid waters. "And so we leave. We move on. They follow. We move again. Each time fewer of my people arrive at the next untainted reef."

"That can't continue forever."

Scarlett winced at Doni's lack of tact.

"No, it can't," the nocsi said, playing a melody on the strings that made her heart twist. "Last I heard, my people are—"

"Alright, me hearties." Trusty Jack approached. "We're going to drop anchor and hold here. Siân, I imagine you'll be wanting a taste of them oysters. Sorry to see the reef in this state, lass. Bloody regent's got no sense in his head doing what he's doing to the seas."

The nocsi nodded.

"Have a go at some if you like," Jack said, "but stay close to the ship in case we need to rally, savvy?"

"Thank you, Jack." Siân was off to stow the instrument before diving in.

"Now, I want to climb up that rise and have a looksie." He held up the captain's spyglass. "You wanted to see that ship, aye?"

Scarlett nodded. "I'll come, yes."

"I'll come too."

Scarlett caught Jack flashing her a look. *He doesn't miss a beat.*

"Of course, lad," the pirate said. "Didn't think for a moment you wouldn't want to be there to protect your sweetheart."

Scarlett rolled her eyes.

"This way." Trusty Jack led them from the bow to midships where a dinghy had been lowered.

Scarlett descended the rope ladder and took a seat. Doni followed, nudging up next to her on the plank.

Jack's smirk didn't go unnoticed.

The cove was beautiful. Crystal clear water and abundant plant life along its cliffs passed as the pirate rowed them ashore. A small border of white sand hugged the shoreline. Scarlett could imagine spending an afternoon here, the world and its woes falling away.

"Who owns this land?" she asked.

"Most coastline on Emerald Island is the property of gentry," Jack said. "Renters tend it, grazing livestock on the hills and paying tithes. But long stretches are wilder. Seein' as we're close to Port Biathstone, this section's safer than most but the more isolated shores can be right dangerous. Strange creatures lurk in caves, and wolves and other unsavory beasts roam about after dark."

Tingle would have loved it here, she thought, gazing at the secluded cove.

Jack aimed the dinghy so the bow ran aground on the sand. He pulled the boat onto the beach and stretched his arms, taking in the view. "If all goes well, I think I'll take me a proper swim before we row back out." The pirate winked at Doni. "You ought to try it, lad. Water here's right warm and the sand runs deep, farther than your height."

"I can't swim," Doni said, lowering his eyes.

"Well, blow me down." Jack raised an eyebrow. "You were lucky that dinghy was there when we dropped from Longshore." He leaned down eye to eye with the gnome. "And even luckier your lass there had you in her pocket."

There was that pang again. She'd forgotten that Doni had never learned to swim. And yet, he didn't mention it. Even after knowing the plan would take them into the sea that night.

Jack caught her eye and smiled.

You too now? She groaned inside. *This is all I need.*

"Show a leg, me hearties." The pirate started off. "We need to get up with time to get back and out of the cove if there's unforeseen problems."

'Unforeseen problems,' she thought. *Interesting way to put it.*

Scarlett let Doni go ahead and followed at the back. A faint path meandered on a switchback up the cove's south side. "What kinds of birds are these?" she asked when they reached the midpoint among the nests. One of the elegant orange and white creatures hovered a few feet off the cliff face, chirping in defense of its territory.

"Those be cove doves, lass. But most refer to them by their nickname."

"What's that?" Doni asked, huffing and struggling to keep pace with the larger pirate.

"Love doves." A chuckle from the front of the line followed.

"Why do they call them that?" Doni asked.

"Males chase the females all season. They pick one lass and give her their heart."

Scarlett shook her head in defeat.

"Takes the females a long while but eventually they see what's right in front of them. And then... well, you know how it is, lad." Trusty Jack slowed and bent his knees.

Scarlett peered over Doni's shoulder at the pirate's crouched form.

"Now, let's have a looksie. Stay low." Jack waved them forward.

Scarlett crested the hill. To her left, a few miles up the coast, rows of houses and streets were packed along the shoreline of a seaside town. Smoke rose here and there from chimneys, and she marked three merchant ships anchored in the harbor.

"Port Biathstone," Jack said, crouching. "Looks to be thriving."

Scarlett scanned the sea. An endless blue blanket shimmered under the morning sun. She passed over Jack's crouching form and continued to the southwest. Her eyes halted at the black ship, closer now, making its way down the coast.

"Jack..."

"Aye, we'll know within a minute or two whether she's got us." He handed her the spyglass.

Inside the circular frame, the ship took shape. A wave of dread ran through her at the sight. A three-masted vessel, massive, with black sails, rose and fell on the swells.

"What ship is that?" Doni whispered.

"*R.I.P. Tide*," the pirate said.

Scarlett lowered the spyglass.

"As in 'Rest in Peace'..." Jack's chilling gaze cut into the otherwise pleasant morning sun. "Captained by the most fearsome pirate alive."

"The Scourge of the Jewel Sea," Scarlett said.

"Aye," Jack spat. "And her ship's heading right for us."

"Can they fit in the cove?" Doni asked.

"Nay, lad. That there's a galleon. But she can anchor in deeper water and wait. Or..." the pirate let the word hang in the air, "send in the smaller boats to try and take the sloop."

That's all we need, Scarlett thought.

"Blimey," Jack muttered.

"What is it?"

"Galleon's turning. Looks like she's bearing northeast."

Relief rushed through her. "We're safe?"

"I think so, aye."

"Thank the gods," Doni said.

"Ship's about now," Trusty Jack said. "You should be able to see the captain at the helm."

Scarlett raised the spyglass and peered about the deck, scanning left and right until— "Wait," she said, spotting the captain. "... I don't understand."

"That be Captain Pitch. Half-orc and a half-ogre."

Through the circular lens, a towering figure stood at the *R.I.P. Tide's* wheel. The topknots of half-orcs on deck, themselves over six feet tall, reached only to the captain's shoulders. She wore a large tricorne hat and black leathers with a long coat and tails. Polished bones lined her outfit like armor, sewn into the fabric. Scarlett's eyes homed in on a large silver staff topped with a horned skull strapped to her back. Even at this distance, the weapon sent a chill through her bones.

"She has a staff," she said, peering through the lens.

"Aye. Pitch is a sorcerer, she is."

A sorcerer? Scarlett shivered. So, this is the one she'd heard about on her crossing to Mayrotten Island.

"Now ain't that odd..." Jack said. "Let me see that spyglass, lass."

Scarlett handed it back. "What is it?"

"Merchant ships... with a naval escort. A bit further out to sea."

She narrowed her eyes and focused nearer to the horizon. He was right. It looked like two merchant ships and one frigate flying the navy colors.

"Something's amiss here," the pirate said. "That don't add up."

"What doesn't?"

"Even if the *R.I.P. Tide* didn't see us, she'd take out that lone Navy boat for breakfast. With two merchants running goods? 'Tis easy pickings... and yet she's sailing on."

"Towards Ruby Island?" she asked.

"Aye... 'tis strange indeed." Trusty Jack lowered the spyglass and met her gaze. "Unless I'm a troll's uncle, those merchant ships with their Navy escort are heading to Port Biathstone."

"Then we've got a problem." Scarlett said. "We can't go waltzing into harbor with the Navy there."

"Aye, I say we leave the ship in the cove and go on foot," Jack said. "Keep a low profile and get a carriage to Liddleton."

"But that will take hours," Doni said. "We don't have any time to lose."

"No, we don't," Scarlett said. This was going to dig into their already tardy schedule. "We're going to be cutting it close getting back to Redtown before the inauguration."

She glanced at Doni. His face was full of enthusiasm, as usual.

Just once can he make it easy on me and not look so adorable.

"Let's get back to the ship," she said. "Jack, I'm thinking you, me, and Big Rig head to Littleton. We leave Siân and—"

"What about me?" Doni asked.

"You need to get your things packed up."

"I'm coming with you to Port Biathstone?"

"Yes." It wasn't a lie.

"Why do I need my things?"

"Because you're not coming with us to Liddleton." It pained her to say it, even more so when she saw the look on his face.

"Why not?"

"Because you're going back to Redtown."

SCARLETT HUSTLED THROUGH PORT BIATHSTONE, HANDS GRIPPING the large sack weighing down her back. She'd had to wait almost two hours for the shops to open after lunch. More time lost. Every step of this operation was plagued by a setback. So far, they'd been relatively minor but together they were taking a toll. According to her calculations, two full days had been lost putting them considerably behind schedule.

Her short legs trod the cobblestones of Port Biathstone's winding streets, retracing her route to where she'd left the others on the outskirts of town. After fifteen minutes, the patterned pavement gave way to dusty dirt, the town's row houses replaced by less frequent single-standing homesteads.

By the time she wandered off the road and through the palm trees and tall grasses, she was soaked in sweat.

"Over here, lass!"

Jack's tattooed forearm emerged from behind a boulder.

"Where have you been?" Doni asked. "You were gone for—"

She held up her hand. "Apparently everyone takes lunch here. A *long* lunch."

"Everyone eats lunch." Doni shrugged.

Jack put a hand on the gnome's shoulder. "Aye, I should have remembered. South Emerald folks take a 'nooner' at midday for two hours. It's because of this bloody heat." He squinted and nodded at the blazing sun.

"I could use something in my belly, if I'm honest," Big Rig said, sitting with his back against the boulder. "Oh, to think of the delicacies I'm going to consume now that I'm out..." His expression brightened. "No more of Bloomie's flavorless stews for me."

"Ain't no one eatin' any more of Bloomie's stews, lad," Jack said.

"Ha!" Big Rig aimed a finger at the pirate and cackled. "Truth to that, scallywag!" The dwarf rose, grunting with the effort.

"Here." Scarlett plopped down the sack and handed each of them a set of clothes.

She didn't miss Doni's expression when he examined the more casual attire she'd purchased for him.

"Just to play it safe," she said, meeting his eye. "It may be that someone gets questioned about us in Longshore, maybe at The Crying Gull. If they describe what we were wearing..."

Her guild companion nodded. At least he understood the prudence of it.

"These are quite fancy," Jack said, examining a well-tailored shirt. He placed it against his chest and turned to his dwarven companion. "Pardon me," he said in a snobby and nasal voice, "but you wouldn't happen to be Mr. Riggins, by chance?"

"Indeed, I am good sir." The dwarf plopped the top hat on his head. "Would you care to join me for lunch? I believe we're dining on crab fritters overlooking the bay."

The two erupted into laughter.

Scarlett rolled her eyes and went off to change in private. When she returned, wearing a flowered cotton dress, all three were properly suited and ready.

"It will please you to know, Mr. Riggins," she pronounced his name with the same air of condescension the two had used in their earlier performance, "that I have provided us with a small picnic." She handed out some wrapped sandwiches and flasks of lemonade.

"Oh, you are a lass!" Big Rig's usual gruff tone was back. He accepted the items, a look of childlike joy on his face. His eyes went wide when he unwrapped the sandwich. "Jacky boy, you see what she done brought us?"

The pirate unfolded his paper square. "Is that real cheese and oysters, lass?"

"It is." She bowed. "Keep it between us. I wouldn't want to upset Siân."

"My ropes are tied, Ms. Tanash," Big Rig said, taking a hearty bite. "Far as I'm concerned, it was fish stew and..." The dwarf lost his train of thought, chewing and grunting, as he savored the sandwich.

Thirty minutes later, their bellies full, they arrived at the carriage station on the north end of Port Biathstone.

"Here." Scarlett returned from the rickety office and handed Doni his transport slip. "This will take you north on the coastal road to Wioma Bay. From there, you can catch the schooner back to Redtown."

The gnome nodded, accepting the ticket.

Scarlett checked the street. When no one was looking, she slipped Doni a scroll. Even if there were spies in the shadows, the action would have gone unnoticed. The exchange was a practiced Thieves Guild handoff taught as soon as one became a member.

"Get that to the local guild den in Redtown," she said. "They'll make sure it reaches the Guild Master in Drakeland across the sea." She locked eyes with the gnome. "As soon as you arrive, Doni."

"I will."

"Carriage to Liddleton! Departing in two minutes."

Scarlett glanced at the horse and buggy. A portly, unkempt man in suspenders waved at their group.

"Give us a minute, would you?" she said to Trusty Jack and Big Rig. "I'll be right there."

The two well-dressed pirates nodded and made for the carriage.

Scarlett took the gnome's hand and squeezed it. "Take care, Doni."

"I will," he said and squeezed back.

"Listen, what happened on the dinghy was a mis—"

Doni leaned in.

Scarlett reared back and turned, his lips landing on her cheek.

"Liddleton carriage departing!"

Doni's eyes were a storm of confusion.

"Miss, if you're coming..."

Trusty Jack and Big Rig, standing next to the driver, waved her to hurry.

"I have to go." She let go of his hand and scurried to the carriage.

"Apologies," she told the driver.

"Not to worry, Miss." The man helped her up.

Big Rig and Trusty Jack sat next to one another on the rear side of the compartment, looking both convincingly disguised and ridiculous at the same time.

A snap of the reins, followed by a jolt as the wheels began rolling, and they were off.

"Well, it is a nice afternoon, isn't it?"

Scarlett narrowed her eyes at Jack. Despite the attempt to deflect from the obviousness of the incident with Doni, his comment made her feel *more* uncomfortable.

"Strange that Lana is in such a quiet hamlet," the pirate added.

Big Rig's one good eye focused on Jack.

"He doesn't know," she said, bouncing as the carriage hit a rut. "I told him it would be complicated but nothing more specific."

"Ha!" Big Rig slapped his freshly pressed pants. "This is going to be the best entertainment I've had in a decade."

12

SPLICE THE MAINBRACE

"**L**iddleton!"

Jack woke with a start.

Across from him in the buggy, Scarlett smirked.

"What?"

Honk! Zzzzzz... Honk! Zzzzzz...

Big Rig's bald head lay nestled under Jack's arm, the pirate's lap as his pillow.

"Wake up ya' scurvy dog!" Jack shoved the dwarf over.

"What is it?" Big Rig came to, looking about. "Shift change? We nearin' port?"

Scarlett covered her mouth and giggled.

"Listen here, lass..." Jack pointed at her. "If you ever—"

The carriage door opened and the driver's head poked inside. "Liddleton, folks. You all getting out? If you're going on to Tenoki it'll be another eight coppers per passenger."

"Oh, indeed. Liddleton is our stop," Scarlett said in a performative tone.

Jack kept his expression straight.

"It appears we've arrived, my good sir," Big Rig, now awake and aware of the situation, said. "Ye shall be... um... well..." he grumbled. "Just get out," he whispered, nudging Jack with his elbow.

We're doomed, Jack thought. He stepped out from the carriage and helped the dwarf down the steps.

With a snap of the reins, the carriage was off, lumbering down the dirt road.

The three stood in silence as it rounded a bend and vanished.

Jack gazed about, taking in the rainforest. That familiar mixture of tranquility and foreboding of the Jewel Island's jungle interiors rose, filling the void left after the incessant creaking of the carriage on their journey. Intermittent bird calls interrupted extended and eerie silences, accented by the occasional howl of a Galanki monkey.

He always felt like an interloper in the jungle. Uninvited and... watched.

"So much for Liddleton," Big Rig said, approaching a rickety road-side stand. A stool behind it stood empty. The dwarf picked up a sign that had fallen from a rusty nail and held it out for Jack and Scarlett to see.

"Looks like there's a return carriage from Tenoki to Port Biath-stone at seven o'clock this evening," Scarlett said, reading the scribbled schedule. "We need to be done and back here by then. Otherwise, we'll be stuck in Liddleton for the night."

"Not sure there is a Liddleton," Jack said. Hints of cleared pasture and bright sunlight peeked through breaks in the dense jungle. The so-called "hamlet" was merely a stop along a sparsely populated agricul-tural section of the island.

"I feel like a fish out of water this far inland," Big Rig said and kicked a rock down the road.

"Same lad," Jack said. "These fancy threads ain't helping either." He twisted and shifted, fighting the tightened collar of his starched shirt.

"Bloody hot," the dwarf said, smacking a mosquito on his neck. "With this humidity there'll be rain clouds by late afternoon."

"Then we better get going." Scarlett started off down the lane.

"To where, lass?"

She pointed ahead at the side of the road.

Jack made out a wooden sign poking through a cluster of hibiscuses with the words *"Home of Rest"* carved in fancy script. Underneath it was an arrow aiming in the direction of an intersection leading east.

"I think we may have overdressed for the occasion," he said, and nodded for Big Rig to follow.

"Nonsense," Scarlett said. "We're solicitors, remember? We deal in estate holdings and inheritance." The gnome turned around and walked backwards. "We do quite well for ourselves."

Jack shook his head. With what she and the dwarf had told him about Lana's situation on the ride from Port Biathstone, he couldn't imagine this plan was going to work.

"Like you said, lad, this is going to be one right amusing afternoon." Jack pulled out two cheroots and handed one off to his quartermaster.

The dwarf's bushy eyebrows furled, scrunching his face under the top hat.

"What?"

"How you plan on lighting these, mate?"

"Bollocks," Jack said. He yanked the smoker from his mouth and tucked it back in a pocket.

"It's ahead," Scarlett said, picking up her pace. "I see a stone wall."

That's not enough to keep Lana inside, he thought. How the half-orc was going to react to seeing him alive had him far more concerned than his re-introduction with Big Rig inside Longshore's dungeon.

The gnome signaled to halt and motioned them to the side of the lane. She pointed ahead. "Two guards at the entrance."

"Let's go talk to them," Big Rig said, "that's the plan, ain't it?"

The thief peered about. "Let's have a look around. Follow me. But first..." She put both hands on her hips and eyed them.

"What?" Big Rig said.

"*Don't* muddy up your clothes."

"You sound like me mum," the dwarf said.

Scarlett raised an eyebrow.

"Aye, we'll be careful," Jack said.

Cautiously, the three made their way off the path and through the rainforest.

"Do you hear that?" Scarlett asked, stalking her way towards the stone wall.

Jack shook his head, recalling the gnome's advantageous hearing during the breakout at Longshore.

The thief led them left, further from the gate.

Jack caught sight of a bell tower and a three-story structure inside the walls. If he had to guess, he'd say it was a former monastery converted into a convalescent home.

"—and now step forward... raise arms into crane takes flight."

"That's Lana!" Big Rig whispered, crouching next to him.

"Aye, no doubt." Jack scratched his head at her unusually calm tone.

They reached the wall and put their backs against the stone, staying low.

"Shift left... feel the energy swelling. And now step forward... raise arms into crane takes flight."

"We did that already," a human voice said.

"What are you on about?" Lana's words spat forth without the ease and grace of her previous instructions.

"We did that already," the human repeated.

"No, we didn't."

"Yes, we did. We *just* did it two seconds ago."

A chorus of voices, in a variety of species, muttered affirmation with the human's claim.

"Don't tell me what's what!" Lana's voice boomed. "Do you think I'm—"

"Ms. Luholi!" a commanding voice said. "Mind your tone."

"Same old Lana," Big Rig whispered.

A half-orc growl echoed off the stones. "Yes, headmaster. But they're sayin' I was repeating—"

"How about you take it from there? What's the next technique?"

"Snake bites the ankle," she said. "And that's what I'm going to do if any of you try and tell me—"

"Alright, I think that's enough for today," the headmaster said. "Lana, come with me, please. The rest of you get yourselves back to the patio and assemble for dinner."

"Okay," Scarlett said. "She's here. We've got that far. And, if she has access to the yard and can move freely inside then this should be a breeze."

Jack shook his head.

"What?" Scarlett whispered.

"Nothing. Just... you do the talking." He pointed at her. "Us two will do the noddin'."

Big Rig nodded.

"Agreed." She waved for them to follow and scurried back to the road. Within five minutes they were approaching the front gate.

"Good afternoon," Scarlett said to a human guard at the entrance. "We're here to see one of your patients. A Miss Luholi..."

"And you are?" the guard asked.

"We're from Tithers, Polk, & Greybeard," Scarlett said. "Solicitors and representatives of the patient's family estate."

"I'm Mr. Greybeard," Big Rig said, and removed his hat in a dramatic bow.

Jack struggled not to make a face. *This is going to be a disaster.*

"We have some unfortunate news about her aunt." Scarlett sighed. "Well, her *late* aunt. There are some documents to sign and an inheritance to discuss."

"We were told of no such appointment." The half-orc flanking the human stepped forward. Her eyes ran over Jack before examining Scarlett. "Where you from, eh?"

"Topaz Island," Scarlett said. "Our office is in Palm Cove."

"You don't sound like you're from Topaz."

"Well, that's our local headquarters in the Jewels," she said. "We're a subsidiary of a larger firm in Drakeland across the sea."

"A what?"

"A subsidiary. We have no appointment because the death was quite sudden. Tragic, really... and there's a limited timeframe to have the estate processed so the patient can receive the inheritance."

Jack read the half-orc's expression. She wasn't budging. *Southern Emerald native by the sound of her. Worth a shot.* "Believe me," he said, using his best Topaz accent, "it's not our choice to come on short notice. It's the new guidelines coming out of Redtown. Quite a nuisance for us on the smaller islands. It's not like we have the same access to notaries and banks as on Ruby."

The half-orc's expression softened. "You're telling me," she said. "Same here as on Topaz." She nodded at her companion, who opened the gate.

"Bodon here will take you in," the half-orc said. "Supposing you'll need to see the headmaster?"

"Indeed," Scarlett said. "And, thank you. The walk from the carriage stop has put us in quite a state." She dabbed her forehead with a kerchief.

Big Rig removed his top hat. "I, as Mr. Greybeard, also thank—"

Jack yanked the dwarf along.

❦

TRUSTY JACK TOOK A SEAT NEXT TO SCARLETT ACROSS FROM A stern-looking half-elf. Her face reminded him of those shrunken apple heads sold by passing caravans along the coastal circuit. As if struck by lightning, her gray hair stood on end in wiry two-inch strands. One seat short, Big Rig remained standing. The dwarf fiddled with his top hat like he'd been summoned to answer for a schoolboy offense.

The headmaster's office held a strange tension, a palpable care and sympathy for elderly folk blended with a strong desire to preside as a disciplinarian. Dusty books lay stacked on shelves, their titles ranging from guidelines for incarceration to the needs of the convalescent. Alchemical devices of all shapes and sizes littered the available tables and countertops. Dried herbs and flowers hung from thick wooden rafters, giving the office a feel of an antique laboratory.

Jack lost himself in the beams of colorful light interrupting the dreariness. Red, green, yellow, and blue reflections dappled the walls and floor from a stained-glass window set under a pointed arch. He recognized the central figure: Gratarius. His hunch had been correct. This was a former monastery to an old divine, one of the eight who walked the world spreading spiritual knowledge of their sacred pantheon. Those days were dead going on almost a thousand years, replaced by a modern world that, while still respectful of the spirits whose traces of magic lingered, had shifted from devout worship of intangible beings to a celebration of more practical ethics and a belief in the firm hand of a noble elite.

The headmaster placed her withered and wrinkled hands on the desk. "So, I'm to understand you're here related to our correctional intern, Ms. Luholi?"

"Indeed," Scarlett said. "We'd like to speak with her about some unfortunate family news. And an opportunity for her to return with us back to—"

The headmaster held up a hand. "I don't think that is a good idea, Ms....?"

"Polk."

Jack felt a wave cresting. This wasn't going to be a downwind run.

"Ms. Polk," the headmaster said, "Are you aware of Ms. Luholi's history?"

"Indeed, I am. As a representative of her extended family, myself and my colleagues here are informed about the Luholi's in the Jeweled Islands. We've been briefed on Lana's extensive training in her youth at the monastery, followed by her expulsion due to anger issues and a penchant for violence, as well as her subsequent stint on a pirate vessel by the name of..." she looked at Jack. "What was it?"

He cleared his throat. "*Lady Luck.*"

"Yes, *Lady Luck*. Under the now-deceased buccaneer, Captain James Hawk."

"And," the headmaster added, "a subsequent ten-year sentence in Longshore... converted to an internment in our experimental rehabilitation program."

"Rehabilitation program?" Jack asked.

"Indeed, for her anger issues and memory loss."

"Yes, the latter was related to a blow to the head during the incident involving her capture, unless I'm mistaken?" Scarlett said. "Hit by that bar that swings around with the sail. I can't remember the technical term..."

"Boom." Big Rig's deep voice echoed off the stone walls.

"Yes, thank you," Scarlett said.

"Ms. Luholi's memory loss has passed, thankfully," the headmaster said. "Her violent tendencies and temper remain."

"It's my understanding," Scarlett said, "that according to the agreement with the correctional institution, if Ms. Luholi wishes to exit your care she can do so after seven years at your facility... it's now been five."

"That is correct," the half-elf said.

"However," Scarlett edged up in her chair, "a clause allows for early release if she is placed under the responsibility of her family, with demonstrated financial viability to cover her care, for the remaining years under contract."

"Only if her family is willing *and* if Ms. Luholi agrees to do so," the headmaster said. "Which I can tell you, speaking on her behalf, she does not." The half-elf narrowed her eyes and leaned forward. "Lana is happy here. Does she have anger issues? Certainly. We have been working on introducing her to spiritual teachings in the hope of exposing the source of her violent tendencies." She gazed at the image on the stained-glass window as if it held the answer. "That remains a work in progress. But, nevertheless, Lana is at peace in this home." A withered finger pointed at the row of dried herbs hanging from the rafters. "She tends a beautiful garden."

Lana? Jack thought. *What've they done to her?*

"I don't think her family understands the severity of her condition, Ms. Polk," the headmaster continued. "Her violent urges make her a danger to herself and others. She is best left under our care." The half-elf leaned back in her throne-like chair. "In fact, the warden and I exchange regular updates about her three times a year."

Not anymore, mate. Jack grinned inside his head.

"And while we have not yet informed her, I sent a missive to the correctional offices in Redtown only a week ago requesting an amendment to the contract. It is my hope that she be denied re-entry into society... permanently. Lana is better off living out her days within the peace and calm of this facility."

What in the blazes? Jack thought.

"With all due respect to her relatives," the headmaster continued,

"I think it's best if you inform her surviving family that she will be better cared for—"

"Your request is being processed?" Scarlett said.

"It is indeed," the headmaster grinned. "I expect approval to arrive any day."

"Then you don't have it on hand?"

There ya go, lass, Jack thought. *Shot across her bow.*

The half-elf's nostrils flared.

"I see," Scarlett said. "In that case, considering we are here on behalf of her sisters, who agree to provide supervised care for her..."

Jack shifted in his seat at hearing the gnome's bold lie.

"... Lana has the right to decide whether or not to return to her family." Scarlett folded her arms. "With the inheritance shared by herself and her siblings from her aunt's passing, financial viability is clearly demonstrated. We have signed documents to that effect."

Jack stopped himself from staring at Scarlett. *We do?*

The gnome produced a set of rolled parchments that she handed to the headmaster.

Thieves Guild, he thought. *Crafty buggers.*

"Please bring her in." Scarlett glanced at a clock on the headmaster's desk. "We've got plenty of time until the seven o'clock carriage back to Port Biathstone."

The disgruntled half-elf, having finished scrutinizing the forged documents, went to the door and spoke with a guard.

Jack did his best to stay calm, but he couldn't ignore the jittery feeling in his limbs. He hoped Lana reacted appropriately when she saw him. This kind of ruse wasn't his cup of tea. The tension of undercover work was a whole different beast compared to his pirate mischief. Sure, he was an outlaw, but when he pulled a trick either at sea or with some landlubber on dry sand, it was face to face, staring down his opponent as the one you say you are. Besting some scurvy dog came from similar wits and strategy, but this level of nuance and deceit was worse than a spring storm in a northern channel.

He checked on Big Rig. The dwarf was pinching the brim of his top hat in an endless loop as if working the ropes on a sail.

Hold it together, mate, he thought. Knowing him well, he could see his quartermaster was going to break and blurt something out of character sooner or later.

"Where did you say your firm was located?" The headmaster said, re-taking her seat at the desk.

"Topaz Island," Scarlett said. "It's a subsidiary of our head office in Drakeland. I've been in the Jewels going on three—"

"Ah, Ms. Luholi," the headmaster said, interrupting. "Do join us." She motioned for the half-orc to enter the room.

Blimey, Jack thought. Lana looked nearly the same, a bit more fit and muscular in the limbs. The edges of her octopus tattoo showed under the sleeve of her shirt and brought back fond memories of the all-nighter when they initiated her into the Salty Scoundrels.

"Well don't just stand there," the headmaster said, "come inside!"

Lana's eyes were wide.

"What's with you? You look like you've seen a ghost."

Jack did his best to keep a low profile, but he felt the half-orc's eyes on him. He coughed into his hand and shifted in his seat.

Lana's eyes darted to Big Rig and softened. *Good, maybe she'll put two and two together,* he thought. If not... well this was going to get messy.

Lana took a step forward.

"There you go." The half-elf made an expression at Scarlett as if to say, "You see? Not fit for the outside world."

"Ms. Luholi." Scarlett stood and approached the half-orc. "My name is Ms. Polk. These are my colleagues, Mr. Tithers," the gnome gestured at him, "and Mr. Greybeard."

Big Rig bowed.

"We're here on behalf of your family. I have some unfortunate news."

Jack could see it in Lana's face. It was too bizarre. All of it. She was going to crack.

Come on, lass, he thought. *Keep it together. We're here to get you out.*

"Your aunt has passed. I'm very sorry." Scarlett put a hand on the half-orc's arm. Lana pulled back like a frightened child.

The headmaster's expression grew smugger. "As I said..." the half-elf muttered. "Unfit for social reality."

"Your siblings," Scarlett said, "are willing to sign you into their care.

You can exit this facility and remain under their supervision, with monthly check-ins by a correctional officer, until the contract expires. But you must agree to it. And," the gnome looked at the headmaster, "you need to decide now, Ms. Luholi... while there's still time."

Jack could see that didn't go over well with the half-elf.

"I... I really prefer to stay here," Lana said.

Bugger all! Has she really gone mad?

"Can't they sell my share of the estate and donate the proceeds to the *Home of Rest*? It would be lovely to expand the garden and bell tower." The half-orc made an appeasing expression at the headmaster.

"There. That's that," the half-elf said. "I thank you for your visit, Ms. Polk and company. I'll have the guard show you out. And there's more than enough time for you to make that carriage."

"Ms. Luholi, if I may..." Jack found himself rising and speaking. *Nothing for it.* "Sometimes our lives take unexpected courses, as I am sure you know. A person finds themself in a position that, while others assume one thing about them, isn't what happened and in fact, to everyone's surprise... including their own, they're alive and doing well." He met her gaze. "To our relief, people in our lives we assumed lost are still there, ready to help and offer aid. *Your family*..." he narrowed his eyes, "is offering to do that for you now. Would you like to be with *your* family?"

The half-orc's eyes brightened.

You savvy, mate?

"It sounds right nice, it does," Lana said in her usual scratchy voice, "but if it's all the same, I'd rather stay here and finish the sentence so it's official."

"This is most disappointing," Big Rig said, breaking his silence. He aimed his next words at the half-orc. "Have you lost your marbles?"

"Excuse me?" The headmaster rose. "How dare you speak to her that way?"

Oh no. Trusty Jack stood, ready to step in if needed.

"No, it's ok, Headmaster," Lana said. "My sisters can be pushy. I'm sure they told them to expect me to be ready and willing to depart with them."

Big Rig grumbled something inaudible.

"As we used to say in my sailing days," Lana said, "Cheddar always tastes best at six-thirty."

Jack put his hand on Big Rig's shoulder and squeezed. "An odd expression," he said, doing his best to act confused by the phrase.

"We pirates had a lot of those." Lana grinned. "The other one I always liked was, 'waves to the west never crash.'"

"Nonsense." The headmaster shook her shriveled head. "That life is behind you now. Do not speak of it again."

"Well," Jack said. "It is disappointing to have to inform your sisters of your decision."

Scarlett swung around, her dress twirling.

He held up a hand to stop her retort. "But we respect it, of course." The pirate stepped forward and offered his hand to the headmaster, who shook it. "Thank you for your time."

The half-elf held his grip a bit longer than necessary. He hated when people did that.

"Thank you for coming." The headmaster's eyes rose from his hand to his eyes. "Mr. Tithers, was it?"

"Indeed." He smiled and bowed. "Come along," he said to his colleagues. "We can pass the time observing the flowers along the road before catching the carriage."

He'd spent enough time with Scarlett by now to know she was struggling with the defeat. He placed a hand on her shoulder and tightened his grip, leading her out. Big Rig, on the other hand, plopped the top hat on his head and strolled out whistling a shanty.

☙❧

"How long, lass," Jack whispered to Scarlett, "back to the carriage stop?"

He nodded at the half-orc guard as they passed through the front gate.

"Fifteen minutes at a casual pace."

"If we hustle?"

"Ten. You want to tell me what's going on?"

"Going to be tight," Big Rig said.

"Are you two mad?" She halted. "There's plenty of time. It's..." she glanced at the bell tower, "a few minutes after six. You realize that you're going to have to go forward without your first mate. We can't spare any more time."

"Keep moving," Jack said and led her along. "But take yer time, like we're enjoying the sights."

Scarlett's stride eased.

"Aye, that's right," he said. "We be schemin'." He pulled a branch with red flowers to his nose and inhaled. "Soon as we're out of sight, we're heading for the western wall."

Scarlett picked up on the ruse, playing along. Now she followed suit, pointing at another flower further down the lane and making for it excitedly.

Jack risked a glance back. The two guards at the entrance stood, half-bored and most likely happy to see them gone.

The road curved and a minute later the gate was out of sight.

"Come on." Jack pulled her into the underbrush. Big Rig took the lead, shoving through the jungle in earnest.

"You're heading off course, mate," Jack whispered, catching sight of the bell tower through the foliage.

"Don't tell me my bearings!" The dwarf swatted aside leaves with his top hat. "I can navigate a ship in pea soup!"

Jack yanked Big Rig's blazer and aimed him so he could see the tower.

"Well, sink me." The dwarf's eye turned salty. "It's only because we're not at sea!"

"Aye." Jack grinned. "Of course it is."

"Do you two want to let me in on what is going on?" Scarlett asked.

They reached the wall at the western edge of the property and halted.

"Cheddar cheese is what's going on, lass." Jack winked.

"Aye." Big Rig did a little jig. "Almost six-thirty."

"This is crazy," Scarlett said, her hands on her hips. "I know there's something afoot here and—" The gnome's ears twitched.

A moment later, Jack picked up a clanking sound on the other side of the wall.

"Watch yourselves," a scratchy voice said.

Big Rig caught Scarlett's attention and pointed up.

Plunk!

A corked wooden cask landed next to the gnome.

Plunk!

Then another.

"What in the blazes..." Big Rig peered up at the wall.

Thud! A large sack crashed on his head, flattening his top hat and sending him to the ground. Before he could stand, the half-orc, with surprising grace, leapt over the wall and rolled out of her fall, rising with her arms wide in greeting.

"Are you cracked?" Big Rig charged at her, looking at his flattened top hat. "You made us go through that performance and risk missing the carriage for some bloody grog?"

"Not just any grog, mate. This is Molly's Molasses."

The dwarf's eye went wide. "Shiver me timbers..."

"Aye," Lana said, leaning down. "Headmaster's got a stash in the cellars."

Jack licked his lips. He hadn't had that rum in over fifteen years. Nothing finer in the Jewels.

"Well, alright," the dwarf grumbled, attempting to fix his hat. "I'll make an exception this time."

"Ha!" Lana slapped him on the back.

Big Rig tumbled to the ground.

"I won't lie," Lana said, helping him back up. "It's good to see you, Rig. And not behind bars in Longshore." The half-orc, spotting Scarlett, squatted and held out a massive green hand. "Lana Luholi."

"Scarlett Tanash," the gnome said and shook it. "Ouch!"

"Sorry, lass. Me strength gets the better of me sometimes." Lana looked at Big Rig and then back at the gnome. "Oh... wait here now. Are you two doing the dirty?"

"A gnome?" Big Rig barked. "Do you offer me insult?"

Scarlett's mouth dropped open.

"Meaning no offense to you personally, Scarlett," the dwarf added.

"I'll have you know that my standards are higher than that wall," she said, regaining her composure. "Which a dwarf couldn't climb if—"

"Now then..." Lana took a step towards Jack. "Be my eyes deceiving me or is that Captain James R. Hawk in the flesh?"

Before he could reply, Jack was launched into the air. Lana caught him and squeezed, his ribs crushing from the hearty hug of his former first mate.

"Down... put me down, Lana," Jack grunted.

"Ain't you a sight for sore eyes, Cap!" Lana scanned over him. "You've come up in the world." She ran the collar of his shirt between her thick green finger and thumb.

Jack slapped the hand away. "Can't wait to get out of these bloody threads and back into me tricorne and cottons."

"Aye, you've got some explainin' to do." She eyed one of the casks at her feet. "And it'll require us raising three sheets to the wind."

"Apologies if we gave you a fright back there, lass," Jack said. "Didn't know any other way of doing it... yer auntie is alive and well, by the way."

"All the more reason to get loaded to the gunwales!" Lana's eyes went to the barrel of rum and widened with anticipation.

"I don't mean to break up the party," Scarlett said, "but we have to go if we're going to get that carriage to Port Biathstone."

The half-orc licked her tusks and looked from Big Rig to Jack. "Please tell me we're goin' to sea, lads?"

"As sure as the morning breeze blows," Trusty Jack said. "Got me a quartermaster right here." He pointed at Big Rig, who puffed his chest. A button on his shirt popped and flew into the underbrush.

"Damn humidity's fault, that is," the dwarf muttered.

"And this here's our benefactor whose got us a ship." Jack indicated Scarlett who was still adjusting to the size and strength of the half-orc before her.

"Not just any ship." Big Rig's face brightened.

"*Lady Luck?*" Lana asked.

"Aye, she sails. Waiting for us in Benevolence." Jack felt a rush of salty spirit course through his veins. High ho, but they were all back!

A tug on his shirt broke the revelry. Scarlett nodded in the direction of the road.

"Come on," he said and started off.

Lana hoisted the sack over a shoulder and shoved one of the casks into the dwarf's stomach. "Carry that, Rig." She tucked the second cask under an arm.

"There's a catch, Lana." Jack pushed aside thick leaves and forged a path through the undergrowth. "We be sailing into the mists. We're going to Dragon Tail Island."

"Whatever mate." The half-orc shrugged. "Weigh anchor. 'Yo ho ho' and all that. I'm in."

That's a first mate for you, he thought. *Through thick and thin.*

"*Lady Luck*!" Lana said. "I can't believe it."

"Aye, 'tis true as true," Big Rig said from the back of the line.

"Lana, why in bloody blazes are you still here?" Jack asked. "You could have jumped the wall anytime. Those guards patrolling the grounds would be easy pickin' for you."

The half-orc shrugged. "Me sisters and auntie dangled a carrot, Cap. They said if I stayed the full seven years, workin' through me anger and whatnot, they'd reinstate me into the will."

"You were written out?" Scarlett asked.

"Aye, being a pirate done it. The offer was their way of keeping me from runnin' off to sea." She adjusted the rum barrel under her burly arm. "I let them think it was working, but I was onto them. Truth of it was, I didn't have the heart to sail again without me hearties."

Aye, Jack thought, his own heart warming. *Companions true, all of us.*

"In the headmaster's office you mentioned wanting to finish out your sentence," Scarlett said. "I assume to receive the inheritance?"

"That was the plan..." Lana licked a tusk. "Until you blokes showed up unannounced."

"From what I gathered in reading through the materials to prepare for today," the thief said, "that would be a substantial sum."

"Scupper that, lass! Forget the inheritance and that anger management tosh," Lana said. "I've got me mates back!"

"Aye," Trusty Jack said. "Now let's get out of here and back to the ship." The pirate pushed through the jungle undergrowth and onto the road.

"Cap." Lana grabbed his shoulder. "Best we stay off—"

"Hey!"

Two guards from the gate emerged around the bend leading back to the Home of Rest.

"I knew you all looked fishy!" The half-orc who had interrogated them on arrival slowed her steps and cracked her knuckles. "You be a pirate!" She nodded at Jack's tattooed fingers. "You done slipped up shaking hands with the headmaster. And you," the guard nodded at Big Rig, "are an escaped convict. Just got word about you lot this morning from the carriage driver heading to Tenoki. Broke out of Longshore, eh?" Her fists rose. "I'm going to knock your teeth out and collect the bounties on your heads."

Her companion, the human guard, caught up to the group, a short sword and shield held at the ready. "And this one'll get herself sent back to Longshore with the rest of you for attempting to escape." He nodded at Lana. "Never liked you... fancy dancing in the yard all day long, claiming it's some sort of fighting art. Well, I got news for you." He looked from Big Rig to Trusty Jack. "They're payin' for your heads, dead or alive."

"The game is up," his half-orc companion said, tightening her fists. "You're coming with us."

Shouts echoed down the lane. Jack counted at least four more guards making haste toward them.

"I don't think so mate," Lana growled out. "Me hearties have come for me, and I'm leaving this here dung heap and going to sea."

"Enough of this," the half-orc guard said. "Get 'em!"

The human guard lunged, his blade heading for Jack's gut.

Lana, moving like a blur, dropped the cask and sack, flipped in the air, and landed between them. Her green arms spun like windmills and the sword and shield flew off into the underbrush. The guard followed, letting out a desperate yelp as he soared into the greenery, landing with a thud.

Jack balled his fists and made for the half-orc. "Now, ya scurvy dog, I'll knock *your* teeth—"

A green streak crossed in front of him. Lana twirled in the air and—

Pow!

A flying spinning kick sent her calloused heel into the half-orc's jaw.

The guard teetered, dazed, before thudding to the dirt. She lay splayed out with her limbs pointing like the four cardinal directions.

"You have no idea how good that felt!" Lana balled her fists and flexed her muscles. "I've been punching and kicking air for years, Cap. Years!" She giggled, giddy with the rush. The half-orc's eyes went to the cask that Scarlett had picked up. "Crack that open, mate, let's—"

"Come on!" Jack said, dashing to the main road.

"We'll never make the carriage!" Scarlett hurried along, struggling in her dress.

"There it goes!" Big Rig pointed, huffing and holding his flattened top hat on his head.

The horse and buggy slowed as it neared the stop for Liddleton.

"Wait!" Jack shouted. "We're coming!"

He tore ahead, Lana close by his side. Rounding the bend, he caught sight of two human passengers disembarking.

The driver craned his neck from the seat up front. The man's eyes went wide. Lana tended to do that to folk, especially when she'd been brawling. Her grog-blossomed cheeks might be less prominent than they had been years earlier, but the rush of violence sent blood streaming through her face.

"These your bags?" Jack asked, huffing, and pointed at the luggage on the back of the carriage. The two disembarking passengers nodded. Lana tore them free of the ropes and hurled them to the side of the road.

"Hey!"

She leaned in and growled. Both passengers scattered.

"Get in!" Big Rig said, opening the door and helping Scarlett inside. Lana jumped in and the carriage teetered up on two wheels.

"In the center, ya scallywag!" Big Rig shouted from inside the cab. It fell back onto four wheels.

"Sorry, mate." Jack grabbed the driver and tossed him off the carriage.

He checked on the guards. Five were close, wielding swords and axes. Two more with bows knelt and took aim.

"Yah! Yah!" He cracked the reins. The horses charged forward down the lane.

Whoosh! An arrow sailed past his ear.

"Hold tight in there, me hearties!" he shouted and snapped the leathers, encouraging the steeds.

The horses, spooked by the commotion and harsh command, barreled down the lane.

"The Salty Scoundrels are back!" Lana shouted.

Jack looked back in time to see the half-orc's head duck back into the carriage, the guards diminishing forms vanishing in the yellow dust.

13

AS THE CROW FLIES

※

Marian stood before the locked case in the treasury.

I'm spending far too much time at the palace.

It was impossible not to with everything related to the upcoming inauguration—the luncheon with her immediate family, yesterday's ceremonial review, and the dreaded rehearsal that loomed in two days' time.

But today's visit was her own doing.

She traced a finger over the case's ornate trim and peered through the glass. The golden arrow lay on blue velvet, its folds like the swells of a rolling sea.

A nice touch, she thought. Refer to the sordid narrative related to the archer turned pirate without tarnishing the revered icon's tournament glory.

Probably her father's idea. Bonnie wasn't that subtle.

Even with its historical significance related to the island's glorious past, the arrow's contemporary function as a trophy pointing to a human prize was below the level of dignity of the palace. In a room filled with relics, ancient weapons, and even the heads and limbs of the island's fell beasts, the arrow's presence felt forced, like an out-of-place guest at an elite social event.

And that had always been you. She smiled ruefully.

The handsome young man with flowing blond hair and the chiseled chin... dashing in his white cotton shirt and blue handkerchief tied at his neck. A farm boy with extraordinary skill in archery and a radiant charisma that rattled even the most stoic of noble elders.

The love affair's narrative returned in vivid memories. The first spark... those brief gazes between them at a series of qualifying tournaments. She, seated in the royal box, her mother aware of the exchanges but keeping silent. And then, a subsequent surprise encounter in the palace garden when the bold and confident youth had snuck past the guards and climbed the walls for what was the first of many secret meetings. Her early years alone in the garden had turned advantageous for these later romantic flirtations, dispelling what might otherwise have raised suspicion during the long hours they shared together amongst lush greenery in hushed conversation. So many nights spent kissing under the full moon of summer, the citrusy scent of Tak-Tak flowers wafting in the air.

And then, to the shock of the nobility and especially her father, James had won the grand tournament. He'd made an impossible shot when a point behind. She could still feel the tense silence after the arrow struck home. It was as if the crowd had been too shocked to process it. And then, gasps of acknowledgment evolved into raucous applause, especially from those on the hillside who made up his common folk brethren. James's win was more than a personal victory; it was a symbol of hope and a demonstration of the determination and strength of the everyday people who represent the island chain nation.

The farm boy had transformed into a bold young man, growing confident. Nobles flocked to him at the celebratory social events, and his charm and charisma went on full display. When he sat at the regent's table at the palace and offered the arrow as an explicit token of his affection, Marian knew there was no turning back.

She laughed to herself. That had been a moment never to forget.

From there, her own defiant streak took on new purpose, and with her mother's support, a clandestine courtship became open and acknowledged. She'd pledged herself to James Hawk and it had driven her father into a fury. It was love, first and foremost. But there was also a personal satisfaction in the gesture of patriarchal defiance. Immature, now that she thought back on it. It wasn't only paternal authority; it was the whole system. Privilege for some at the expense of others regardless of gender. The classism was an embarrassment, and something she never wanted. And so, she'd accepted the course willingly and with gusto, as if it were meant to happen. For it had been, after all, sparked out of love.

Her poor mother had done everything on her behalf, shouting and defending a daughter's decision on the balcony in front of her and Bonnie and in the bed chamber in private. But always the question remained: what would the regent's daughter do with a farm boy for a husband?

And then, like a fast-moving squall blowing through, none of it mattered.

The day of their wedding arrived, and with it the news that James Hawk had been charged with murder. Caught by the Red Knights after robbing a wealthy couple, themselves newly married, on the road between Pelton Village and Redtown. The newlyweds had been stabbed to death, their belongings pilfered. The farm boy had been easily found hiding near a creek. On his person was the couple's sack of jewels and a wedding ring, as well as a bloodied dagger.

"A desperate man taking desperate measures," her father had said, apologetically.

Shock had turned to grief. And from there, her time of reflection transformed into determined intention. Wanting nothing to do with the noble life, and any of the pomp and circumstance, she'd done the unthinkable: signed off her hereditary line and left to join the mage's guild and become a healer.

Everything had blossomed anew. The healing arts had proved to be her calling. All the years learning plants and fauna in the palace gardens, along with her privileged education, had made for accelerated guild training. She quickly learned to attune to the island's magic, and that along with her skill at alchemy, had made it possible to get out into the city and do good work. The years had passed filled with reward. She was making a difference, not by making decisions that controlled politics and the economy, but by being *in* the world *with* the people. Small and humble aid and comfort for real, tangible pain and suffering. Men had come and gone in brief but passionate relationships. And she'd been blessed with a circle of strong, loyal, and loving friends.

And yet, here she was in front of the display case.

Even though the man had turned criminal and had proven it ten times over by escaping prison and becoming a pirate, she still found herself unsettled by the news the girl from the palace kitchen had brought her.

That face, she thought, remembering the sketch. And what Lithana said she'd overheard Master Rin tell her father.

A tour group entered the opposite end of the treasury, led by one of the palace guides.

"Where's the blood iron blade?" a gnome with a red moustache and beard asked.

The elf gestured to a marble centerpiece under the domed ceiling.

"It would be there," the tour guide said, "but the noble family has recently removed it from display. It's now in the private possession of the Fitzwaters."

Grumbles followed from the group of visitors.

Marian's hand went to her waist, fingers gliding over the ruby encrusted handle of her dagger.

"Come and see the cooled Magma Giant's head," the tour guide said to a young half-orc. "If you dare."

Marian moved off, nodding to the guard who let her pass into the restricted area leading to the south hall. She crossed the grand hallway, its row of framed portraits eyeing her from the walls and climbed the spiral stairs to the second floor.

A moment later she stood before a thick, mahogany door. She lifted its ornate handle and knocked.

"Come."

"Good morning, Master Rin."

"Marian." The elf put down her feather quill and rose from her desk.

"I'm not interrupting, am I?"

"Not at all." The arch mage gestured to sit.

Marian got comfortable in the chair across from her.

Master Rin threw her white hair back over her shoulders and sat.

The doors to the veranda were open, a late morning breeze billowing the thin curtains and sending soft light into the office. Books and sundry items pertaining to the illusory arts filled the shelves. Behind the arch mage, a portrait of Nimárwe, the grand wizard of the Golden Elves, presided over the office. The high elf stood on a promontory overlooking the sea, her robe alight with the setting sun. She held an exquisite staff topped with a golden gem in one hand, and an elegant bow gripped in the other. A quiver of arrows lay at her feet. In the distance, the city of Redtown stood burning but safe under the protection of three golden dragons who circled above the streets. The body of a massive drake, pale as a ghost, lay dead at the wizard's feet.

"To what do I owe this pleasure?" Master Rin clasped her bone white hands together on the desk.

"I'm concerned about the fever."

"This again?" The arch mage leaned back in her chair. "Marian, it's a natural part of life. Ebb and flow, as they say."

"I was treating a girl in Eel Town... using the remedy I mentioned with ravensfiddle, yester blooms, and rosemary. The child's arms had a strange rash blooming; one I'd not seen before."

"Did your recipe help?"

"Yes." Marian glanced at the veranda. "But then the mother summoned me back. Despite all my efforts, both alchemical and through spells, the girl..." Her stomach wrenched with the thought it. She shook her head, defeated.

"Death is a natural part of the cycle. Certainly, Telathia teaches your members that all cannot be saved no matter how powerful your arts of healing are?"

"Yes, of course. I just..." she leaned forward, "I was hoping you could make my father see how serious this is. The mother told me she knows of three more children who've come down with fever. It's spreading, Master Rin. And if it gets onto a ship and—"

"I am not going to burden your father with this, not now. Perhaps after the inauguration. It's only two weeks away."

"That might be too late," Marian said.

The arch mage smirked. "It's two weeks, Marian." Master Rin rose and gestured towards the door. "And speaking of which, I have a pile of papers related to the transition that need my signature."

Marian stood.

It was now or never.

"It's been a long road, hasn't it?" She strode to a model of a ship on a shelf, leaning in and examining the workmanship. "To think my sister will be queen someday..."

"Indeed," Master Rin's voice said behind her. "It could have been you."

Marian's eyes narrowed. "She's got a much better temperament for it. And her honesty is unwavering."

No response from the arch mage.

"Is there something else we need to discuss? As I said, it's a busy time."

"She did me a great service that day off Benevolence." Marian ignored the elf's question. "Closed a chapter to an earlier part of my life." She turned.

Master Rin stood, hands clasped.

She knew that posture. It screamed discomfort. "You were there, weren't you? I always forget that."

The elf nodded.

"I've never asked," Marian said. "It feels awkward discussing it with my sister. Did you see him die?"

"We all did, my lady."

Marian kept her composure, hearing the use of her more formal and now irrelevant title.

"Trust me," the arch mage said, "It was not something you want to—"

A knock interrupted them.

"Come."

Marian wasn't surprised when Sir Roderick, in full armor, appeared in the doorway.

"Sir Roderick?" Master Rin asked. "To what do we owe this pleasure?" The elf smirked at Marian, the tone of knowing lost on none of them.

"Arch mage," the Red Knight said in greeting. "My lady." Sir Roderick bowed in her direction, his bald crown on full display.

"Good morning, Sir Roderick," Marian said.

"I was informed of your presence at the palace." The Red Knight's face reappeared. The burns and scars caught the morning light. "You really should send for me to escort you through the city when you wish to visit."

"Yes, well this was spontaneous... and unplanned. I was in the upper district and something was weighing on my conscience." She met Master Rin's gaze, ostensibly referencing her concerns over the fever running through the city.

"Of course." The knight's chin lowered, helm tucked under his arm. "The good news is, I will be able to escort you back."

"Good news, indeed." Now she was the one hiding a smile. "Master Rin and I were just finished, weren't we?"

The elf nodded.

"It's quite hot, my lady. Shall I—"

"On foot, Sir Roderick," Marian said and exited the office.

The clanking of the knight's armor echoed behind her.

She had no reason to doubt Lithana's information. And, she'd seen the sketch with her own two eyes.

And you, Master Rin, she thought, *just told me a lie.*

⚜ 14 ⚜

MAKE UP LEEWAY

✦

The sea elves had been busy while they were ashore. After removing the false plank and outfitting the original sails, they'd managed to paint the deck's railing. With the switch of the canvases—'*Felicity*' proudly displayed on the bow—and the new colored trim, the sloop had left its cover identity in its wake.

Jack was impressed by the wit of the southern sailors and took note of their clever tactics for future situations on *Lady Luck*.

If and when she's mine again, he thought, standing at the railing and gazing at the darkened sea.

No moon shone. A blanket of clouds covered the stars, leaving only ambient light from the candle boxes hanging on the ship's ropes.

They'd departed the cove the previous morning under cover of darkness. An hour before dawn, the island coast had been no more than a shadow. He and the others had returned with Lana, rum casks in tow, in the wee hours of the night. The carriage had been ditched at the nearest road to the shoreline where the ship lay anchored. The howling of wolves in the hills had hastened their pace, and they'd managed to put their feet back on the sloop's deck without incident.

It had been good sailing after they'd lost sight of Emerald Island. Then, late in the afternoon on the second day at sea, the breeze had shifted. A sky of patchy clouds had grown wearisome and gray. The dreaded northwesterly wind blew in and met its southeasterly counterpart. The infamous phenomenon known as the 'crossing swords' introduced itself to the crew and their guests, turning the sea to glass.

Now they sat, stalled... barely making headway in the first hours after sunset. Short of a miracle, Jack knew from experience that the standoff wouldn't resolve itself for two days.

Scarlett was a wreck over the news. The gnome had paced about, muttering curses and ranting over the tightness of their schedule. After what seemed like hours, she finally settled against a crate and had been staring off to sea ever since.

Trusty Jack and Big Rig had both flipped a copper penny overboard hoping to counter the bad luck.

Lana, being Lana, had shrugged it off. The first mate was content simply to have the sea under her feet again. Her pirate bones were regaining strength with every passing hour.

Shan't be long until she's full-on again, he thought. *Then that sea dog could probably pull us all the way to Redtown.*

Trusty Jack leaned over the railing and peered at the water lapping the hull. His nostrils tingled from the pungent aroma of salt hanging in the air.

Cackles and laughter echoed across the deck where the others were gathered at the ship's bow.

It was hard to believe his former mates were back together.

Myron, the missing member of the Salty Scoundrels, flashed into his mind. The poor cook would have enjoyed serving up a meal for the reunited pirates. All these years and Jack had never forgotten the sight of the man's blood spilled over *Lady Luck's* deck the day they'd been betrayed and routed by Bonnie and the mage.

He spat over the side of the ship, a fiery vengeance stirring in his belly.

Simmer down, lad. Get your ship back and sail away.

"My quarters are yours, Jack." *Felicity's* captain appeared next to him. "Take as much time as you need," she said. "I'm going to stay out here and try to woo the wind with dirty words."

Trusty Jack laughed. "Aye." He examined the cloud cover. "It's looking like two suns and moons at least."

Ashana removed her tricorne and ran a hand through her shoulder-length blonde hair. Jack tried to guess her age but with sea elves it was always difficult.

"I'm one hundred and seven, since you were wondering." She put the hat back on her head. "Which makes me probably about the same as you for my species. Been at sea most of my life, save for a stint as an apprentice. Was born on a sloop not unlike this one." The captain patted the rail.

"You've got a fine ship here," he said. "And fast, too."

"Well, when you get yours back maybe we need to see who's the better sailor?"

"That be a challenge, Captain?" Trusty Jack turned to face her. He hadn't noticed it before, but her eyes were like sapphires... alluring and strong.

"Indeed," Ashana said, "and I think I know what I'd take as my prize after I pull the wind from your sails." Her gaze broke with his and lowered to his chest, continuing all the way to his boots.

"*Lady Luck's* a fast ship," he said. "And her captain knows every inch of her."

He cringed inwardly. *Bollocks,* he thought, *that came out awkward.*

"Sounds like good sport." The sea elf touched his arm as she passed. "I look forward to it." Ashana's fingers dragged across his cotton sleeve before she sauntered away, heading toward the helm.

"Blimey," he whispered. *Wasn't expecting that.*

Laughter echoed across the ship. He caught sight of his companions leaning on a stack of crates in conversation. Scarlett sat away from the group, fiddling with something in her hands.

Jack gazed north. His mind turned to Redtown. The city. The palace. His past life and losses. *Is she still there?*

More laughter and a hearty, "Yo ho ho!" from Lana bounced over the becalmed sea.

Jack checked to stern. The captain caught his eye from the helm and nodded.

Was it all a foolish youthful dream?

Deny it as he might, even with the ship in dead water, he still felt the pull of Redtown. Because of her. If there was time, he would at least inquire.

"I've got the lads and lasses gathered."

Trusty Jack turned to find Big Rig before him, a cask of Molly's Molasses tucked under his thick arm. He bounced his eyebrows in anticipation of cracking open the top-shelf rum.

"Keep the pours small until we get through business, Rig," Jack said and patted him on the shoulder. "I don't need Lana loaded to the gunwales while we're trying to talk strategy."

"Oh, the taste of it though, Jacky boy!" Big Rig lumbered along beside him as they made their way to the captain's quarters. "Do you remember it, lad?"

"Aye, like honey mixed with chocolate. Me lips are smacking with the thought of it."

Lana, Scarlett, and Siân arrived on cue.

Jack removed his tricorne and made his way inside. Navigational maps and tools lay splayed out on a desk on one side, with a shelf of books, a chest, and other sundry personal items on the other. To stern, three windows ran parallel across the back wall. Below lay a cushy and cozy bed, its presence made awkward by the provocation of *Felicity's* captain.

Next to the mattress, inside a locked weapon's case, was an intricately carved wooden staff topped with an orb that swirled with iridescence like an animate opal.

Blimey, she's a mage, he thought.

"Right nice captain's quarters," Big Rig said.

Jack gestured for everyone to sit.

"Crack open that cask, Rig!" Lana's biceps flexed as she rested her forearms on the table.

"Easy there, lass. There's business to attend to," Jack said, and sat down. "We need to keep our heads about us."

"Come on, Cap! One toast for old time's sake." The half-orc went from face to face looking for support.

All eyes were on him, nodding. Big Rig looked as giddy as a lad on his first fishing outing, waiting to cast a line.

"Alright, ya scallywags." The pirate acquiesced with a shake of his head.

"Yo ho ho!" Lana shouted to cheers from the others.

Scarlett had her usual smirk of amusement on her face. "What are we toasting to?"

"Perhaps one of my recent compositions would fit the occasion?" Siân said, clearing her throat.

Big Rig grumbled, retrieving a set of shot glasses from a nearby cabinet.

"Save your eloquence for when we're done and sitting pretty, bard," Jack said with as much tact as he could muster. "This calls for pirate words."

Hearty "ayes" and nods from the quartermaster and first mate followed.

Jack accepted a shot glass from the dwarf, who poured rounds for all.

"Now, hearties." Jack's tone grew earnest. "Raise your glasses."

He motioned to each of them, going from one to the next. In the cabin's candlelight, long shadows passed over the table from arms held high. Light glinted off the rum-filled glasses, dancing across their faces, and stirring his pirate heart.

"To adventure, to fortune, to companions true. And..." he turned to the windows at the back of the cabin, "... to some bloody wind."

"Yo ho ho, Cap, them's salty words!" Lana said.

"Cheers to that!" Big Rig bellowed and rose, reaching across to clink the first mate's glass.

Scarlett and Siân echoed the sentiment.

Jack knocked back the rum. The elixir rolled down his throat without so much as a singeing. He kept his mouth shut and closed his eyes, savoring the rum's piquant richness.

"Aye, that's a taste I've missed," Big Rig said with a sigh. "It's got some age on it, that does. Smooth as a downwind run."

"Give me another, mate. My belly's achin' for it!"

Jack opened his eyes at the sound of the half-orc's voice.

"Steady on, Lana." He licked his lips, fighting the urge to support her request. "Trust me." Jack's eyes went around the table. "You're all going to want to get loaded to the gunwales after you see what our thief has in her pocket."

⚜

THE SHIP CREAKED, BREAKING THE EERIE SILENCE.

Lana and Big Rig sat frozen as statues, eyes wide.

Siân, paws braced against the table's edge, tutted with her two front teeth.

The scene in the captain's quarters had the look of a painting, a dramatic moment suspended in time by a painter's brush.

Scarlett's tiny palm lay flat on the table, a few inches back from where she'd placed the compass. She slid her hand back until it fell into her lap.

"Aye," Trusty Jack said, his voice a whisper. "'Tis the ghost icon, that is."

"That means..." Lana's words trailed off, her eyes fixed on the compass.

"How else did you fancy us finding our way through the mists?" The pirate leaned back in his chair.

Scarlett caught his eye, the silent question spoken by her expression.

"Go on, lass. Open it."

The gnome reached forward and clicked the switch.

Everyone leaned in.

"There's no needle," Siân said.

"Aye," Jack said.

Understanding dawned on Big Rig's face. No doubt, the dwarf remembered his query about smithing in Longshore's dungeon.

Trusty Jack checked the compass. The pin neither shook nor rattled. As he hoped, they were too far from the mists for the enchanted device to link to the source of its powerful magic.

"So that's why we're going to Redtown." It was Siân, who twitched her whiskers. "You want to steal the blood iron blade... and replace the missing needle."

Clever bard, Jack thought. The nocsi knew her legends.

"Indeed." Scarlett settled back into her chair. "The plan is to abscond with the dagger. Mr. Riggins can then forge a replacement fitting the dimensions and weight needed for the compass to give us a bearing."

The quartermaster, still leaning forward, ran his gaze over the device. He tucked his beard against his chest and settled his cheek on the table. His eye homed in on the mechanics.

"You can pick it up if you like," Scarlett said.

"I'd rather not, lass," he said. "And aye, I can forge it. But I'll leave the installation to you, Ms. Tanash. Under my direction, of course."

The gnome nodded.

"Great, so we steal the dagger. He forges a needle. Then what?" Lana's eyes were on the cask.

"Then," Jack said, pausing to emphasize the need for patience. "We get ourselves to Benevolence and outfit *Lady Luck* with supplies. And rouse a crew to sail her." He turned to Big Rig. "Can you muster one, mate?"

"In Benevolence? It's been a long time, Jack," the dwarf said, sitting back. "Depends... if Grumpy Jim's cantina is still open, he'll be able to steer me right."

"How many do you need?" Scarlett asked. "Crew members, I mean."

"*Lady Luck* runs best with twenty hands," Big Rig said, "though she can sail with ten in a pinch." The dwarf's expression grew animated, "One time Jack and I ran her ourselves, but that was something I'd not like to repeat."

Jack nodded, remembering. "Aye, if we get ourselves around fifteen sea dogs we'd be in good shape. Any less and I would worry about defending the ship if we were engaged or boarded."

"This all seems settled then," Lana said. "Now, how about we pour another round, Cap?"

Jack held up a hand. "Almost lass... we need to trim the sails a bit first."

The half-orc grumbled.

"Talk to us about Redtown," Jack said to Scarlett. "How is this going down?"

"I sent Doni ahead to do the scouting and prepare. We can go over the plan and get his updates on arrival. I think it's best to wait until we hear his report before firming up specifics. But the general idea will be to enter the treasury museum in disguise. From there it's really a matter of being able to bypass security in the palace and get back out undetected. He'll be able to provide details, but you'll be in our hands for this part."

"You trust him?" It was Lana. "Meaning no offense, Scarlett."

"Doni's a good lad," Jack said. "Put his life on the line to get us out of a fix in Longshore." He caught Scarlett's eye and winked.

The gnome blushed.

"He's got a special talent too," he added. "Can shift. Right handy in a pinch."

Big Rig and Siân both nodded their agreement.

That seemed to put the half-orc at ease.

"We're in a good position," Scarlett said. "We've got two expert thieves, both guild members who can exploit connections in Redtown. Expert sailors skilled with swords, blades, and fists. And a performer and fast talker who can work both as a face and a distraction." She gestured at Siân. "I'd have preferred to add a mage to the group but even without one it's a strong base for success."

"If we accomplish this," Siân said, "and I mean all of it... then what?"

"You mean after we find some wind?" Big Rig said.

"Very funny, Shorty. I mean after that."

"Oh," Big Rig said, "so after we pull off the Redtown heist, get to Benevolence, forge a compass needle and muster a crew, and sail through an ancient mist of dark and dangerous magic to find an island hidden for a thousand years. Then we survive whatever curse and traps lie in wait. As well as overcome whatever magical or physical guardians might—"

"We get the idea, Rig," Jack said. *Blimey, you're not helping, mate.*

"Yes," Siân said, "after all of that."

"Then it's back to the Jewels," Jack said. "With a boat full of treasure and the dragon's blood." This time *his* eyes went to the cask.

Deny it as they might, the gold and glitter of that word... 'treasure,' was as tasty to the pirates as the rum. All three of their eyes brightened dreaming of the future bounty.

"And then?" the nocsi asked.

"Blow me down, bard!" Big Rig threw his arms out wide. "'And then?' 'And then?' This is as bad as being locked up with you in Longshore!"

"Hopefully, the regent is out," Jack said, calmly. "Scarlett's client gets their wish with a change of leadership at the palace, and your people have a better chance at keepin' the reefs alive."

"Perhaps even start a recovery effort on some of the less fortunate coasts," Scarlett added. "I could put in a word on your behalf."

Now, the nocsi's eyes brightened.

"And then?" Siân tutted at the dwarf.

"You'll get your share of the booty, lass," Trusty Jack said. "And there'll be plenty of time to tell my tale for your chronicles."

The nocsi picked up the elven lute leaning against the table and strummed a chord. "And what a tale it will be." Siân eased back, plucking a soft melody, appearing to have finally put her line of questioning to rest.

"If we live to tell it," Big Rig grumbled.

"And then?" This time it was Scarlett. "I mean, what will you three do?"

"Who cares, mate!" Lana said. "We'll have *Lady Luck* and a pile o' gold. The Salty Scoundrels will be back on the high seas. You heard the captain's toast." The half-orc raised her empty shot glass. "'To adventure, to fortune, to companions true.'"

Jack took Lana's shot glass and filled it with rum from the cask. "Thinkin' maybe we'll cross the great water to Drakeland," he said. "Always fancied sailing the mainland coast and seeing the capital city with my own eyes." He smiled at Scarlett. "Might even sail up north and get me one of them glow stones from the Fjords of Raukulnen."

"Fjords of Raukulnen?" Lana accepted the shot glass and knocked back the rum. She held it out for another. "My teats would poke out the dwarf's eye in that cold!"

The entire group broke into laughter.

15

CLAP OF THUNDER

"Jack."

The pirate's head rang like a bell, jolts of pain shooting through his skull.

"Jack..."

More shaking and more pain.

"Jack!"

"Blimey! What in the blazes..." Through blurry vision, Trusty Jack made out a dark shape swaying back and forth. He squinted. In the sunlight beaming through the hatch, Big Rig's wrinkled face towered over him. "I feel bloody awful," he muttered. His stomach churned like a stormy sea as the hammock rocked back and forth.

"You're not the only one, mate."

The flap of a canvas echoed from above decks.

"There's wind," Jack said and sprung up, plopping his feet on the floor.

"Aye," Big Rig said, "and more besides."

"What do you mean?" Jack rubbed his eyes. *Did we finish all that rum?* The last thing he remembered was being arm-in-arm with Lana and Big Rig, serenading the sea as the first light of dawn edged the horizon.

"You better come and see for yourself," the quartermaster said.

Jack pulled on his boots and made for the ladder.

There was wind alright. He had to hold onto his tricorne on deck.

"That's out of the northeast," he said, eyeing the sails.

"Aye, one for the books," the dwarf said. "One day since the swords crossed and she decided to blow in. Never in my lifetime have I seen it happen." The quartermaster waved him to stern where the captain stood on the poop deck.

The hangover was brutal. It had been years since he'd drank that much rum—heart racing, sweating, and a stomach that felt like it had turned green.

"Hold on, Rig," he said and bolted to the railing, "I ain't gonna—"

Vomit projected from his mouth and splashed into the sea.

"... make it."

A hearty slap on the back almost sent him overboard. "That's alright, mate. Lana and I chundered, too. And, you just made me ten coppers."

He eyed the dwarf, heaving in breaths between retching. "You bet against me?"

Big Rig winked. "Come on. You need to see this."

Trusty Jack lumbered his way up the steps to the stern railing.

"Trouble." The captain held out the spyglass.

Jack aimed the eyepiece where she'd directed him. "Bloody Navy..."

"That about sums it up," Ashana said.

He raised the spyglass to the main mast of the approaching man o' war. "That's the admiral's colors flyin'."

"Indeed," bellowed Big Rig in his deep voice. "That ship's captain would be none other than Admiral Bonnie Fitzwater."

Jack handed back the spyglass. He checked *Felicity's* sails and course. "Man o'war's on a downwind run. Heading out of Redtown by the course of her."

"Aye," Ashana said.

"And we're on a tack making for Redtown."

"Aye."

"You think she's aiming for us?"

"Aye."

This call and response wasn't going how he had hoped.

"What's happening?"

A mess of crimson red hair appeared at his waist, a pointy ear breaking through the tangles.

"How are you feeling this fine morning, Ms. Tanash?" he asked.

"Very funny. I assume this is not an ideal situation?" The gnome could barely see over the railing.

"It is not," *Felicity's* captain said.

"We've got two options," Big Rig said. "Minding your pardon, Captain."

Ashana waved no offense and gestured for him to continue.

"We cut and run, in which case they give chase. *Felicity* can out-sail her, but it would be a long track, and one that takes us further from Redtown."

"It also means we mark ourselves and blow any cover we still have," Scarlett said.

"The other option," the dwarf said, "is to let her come in close and deal with what happens."

"And that would be?" Scarlett asked.

"My guess is she'll want to tie alongside and do an inspection," Ashana said, holding her hat as a strong gust blew past.

"Looking for what?"

"For you," the captain said.

Bonnie, Jack thought. If she laid foot on *Felicity's* deck could he let her go? His hand gripped the handle of his cutlass.

Another covered it, tiny fingers clasping tight.

Jack peered down to find the gnome shaking her head.

"There is always a chance she lets us pass," Big Rig said, and spat over the side for luck.

"Can you hide us on board, Captain?" Scarlett said.

"It's possible, but risky," Ashana said. "It will mean dispersing you into various corners and crates." The sea elf's head went back and forth like a pendulum. "All a numbers game. We'd be playing the odds if they do a random inspection."

"Those be tough odds," Big Rig said.

Trusty Jack narrowed his eyes at the man o' war. *Bonnie Fitzwater.* *Within my reach.* "Then again," he placed a hand on the dwarf's shoulder. "We be pirates. Gamblin' is in our bones." Jack looked at the sea elf and the gnome. "Minding' *your* pardons. I mean Rig and me."

"You want to risk it?" Scarlett asked.

"I think we have to," Jack said. "Although I want a contingency plan."

"Agreed," Ashana said. "I've been thinking about that these last few minutes." Her eyes, their yellow sapphire-like brilliance glinting in the morning sun, met his. "That nocsi is an extraordinary swimmer... which gives me an idea."

"Oh?" Scarlett's ears perked up.

"A bit of sabotage," the captain said. "Enough to buy us time to flee if need be."

"How long do we have to decide?" the thief asked.

"Time's up." Ashana said, peering through the spyglass.

"I say we do it," Scarlett said.

"Agreed." Jack sent Big Rig to get Siân.

Ashana was off to retrieve whatever items would make up the ruse.

Jack took one more look at the man o'war.

Sure enough, the flag to halt and be boarded was on its way up the ship's mast.

With every moment they drew nearer, the tension rose within him. Bonnie Fitzwater, on that very ship. Fourteen years of misery and drink. Of isolation and—

"Jack." The same tiny hand took hold of his fingers. "If the admiral comes on board, I need to know you won't risk everything for personal revenge."

The storm in his stomach from last night's carousing turned angry and violent.

"*Jack...*"

"Aye, lass. You've got my word. But..." He balled his fists. "If things go south, and we're crossing swords and blood's spilling, she's fair game."

"Agreed."

"Hurry, both of you." It was Big Rig. "Follow me." The dwarf lumbered down to the main deck where the captain, Siân, and the others had gathered.

"You know what to do?" The captain handed a flask to the nocsi.

Jack didn't miss the opal-topped staff, free of its locked case, leaning against the door to her quarters.

"Indeed, I do," Siân said. "This is exciting!"

Jack rolled his eyes. *That's one way to put it.*

"Remember, release the worms *only* if you hear the bell," Scarlett said.

"And be extremely careful," Ashana added. "If even a drop splashes on you, you're done for," the sea elf said.

"Understood." Siân strapped the bottle to the makeshift leather band across her chest.

"What's this about worms?" Jack said.

The captain peered in the direction of the approaching man o'war. "No time for specifics. The nocsi is going to be ready to give their rudder a serious problem if we need it. One of my own concoctions."

Scarlett nodded at him, indicating her approval of the ruse.

Good enough for the guild thief, then good enough for me. The gnome had earned his trust after the two previous operations and all the unexpected turns and mishaps. "Alright. If all goes well," Jack said, "these Navy bilge rats will board us, have a look about, stick up their noses, and go on their merry way."

"If that happens," Ashana said to Siân, "you stay out of sight underwater and make your way back here once the man o'war ties itself free."

"Come back up on that side, lass." Jack pointed to port on *Felicity*, which stood away from the approaching ship. "Not to starboard, savvy?"

"Oh." The nocsi tutted with her two front teeth. "I hadn't thought of that. Quite prudent."

Aye, Jack thought, resisting the urge to call her a landlubber.

"How long can you stay under the surface?" Scarlett asked.

"My species is capable of almost ten minutes without a breath. However," Siân raised a furry finger, "when I was in my tweens, I won second place in the reef trials for staying under for eleven minutes. Now, Grulinden was able to—"

"Save the tales, bard. And hopefully you won't need that much time," Jack said. "You can pop up at their stern by the rudder when you need to while you wait. But on the return swim, if all goes well, and you have extra air left, use it. They might keep eyes on us even as they sail off."

"You do this, and you'll be a Salty Scoundrel for sure!" Lana picked up the nocsi and shook her.

"Easy!" Jack said. "Put her down, Lana!"

A chorus of sighs sounded as all eyes settled on the corked flask, still intact, after Lana dropped Siân to the deck.

"Where in blazes are you going to hide *her*?" Jack indicated the quick-to-anger half-orc.

The captain shook her head as subtly as possible.

He got the message. Better to not reveal that until they had to.

"Time to get out of sight, everyone," Ashana said.

"Good luck, hearties," Jack said.

The dwarf, half-orc, and gnome all reciprocated.

"Oh! I have a poem that's perfect for this occasion," the nocsi cleared her throat.

"Off you go!" Big Rig lifted her up and threw her overboard.

"Not subtle, mate." Jack shot him a stern look.

"But, oh so satisfying. And look." He pointed at his ear. "Ain't bleeding."

"Get going." Jack shoved him in the direction of his hiding spot. "You too, Lana. And don't give the sailors a hard time of it, savvy?"

"Aye, Cap," the half-orc grunted.

"Jack?" It was Scarlett.

"Yes, lass?"

"I want you to hold something in case—"

"Oh no." He held up his hands and backed away. "Not for all the gold in the sea."

"No, you don't understand..."

Jack walked towards the stack of crates at midships. "Oh, I do, lass. And the answer is no. You ain't pawning that cursed thing off on me.

Plus," he turned and smiled, walking backwards, "we've got one more cask of Molly's Molasses to finish tonight."

"You can't be serious?" she asked, her skin turning somewhat green.

"Yo ho ho!" He removed his tricorne hat and bowed.

Now, Bonnie, he thought, slipping into the crate and waiting for the sea elves to stack a few over him. *If you step foot on this deck and the plan goes afoul, I'll gut you straight through.*

৩৫৩

JACK SAT IN THE DARK. THIN LINES OF LIGHT BETWEEN PLANKS revealed *Felicity's* deck and hints of the captain's legs, close by. Her elegant wooden staff ran in vertical segments through the seams in the musty crate.

"Here we go, Jack," Ashana said. "Sit tight."

Where Lana and Scarlett were, he didn't know. Somewhere to stern, he guessed, hid away in the holds below deck. Big Rig, despite cursing about the dust and dirt, had reluctantly agreed to a nearby crate. When the sea elves handed him two small hand axes before closing the top, his mood brightened considerably. Hopefully, those blades, and Jack's own cutlass that lay next to him, would be free of blood today. Even with his desire to stick a knife through Bonnie's heart, the idea of taking on a man o'war armed to the teeth with marines wasn't on his pirating wish list.

But if we manage to run and I got my hands on one of those elven longbows...

He shook his head. A foolish idea. Selfish. Putting everyone's lives at risk for a personal vendetta. Not the pirate way.

"Good morning, officer," *Felicity's* captain said. The clanking of boots on deck interrupted the whistling of the breeze.

"Inspection, Captain," a deep half-orc voice said.

"Of course. Ship's yours as you see fit. Make your checks."

"Thank you. Look around!" the officer shouted. "And make it quick."

The crate overhead screeched. Light appeared through the seams on the lid.

We're made! Jack thought, hand going for his cutlass. His fingers wrapped around the handle with the silence of an assassin.

With a thud, the light vanished. The half-orc's bottom bent the planks on the top of his crate.

"The lads won't be a moment," the officer said, getting comfortable. "Not really interested in cargo. We're looking for a group of escaped convicts. Have you seen these faces?"

Through the planks, Jack followed the green hand as it offered the captain a sheet of paper.

Longshore. Jack grimaced. *Aye, the price of infamy...*

"Unfortunately not," Ashana said. "Handsome fellow though, the man I mean."

Jack smirked to himself. His grip on the weapon eased.

"I'd imagine they're long gone by now," she said. "Would be foolish to hang around Ruby Island with everyone looking for them."

"Agreed," the officer said, "but we are required to check. What's your destination? You look empty."

"Redtown. Picking up passengers and a small shipment before heading to Drakeland."

"Well, there's three merchants in front of you. Full of sea kelp and shellfish from the reefs."

"Oysters, eh? Must be nice."

"Not on my budget," the officer said. "Admiral enjoys them."

"She on board? I saw the colors."

"Aye, somewhere below deck. Can't be bothered with these petty stops."

Bollocks, Jack thought. His urge to break free and cross to the man o'war lost out to his greater purpose. *Think of Lady Luck and the open sea, lad,* he thought. *Let it go...*

"Looks good, sir!" a voice shouted.

"Right, that should wrap it up. Enjoy your stay in Redtown, Captain." Dust fell from the planks as the half-orc stood.

"Achoo!"

"What was that?"

Big Rig's crate, Jack thought. *That dwarf's going to blow our cover!*

"Only my quartermaster over there," Ashana said. "He's been fighting a nasty cold. Sneezing since we left—"

"Achoo!"

"That's coming from a crate."

Trusty Jack slid the cutlass from its hilt, careful not to bump the planks with his elbow.

"Mr. Thompson! Bring some marines."

Jack crouched against one side, his boots ready to kick out the wood.

"I really don't think that's necessary," the captain said. "I've got the manifest in my quarters if you'd like to see it."

Her hand signaled to Jack. He tensed his thigh muscles, ready to send his heels through the side.

"Sir!" a new voice said.

"Mr. Thompson, I'm going to need your marines to—"

Purple lightning flashed.

Two voices screamed and then... silence. Only the wafting of the breeze.

"Alarm!" a voice shouted. "Stations!"

Trusty Jack kicked out the side and rolled up onto his feet, cutlass in hand. The half-orc officer and a human marine lay splayed out, charred and smoking on deck.

"Time for Plan B," Ashana said, staff wielded tight.

Big Rig crashed free of his crate as shouts rose from the marines on deck. The dwarf's two axes swung in a practiced intersecting arc, blood lust in his eyes.

"Achoo!" He sneezed and twitched his nose. "I told you I didn't want to be in there!"

"Watch out!" Ashana yanked Jack out of the way as an arrow from an archer in the man o'war's crow's nest embedded itself into the deck.

"Now what?" Jack took in the growing chaos.

"We cut loose and ring that bloody bell!" the captain said.

The marines on board engaged *Felicity's* crew. Jack gripped his cutlass as one charged. He raised the blade but it never came down. Big Rig leaped in front of him and, with a graceful motion, took out the soldier's leg with one ax and their sword arm with the other.

"Come on ya' scurvy dogs!" the dwarf shouted and bolted off to aid the sea elves.

Trusty Jack scanned the man o'war for Bonnie. No sign of her.

"Look out!"

He turned and again, before he could swing his blade, the captain shot a bolt from her staff and charred another marine.

"Get under cover!" Jack said, as arrows rained down. He pulled the captain alongside so they were shielded from the assault by a line of crates.

"We're cut loose, Captain," a sailor said, appearing next to them and crouching down.

"Excellent. Now ring the bloody bell!" Ashana said.

"Look! To stern!" Jack pointed.

The sea elf at the bell lay on the deck, blood flowing from an arrow wound.

A green blur drew his eye. Lana had emerged from below deck. She moved as if dancing, spinning and punching, laying out marines. The half-orc let out a roar like thunder and sent a soldier overboard with a side thrust kick. She stayed motionless a moment after making impact, leg extended at face height.

Aye, she's full-on pirate now.

Jack risked a peek over the crates. *Felicity* was indeed free of the man o'war, the gap between the ships growing. "We've got a new problem," he said.

"What is it?" Ashana joined him, peering over the boxes. "Not good," she said. "That's a red mage."

On the other ship, an elf in a crimson robe motioned with his arms, conjuring a spell. A surge of fiery magic swirled in his hands.

Big Rig's unmistakable shouts and cursing echoed over the deck as the dwarf sliced his way through the now stranded marines at midships.

"Ring the bloody bell!" Jack shouted at Lana. "The bell!" he said again and bolted to stern.

Scarlett appeared from a hatch.

He pointed as he ran. "The bell!"

The gnome dashed to it.

Clang! Clang! Clang!

Jack rolled to avoid an arrow and came up at the helm. "Let me at it!" He shoved a sea elf aside. "Foremast to half!" he shouted. "Main on full!"

"Aye!" a chorus of sea elves responded.

Jack spun the wheel.

"I can buy us some time," Ashana said, arriving and picking up on his maneuver. "Ship's yours." The captain dashed to the starboard deck facing the man o'war. She raised her staff. The opal-like orb glowed, sending a translucent bubble outward along the edge of *Felicity's* railing.

Boom!

The red mage's fireball slammed into the magical barrier.

Ashana collapsed, blown down by the powerful spell.

Jack checked the man o'war. *There you are.*

In full regalia, plumed hat and all, Admiral Bonnie Fitzwater stood at the ship's helm.

With *Felicity's* bow edging towards the retreating Navy vessel, their two gazes met.

Fourteen years later, and now they were helm to helm, staring each other down.

"Old salts die hard, Bonnie," he said and removed his tricorne hat, performing a dramatic bow.

Even at this distance, he could see her eyes go wide.

Shouts and commotion overtook the man o' war. Bonnie spun the rudder left and right, the desperation apparent in the rapidity of the actions. The red mage spoke animated words in her ear. A group of sailors ran to the ship's stern and peered down, shouting and pointing.

"Way to go, Siân!" Lana's voice boomed across *Felicity's* deck.

The man o'war drifted away, its stern edging into view. Long and spindly worms writhed about over the rudder, devouring the wood.

A chorus of cheers rang out on *Felicity*. Jack followed a gray blur dart through the azure water and under the hull, heading to port.

"Throw her a line, Lana!" he shouted.

"Aye, Cap!"

"Rig!" Jack scanned the deck.

The dwarf appeared panting, his axes bloody.

"Take the wheel, mate." Trusty Jack handed over the helm and ran to the sea elf captain.

"You alright, lass?" He tapped her cheek and shook her.

Ashana's eyes opened. "This is where you are supposed to kiss me," she said and winced with pain.

He laughed. "Your wood worms did the job. Man o' war's rudderless and drifting south with the wind." He pulled her up and helped steady her on her feet.

"Keep us moving away," she grunted. "Get the sails to full. We're not out of range of—"

Boom!

Beams and sails crashed down onto the deck.

"—the red mage," she said.

"Foremast down!" a sailor shouted.

"Show a leg!" Big Rig barked. "Full sails on main. Get that fire out, lads!"

"I think we're far enough now," Ashana said, leaning on Jack's shoulder for support.

Trusty Jack stepped with her to the railing. His eyes went to the helpless man o' war.

Bonnie Fitzwater's gaze burned across the sea.

Jack's own doubled its temperature back at her.

"So that's Admiral Fitzwater?" Ashana said. "I like her hat."

Jack laughed, the rush of victory overtaking his desire for revenge. "Three cheers for *Felicity*!" He raised a fist.

"Ho! Ho! Ho!" the sailors shouted.

"And here's to the newest Salty Scoundrel!" a husky voice said.

Trusty Jack turned to find Lana carrying the soaked and dripping nocsi on her shoulder.

"Well done, lass," he said.

"She's in now, ain't she, Cap?" the half-orc said, placing Siân down.

"Aye, she's in." Jack placed a hand on the nocsi's shoulder. "We'll give you a proper ceremony in Benevolence."

"Ha!" Lana's face lit up. "We should toast now! I'll get the cask!"

Before he could stop her, the first mate bounded off to retrieve the Molly's Molasses.

"Not perfect as an escape, but more than adequate considering," Scarlett said. "Are you alright, Captain?"

Ashana nodded. "I will be. That's more magic than I've used in a long while. And, it's the strongest I've ever faced. It was only the distance that saved us."

"That and your schemer' with the worms, Captain," Jack said, indicating the nocsi and the dangerous concoction.

"We can limp into harbor," Big Rig said, approaching. "Your quartermaster's got the helm, Captain. Foremast is gone, but with the wind we can tack our way into port."

"We're going to have to disembark quickly and let you get away before they send news back to Redtown," Scarlett said. "I fear this will be goodbye, Captain, for your own protection."

The sea elf nodded. "Aye, that is true."

Trusty Jack felt the captain's gaze on him but he kept his eyes on the sea. "Shan't be long," he said. The pirate pointed ahead. Wispy clouds and the island's signature twin volcanos peeked over the horizon. "That be Redtown."

"Jack, that ship heading out from the capital." Scarlett indicated a small merchant vessel in the direction of Ruby Island. "Why is it flying a yellow flag?"

A silence fell over the group.

"Jack?"

"That means it's on board, lass."

"What is?"

The pirates face grew earnest. "Fever."

16

BILGED ON THE ANCHOR

❦

Tacking took longer than expected.

Redtown grew closer over the course of the afternoon, but Scarlett felt like they were moving at a snail's pace. Big Rig explained to her that, distance-wise, tacking meant sailing roughly one and a half times farther than if you went in a straight line. The back and forth cutting across the wind was tedious, but according to the quartermaster, if one wanted to be a proper sea dog, then patience was a virtue worth investing in.

"Is it always this slow?" she asked.

"Depends on many factors, lass," the dwarf said, holding his beard in the breeze. "How close to the wind you're sailing, the strength she's blowing, how long since you careened the ship."

"Careened?" Scarlett pulled aside the tangles of red hair blowing across her face.

"Aye, putting a ship on her side... cleaning off the barnacles and seaweed and whatnot." The dwarf's one eye sparkled. "Do you know once, on a lee shore on Opal Island, we found an aqua sprite stuck to *Lady Luck's* hull? That was a sight to see! The wee lad was so thankful to be set free it stayed with us for almost a month. You could see it glowing off the bow as we cut the water."

Scarlett felt the pang of loss, remembering Tingle's heroic demise.

"What's the matter, lass?" the dwarf said.

"Nothing." She wiped a tear and smiled.

"Aye, well, you'll be seeing your sweetheart tonight. That'll cheer you up." Big Rig elbowed her playfully.

She pushed his arm away. "Doni's not my sweetheart."

"Sure, lass. Whatever you say." The dwarf tapped his nose and lumbered off. "Two hours and we'll be in harbor!" he shouted back to her.

Scarlett looked to stern, gazing southwest. Nothing but clear and empty sea.

"Not to worry about that man o'war, lass," Jack said, joining her on their starboard tack. He braced himself on the rails of the heeling ship. "She's in double-trouble. Wind's pushing them further away and they've got to deal with that lost rudder." He winked. "It might take us some time, but we'll reach the harbor safely." The pirate placed a strong hand on her shoulder. "They can't send a crow. If they did release one, it would fly to Topaz."

"Why?" She caught sight of the merchant ship with the yellow flag in the distance.

"It's closer o'er that there horizon." He pointed behind them. "Right handy if you're lost. Aims you towards the nearest land. But for their situation? Well, the admiral's left high and dry."

Scarlett examined the pirate's profile. Late afternoon light cast shadows on his chiseled features.

His eyes narrowed and he spat overboard. "The admiral will get her due, she will."

She could imagine the frustration of being so close and having to let the opportunity go. *Pirates and their revenge.*

"You're smiling lass. What's so funny?"

"It's this." She gestured around her at the ship and crew. "If you had asked me where I thought I would be a year ago, I certainly wouldn't have answered, 'sitting on the rails of a ship, on the run from the Royal Navy, with a legendary pirate by my side.'"

"*Once* legendary," he said. "Now? Just a man looking to get his ship back and find his freedom."

"Is that all you're after, Jack?"

"What in blazes is that supposed to mean?" He held his hat as they came about for a port tack.

"Nothing." She gazed out at the new version of a similar view of open water.

For the next two hours, the tacking continued until they reached the outer harbor of Redtown.

Dusk had settled in and with it, a signature calm that Scarlett had come to adore aboard ship. She took her usual spot at the bow to submit to the crepuscular spectacle. More than fifty ships lay anchored at intervals in the bay's calmer waters. Jack and Big Rig grew animated as they passed an extraordinarily large naval galleon. The two were like schoolboys, pointing at features and discussing what looked like retractable beams on its rear mast.

Along the shoreline, tropical palms mingled with craggy rocks and stretches of white sand. Rustic fishing huts dotted the landscape. Smoke from fire pits on the sandy beaches drifted over the bay, and the scent of roasted plantains and fish wafted across the still water.

As *Felicity* neared its mooring, Scarlett gained a better view of the docks. Even at dusk, the harbor was alive with activity. Smaller boats moved about, illuminated by candle boxes, transferring passengers to the larger ships or bringing in supplies and goods to market.

She grew hypnotized by the graceful arcing flight of a greka that hung over the central docks. The massive red bird soared above the buildings as a shadow, conjuring an image of a ghostly dragon in miniature. She, like almost everyone educated in ancient history, knew the legend of the Golden Elven wizard who slayed the fell beast that had threatened the city.

The gnome tracked upwards, beyond the lower districts that lay in shadow. The palace and ring of greenery were aglow with the last fire of the setting sun.

"Scarlett."

Jack waved her over as the ship dropped anchor.

"Dinghy's all set, lass. Time to get our feet on dry land," he said.

"The quartermaster will row you ashore," Ashana said as they prepared to disembark. "Take these." She handed Scarlett a stack of cloaks.

"And you?" the gnome asked, accepting them and passing the clothing out to her companions. "Where will you go?" Scarlett handed the sea elf a sack of gems that she and *Felicity's* first mate had weighed out in the captain's quarters.

"Home, I think," Ashana said. "We'll take a run past Benevolence and make repairs first." The captain removed her hat and ran a hand through her blond hair. "It's been almost two years since we've been south. The business up here is good, but I could do with time in the tropics."

"Ain't we in the tropics?" Lana asked, gesturing at the harbor.

The captain smiled. "Aye, but if you ever come south, you'll get a taste of the *really* hot and humid climes. Would even slow you down, Lana."

Grumbles of doubt from the others reached Scarlett's ears.

Ashana held out her hand. "Pleasure doing business with you, Ms. Tanash. Look me up if you come south. If you find yourself in Port Joranda, tell the dock master Ashana of *Felicity* will sign for you."

"Thank you, I don't expect to but one never knows."

"Well, Jack," the captain said, "looks like you saved yourself from humiliation."

Scarlett caught the pirate blushing.

"I'm referring to that sailing race between *Felicity* and *Lady Luck*. Not what you were thinking." Ashana slapped Lana's tattooed shoulder. "Dirty lot."

The half-orc roared with laughter.

"What's this, Jack?" Big Rig said. "You running from a challenge?"

"Nay, lad. Victims of circumstance." The pirate held out his hand. "You're one heck of a sea dog, Ashana. Was an honor to sail under your command."

"And under yours, albeit briefly." The captain eyed Big Rig. "That goes for both of you."

"You'll get a look at *Lady Luck* if you stop in Benevolence," Jack said. "Then you'll see that runnin' south was the right decision."

"Hah!" Ashana plopped her hat on her head. "Now get going, all of you. And good luck with whatever it is you're up to." She leaned into Scarlett's ear. "Something tells me I'm going to like the result." The sea elf winked a golden eye.

Big Rig descended the ladder, followed by Siân and then Lana.

"Steady on, lass!" Big Rig shouted from the dinghy. "You'll tip us!"

"Shut your trap, dwarf!" the half-orc barked. "You want the rest of this rum, don't you?"

"Just like old times." Trusty Jack rolled his eyes and went down the ladder.

"Take care of him, Scarlett," Ashana said, voice a whisper.

"Jack? He doesn't need anyone's help."

The captain peered over the side. "I'm not so sure about that. There's blood leaking from that pirate's heart."

⊗

THE DINGHY GLIDED ALONG UNNOTICED. A WELCOME CALM LAY over Redtown's harbor. Random music of nautical vessels at anchor bounced off the still water, accented by the occasional rise of laughter from inside quarters where captains and crews dined by candlelight.

To Scarlett's relief, the growing dark, along with the cloaks provided by *Felicity's* captain, maintained their anonymity. A good thing, too. Stepping foot on the dock, she confronted her own face along with the others on a WANTED poster nailed to a post.

Lana was the only member of their party not depicted. Apparently, news of the half-orc's liberation on Emerald Island had yet to reach the capital. Of all the Salty Scoundrels, the former monk was the most gregarious and unpredictable.... and the most eye-catching with her size and boisterous persona. Scarlett made a note to keep that in her back pocket. Whether it would be a potential advantage or disadvantage was yet to be determined.

"*Unknown Accomplice*." She read the words underneath a rather convincing sketch of her face as the others disembarked. It had a nice ring to it. Her Thieves Guild allies would be impressed.

And, speaking of allies, what concerned her was Doni. Hopefully, the gnome had secured a safe house nearby. Considering they passed two more posters before clearing the docks, her fellow thief should be more than aware of their fugitive status.

"What's that stench?" the half-orc said.

Scarlett winced, not from the nauseating odor, but from the volume of Lana's voice. *And that's why it's best she's not on the poster.*

"You don't want to know," Big Rig whispered and pulled the first mate along.

Lined up in rows along the adjacent dock were no fewer than twenty wooden stretchers draped with blankets. None of the covered bodies was much larger than she.

Scarlett kept her composure, but the thought of lives lost so young left an indescribable and unsettling feeling in her stomach. She tugged on Trusty Jack's sleeve to make sure the pirate took notice.

A silent nod from his hooded figure confirmed his response. "Come on, lass," he whispered. "Let's move and get out of sight."

Scarlett covered her face with her cloak as they passed another row of stretchers along the wharf. *They're taking them away at night*, she thought. *Trying to hide the spread...*

The group scurried along the waterfront until they reached the central thoroughfare leading up and away from the docks.

"Now, lass," Jack said, halting in a darkened spot on the cobblestone street, "where we meetin' Doni?"

Scarlett peered ahead. Candle boxes ran like fireflies, lighting the way as the Eel District's streets rose heading inland. "This way," she said. The daily window for Doni to be waiting for a potential rendezvous was still open if they hurried.

"Hey Rig," Lana whispered as they walked. "What do you say we take a sip, mate?" The half-orc pulled the cask from under her arm and indicated the cork. "I can pour into your mouth. Then I'll get down on me knees, and you can do the same."

"Are you bloody mad?" Big Rig whispered, scratching at his cloak. "I think this is made of horsehair. I'm getting the itches all over."

"A shot of Molly's will cure what ails ya'," Lana said.

"Steady on, you two!" Jack grabbed the half-orc's hand before it reached the cork. "Not here."

Scarlett spotted the shadowy alley between the Times Told Tavern and the Eel Town Apothecary a block ahead. "This way." She waved the group on. "And keep your heads down."

Evening was in full swing in Eel Town. Carts bounced down the cobblestones, heading to the docks to load freshly arrived goods. Laborers followed familiar paths on their daily journeys home after work, while others milled about outside the street's social establishments and shops.

"Doni," Scarlett whispered when she reached the alley.

A rodent scurried along the wall, heading back towards a heap of trash.

"I don't see anyone," Lana said. The first mate strode to the back wall and looked about. She held up her arms. In the dim light, with her muscular frame under the cloak, the pirate looked like an intimidating member of a secret order.

"Doni? You here?" Scarlett repeated.

The half-orc rejoined the group.

"I only answer to the password," a familiar voice said from behind the pile of trash.

Scarlett rolled her eyes.

"Blow me down!" Lana said. "No one was there, Cap. I swear on me spirit, I do."

"Aye, that's Doni, that is," Trusty Jack said. "Come on out, lad." The pirate turned to the others. "That there rodent you saw a moment ago... *that* was our thief."

"Aah's" were whispered and three hoods—Siân's, Lana's, and Big Rig's—nodded in unison.

"*Achoo!*"

"Not again, mate!" the pirate growled out.

"It's bloody horsehair, Jack!" The dwarf scratched his arms and twitched his nose. "Driving me skin to hives, it is!"

"Do you have the password?" the voice said.

Scarlett strode to the back of the alley and yanked Doni out from behind the trash.

"Nice to see you, too." The gnome ran a hand over a curly end of his russet mustache. "I was following protocol. According to the guild manual, you should never reveal yourself to another member unless they provide—"

She dragged him back to the group. "Lana, meet Doni. Doni, meet Lana."

Her colleague's eyes went wide.

"Aye, most folks have that reaction," Jack said. "Don't get on her bad side." He slapped Doni on the shoulder. "How are you, lad. Glad to see someone here, I'm sure." The pirate winked in her direction.

Not now, she thought.

"Achoo!"

Scarlett, along with everyone else, eyed the dwarf.

"Don't give me that look! You don't know what it's like having an allergy!"

"Doni," Scarlett said. "We need to get off the street."

"You're telling me," the gnome said. "Your faces are everywhere." He took a step closer. "Not that I mind seeing yours every block, mind you." He bounced his eyebrows.

"Do you have a safe house set?" she asked, ignoring his remark. "Please tell me it's close."

"I do."

"Good, let's go." She nudged him ahead in the direction of the street. "You can update us on—"

"About that..."

Scarlett halted at the now familiar and dreaded phrase. "Doni...?"

"I did everything you asked!" He held out his hands in his defense. "It's not my fault."

"What's the problem, lad?" Jack asked.

Lana, Siân, and Big Rig were huddled against the wall. The half-orc held out the cask, tipping it and pouring rum for the nocsi.

"Oh, that *is* good," Siân said, wiping her mouth with a paw. "I think this batch is better than—"

Trusty Jack smacked the bard on the top of the head. He pointed a finger at Lana. "Cork it," he said.

"But Cap, I didn't get a shot yet and Rig's—"

"The cask *and* your mouth!" The pirate's voice had a captain's tone.

"Aye, Cap." The defeated half-orc plugged the cask to grumbles from the dwarf and the nocsi.

"Out with it, Doni," Scarlett said. She already knew it wasn't good news by the way he was fiddling with his fingers.

"Achoo!"

She gestured to ignore the dwarf's sneeze and speak.

"I'll come right out with it," Doni said. "The blood iron blade isn't in the treasury."

"What?" Scarlett and Jack said simultaneously.

The entire group shifted focus, and Scarlett found herself crowded by pirates on all sides.

Doni took a step back.

"Give him room, lads," Jack said, waving them off. "Go on, Doni."

"I scouted the palace. Took a tour and walked through the museum. The pedestal is there but the case is empty."

Scarlett's mind struggled to process the news. *It had to be there. It's been there for decades.*

"When I asked the tour guide about it, she said..." he reached into a pocket. "I wrote it down because I knew you would want it in her exact words." He held up the paper and aimed himself so it caught the light from the window to the apothecary next door.

"And I quote, *'The noble family has recently removed the blood iron blade from display. The dagger is now in the private possession of the Fitzwaters.'"*

"Blimey," Jack said, shaking his hooded head.

"It could be anywhere in the palace," Siân said and tutted through her front teeth.

"Or, with the admiral or the—" the dwarf sneezed, "regent."

Silence fell over the alley.

Scarlett checked the street. Folks came and went, passing by at a steady rate. They needed to get out of sight. "This is a disaster," she said. "I need to think."

"Well, while you all have a good think," Big Rig said, "I'm going into that bloody apothecary and get me some herbs. Otherwise, I'll be laid up for days recovering from this blasted horsehair." The dwarf stomped off towards the corner.

"No!" Jack said. "Lana!" The pirate motioned for her to stop him.

The half-orc yanked the dwarf's shoulder. Big Rig's cloak came clean off and hung in her thick green hand. An entire street of passersby turned, the dwarf on full display.

"Look!" Someone shouted from across the street. "It's one of them wanted ones. From the posters."

"Sink me!" Jack said. "Where's your safe house, Doni?"

"Two blocks up," the gnome said, "follow me."

Scarlett turned in time to see Lana growl at the crowd, sending them fleeing like a frightened school of fish.

"Achoo!"

The half-orc threw the cloak at the dwarf. "Put that back on!" To Scarlett's surprise, the dwarf covered himself back up.

"This way, quick!" Doni urged them up the street.

Scarlett ran after Jack, pulling up the rear.

"Thank you, Rimo," a female voice said as they rounded the corner, "The Order is grateful for your herbal—"

Crash!

Scarlett smacked into Jack's back and tumbled to the ground. She rose to find the pirate face-to-face with a half-elf in a blue robe. The woman's hand gripped a weapon at her waist.

The two stared into each other's eyes.

"Marian?" the pirate said, from under his hood.

"James?" The mage took a step back, her long black hair and face catching the candlelight.

Scarlett found herself drawn in by her eyes. The half-elf looked like a gentle yet fierce panther, if such a thing were possible.

"Halt!"

A group of city guards clanked up the cobblestones.

"Come on!" Siân waved a paw and ran off after the others.

"By Order of the Regent and the City Guard, I said stop!"

"We have to go, Jack." Scarlett yanked his sleeve.

"Marian, I... we..." the pirate's words were left hanging in the air as they dashed off.

17

ALL AT SEA

✦

"**A**re you hurt?"

Marian stared at the city guard.

"Were you robbed?"

"No." Her hand touched the strap of her bag.

"Did you get a look at them?" the guard said.

"I..." Her mind was a storm of confusion. "Sorry, I have to go." She pushed past him.

What just happened?

James Hawk was alive. The man supposedly killed by her sister's hand walked among the living.

Her old lover's face lingered as she pushed through the crowd. Townsfolk gathered outside taverns and shops, gawking and gossiping about the disturbance. A brigade of soldiers marched up the street, their commander shouting orders to search the nearby buildings.

James Hawk, she thought. *How many years has it been?*

"Marian?"

She turned to find Louisa and Qin, two fellow blue mages, approaching.

"What's all this commotion?"

"Fugitives," she said, hands trembling. "Spotted on the street."

"From the posters?" Qin, a tall human, said.

"I... I don't know." Marian removed the strap from her shoulder and held out her bag. "Can you take these herbals and distribute them for me? I need..."

"Of course," Louisa, a half-orc, said, accepting them. "You look like you're in shock." The mage placed a green hand on her shoulder. She checked her eyes and gave her a once-over. "Maybe you better stay with us, Marian."

"No, I need to walk." She pointed at the bag. "The addresses and names for those vials are on a scroll."

"We got it, don't worry," Qin said, smiling. Louisa nodded in agreement.

"Thank you both." Marian gestured with clasped hands, mage-style, and turned north, heading up and out of Eel Town.

They lied to me. Her eyes narrowed. *My sister and my father lied to me.*

Lithana had heard right. Master Rin's words in conversation with the regent were now confirmed.

The clangs of plate mail and stomping of boots echoed off nearby buildings as more soldiers headed past her to the lower city. Their silver armor glimmered from the candle boxes lining the street. A blonde-haired guard, whose frame and gait were alike to her old lover's, drew her in. James's features, partially obscured under the hood when they'd collided, returned as a mental image. That familiar jawline, like a bird of prey, and his sharp green eyes. But his face had changed. The youthful exuberance she had known was now a weathered canvas.

The sea will do that, she thought.

Something told her there was more than salt and waves in that transformation. A lifetime of hardship was written on his features. She could only guess what kind of criminal acts and dubious dealings he'd participated in while pirating that had caused it.

She stomped up the cobblestones.

This changes nothing, she thought.

Her steps slowed.

Don't kid yourself. Everything had changed in the span of a heartbeat. Not with him, but with her family. They had treated her like a child... and a fool.

Before she knew it, she was opening the door to the healer's guild.

Marge floated out from the kitchen, the sprite's usual warm glow illuminating the hallway and row of mailboxes.

No ghost on her ledge tonight.

"Hello, Marge," Marian said in a whisper.

Moving like a cat, she made for the stairs, heading up to—

"I'm awake."

Marian's foot hovered above the first step leading up to the bedrooms.

"Come in and have some tea."

Marge appeared over her left shoulder, swirling in a hypnotic pattern. Marian followed the sprite into the kitchen. The guild's headmaster sat at the table, stirring a miniature cauldron. Familiar flower petals and sundry stems and sprigs floated on the surface of the mage's usual evening brew.

"You're home early." The elf flicked her long and frail fingers. A brief glitter passed over the surface of the concoction and bubbles rose as it instantly boiled. "Empty house tonight," the headmaster said and poured herself a cup from the pot. "Everyone's in the lower districts, working. All except Desdianté, of course. He's taking a break but will be back to his usual potion mischief in the basement before long." The elderly elf wrapped her robe about her and sat. "I don't know how more folk don't see it, Marian. That fever is getting worse again... and fast."

"It rises with renewed vigor, Headmaster," she said. "A malignant spirit lingers in the shadows because we have turned a blind eye to it." She shook her head. "I am sorry for returning. I handed off my herbal doses to Louisia and Qin. They'll be taking care of my rounds tonight."

The elf's eyes softened as she sipped her tea.

"It won't happen again." Marian joined her at the table. "Something unexpected shook me and I need some time to deal with it." She adjusted her blue robe with a trembling hand.

"You of all members do not need to justify a break." The headmaster gave her that stern and knowing look that only the wise and elderly can. "As it is, you've helped with the latest outbreak more than anyone in this guild."

"It's not enough," Marian said and poured herself some lemon water.

"That is not your, or any of our faults. We both know where the blame lies."

She always respected the fact that the old mage never minced her words, nor did the elf dance around the Fitzwater family's dubious role in the politics of the city.

"And speaking of that," the headmaster said, "how are you doing with the upcoming changes in the palace?"

"It is what it is." Marian took a large swig of lemon water. James's face returned. *He's alive?* It still wasn't sinking in. It was as if a part of her had known, after all the signs over the last week, but tonight... an idea, an abstract concept, had come back to life. He had stood there before her very eyes. Where had he been for all these years? *And why did he never come back?*

"Child." The mage reached a wrinkled and bony hand across the table. In the candlelight the elf's frail figure, wrapped in her night robe, was like a ghost—a spirit risen to walk among the living. "I am no fool. I know why you ended up here. It wasn't only your passion and interest in healing."

Marian opened her mouth, but the elf held up a hand.

"It is a noble mission, yours. The care you have for the people of this city shows in everything you do, Marian. And that was not possible from the palace. You made a choice and a respectable one."

Where is this going? she thought. They'd sat at this table a hundred times over the years but never had the headmaster been so forthcoming.

"It will not be ideal when your father is crowned," the elf said.

"I don't understand?"

"Something important has happened, or am I mistaken?"

Marian couldn't quell the rush of emotions and thoughts running through her head from the encounter with James and... *who?* she thought. *Who were those other hooded fugitives? And why were they in Redtown?*

"I saw someone, Headmaster... that I haven't seen in a long time. If I'm honest, it's shaken me. But I won't allow it to take hold over me." She dug her fingers into the table. "My self-worth and my charge to the people of this city won't be diminished by it." She shook her head, growing angry at James for showing back up in her life. Yes, it had been a chance meeting. But what gave him the right to do this to her? To intrude without having the decency to make a conscious effort to explain himself... and after all this time.

And then there was Bonnie. And her father. They'd lied to her... for years. *What kind of family does that?* Marian could hear her sister's words. "We wanted to protect you... we did it for you. We—"

"And you are conflicted. It shows on your face." The headmaster poured herself more of the brew.

"No," Marian said, the defiance swelling inside of her. "I'm angry that my life is pushed off-course by someone who doesn't deserve my time or respect."

"Ah, so this is a crisis of forgiveness." The elf sipped her tea. "It is easy to shun forgiveness in your youth."

"I am hardly young," Marian said, eyeing her.

"Years still lie before you, child. And therefore, the potency and imminence of regret is like a distant sail on the horizon."

"Telathia's teachings tell us—"

"Nice try," the elf said, smiling. "I commend you for the tactic. But we're not allowing our divine to be the shield on this one."

Marian reared back in her seat.

"Oh, come, now. You know as well as I do that we make our own ways through this world. The old gods linger in magic, but they do not cast retribution against us for straying from some ancient purpose. Those days ended when Nimárwe slew the ghost dragon right here in this city."

Marian found herself at a loss for words. Never in all her years in the guild had she heard the headmaster be this candid. Or, speak words so close to what might be considered irreverence by their order.

"A marriage exists between truth and forgiveness," the elf said. "Once you have access to the truth, the road to forgiveness is revealed."

"All I possess are lies," Marian said. "Years and years of them, piling up."

The elf nodded in a knowing way. "If you demand the truth of others, you might get it. Or, you may need to find it yourself. Either way, that is the road to resolution." She raised her teacup and sipped with a precocious gesture. "At least, that is what this senile old elf of two hundred and thirty-five years thinks."

"I don't have time for this now." Marian shook her head. "Not with the upcoming inauguration and the fever running rampant."

"It's never the right time. There's always something."

She hated it when people said that. It was like laying down a perfect hand in cards. No response could be made to counter its veracity.

"The truth hurts, Marian. But its pain is unique. Not a chronic ache, but a surge of potent suffering. The reward is the relief it brings afterwards... it's a matter of whether you can survive the experience and live with the new understanding it brings."

The headmaster reached across the table. Withered fingers tightened on Marian's wrist.

"I want to tell you something," the elf said. "And I want you to listen and keep your mouth shut until I finish. Understand?"

Footfalls, soft and scraping, drifted from the staircase in the hall. Desdianté, the reclusive night elf, entered the kitchen.

"Give us some privacy, would you, dear?" the headmaster said to the potion-obsessed mage.

"Of course." Desdianté bowed and moved on. The soft shuffling of feet on the stone steps to the cellar followed.

The headmaster locked her glowing amber eyes on her.

"You've always been different, Marian. From the time you walked through the door to the way you excelled during your training. Something sleeps inside of you, something beyond the work we do here. I've always known a day would arrive when an opportunity to alter the course of your path in life would present itself. I don't know what it is, or where it might lead, and it isn't my business ..." the elf tightened the grip on her forearm. "But something tells me you do."

Bony fingers released their hold and slid back across the table.

"Take some advice from an old elf who watches and hears everything. Including young mages slipping up the stairs after late nights out with their friends."

Marian scoffed. The humor was a welcome relief, as if the pent-up tension released with the exhalation.

"You," the headmaster said, "are not bound to this Order."

"What are you saying?"

"I told you to listen and not speak, did I not?"

Marian shrank under the elf's earnest stare.

"We all have our callings. Some find theirs early. Others, take some time.... and others still, find that a part of their life is called to one thing, but then another chapter leads them elsewhere."

The headmaster rose and placed her mug in the sink.

"I'm a mage of this guild," Marian said. "I took an oath."

"You did," the elf said, her back to her. "You know as much as anyone that words contain power. But, at the same time," the elf turned and faced her, "they are only words, dear."

The statement lingered in the air, as if weightless.

"Don't let them get in the way of the truth, Marian." The elf gestured with her hands. "Even that chain around your neck can be taken off. It will neither change who you are, nor prevent the path to whom you might become." The old mage shuffled to the doorway. "It is, after all, only a chain."

Marian stared at the empty parlor as the elf turned and made for her quarters. Marge passed, making her way to her usual spot near the entrance to the guild.

The cauldron on the table stirred. The surface of the remaining brew trembled and swirled. Steam rose from the pot and, with a magical glimmer, transformed into a familiar voice.

"We are never bound to others. Except through love."

The click of the door to the mage's bed chamber echoed down the hall.

18

HANG THE JIB

"**W**e're in the clear," Doni said and hastened down the steps.

Jack and the others had been in the cellar-turned-safe house for an hour while the heat of the chase outside cooled.

"I haven't seen a guard pass in at least ten minutes." The gnome shut the thick wooden door behind him. He set the double bolt.

Jack sat, along with Scarlett, Big Rig, and Siân, at a large rectangular table. Against one wall, arms folded and eyeing the cask in front of him, was Lana. The half-orc hadn't spoken a word since they'd arrived. Her hulking frame flickered in the dim candlelight illuminating the underground hideout. For the last fifteen minutes, she had been chomping apples from the barrel next to her, taking her time and emphasizing each bite until Big Rig lost patience and pulled rank, demanding she stop. Jack had seen this behavior before. The bitterness between them wasn't personal. Well, it was, but not tonight. Lana was fighting her craving for the cask of rum and Big Rig's discomfort was as prickly as the itches from the horsehair allergy irritating his skin.

The others had sat and eaten in silence. Doni did his job well. The cellar was stocked with provisions. Salted fish, various tropical fruits, and loaves of Redtown Rye, made from coconut milk, molasses, and flour, lay scattered and half-consumed across the table.

"Old Grindlemore has been helping out the guild for years," Scarlett said, breaking the silence. She washed down the last bite of her bread with a swig of lemon water. "Even if the guards enter the bookshop above us, the night elf will cover and send them away." She eased back into her chair. "And if they get pushy, the secret passage to the cellar is far beyond their skills of detection."

"Was that a ward glowing around the edges when Grindlemore closed it behind us?" the nocsi asked, peeling a plantain.

"Indeed," Scarlett said.

Jack was only half listening, lost in a storm of confusion. Barraged by gusts of potent and painful memories, he struggled to find his bearings. Every so often, a warmer breeze pushed through the tempest, a flash of earlier times between him and Marian dispelling the dark clouds and bringing forth fonder memories of the love they once shared.

Those eyes, he thought. They shone the same as they had all those years ago. Marian looked well, and for that, he was happy. The whole incident had happened so quickly that he'd had no time to think. The words he left hanging in the air when they fled were a bumbling embarrassment.

She took you for a criminal, he thought, picturing her hand going for her weapon. *And she wasn't wrong.*

"Jack? Are you listening?" Scarlett asked.

"What's that, lass?"

"We need to talk about what to do now."

Jack shrugged. "Ain't naught we can do."

"Aye, I think we're dead in the water." Big Rig reached for the cask but stopped shy of it.

The pirate nodded and waved for Lana to join them.

The half-orc was at the table and seated before he could blink.

"Blimey, mate," Jack said. "What're you going to do when it's all gone?"

"Have me a go at finding more." Lana held out her glass. "We're in

Redtown, Cap. I'll bet there's barrels of Molly's Molasses cellared higher up the hill. Rich folk love to brag about the age of their grog."

The dwarf filled her shot glass and the others all around.

"No toasting," Jack said. "Not with this news."

Ayes and nods echoed around the table.

"Well, it seems the only thing to do is figure out where the dagger is," Doni said, edging his seat a little closer to Scarlett.

Jack almost smiled, but his amusement at the gnome's flirtation was cut short by the intrusion of Marian and their chance meeting. Her image lingered like the scent of wildflowers. He couldn't free his mind from her face... *What was she doing in Eel Town? Must be the fever. She'd be up all hours treating those children.* His eyes ran over the memory of her face. Then, down her neck to the graceful curves of her shoulders. She'd worn a pendant that fell to her collarbones. It looked to be a jewel of the Order of Telathia, some kind of symbol or talisman of her commitment as a healer and guild member.

Jack's eyes continued wandering over the lingering image of his former lover. Down her chest to her waist, and her hands.

Free of rings. Instead, gripping a—

"What is it, Cap?" Lana said and halted pouring rum. "You look like you seen a ghost."

"Shiver me timbers..."

"Jack?" Scarlett edged forward in her seat.

"Describe the dagger," he said.

"What?"

"Describe it!"

"Easy, lad," Big Rig held up a hand.

"Sorry, lass," Jack said. "The blood iron blade... the details."

"A blade like any other," Scarlett said, "but with a faint red tinge to the steel."

Jack nodded in earnest. "And?"

"A ruby-encrusted hilt, curving like a horn towards the tip."

"The pommel?" He made as if gripping an imaginary handle. "An ornate dragon's tail?"

Scarlett's eyes spoke of confusion. "You've seen it before?"

Jack's mind pitched about like a sailor thrown overboard into a stormy sea. Elation and anxiety rose and fell like powerful ocean swells. "Aye, I've seen it."

"Was this before you were in prison?" Doni asked. "When you—"

"I seen it tonight!" The pirate slammed a fist down.

Gasps around the table sucked the air from the room.

Scarlett's eyes went wide. "The weapon... the one she went for when you collided."

"Aye," Trusty Jack nodded. "'Twas the Blood Iron Blade right as day, it was."

"Blow me down," Big Rig said, shaking the nocsi's shoulder with a burly hand.

"I'll drink to that!" Lana said and knocked back her rum.

"I can't believe it," Doni said. "So... I'm not in trouble?"

"You were never in trouble," Scarlett said. The thief put a hand on her colleague's shoulder. "It wasn't your fault it was removed from the palace."

The gnome's face softened with relief. No one missed the glimmer in his eyes at her touch.

"But..." Siân began.

"But what?" Big Rig said, shooting his rum.

"That means we have to steal it from—"

"We can't steal it," Scarlett said. "I mean, we could try, but it would be near impossible. It's warded to her, for sure. That blade holds far more than ordinary magic. If we tried she'd know immediately. And, with her rank in the Order, you can guarantee she's a powerful spell-caster. The potential wrath she could unleash—"

"We're *not* harming Marian," Jack said, staring Scarlett down.

"Easy, Jack." The thief held up a hand. "I'm on your side here. I agree that engaging in theft and its potential consequences is not the answer."

"But she's a healer?" Doni said. "She doesn't possess harmful magic."

"Don't be fooled," Siân said. "Healing mages can cast powerful spells that pull life and power as much as revitalize and nourish it. Same with their potions. They can be turned into potent poisons. It's the Order and their oaths that direct their magical actions and choices."

"We're *not* hurting Marian." Jack balled his fists.

"We are all in agreement on that," Scarlett said to nods around the table. "But we need that dagger."

"So, what do we do?" Doni said.

"I can think of only one option," Scarlett said.

A sea of eyes flickered in the candlelight. Jack felt like a mackerel surrounded by sharks.

"Oh no, scupper that," he growled. His insides churned at the thought.

"Jack," Scarlett said, "it makes the most—"

"Out of the question." He folded his arms and leaned back. *Not for all the fish in the sea.*

"Cap, mind my pardon," Lana said, "but you're the one for this, from what I can see."

He shook his head.

"I hate to put you in this position, Jack," Scarlett said. "I really do..."

"Don't worry, lass. You're not putting me in any bloody position. It's not an option." He slammed his rum. The elixir ran down his throat, adding fire to the rising flames in his belly.

"Why would she help us?" Big Rig asked. The dwarf's chair screeched as he aimed himself at the thief. "You expect her to hand over an ancient artifact, a powerful and valuable one to boot, so you can do what... challenge her family's authority?"

Jack leaned forward. "Well, lass?" His eyes homed in on her like a bullseye.

"Not challenge it," the gnome said, going from face to face. "Over-turn it."

"And why would she agree to that?" the dwarf pressed her.

Jack knew to let the quartermaster have the helm. Either more was forthcoming or they were going to walk away. *Would that be so bad? I've got me mates. No ship, but we would manage. As for Marian, well...*

"Because she does not agree with what her father..."

Jack found himself the focus of the thief's gaze.

"... and her sister have done, are doing, and want to do in the Jewels."

"You know this how?" Big Rig asked.

"It's my job to know this," she said. "My guild deals in information. And my client—"

"Who is your bloody client?" Jack couldn't hold his tongue any longer.

Scarlett leaned back in her chair and sighed. "When we get to Benevolence all will be revealed."

"What in blazes does that mean?" Jack said.

"I will explain everything in Benevolence. Or, rather, you will understand everything once we arrive... your ship is there." She went from face to face. "And so is my client."

"You still haven't answered my question, lass," Big Rig said. "Why would she give us the blade *now*?"

"She won't give us the blade. But she might give it to Jack. And frankly, Mr. Riggins, I'm all out of other options at this point. I believe you pirates refer to this as, 'scraping the bottom of the barrel.'"

"What if you and Jack were to do this together?" the dwarf said.

"What?" Both he and Scarlett replied in chorus.

"Aye, seems to me Jack does the talking and you do the walking."

"I don't follow," the thief said.

"Rig, you're talking bilge, lad," Jack said. "I ain't doing nothing of the sort."

The dwarf raised a hand in a gesture of patience. "If you would, Captain. Allow me a moment."

So, he's working a schemer. The mention of his rank told him the quartermaster had a plan. What it was, he didn't know, but he would give his old friend the helm.

"By walking, I mean you, Ms. Tanash, appear to be privy to information that we are not. Enough of it that you are willing to put the captain in a personal pinch to risk our success."

"Go on." She folded her arms.

"Let the captain approach her, if he fails to—"

"Scupper that!" Jack said. This wasn't what he was supposed to be doing!

Again, his old friend raised his hand in a respectful manner, asking for patience.

"If he fails, you agree to step in..." the dwarf caught his eye, "separately and alone, and lay it all on the line to attempt to persuade her."

"Why would that work?" the thief said.

"Not saying it will," Big Rig said. "But if you're asking the captain to risk his neck on this, I think it only fair you throw in and agree to do the same."

Scarlett's cheeks flushed. Whether it was from anger or embarrassment, Jack couldn't tell.

"Agreed," she said.

"It don't matter," Jack felt his own face going red. "Because I ain't doing it."

Again, all eyes were on him.

Jack's temper flared. He locked gazes with the dwarf. *What did you just do, mate?*

"Jack?" Scarlett held out her hands, waiting for his response.

He shook his head. "I told you all 'no.' And I mean, 'no.'"

"Then we're through," Doni said.

"Where does this leave us?" Siân asked.

"No idea mate," Lana said. "I'm as lost as a schooner in fog."

"I think Doni is right," Scarlett said. "This is at an end. Our deal is unfortunately nullified. Therefore, *Lady Luck* will be sold by the guild and we," she indicated herself and Doni, "will inform our client of the change in plans and proceed to securing a second option."

"I'm going to meet our client?" Doni asked, perking up.

Scarlett shot him a look.

"Give us a moment, would you?" Big Rig said to those gathered around the table.

Jack folded his arms.

"Go on," the dwarf said. "All of you. I want a word with the captain in private."

The four others rose.

Lana reached for the cask.

The dwarf's hand intercepted her, gripping the green forearm tight.

"Leave it."

"Come on, Lana," Siân said, patting the half-orc with a paw in consolation.

"We should check in with Grindlemore," Scarlett said to the others, leading them out. "Make sure we're still looking safe from the guards. That's a problem we all still share."

Jack's old dwarven friend stood and filled their shot glasses before taking a seat across the table.

The door clicked shut, leaving the two alone in the cellar.

The dwarf's eyes softened. "Deal aside, I want to talk about you and Marian. Between the two of us, meanin' all respect, you've been carrying this for years." Big Rig's skin creased at the corner of his good eye. "I see it on your shoulders, Jack. I know it's a burden."

"She's not taking me back, Rig. Not after what I've done."

"I know, lad." The dwarf ran a calloused finger over the table's coarse wood. "Ain't about that. You've got a chance to explain yourself to her. She deserves that. It ain't going to be an easy parlay, lad. But no matter how she responds, if luck is with us and she agrees to help, we'll get our ship back. We can leave it all behind and sail away." The quartermaster leaned back in his chair and placed his hands on his head. "And even if she refuses... and she most likely will, you'll be free of it. You'll have said your piece." The dwarf leaned close to the candle between them. "You can't have that cargo weighing you down forever."

Jack twirled his shot glass with finger and thumb, concentrating on the way it caught the light.

"Think of Marian, lad. I'm sure this would bring her closure."

Jack's heart wrenched at the thought of the burden this mess, and his subsequent ignorance, had potentially done to her. For years he'd sailed the Jewels without seeking her out after his escape from Longshore. And then, he'd miraculously survived being marooned at sea. And what had he done after enduring a living nightmare? He'd ran. He'd avoided going anywhere near Redtown, or any other civilized port related to his past.

"You remember when we were cellmates?" the dwarf asked, lifting his shot glass and examining the rum's hue in the candlelight. "What did I say to you when you first arrived at Longshore?"

"Was that before or after you put me in my place for trying to take your bottom bunk?"

The dwarf chuckled. He took a sip of rum and narrowed his one eye. "After."

Jack knocked back his drink. "You told me sailors worth their salt never turn their backs to the breeze."

"Aye." The dwarf shot the last of his Molly's Molasses. "Ain't no treasure downwind. Life's always a fight."

The dwarf's shot glass clinked on the table, and his chair screeched. The quartermaster's heavy footfalls bounced off the walls.

"The ship don't matter. Ain't about that, lad."

With a gentle click, the door shut.

Jack sat in silence.

He lost himself in the candle's flame, its flickers hypnotic and mesmerizing.

He'd had moments like this before in his fifty-odd years of adventure. Fewer of them than the fingers on his hand. Defining moments that changed a man and the course he'd set for himself.

You knew this was coming as soon as you agreed to leave Mayrotten Island. One phrase of acceptance in The Dreg had sealed his fate. He'd weighed anchor and there was no way he was going to get through the Jewels without it all returning, piece by piece. As much as he tried to deny it, the road to Benevolence and *Lady Luck* ran through Redtown. And that meant Marian.

"Nothing for it," he muttered and shot back the last of his rum. "Time to trim the sails."

෨෪ඁ

"Good luck, lad." Big Rig squeezed Jack's arm.

Scarlett slipped back into the alley and joined them in the shadows. "Doni was right," she said. "She's been inside the library for at least an hour. Seems to be a weekly routine."

Jack's stomach pitched about. Storms at sea? A naval frigate running down *Lady Luck*? That was the kind of conflict and fear he faced without so much as flinching. But this?

"Remember, it's important to emphasize the regent's role," Scarlett said. "Marian needs to understand you aren't responsible for your time in Longshore. It will be a hard sell but try and convince her for your own sake as well as ours."

He nodded.

"When the time is right, mention the dragon's blood for the reasons I shared with you," she said. "Just hold off on that until you've resolved the tension about your absence."

Right, Jack thought. *It's only been over thirty years in the making.* "This is bollocks." He looked from Scarlett to Big Rig. "I'm tellin' you both," he grumbled, "she ain't going to buy in."

"Marian's coming out," Big Rig said, peering around the corner.

"We'll be right here," Scarlett said. "Good luck."

Trusty Jack mustered his courage and strode from the alley. In the fine clothes Doni had procured for him, the pirate looked like a proper upper-class gentleman on his way home from a day overseeing a profitable business. Velvet gloves and a stylish hat served double duty, hiding his features and covering his tattooed hands, while offering him a distinguished air. As uncomfortable as he was doing it, Jack tapped the ornate walking stick on the cobblestones with every step. Despite both he and Big Rig claiming the noise drew undue attention, the two guild members insisted he use it. Not only did it fit the cover identity, they said, but it offered him a weapon should things go awry.

Marian descended the steps of the library.

Jack hastened his stride to intercept the mage. He checked the guard at the corner. A female elf in plate armor stood at attention, focused on a set of carts laden with goods being unloaded across the street.

From underneath the brim of his fashionable hat, Jack followed Marian as she crossed to a line of shops. His former lover halted at a large window, observing the objects on sale.

Butterflies swirled in his stomach. Lightheaded, it was as if he'd left his body and watched himself approach.

"Hello, Marian."

The mage kept her gaze on the display.

"It's me, Jack... I mean, James."

"Pretending to be someone else." Her long black hair caught in the light of a nearby candle box. She didn't turn to face him. "Must be easy for you."

"I want to explain, Marian..."

"Explain what, exactly? That you're a pirate and a criminal?" She turned and their eyes met.

Jack opened his mouth but nothing came out.

"Or, that you're a coward for choosing to run away and forget your past?"

The one-two combination had him on the ropes. It was where he deserved to be and the emotional pain had him wobbly on his feet.

"Why are you here, 'Jack'?" Marian's panther-like eyes grew fierce. "To free your guilty conscience?"

"No, Marian." He checked the guard down the street. "I want to..." He thought of Big Rig's words when they sat alone in the safehouse. "You deserve to know the truth. I've left this too long, and it's done hurt and harm to you."

"You don't know *anything* about what's been done to me, James. And don't you *dare* presume to." She closed the distance between them.

The compressed energy was palpable, a strange mix of regret, fear, and desire. Despite the years, Marian was as beautiful to him as ever. His fingers itched to take her hands in his, as much as he also wanted to take a step back.

"Look at what you've become. You're a criminal."

"Aye," he said, finding solace in anger. "I'm a pirate, I am. And proud of it." He thumbed his chest. "I live in a far better system than the one your family runs that treats the lower classes like pawns." He puffed his chest. "I might be a pirate, Marian. But I'm an honest one. I've been an honest man all my life."

"You murdered two people, James... for what? A ring? Money?"

"I was framed!"

"By whom?" She spread her arms wide.

"Your father!"

"Please... don't lie, the knights apprehended you red-handed."

"What?" He took a step back. "No, Marian... who in blazes told you that yarn? I was handed off to the Red Guard. The Knights ain't done nothing. All they did was bring me to Longshore."

"Then who was it?"

"Hired thugs. Brutes... some kind of professionals."

"You just lie and lie." She shot him a look of disdain. "Piracy suits you."

Jack deflated. "You don't believe me?"

"It doesn't matter. What does it change now?" She shook her head. "You chose your path and it was one full of crime and without any regard for me."

"Blimey, Marian! Up until your sister set me adrift on a bloody raft the size of me thumb, I was doing good work. Was I stealing? Aye, from a robber running the Jewels... your father!" He pointed at her. "The poor needed that tax money. To buy food, clothes, and to scrape by with a decent life. That's what that money was meant for. Not for bloody Harpy Oysters!"

Now her mouth was open, but no words came forth.

"You might not believe it, but we were working to a common purpose, Marian. I know you signed off on your noble line. Sometimes you can't work within the law because the laws keep you from doing what's right." He balled a fist. "I stand by that, I do."

Marian gritted her teeth. "And so you went sailing through the islands, making a name for yourself," she said. "'Trusty Jack' the good pirate... caring about everyone except the one you vowed to love."

The words pierced his chest and punctured his heart. The truth of it left him unable to respond for a long moment. He looked into her angry eyes.

"I loved you, Marian," he said.

"Another lie."

"Never," he whispered. "Not that, lass."

"Where were you all this time, James?"

"I..."

"You could have come and found me."

"And would you have believed me?" he said, voice cracking. "As far as you knew, I was an escaped convict. A killer..."

"You never even gave me the chance to try. Instead, you left me without an answer. Having to hear about your criminal exploits sailing the islands from my sister and my father." Marian's jaw tightened. "I walked by that arrow in the palace for *years*. Years!" She took a step closer. "And don't think for a minute that I left the royal line because of you. I left because of me!" She pointed at her chest. "Because it was what *I* wanted to do, and the way that I could best serve the people of these islands. You ran away from your problem. And now I learn that you've been missing for another fourteen years?" She spread her arms wide in a gesture of futility. "Fourteen years, James? Where have you been?"

Jack lowered his head. "I'm sorry, Marian. I can't say nothin' else now, I know. But I'm here to offer that, I am."

"I thought you were dead," she said, voice breaking. "That would have been better than this."

Jack's eyes ran over her features. A well of emotions was held at bay by the mage's fortitude.

She shook her head. "You've broken my heart a second time, James. I could live with you dead and gone. Now, I have to live with you alive, knowing that for all this time you chose selfishness over me... over love. That pain hurts worse than the news of your death."

Jack's insides collapsed. Even the anger at being coerced into this by his mates couldn't rise through the weight and despair pressing down on him.

Marian's face shifted. Her lips tightened and her stare grew fierce. "Now get out of my sight before I call the guard." She pushed her face within an inch of his. "And don't try and follow me or contact me again. If I see your cowardly face, I will stab you with my own hand." She put a finger on his chest. "Right in your black heart."

She shoved him out of the way and stormed off.

Jack stood motionless. *I've made such a mess of it all.*

His past, their past, lay scattered like flotsam and jetsam after a raging storm. The debris, all of it, was his in name and action.

She hates me. And she deserves to.

In the window's reflection, his conscience stared back at him. *At least she heard my words.* He removed his hat and wiped the sweat from his brow.

"I'm guessing that didn't go well?" Big Rig's voice cut into his brooding.

"No, lad," he whispered. "I didn't even get through—"

"Put that hat back on. Do you want someone to spot you?" Scarlett said, appearing on his other side.

"It's in your hands now, lass." Jack placed the hat back on his head. "I might as well be walking the plank."

19

SWING THE LEAD

S carlett made her way out of the lower city and climbed the grassy hills that hugged Redtown Bay. By the time she'd reached the secluded knoll, the sun had spoken its daily farewell and departed for the far side of the world. No more than a faint glow persisted from below the horizon. That fading light crossed the open sea to the edge of the coast, casting purple shadows on the scattered palms along the shoreline.

She allowed herself a moment to savor the view. A harmony of sensory delights rose from the combination of the fading day, the rhythmic lapping of the sea, and the crisp and clean salty air. She had grown to love the island chain and its unique topography. So much so that the thought of returning to Drakeland brought forth a strange regret, even though its coming would signal the completion of her mission in the isolated archipelago.

If it's successful, she thought.

Returning in failure wasn't an option. This was the most substantial assignment she'd been given by the Thieves Guild. She had been in its inner circles long enough to know it was based on more than the high-priority nature of the mission; it was a test. Within the year, one seat out of the ten comprising the Two Hands at the top of the guild's Finger ranks would open. Her candidacy was at stake, and she intended to demonstrate she had the wits, cunning, and tenacity to join those who influenced the shape of politics, power, and wealth throughout Arsel.

Scarlett took a deep inhalation of pungent sea air and pulled the pouch from her vest pocket. Following the same ritual she had used on the cliffs at Longshore, she held out the sprig and whispered the incantation. Once again, the rosemary twig rushed skyward. This time though, the nighthawk that circled and descended arrived with a scroll wrapped on its leg above the talons. She removed and read the missive. At least her client's update wasn't worse than the one she would attach to the bird of prey. That note would cross the twin volcanic peaks to the guild-sanctioned courier at the southern tip of Ruby Island, who would transfer it to an albatross for the flight across the open water to Benevolence Bay. Everything hinged on her attempt to persuade Marian Fitzwater where the pirate had failed. If they could procure the dagger, then all else would fall into place. They might even make it to Dragon Tail Island and back in time.

An hour later, Scarlett stood with her back to a wall on the edge of Redtown's guild plaza, another of the many shadows cast along the side street in the night. The rush of flaming water from the dragon fountain broke the silence in the less frequented mage's district, its crimson light casting an ominous glow on the lane's opposite wall.

Scarlett peered around the corner. *Finally*. Marian Fitzwater said goodbye to another mage and strode around the fountain toward the healer's guild.

The gnome took measure of the distance from her hiding spot and edged back into the shadows. Using her thieving expertise, she counted the half-elf's paces in her mind and, when she'd reached the appropriate number, edged the sleeve of her robe into the light to—

"You picked the wrong mark, thief." The sound of a blade leaving its scabbard followed.

Scarlett smirked at her success. She stepped from the shadows, hands open at her sides. "You are correct, Ms. Fitzwater. I am a thief, but I'm not here to rob you."

"A rogue in the shadows who doesn't intend to steal? I've heard a lot of tosh of late, but that might be the biggest lie yet."

The gnome chortled under her hood. She knew by the mage's stance that the healer had formal training with a blade. Not only that, but her presence radiated an intimidating and calm confidence. *Like a panther*, she thought, not for the first time. And that wasn't even considering her abilities as a spellcaster. Without question, the gnome was little to no threat to the mage.

"I'm here to offer information about the grave issue plaguing the city and ask something of you in return." Scarlett stepped into the light. The dragon fountain's flaming waters cast blood-red reflections over the cobblestones. "And to talk to you about Captain James Hawk."

"And that is where this conversation ends." The mage gestured with the blade. "Run along, thief. I have no interest in talking about that scoundrel."

"If you'll allow me, Ms. Fitzwater, I'm here with an offer. One that Captain Hawk intended to make but was—"

"Blown off-course?" the mage said, full of snark.

"Quite."

"I have no interest in hearing your offer, Ms.?"

"Tanash. Scarlett Tanash. I'm an agent employed by a private party who wishes to remain anonymous."

"How shocking." More snark. "By chance, he doesn't happen to use an ironic nickname and wear a tricorne hat?"

"No." Something told her she was going to enjoy their exchange, regardless of its outcome. "But my goal does involve the hiring of a captain to sail me through dangerous waters. And James Hawk has agreed to do it."

"For what in return?"

"His ship."

"Typical," the mage muttered. "Sounds about right. Then he can run away. He's good at that."

"Frankly, Ms. Fitzwater, I don't give a damn what he does after our contract expires."

"Get to the point," Marian said, "because otherwise this point," she aimed the dagger at her, "will gut you."

"That blade is the point, Ms. Fitzwater." Scarlett felt pretty good about that one. Marian seemed to as well from the flicker of amusement that passed over her face. "I assure you, this is a civil request."

"Make it, then."

"I am in the process of addressing a crisis in the Jewel Islands. A crisis that involves your father's leadership."

Scarlett examined the mage's body language. As she thought, her statement was enough to keep the half-elf listening.

"The crisis you are fighting is not only inside the palace. It's in Eel Town, and it's spreading."

The mage took a step closer. In the light from the fountain, her features revealed an earnest stare. "Tell me what you know."

Scarlett hid the conflicted feelings swirling inside of her. This topic was part rhetorical strategy and part genuine concern, as mixed and muddy as Marian and Jack's past. "We came ashore at night... to Redtown. There were bodies lined up under stretchers on the dock."

"How many?" Marian's tone softened.

"Too many. In total, over twenty."

"Twenty?" Marian strode in a slow circle. "When was this?"

"Two nights past. Tonight, I checked again."

"And?"

"More than that."

Marian's brow furled. Her lips moved, speaking near-silent words.

Scarlett's ears picked up numbers being whispered from the mage's mouth.

"That's a fast spike," the half-elf said.

"There's more. We passed a ship leaving harbor on our way in. It was flying a yellow flag."

The healer's eyes widened.

"I'll get right to the point, Ms. Fitzwater. That dagger in your hand is why I'm here. It can be the solution. The blade holds the magic to guide us to a source of great healing. Enough to wipe that malignant ancient magic from the islands forever."

"You think an elven blade will cure a plague that's lurked in the shadows and festered for a thousand years?

"I know, my lady, that you are familiar with the legend of the dragon's blood."

The mage stepped back. "You seek Dragon Tail Island?"

Scarlett grew bold. She lowered her hood and let the fountain's flame-like light illuminate her crimson hair. "The blood iron's magic can guide us through the mists. All else we need is already in our hands."

The mage held out the dagger. Its ruby-encrusted hilt shimmered.

"We have our captain in James Hawk," Scarlett said. "I have a ship. We just need a bearing. All it will take is that blade." She pointed a tiny finger. "If you provide it, on our return, I will exchange what you gave us for two things."

"The dragon's blood is a magical cure-all," Marian spoke the words like a declaration that solved a puzzle.

Scarlett nodded at the mage's knowledge of the elixir's power.

"It could be harnessed and distributed," the mage continued, "with the correct tincture recipe..."

"I'm sure your guild has that ability. Its potency would wipe out every trace of fever," Scarlett said.

The mage eyed the weapon in her hand. "And the dagger's fate?"

"It would need to be destroyed."

Marian turned the weapon back and forth, the blade gleaming in the fountain's light. "When I signed off from the royal line, I was allowed one item from our family collection. I never bothered with it until a few weeks ago when my limit was tested. Do you know why I chose this dagger, Ms. Tanash?"

The gnome kept silent, choosing to defer to the mage for an answer.

"Because it was the second most prized possession in my father's collection. The first being a golden arrow." She held up the blood iron blade. "This, I took for spite. Nothing more."

"Then let it do something worthy of its legacy. We can work to a common purpose and rid the islands of a tragic and dangerous magic."

"And the pirate?"

Scarlett cocked her head at the mage's choice to avoid Jack by name. "None of my business. I am not asking you to relive the past. Nor to have direct interaction with him. You need not ever see him again. That said, I can tell you that Jack's true to his word. And despite being a pirate, he's honest. And fair."

The mage scoffed. "You know this how?"

"I've witnessed it through deed and action. Thrice in dangerous circumstances on our journey he's put his life on the line for me, and for others he cares about." The gnome raised a red eyebrow. "Would it interest you to know that my client requested him for that very reason?"

"And why would they do that?"

"My answer will have to wait, Ms. Fitzwater. But if you agree to this, all will be explained. For now, I will say that Captain Hawk's kindness and caring is the reason my client's vision for a better future in the Jewels is possible."

Marian shook her head. "You realize how absurd that sounds?"

"With all due respect, I think you know there are lies turning into truths with every sunrise of late."

Marian examined the dagger, rotating it in the fountain's crimson light.

"You know he was framed?" Scarlett said.

"Is this about the Red Knights not capturing him?"

Scarlett shook her head. "I know nothing of that part of the tale. But I heard with my own ears the warden's admission at Longshore."

"Admission of what?"

"To helping set up and imprison your fiancé."

"You said two things," Marian said, ignoring the line of evidence. "An exchange would mean you provide two things to me. You've mentioned one." She put the dagger back into the scabbard at her waist.

Now it comes to it, Scarlett thought. The test of how deep Marian's commitment and passion to change politics in the Jewels went.

"My mission's central purpose is something I believe you also support."

"And that is?"

"Regime change."

The mage's eyes narrowed. "A bold claim."

"I am not talking about assassination," Scarlett spoke as quickly as she could to get that off the table. "I am talking about justified revolution. Political renewal from the ground up."

Marian stood motionless.

Come on, Scarlett thought. "This is only possible if we move quickly, in time to halt the inauguration. If that happens, it will be near impossible afterwards." *I'm all-in now. I've made myself doubly a target of the regent and his guards.* "I am not asking for explicit support. I understand the personal danger for you. I'm requesting that blade, and as I said, the price I can offer is the cure to the fever and... a new political system that serves the best interests of the people."

"Your client wishes to rule?"

"Not in the least," Scarlett said. "My client wishes to replace a tired, abusive system based on class and privilege with a democratic one. She——" Scarlett stopped, realizing her accidental outing of her client's gender. "She has no desire to preside over anyone."

"You may be sincere, or you may just be the most articulate and persuasive thief to step foot on these islands." Red light danced like flames on Marian's black hair and blue robe. "As much as my guild's mission is aligned with curing the fever, and as much as I despise the upper class's control of politics, I cannot support your endeavor, Ms. Tanash... nor hand over this heirloom. Your offer relies on vague references, formidable obstacles, dangerous magic, and a band of criminals to accomplish the near-impossible in the shortest of time frames."

"That about sums it up," Scarlett said, feeling a wave of "pirateyness" rush over her. "Say what you will about buccaneers, thieves, and those who live outside the law. One thing we don't do is back down or submit, especially not to corrupt authority and rule that does more harm than good, especially for the less fortunate."

"Why should I risk this?" Marian said. "The foundation of your offer is full of confusion, lacking in graspable truths."

"We thrive on risk, Ms. Fitzwater, knowing the rewards it offers. Seems like saving lives now and saving those of future generations is a treasure worthy of risk, even if it means gambling on trust."

"You certainly have the gift of rhetoric, Ms. Tanash."

"So, you're convinced?"

Marian didn't respond.

"If you need time, take it," Scarlett said. "You can always contact me through the proprietor at Home of Tomes in Eel Town."

"Good evening, Ms. Tanash." Marian turned to leave. "And I don't need to remind you of the power of the dagger. Do not make the mistake of trying to take it, by cunning or by force."

Twice sunk, Scarlett thought, watching her go. *Isn't that what Jack called it on Mayrotten Island?* She knew enough to understand the mage was not convinced.

"And remind your captain..." the mage's words drifted across the cobblestone plaza, "I'm to be given a wide berth." The mage reached the entrance to the guild hall and vanished inside.

20

TRUE COLORS

M arian scanned the available produce in the wooden slots of the market stall. At this late hour, not much variety remained and what did were the runts of the daily harvest. "Surprised to see you here."

Marian turned to find her friend and fellow mage, Alara, approaching. "Thank you, I'll take these three Ponangs," she said to the merchant and handed the elderly gnome a stack of pence. She turned to Alara. "I'm grabbing a few last-minute items for a dessert."

Alara fell into step next to her as she headed back to the guild hall. "Do I have a funny story for you," her fellow mage said. "Apparently, our headmaster—"

Marian spotted the kitchen girl from the palace making a poor attempt to lurk indiscreetly outside the healer's guild.

"Alara, I need to go," Marian said, interrupting. "Sorry."

"I'm cutting it close myself," the red mage said. "We've got a meeting about your father's upcoming inauguration. We're doing some demonstrations of destruction magic during the celebrations."

Typical, Marian thought. *My father and his shows of force.*

"See you tomorrow night at the Palmetto. Remind me to tell you about it." Alara scurried off. "Trust me, it's hilarious!" the mage shouted, her red robe fluttering about as she headed around the fountain.

Lithana waited at the building's corner, wringing her hands.

Marian motioned to follow her inside.

Before she shut the door behind them, Marge was in her face.

"Good afternoon to you too, Marge," Marian said. "You remember Lithana?"

The sprite whizzed around the girl's head before settling by the mailboxes in the hallway.

"This way," Marian said, heading upstairs.

Afternoon light beamed into the second-floor hallway. The ornate leaden window at the end of the corridor cast shimmering rays of blue, red, and green reflections, dappling the passage in a mesmerizing display.

"Amazing," Lithana said. "Is that Telathia?" The girl pointed at the figure depicted in the stained glass.

"Indeed." Marian opened the door to her room and gestured for the girl to enter. As a rising member of the guild, she'd upgraded to one of the five large suites within the residence two years prior. A comfortable, wide living space with a sofa and chairs led to a split where a kitchen opened left and her bedroom and bathroom occupied the right portion of the apartment. The guild hall's aged mahogany walls were decorated with a variety of prints and ephemera related to the history of the islands and various botanicals associated with the mage's alchemical endeavors.

"Before I forget..." Marian counted out five gold pieces and held them out for Lithana.

"Oh, no, my lady." She shook her head. "I couldn't."

"You can and you will. You don't want to leave as a toad, do you?"

The girl's eyes went wide and she accepted the coins.

"Now sit." Marian indicated a chair and took a seat on the sofa across from her. "What did you find out?"

Two days had passed since she'd been at the palace to talk with Master Rin. Despite her effort to leave things alone, Marian found herself stopping by the kitchen before departing for the lower city. A genuine greeting to Chef Molard had served as an ostensible excuse to enter the staff area and locate Lithana. She had instructed the girl to listen for anything out of the ordinary in the offices.

"An argument, Miss. Between the regent and your sister, the admiral."

Marian edged forward on the sofa. "Go on."

"Your father was angry with her."

"Why?"

"Over a man. They kept referring to a 'him.' But then the regent called him a pirate."

James.

"Back up and tell me what you overheard."

"The admiral said, 'I wanted to teach him a lesson. He deserved to suffer.' And your father started shoutin', he did. Something about arrogance and threatening their legacy. I remember he said, 'All because of your conceit.' I don't know that word, Miss. That's why I remembered."

"It means to have too much pride," Marian said. "So much so that it can lead to decisions and actions not in your or others' best interests."

In this case, my father's... Bonnie didn't kill James... was it really conceit? Whatever the reason, this proved without any doubt that her sister had been lying about James to both her and her father for fourteen years. *And, Master Rin knew*, she thought.

"And then the admiral said, 'He's alive. I saw him with my own eyes on the ship.' That's when your father started cursing... right nasty words, Miss. Enough to make me blush. Then, the admiral mentioned a battle and that the crew used magic and got away. That's when the regent said something about Longshore Prison and the wanted posters." The girl's eyes lit up. "They were referring to Captain Hawk, weren't they, Miss?"

Marian sighed. She owed the girl the truth, but it meant fueling the fire of rumors amongst the masses. Her stomach boiled to think they saw the pirate as some kind of folk hero back from the dead.

"I think they were referring to him, yes," she said. Lying was not the answer. She would be nothing but a contradiction if she did it after her recent conversations with James and the gnome. "Lithana, remember there are legends and then there are real people. Take my father, for example. You know of the regent and consider him a professional leader, and then you heard him using foul language as a man. We are all real people with faults. No one is perfect."

"Trusty Jack is," Lithana said, eyes aglow. "He's the perfect pirate."

Youth, Marian thought. "Was there anything else?

"Just a good scoldin' that the regent gave your sister."

"I'm familiar with those," Marian said.

"Your sister left and I delivered the breads to the guards. Only other thing was an old half-orc that came in when I was returning to the kitchen."

"A half-orc?"

Lithana's fingers tightened on her thighs. "I didn't like the look of him, Miss, so I left the office halls right fast, I did."

"Can you describe him?"

She shook her head. "I didn't want to get caught, Miss. He was frightening, he was... dressed in black leathers under his cloak. Strange piercings through his lips and nose. I kept my eyes down and hurried out."

A sickening sensation filled Marian's stomach. *It couldn't be. That devious rat hadn't been around for decades.*

"I heard one thing from down the hall as I left."

Marian listened, her mind on the memory of the old mercenary who did her father's dirty work in his early days as regent.

"Your father said, 'We may have a problem with the pirate.'"

Pirate... did he mean James? Her former lover's words about brutes who supposedly rounded him up returned. *Could that have been related to the half-orc?*

"You alright, Miss?"

"Yes," Marian adjusted her robe. "What about Master Rin? Did you hear anything about the fever?"

"Nothing, Miss. But Master Rin was upset yesterday. I heard her talking with a ship captain. I think his name was Garner. They were arguing about costs per passenger." The girl's brow furled. "'Twas funny,

Miss. They kept saying 'bodies'... seemed cold to me to refer to travelers as such."

Marian frowned. *The gnome spoke the truth about the harbor. This is a cover-up.* "Sometimes those obsessed with business have clouded judgements and lose sight of their compassion," she said. "It becomes blurred by profit and self-preservation."

The girl cocked her head.

"It's better to leave that one be, Lithana. Is your family doing well? Your little sister, healthy?"

"Yes, she's well as can be, thank you, Miss."

That was a relief. With what the gnome had shared last night it wasn't going to be long before most children in the lower city fell ill.

"Miss, if I may... can I ask a question?"

"Of course."

Lithana pointed at the wall over Marian's shoulder. "That picture. I seen the same one in Master Rin's office at the palace."

"You don't know who Nimárwe is?"

The girl shook her head, cheeks flushing.

"Do you know about the ghost dragon?"

"Only that the city almost fell to it, and the elves of old saved Redtown."

"Well, this is as good a reward as that gold in your hands. Knowledge is something you keep forever. Once you have it you don't give it up like those coins." Marian pointed at the stack in the girl's palm. "Come here." She stepped over to the engraving that was a smaller replica of the original painting in Master Rin's office.

"Nimárwe was a golden elf, the high wizard of the mages. She had incredible powers linked to the elder gods who once presided over the Jewel Islands."

The girl's eyes ran over the engraving, her face filled with wonder.

"Each god had a distinct spirit, an essence... like the sauces you cook down for hours in the kitchen."

The girl nodded in understanding.

"They say that the Jewel Islands were once gems on a divine's necklace. And that during a fight among gods in the sky kingdom, it was torn from Telathia's neck and fell to Arsel, landing in the open sea."

"That's why they're called the Jewels?"

"Indeed. Each island takes its name from those gems. Emerald, Topaz, Ruby, Sapphire... they contain divine currents that we refer to as 'magic'... traces of the gods' powers that linger in our material world."

"And the dragons?" Lithana asked.

"No one knows how or when they first came to Arsel, but they are in the records since the arrival of the golden elves in the Jewels."

"Where did they come from?"

"The elves? From Arsel. Divine light, cast from the Sky Kingdom, shone off the mainland coast and led them to sea. Lured by the gods, they ventured forth on a voyage of discovery, following the unworldly beacon across the deep blue. After weeks of empty sailing with doubt rising in their hearts, the Jewels appeared on the horizon, breaking the flat and endless waters, and became their home... a land where they lived as heightened beings attuned to the islands' magic as none other could. Golden dragons were in abundance in the archipelago and the elves found kinship with the drakes. The two species lived together for thousands of years in peace and isolation."

"Until?" Lithana's eyes were on the ghost dragon sundered at Nimárwe's feet.

"Until the peace of their world was broken. Turmoil amongst the gods caused Hanis-tá, the jealous divine, to seek retribution. He sent a festering and death-spirited magic down to Arsel. It came in the form of a ghost dragon. Neither living nor dead, an in-between being that had only one purpose... to crush the golden elves and destroy their kingdom as revenge on his divine siblings."

Marian approached the engraving and examined the image of Nimárwe. The elf stood over the ghost dragon triumphant. The famous bow in one hand and a quiver of arrows at her feet. "But the high wizard took the creature down, with some form of powerful magic now lost to us."

"Why didn't they run, Miss? From the islands?"

"Nimárwe wasn't just a wizard. She was royalty." Marian shifted uncomfortably at the association with her own family's role as regents. "It was her job to protect the city."

"Against a ghost dragon?"

"There are responsibilities that come with privilege, Lithana. But that is another conversation and one I don't want to have now." *Or ever.*

"What happened to the ghost dragon?" Lithana said.

"That is where the story takes a tragic turn." Marian looked to the girl. "The elves took the bones to a remote island over the eastern horizon. There, they buried them deep in a vault along with a vial of Golden Dragon blood, the most pure and powerful form of healing in the world, alongside priceless offerings to Telathia to protect them and keep the evil at bay. The spirit of Hanis-tá and his dragon were banished, but even so, the power of that lingering magic was strong enough to remain. You've heard of the mists?"

"Oh, yes, Miss." Lithana nodded. "Pa would tell us of it 'fore sleep. 'O'er that horizon be Dragon Tail Island,' he would say. 'Nothing but death waits there.'"

"I'll bet he told you to stay out of the eastern sea."

"He did. And from Mayrotten Island too."

Marian nodded. "That mist is the lingering spirit of Hanis-tá's magic, and its invisible traces reach the farthest tip of the Jewel Archipelago."

"Miss, you said the tale was tragic, but the elves sent the bones away and locked them on the island?"

"This is where the tale reaches to the present... to you and me." Marian walked to her desk and picked up a vial of the tincture used to help with symptoms of the fever. She held it up for Lithana to see.

"Before they burned the dragon to its bones, the creature's blood leeched into the ground. A diseased magic ran into the soil on Ruby Island. It's the cause of the fever that lingers still."

"Pardon my asking, Miss. But isn't blood iron made from it?"

"Luckily, it is not," Marian said, pulling her robe around her waist to cover the dagger. "That is forged from golden dragon blood." Marian's mind went to the gnome and the proposal. "But the elves made a compass from the ghost dragon's blood before they burned it, as a way of locating the island should they ever need to return. The needle balanced the evil magic of the compass, controlling its deceit and chaos. It points to the island, cutting through the mists, leading to the last remaining golden dragon blood in the world."

"Why would they ever want to return to Dragon Tail Island?"

"It is said—"

The clanking of plate armor broke the silence.

Marian held up a hand, asking for quiet.

A knock came at the door.

"My lady?"

"Sir Roderick?" the mage asked.

"Yes, my lady," the Red Knight's voice came through the door. "I need to speak with you. It's urgent."

Marian put her arm around the girl and led her across the room.

"You need to go, Lithana. Thank you for this. We can talk more about history any time you like."

"Really?"

"Of course," Marian touched her cheek, seeing something of herself in the youth. "I am happy to share what I know with you."

Lithana's eyes lit up.

"One moment, Sir Roderick." Marian went to her desk. "Here." She handed Lithana another gold coin. "Take this to Mirtha, the book merchant on Fisher's Row. Tell her to give you a copy of *Ruby Island History, Vol.* 1. I will help you with the difficult words like 'conceit.'" She winked.

"Thank you, Miss."

"And if you hear anything else, please return."

The girl nodded.

"Be careful at the palace," the mage whispered and opened the door.

The Red Knight bowed.

"Come in, Sir Roderick," Marian said.

The knight's one good eye narrowed as the girl scurried out and past him. "Why is she here?"

"My guess is the same reason you are." Marian gestured for him to enter. "This day has been filled with disturbing revelations."

"More have arrived, my lady." The Red Knight strode into her apartment and stood at the center of the living room, helmet under an arm.

"Sit," she said.

"I'll stand, thank you."

Of course you will, she thought and took a seat in the chair where Lithana had been a moment earlier.

"Is this about my query regarding James Hawk's capture?" Marian said.

The Red Knight's face turned grave. "It is." The burn scars on Sir Roderick's face stretched. His aged onyx skin seemed to fall, acquiescing to gravity in a way Marian had not seen before. The old knight adjusted his eye patch and cleared his throat.

"It was not easy, my lady, but I located a retired member of my order whom I trust."

To Marian's surprise, he sat down on the sofa.

"This dwarf was a longtime sergeant of the high guard, privy to our most secret assignments."

Marian studied the man. He looked as if he'd been forced to surrender under humiliating circumstances.

"What is it?" she asked.

"The information you gave me is correct. The Red Knights did not apprehend James Hawk. The man was handed off to the high guard by a small team of mercenaries." He raised a scarred eyebrow. "Led by a rogue swordspeller named—"

"Kakani," Marian said.

The Red Knight nodded.

"I can't believe it," she whispered. Everything was falling into place, but the weight of the revelation and what it meant was overwhelming.

"I was not sure if he were someone you would remember, my lady."

Oh, I remember him. Even as a young girl, how could she not? Lithana's fright only a day ago proved as much. The half-orc was a cold-hearted sword for hire, with a reputation for bloodlust and a talent for spellcasting focused on the art of torture. "I know a good deal about what kinds of 'services' he provided for my father."

"It seems that Captain Hawk was set up," the knight said. "Two innocent people were murdered by Kakani's rogues and made to appear as if the young man had been the culprit."

"Why, Roderick?" Her heart was breaking with confusion. Pieces were falling in every direction—betrayal, deceit, victimhood...

"I do not know, my lady." The Red Knight sat up straight, chin held high. "But I know by whom and as a Red Knight who swore an oath to this city, I find it both egregious and immoral."

Marian squeezed her hands tight. Her muscles were already tensing against yet spoken words. "Tell me, I need to know."

"Your father."

Like a fuse reaching powder, the words set off an emotional collapse. The man who had been one half of the pair that brought her into this world had intervened and crushed her one love.

"I am sorry, my lady."

Through her blurring vision, Sir Roderick's face lowered.

My father did this? Strangely, a repressed feeling that had lurked within her for decades rose. Unlike in the past, there was no shrugging it off as nonsense, its persistence and prescience now oddly vindicated. James's arrest had all been so sudden and so... *convenient.*

Marian's inner strength rose. Anger pushed aside her grief.

"Can I trust you, Sir Roderick?"

The Red Knight's scar-stricken face softened with a mixture of concern and mild insult at her query. "I serve the Order of the Red Knights and live by my oath, my lady. I was charged with your protection. Therefore, I serve you. My order serves the city of Redtown."

"Is that a 'yes?'"

His stare grew earnest.

"What about my father?"

"I take orders from the regent. But..." Sir Roderick took in a breath.

"But?"

"May I speak plainly, my lady?"

"It's been my wish for the last two decades, Roderick. Please. If ever there was a time for it." She met his earnest gaze. "It is now."

"You, of all the Fitzwaters alive today, demonstrate the nobility and humility of one worthy of leading from the palace."

"I don't have any desire—"

The Red Knight held up a hand.

Marian halted, his action both a stunning breach of etiquette and a welcome surprise. For once, the man who had always been a true and loyal protector was speaking boldly and as an equal.

"I fear for what is to come of the Jewels should your father take control as king," the knight said. "I am not alone in this opinion among my order. We serve the people, and the palace as an institution that presides over them, but we do *not* serve a person."

Of like mind. "I want to tell you something, Sir Roderick." Marian steepled her fingers at her chin. "Sharing this information with you is risking my life." Everything she knew based on Lithana's information and her encounters with James and Scarlett Tanash flowed from her tongue. She told him of the dagger, the rogues' plans to use it to reach Dragon Tail Island, and what it could mean politically and for the health and welfare of the population's fight with the fever—a plot to prevent tyranny by overthrowing her own father's regime, and the concurrent ability to cure a deadly plague that could take down the young generation throughout the islands.

The Red Knight listened in silence. The face that had softened moments earlier shifted, as if a living being had been morphed into a noble sculpture of stone.

Marian let the words settle. Motes of dust caught in the window's light at the split to the kitchen and bedroom. *My father set James up. Prejudice, elitism, and self-preservation were more important to him than a daughter's love.* James's face when they met last evening, with its mixture of pride and weariness, returned. She felt for him. And those words he spoke about enduring love... yet, pride and her own self-worth parried in defense. That didn't change the years of neglect and absence, running from her and the world and life he'd left in a wake of piracy and criminality. She shook her head, conflicted. *What am I supposed to feel?*

"There is still time, my lady." The Red Knight's words pulled her back from the internal nightmare.

Marian shook her head. "I can't go back, Sir Roderick. Even if I wanted to return to the noble line, it is too late."

"That is not what I mean." The Red Knight rested his hands on his knees. "It is never too late," he whispered, "to do what is right."

"What are you saying?"

"You don't need to sit on a throne to display nobility." Sir Roderick's jaw muscles tightened. "And you don't need a crest," he indicated the flaming insignia on his plate armor, "to have a moral code."

"I don't understand?"

"You were born into circumstance. Why? No one knows. But it gives you options. Do not walk away from them. You can sign away your right to rule, you can turn your back on the palace, but you will always be a Fitzwater. Your family has governed for hundreds of years through your aunt's royal line. It is a proud legacy. Had Queen Ricarda and her son not perished at sea, the present might look different."

That was true. Her aunt had been a kind and generous leader. At the least, she would have taken care to keep the fever at bay. Ricarda's compassion would have led her to maintain a fair tax levied against the islanders, as well as protect the archipelago's natural ecosystem.

"People want leaders, my lady. You have lived a life of privilege. With that condition comes expected sacrifices if one is to remain true. But as a leader, they are not *your* people. That is what your father, with all due respect, does not understand. Your aunt, Queen Ricarda and others in your family before her, governed as royalty with grace and fairness. When a threat rose, be it Orc bands from the jungle, Magma Giants from the volcanic caves, or in the days of old, a Ghost Dragon," the Red Knight nodded at the image of Nimárwe on the wall, "they stepped forward and put their lives on the line. It didn't matter if it was hopeless, nor did it need to be made an official charge by decree for them to act." The Red Knight raised a gloved hand and gestured as if to placate an audience. "This was never folly. A wise leader knows when surrender is necessary for the survival of those under their protection." Roderick's voice rose in volume. "But a time comes when one acts despite the risks. Misplaced pride falls to strength and honor." His one eye narrowed. "That is true courage and noble sacrifice! That, my lady is what turns leaders into heroes."

Marian took pause. *Risk,* she thought... this was the second time in days that the word reared its dubious head.

"I asked for you to speak plainly and you have honored that," she said.

"My lady." The Red Knight lowered his head.

Marian rose and went to her desk. She hastily scribbled on a piece of parchment and handed it to Sir Roderick.

"Read it through now," she said.

The Red Knight squinted, his one good eye scanning the note. "You want me to do what?"

"I want you to do all of that." Marian met his gaze. "Speaking as a Fitzwater... of the noble line sworn to protect this city and my fellow citizens, here and throughout the islands. Will you honor my request?"

The Red Knight rose and stood proudly before her. He bowed his head. "In life and in death, my lady."

"Thank you, Sir Roderick. You honor our city. Go. And make haste." She put an arm on his shoulder and smiled. "In this difficult hour, I find our new bond comforting, old friend."

The Red Knight's eye was aglow with pride. He nodded and exited.

Marian stood amidst the silence of the empty apartment. The past and present of her life for the last twenty-some years stood on display: books and prints related to alchemy and healing arts, devotional icons to Telathia and other comforts that had been collected over her travels throughout the Jewels, and trinkets and gifts from close friends and colleagues.

A long-dormant feeling rose inside of her. She'd felt it years ago upon returning to her quarters in the palace after she'd informed her father she was exiting the royal line. Her childhood bedroom, the grand hallways, and even the veranda and her beloved gardens had shifted in perspective. Now, standing alone in the suite, her life as a mage stood before her as if she were gazing into the past.

Marian's hand went to the dagger at her waist, gripping its ornate handle. She turned, a strange force drawing her to the engraving. Her eyes ran over the delicate line work depicting the famous scene.

Nimárwe's expression pulled at her. The artist had captured a beautiful contradiction in her features. Defiance mixed with fear. Exhaustion and elation. Triumph and...

Sacrifice, she thought.

With slow but inevitable determination, Marian touched the pendant at her neck. She held it out, fingers running over the jewel's smooth surface. Afternoon sunlight glinted on the gemstone, sending shimmering reflections across the engraving on the wall. Divine-like light danced across the elf triumphant as she stood over the body of the terrifying drake.

Marian reached behind her neck and undid the clasp. She removed the Chain of Telathia and held it up in front of her.

The pendant dangled and spun, glimmering.

She strode to her desk and placed it in an envelope, adding the headmaster's name to the outside with a feather quill pen.

On a folded piece of parchment, she added a short note:

"I found the truth. And with it, the road."

21

BRING A SPRING
UPON A CABLE

Scarlett surveyed the somber mood around the safehouse table. Trusty Jack leaned back in his chair, arms folded. Big Rig fiddled with a line of rope, tying and untying nautical knots. Siân, having given up the exquisite elven lute when they disembarked *Felicity*, strummed a small lyre acquired from the night elf upstairs. Doni's unease was palpable. The gnome sat at her side, head down, twiddling his thumbs.

Only Lana appeared unaffected by their combined failures to persuade the mage. The half-orc's arms danced through a sequence of martial techniques, the candlelight casting near-animate shapes and beasts as she performed intricate combinations of punches and strikes. Scarlett couldn't help but wonder if such an origin or influence existed in the former monk's combat style.

With a deep sigh, the gnome straightened herself in the chair. *Might as well get this over with.* "I think it's time we accept the inevitable."

No one stirred.

"I take it by the lack of reaction that we already have?"

"Knew that wasn't going to work, lass," Jack whispered, picking at his teeth.

"I am sorry to have to call this to a close," Scarlett said. "I know it's not everything you hoped for, but at least you got your crew back."

Soft mutterings of "aye" rose from the dwarf and the half-orc. Siân plucked a chord in a more harmonious and major key.

"What will you do now?" she asked.

"Get ourselves off Ruby Island for a start," Big Rig said. "Going to prove difficult enough, that is."

"Aye, lad." Trusty Jack pointed in affirmation. "After that we'll head to—"

A knock cut him off. There was a pause, then three more knocks followed.

All heads turned to the door leading up to the bookshop.

With cautious steps, Scarlett crossed to the wooden entrance and unbolted the latch. Step by step, the gnome climbed the stairs leading to the main floor. The magical ward shone at the seams of the hidden passage, illuminating the stairwell with an eerie purple light.

She knocked four times in rapid succession and waited.

"What's happening?" Big Rig asked, his dwarfish beard and head peering up from the bottom of the stairs.

"I don't know," she whispered and waved him back. "Be ready."

The purple edges faded and the panel slid open.

"There's someone here for you," the night elf said. Violet nocturnal eyes glowed in the dim light of the bookshop.

Scarlett peeked around him, but all she saw were stacks of tomes. The lingering scent of burning sage wafted down the stairs.

"They claim you gave them this address," the night elf said.

Her stomach fluttered. *Could it be?*

"Shall I let them in?"

"Send them down," Scarlett said and retreated to the bottom of the steps.

"Who is it?" Big Rig stomped forward.

"Are we made, lass?" Jack grabbed his cutlass.

Lana smacked a fist against her palm and pushed past her captain to be the first to engage.

"Everyone back up." Scarlett held up her tiny gnomish hands and motioned to make space. "In your seats."

No one moved.

"*Now.*" She narrowed her eyes. "Stay calm and let me do the talking." She pointed at Jack. "Especially you."

Shuffling of feet on stone broke the tense silence.

Scarlett turned as a hooded figure appeared in the doorway. Draped in a common wool robe with a swath of fabric covering their face, the mystery guest took a step forward. Almond-shaped eyes, fierce and determined, radiated from the narrow opening above the mask.

Scarlett knew those eyes.

A hand pulled back the hood and removed the face wrap.

Everyone gasped.

"Marian?" Jack said. "What are you doing here?"

The mage nodded at Scarlett and approached. She drew her dagger and placed it on the table.

"Saving my people."

⚜

"THANK YOU, MY LADY." SCARLETT COULDN'T HOLD BACK HER relief. "You can count on us. Once we arrive at Benevolence, I will have a courier send—"

"Oh no, Ms. Tanash." The mage took off the wool robe and threw it over a crate. "You misunderstand. And it's Marian, by the way." The half-elf looked over the stunned faces. "That goes for all of you."

Scarlett checked on Trusty Jack. He looked as baffled as the others, though she didn't miss the twinkle in his eyes at seeing his once-betrothed across the table. "I'm sorry," she said, offering the mage a seat, "what exactly did I misunderstand? You're giving us the dagger, are you not?" The gnome sat in the chair adjacent to Marian.

"Indeed." The mage adjusted her blue robe and crossed her legs. "I'm not sure we've all been properly introduced. James and I know each other, and I assume you to be Mr. Riggins?" She met the dwarf's gaze.

"Aye, Dûr Riggins. Quartermaster to Captain Hawk. But please my... um... Marian, call me Big Rig."

The mage smiled. "As you wish."

"Lana Luholi." The half-orc's chair screeched as she rose and bowed.

"Please, Lana." Marian held up a hand. "No need for that. I'm just another islander like you. I'm guessing you're from Emerald with that accent."

"Aye, that I am." Lana's eyes brightened. "May I say your hair is lovely, Marian. Been itchin' to let mine down like that but with the knucklin' and whatnot it tends to get in me way."

"Knucklin'?"

"Brawling," Big Rig said, and motioned for Lana to sit down.

Scarlett waited anxiously as Marian continued around the table.

"Hello, James."

"Marian," the pirate said. His cheeks flushed but he held her stare.

"I'm Doni!"

Scarlett almost jumped in her seat. This time though, she welcomed her fellow thief's exuberance. It broke the tension of the exchange between the former lovers.

"I'm a colleague of Scarlett's. We're old friends. Going way back to our childhood days." He nodded proudly. "Did you know we were once—"

"Doni!" Scarlett shot him a look.

The gnome shrank in his chair.

"And you must be Siân?" Marian asked.

"How did you guess that?" The nocsi put a paw to her chin. "Oh wait!" She pointed at the mage. "The posters!"

"Indeed. Are you from the eastern reefs or those off Topaz coast?" Marian asked.

"Eastern reefs. My romp's the kelp forests south of Opal Island. I've many a song to sing about my home."

"Well, perhaps you can fill the time for me with some of your tales."

"Oh no," Scarlett said, "Siân is coming with us. She's been inducted into the Salty Scoundrels."

The nocsi picked up her lyre and strummed a bold introductory chord in celebration.

"She'll be sailing to Benevolence."

Marian smirked. "As I said, you can help pass the time." The mage's head went around the table. "I'm coming with you."

"What?" Trusty Jack blurted.

"*I'm coming with you*," Marian repeated. "Ms. Tanash and I have a mutual understanding about the needs of the people in Redtown and throughout the Jewels. But I will be honest with all of you; I don't trust any of you. And so, I am offering you the dagger provided I sail with you to Benevolence, and from there, to Dragon Tail Island."

Did he smile? Scarlett thought. Unless she was mistaken, the corners of Jack's mouth broke into an upward arc.

"You are most welcome, Marian," Scarlett said. "I speak for all of us, I believe?"

Nods around the table, including Trusty Jack.

"And thank you," Scarlett said, "you have appeared as a beacon in our dark hour."

"Save your flattery and optimism, Ms. Tanash," the mage said, her tone light. "Something tells me we are going to need it."

"I'll drink to that!" Lana reached for the cask. "In fact, how about a round, Cap?" The half-orc pushed a shot glass across the table. "Are you a fan of rum, my lady... sorry, Marian? This here's Molly's Molasses. The finest rum in the Isles. Getting mighty near the bottom of the barrel so get it while ye can."

"Can't say I've had it," Marian said, "but I'm in."

Lana slapped her massive green thigh. "Well, I'll be a plucky parrot! It's nice to have another lass around who likes her grog!"

Marian nodded, a small smile on her face.

Scarlett found herself settling. *We're back on track,* she thought. *I can't believe it...*

"Benevolence here we come!" Lana said, filling shot glasses and distributing them.

Big Rig stood. "Captain, if you don't mind, I'd like to make this toast?"

Trusty Jack motioned to proceed.

The dwarf cleared his throat. "To breezes and ladies fair." He gestured the shot glass at the mage. "To rolling seas and safe harbor." The quartermaster put a hand on Trusty Jack's shoulder. "And to our ship, *Lady Luck*."

"Aye!" Lana shouted and slammed a fist on the table.

"Drink up, mateys," Trusty Jack said and knocked back his shot.

Scarlett slammed the fiery rum.

Lana's gaze was fixed on the mage. "Well?"

Marian wiped her lips and placed the glass down on the table. "Interesting. I think..." she rubbed her chin, "it would be wise to have another before I pass judgment."

Lana was up and stomping around the table. The half-orc poured another shot for the mage holding the cask high so the liquid cascaded down through the air. "Oh, Cap! We're going to have a time of it, aren't we?" Lana said and did a jig, shuffling her feet.

Scarlett wasn't sure what to make of Jack's expression. The man looked to be in shock.

Marian leaned over. "Do you have safe passage out of Redtown?" she whispered.

"No," Scarlett said. "We lost our boat after arriving. An incident with the Royal Navy left us with no choice but to release our ship for hire."

"Ah yes, I believe you had a run-in with my sister," the mage said. She looked across the table. "She saw you, by the way." The mage's words rose in volume so Jack and the others could hear. "Once we are safe and sailing, I will share what I know of your situation with the palace and those who seek to stop you."

"Thank you yet again, Marian," Scarlett said.

"As much as I am enjoying this rum," the mage said to Lana, "we need to go."

"To where?" Siân asked.

"I've arranged secret passage on a sugar trader. They'll drop us in Benevolence on their way southeast to Opal Island. And before you ask," the mage raised a hand, "it's taken care of. Ms. Tanash, you and I can discuss resources once we are at sea."

"Thank you, Marian. And please, call me Scarlett."

"If luck is with us, we'll get through Eel Town to the harbor without detection," Marian said. She picked up the dagger and put it back in the scabbard at her waist.

A green arm blocked Scarlett's view of the mage.

The glint of a shot glass between thick fingers came into focus.

"You'll be needin' one more for luck, Marian." Lana winked. "It's a pirate thing."

৩১১

UNDER THE COVER OF DARKNESS AND A BILLOWING MIST, THE PARTY made their way through Eel Town. Hooded and cloaked, they moved as silhouettes. Scarlett worked point at the front of the column, doing her best to avoid the city guards on night duty.

Big Rig and Lana had spent the entire walk from the safe house arguing in hushed voices. The half-orc insisted the Redtown fog was thick as curdled milk, while the quartermaster claimed the designation far too extreme. Curdled milk, the dwarf had explained, was only one grade below pea soup. This fog, the old salt declared, was no more than wedding veil mist. Trusty Jack, recognizing the danger of their words reaching others' ears, put an end to the debate. The captain refused to take a side, instead threatening extra mess duty on *Lady Luck* if they didn't pipe down. When Lana nudged the argument with a whispered, "curdled milk" in Big Rig's ear, the pirate upgraded his threat to forcing them to work two shifts in the mess *together*.

Scarlett took note of how fast that shut both up.

Five more minutes of slinking in the shadows and they had reached the street leading to the docks. Scarlett halted at the corner and gestured for the party to wait against the wall. She peered about, taking in the wharf. Candlelight shone from dock stations where each gangway extended into the bay. Bands of mist lingered, causing the flames to appear as fuzzy and indistinct orbs. Beyond the wharf, golden reflections from decks and galley windows hinted of ships at anchor. An occasional clang of a pulley against a mast broke the quiet.

"Where did you say the merchant ship was?" she whispered.

Marian bent a knee beside her. Siân, Big Rig, Lana, Trusty Jack, and Doni waited behind them.

"At the farthest mooring, near the harbor's entrance," the mage said.

Marian's half-elf eyes met her own. Even in the shadows and fog, flecks of gold like shattered amber glimmered with mesmerizing potency.

"I've arranged for two dinghies to be left at the ready," the mage said. "It's a long row, but I thought it better that the merchant ship have a clear path to cut and run if there's trouble."

"Smart," Scarlett said.

"Chalk it up to an admiral for a sister." Marian winked.

I like her, Scarlett thought, and glanced back at Jack. No wonder he did, too. The regent's daughter was smart, confident, caring, cunning... the list went on. Without question, Marian Fitzwater had the mark of the extraordinary.

"Our boats should be there." The mage pointed at the farthest dock.

Scarlett made out a pier and check-in station before the mist consumed the view. "We've got to deal with those guards." She indicated three soldiers illuminated under a candle box. Armed and armored, the trio stood in casual conversation.

"And those as well."

Scarlett followed Marian's finger. Above the rolling bands of mists, two vague and shadowy forms occupied crow's nests atop naval vessels.

"Archers?" she asked.

"My sister had them stationed there yesterday," Marian said. "Your Salty Scoundrels are quite the wanted bunch after the incident at sea." The mage glanced back at the others. "I am sure being stranded and rudderless before a full crew was not a good look for an admiral."

"As long as we stay out of the light, those archers won't be a problem." Scarlett's tactical vision scanned the docks. *But we need a way past those guards.* Even if they hugged the shops, the candlelight from the arrival station would reveal their presence. "Wait here a moment," she said.

Like a ghost, Scarlett drifted forward, moving from stall to stall and along doorways until she was close enough to get the lay of the land. The thuds and clangs of pulleys drew her attention. A merchant ship sat docked between the guards and their dinghies, unloading a shipment. Her gnomish eyes narrowed and she read the words stamped on a stack of crates: "*Topaz Island Exports: Sea Kelp.*"

She scurried back and joined the group.

"I have an idea," she said. "Siân." The gnome waved the nocsi forward. "There's a merchant ship unloading crates past those guards. Guess what they're hauling?"

"Molly Molasses?" the nocsi said, tutting through her teeth.

Full-on Salty Scoundrel already, she thought. "No... sea kelp."

"Oh!" The bard clapped her furry paws in delight.

"If I can get you there," Scarlett said, "how long would it take to charge your magic?"

"Quite fast. My saliva will begin digesting the kelp immediately."

"I need a big psionic force for this to work, Siân."

"How big?"

"A pile of those crates needs to go overboard."

"A distraction?" Marian said.

Scarlett nodded.

"What about you two?" the mage asked. "How will you get to the dinghies?"

"Siân can swim," Scarlett said.

"And you?"

"Doni." Scarlett waved for the thief to come forward.

The gnome joined the huddle, fingers twisting his russet mustache.

"Can you—"

"Anything for you." He grinned.

Scarlett didn't miss Marian's amused expression. *Her too, now?* she thought.

"I need a grindle-windle," she said.

The gnome's eyes lit up.

"You've done them at the training camp?"

Doni nodded.

"Well, now you're going to do one in the field." She locked eyes with him. "And you better do it well because I'm the one who will be out there and vulnerable."

He stood up straight and fastened the buttons on his vest. "You can count on me."

"I need two grindle-windles, Doni. One to get us to the crates." She pointed at a misty section of the docks. "And one after you hear the commotion."

"Oh." He rubbed his hands. "You need a *double* grindle-windle."

A wave of warmth rushed through her veins. He wasn't scared in the least; only excited to aid her. Without realizing what she was doing, her hand came to rest on his shoulder. "You pull this off and you might get another kiss."

His eyes went wide.

Why did I say that? she thought.

"Shouldn't I get *two* kisses?" Doni said. "It's a double grin—?"

"Don't push it." She handed him two small marble-like balls.

"Ready when you are," Siân said, handing over her things to the mage for safekeeping.

"Marian," Scarlett said, "put Lana in the middle between you and Big Rig. Jack can go first when you make for the dinghies. If something goes wrong, try and keep Lana under control."

"You want me," the mage pointed at her chest, "to keep her," she pointed at the half-orc bruiser, 'under control?'"

"She likes you." The gnome winked.

"I'll have the dwarf do it." Marian sifted through her bag and pulled out several wrapped items.

Scarlett watched as the mage tied a series of herbs and flowers to a white quartz stone and set the bundle in a small pouch.

"I want a spell ready," the mage said. "In case things take a wrong turn."

They usually do. "Alright, everyone." Scarlett motioned the group together. "Gather round."

Speaking in hushed tones, she outlined the plan.

"Good lucks" were shared all around and, after Jack denied a toast proposal by Lana, she and Siân hurried off in one direction and Doni in the other.

Slinking along, she and Siân passed storefronts and scurried behind empty fishmonger carriages to the edge of the candlelight.

"Now what?" Siân whispered, as they ducked behind an extra stinky cart. The bard twitched her whiskers at the stench. "Yuk! Even my taste for fish is grossed out by this smell."

Scarlett pinched her nose and spoke in a nasally voice. "Now we wait for Doni."

Where will he do the first grindle-windle? she wondered, scanning the docks. Right now, Doni was most likely speaking to the magic marble, priming it for the ruse.

"Oy!"

Scarlett's head swung to the source of the shout. She smiled at Doni's choice to use a magically-generated gruff tone. Again, that warm feeling rose. Despite his quirks, he really was making progress as a guild thief.

"Screw the regent! And screw the lot of you that work for him! Rotters, all of ya!"

The illusory silhouette of a half-orc appeared at the opposite end of the docks, raising a fist in defiance.

"This is gonna' make my night," a female human guard said, patting her club in her palm. "Come on, lads."

"Archers!" Another shouted up at the ships' crow's nests and pointed to where the illusion appeared. "Stand ready, only shoot if there's trouble."

"Ain't no trouble," the woman guard said and spat as she walked. "He's drunk and going to get himself a nice little beating." The others chuckled and followed, readying their clubs.

"Now," Scarlett said and moved across the street. She and Siân reached the crates without incident. The thief pried open a plank with her dagger.

Siân sniffed. "Oh, that's fresh and high quality." The nocsi reached a paw in and withdrew a claw full of kelp. "It's been almost a year since I've had this." She chomped it down.

The bard's pupils dilated. A faint green light sparkled from her slim irises. "More... give me more." The otter-like humanoid reached in and gulped down another handful.

"Good enough?" Scarlett checked on the guards. They continued to search the docks but were starting to lose interest.

"It's never enough." The nocsi's paw reached for the opening in the crate.

Scarlett intercepted it. "Enough for what we need?"

"I guess so."

"Then that will have to do. Let's go." She pulled Siân along to a spot within the stacks where they had a clear line to the deck of the ship. "Do it, Siân."

A low hum rose from the nocsi's throat. She opened her eyes and shot out an arm.

Boom!

Scarlett's eyes went wide at the force of the invisible wave of energy.

Splash! Splash! Splash!

"Blow *me* down," she whispered.

"Oh, you have no idea how good that felt!" Siân said, rubbing her belly.

Commotion filled the dock as the sailors reacted to the scattered cargo. Most crates fell to the pier and smashed apart, sea kelp spilling out onto the planks. A few others went into the water.

"Look!"

Scarlett followed the nocsi's paw. The party was heading along the storefronts towards the dinghies.

"Excellent," she said. "Okay, Doni. Give us the second one... wherever you are."

Scarlett waited.

Nothing.

The initial chaos of the ruse subsided into an orderly cleanup effort.

"Siân, go now. Get in the water. I'll be fine."

The bard nodded and slipped over the side of the dock.

Scarlett nibbled on a nail. *Come on, Doni.* The guards who had fallen for the first grindle-windle were running back to the ship, making straight toward the pile of crates where she lay hidden.

Nothing for it! she thought and bolted towards the dinghies.

"Long live the revolution!"

The half-orc's voice from the second magic marble made her smirk. She dashed through the well-lit open section towards the shadows where the others would be prepping for departure.

"How'd I do?" Doni appeared from behind a fish cart running next to her.

"Spectacular. Definitely two kiss—"

A force hit her shoulder, and she tumbled to the ground.

Her vision swirled from the impact. *What happened?*

Shouts behind her grew louder.

Doni pulled her up from the cobblestones. "Run Scarlett!" He shoved her forward.

In a daze, Scarlett dashed off. Warm liquid trickled down her ribs under her shirt and cloak. *Gods, I've been hit. With what?*

A robed figure emerged from the shadows ahead. Intense cobalt light shot from Marian's palm and whizzed past her ear. Scarlett glanced back in time to see a sheet of ice cover the cobblestones. The three guards slipped and crashed down, clubs sliding across the ice.

Pain throbbing in her shoulder, she risked another look. Through blurred vision, Doni's hazy outline stood at the edge of the ice patch.

"How dare you?" The gnome balled a fist at the fallen guards. "I'll make you pay for this you—"

"Hurry!" Marian waved at Doni to get moving.

Stumbling and dizzy, Scarlett reached the others and crashed into Big Rig. The dwarf helped her down and into the boat. Lana and Jack were already away from the dock and pulling Siân over the side of the other dinghy.

"Come on, Marian!" Big Rig shouted.

The mage stepped off the dock and into the boat.

Through waves of unfocused vision, Scarlett tracked Doni's progress. The gnome was halfway across the open street to their boat. More guards emerged from an alley only a few paces behind him.

"Doni!" Pain ripped through her neck and shoulder as her vocal cords strained.

"We have to go, Scarlett," Big Rig said. "Now or never, lass."

"He'll make it." Marian gripped the dock to keep them stable. "Hold a moment."

"We can't take those guards on," the dwarf said, "they'll be on us if—"

Thud!

The gnome tumbled to the ground, an arrow stuck in his back.

"Doni!" Scarlett lunged for the dock.

"No, lass!"

A strong hand yanked her back. Pain ripped through her shoulder from the backward motion.

"Go," Marian said to the dwarf. "I'm sorry, Scarlett," she said, her expression a mix of desperation and despair.

Whoosh!

Doni and the pursuing guards rose off the ground, blown across the street. They smashed into the carts and shopfronts along the wharf.

Lightheaded, Scarlett caught the faint form of the nocsi standing on the other dinghy, hand outstretched.

Fog, as thick as that hovering over Redtown clouded her eyes. She pitched about, woozy. As if watching from outside her body, a gnomish hand reached for the dinghy's railing.

"Doni..." she said, voice cracking.

"I got you, Scarlett." Marian's soothing voice accompanied her gentle touch supporting her from falling overboard.

The shadowy form of the gnome lying motionless, a shaft stuck in his back, faded as darkness took her.

22

FLY BY NIGHT

⚜

Trusty Jack stood at the ship's railing studying the small figure at the bow. The gnome had been there all morning, sitting cross-legged and motionless, as they tacked their way across the open water to Benevolence Bay.

"Someone should talk to her," Big Rig said, appearing at his side.

"Aye." Jack sighed.

For two days, Scarlett had remained below deck recovering from the arrow that had pierced her shoulder. Another reason he was thankful Marian had joined them. The mage's spells and herbal remedies accelerated the healing process to where the thief could now move about and join the others.

Though, if Scarlett's behavior was any indication, the arrow wasn't the concerning wound. Trusty Jack couldn't imagine the grief the gnome felt at the loss of Doni. He had to admit, despite Scarlett's impressive constitution and thick skin, this might prove to be a burden too heavy to carry. He wouldn't blame her if she bowed out of the leadership role. No one in their party would.

"It really should be you, lad," Big Rig said. The dwarf's strong hands gripped the railing as the ship heeled. The quartermaster's stocky frame leaned over the edge of the ship, head aiming to stern. "Making good time," he said. "This merchant's tight on the tacks."

Trusty Jack joined him, allowing his concerns to drift away with the swirling foam in the ship's wake. The refreshing emptiness lay before him.

Jack stared at the horizon, seeking respite from the emotional chaos of the last few days. As if taking flight, he crossed the waters, passing beyond the horizon until a mainland he'd never seen appeared in his mind.

"You ever miss the stone mountains, Rig?" Jack asked, as he and his old friend took in the endless blue. "I mean those of your home back in Drakeland."

"Aye, lad... deep in my heart. But then I remember there's more than sand down in the deep. Peaks and valleys, caves and crevasses made of thick and solid rock... it's all below." He nodded at the water. "That brings comfort to my dwarven blood."

Jack had to admit, he'd never thought of it before. To him, the sea was what lay beyond the edge of land, itself a relief of the physical burdens of rock, dirt, and sand.

"Out of sight, but not out of mind," Big Rig said.

Jack felt the sturdy grip of the dwarf's hand on his forearm.

"Go and talk to her, lad."

His old friend patted him twice before moving on, leaving him alone with the view of the sea. Trusty Jack checked on Scarlett. The gnome sat like a statue. Her cloak fluttered about in the crosswind on their southeasterly tack.

"I think you should speak with her."

Music to his ears. Her real voice; not one inside his fading memories.

In her blue robe, Marian crossed the view to the bow. The mage clasped her hands together on the railing and gazed out at sea.

"I haven't been on a ship in years," she said. "It's refreshing and cleansing."

Trusty Jack joined her, mimicking her pose at the rails. "Aye, it's peaceful out here... easy to forget there's a world over the horizon."

Marian's salt and pepper hair blew about in the breeze.

Jack mustered his courage. "You might have been out of sight, Marian, but you were never out of my mind."

Silence.

Bollocks, he thought. *I'm terrible at this.*

"Let's talk when we reach Benevolence," she said. "For now, I want to focus on healing Scarlett before we reach the world again. Both physically and, as much as possible, emotionally. This entire journey relies on her."

"True, that is," Jack said, happy to delay the awkward and potentially hurtful conversation. "I'll go talk to her. But Marian..."

The mage turned.

"Not now, James." She shook her head. "As I said, it's not the appropriate time."

"That's not what I meant, lass. I was wantin' to propose... well." He took off his tricorne and fiddled with the brim. *Damn! I feel like a schoolboy.* "Would it be too presumptuous of me to suggest we speak over dinner? On *Lady Luck*, I mean. Captain's quarters is right quiet. I would feel more comfortable there."

Marian's expression shifted.

"Meanin' nothing by it." Jack held up a hand. "Just... so we can speak openly." He checked about the deck to see who stood within earshot. Big Rig, Lana, and Siân started acting like they were doing busywork nearby. "And with a bit of privacy." Jack's eyes narrowed at the Salty Scoundrels ostensibly re-arranging a pile of ropes. "Seeing how everything is all eyes and ears on a ship's deck."

The corners of the mage's mouth rose. "I'd like that." Marian let go of the railing and reached into a pocket. "Give Scarlett these tea packets. Tell her to take one every—"

"Coming about!" a sailor shouted.

The ship swung to port.

Marian, hands free from the railing, stumbled forward.

On instinct, Jack caught her before she went down. Face to face, the warm breath that pulsed from between her lips was like an invisible caress. Her mahogany eyes sparkled with those never-forgotten shards of amber.

Jack did his best to hold back the desire rushing through his veins. "Sorry, lass." He released his grip on her arms and helped her stand up straight. "Sailor's instinct."

"It seems I have a lot to learn about ship life," Marian said, adjusting her robe. She turned towards the view of the sea. "And pirates."

He paused, considering the mage's statement.

"Go talk to her, James," she said, her voice fanning his rising flames. "Tell her you're sorry for what happened and try to make her understand loss is often an unfortunate consequence in life."

A pang of regret wrenched his gut.

The ship settled into its tack, fluttering sails replaced by the rush of the sea along the hull.

"Alright," he said, fixing his cotton sleeves. "The truth of it is, as a captain, and a pirate..." He looked at Marian. She stood, back to him, gazing out at sea. "I've had this conversation all too often. It's just... been a while, is all."

He strode forward. In the corner of his eye, he saw Lana's green hand tapping Big Rig, getting the dwarf's attention and nodding in his direction. Siân let the rope fall to the ground and joined them in gawking. Jack stepped with earnest strides, letting his heels hit the deck so each footfall carried through the timbers.

He halted behind Scarlett, peering down. The gnome's cloak fluttered around her on the deck like a pool of water. Sniffles and sobs carried on the wind, passing by his ears to be lost as the breeze drifted to the stern.

"Lass?"

More sobbing.

Jack stepped up to her side. Scarlett's hands appeared in her lap, resting on her crossed legs. A scrap of burlap in her grip fluttered in the breeze.

Swollen and puffy red eyes gazed up at him. She held up the fabric. "I never told him I kept it, Jack," she said, voice faltering.

Trusty Jack read the scribbled and blurring ink above her signature and Doni's—her half of the marriage pact they'd made in their youth.

"I'm sorry, lass," he said and sat next to her.

"Why didn't I tell him?" Her tiny fingers fiddled with the fraying edges. "Now it's too late."

Jack put his arm around her and pulled her in. He checked on the others. Marian turned her gaze back to the open sea, and the Salty Scoundrels went back to their ostensible busywork.

"After this was over, I promised myself I would show him my half and—" Sobs overtook her words.

Jack squeezed, feeling her small head fall onto his shoulder. Underneath the shelter of her hood and his grip, she wept.

"Take as much time as you need, lass."

Her tiny fingers squeezed the scrap of burlap.

"And I'm sorry for mistaking what you were asking me to hold back there in Redtown. I see now what you were referring to. Mighty noble of you. And selfless. Which is what your lad, Doni was. I didn't know him long, but in the time I did, I saw a gnome who never hesitated to do what you asked of him." He pulled her in closer. "And he did it out of love."

Her head went up and down, nodding, tucked into his shoulder.

"Bloody brave, Doni was. At Longshore, and back there in Redtown." He felt her tension ease.

Scarlett pulled back and wiped her eyes. "I know." Her fingers fiddled with the edges of the burlap scrap. "He never stopped supporting me." She sighed. "When I was nineteen, I did something foolish. All my plans... *our* plans... were tossed upside down. To make it worse, I ran away from my mistake and left an entire life and family behind." The gnome's puffy eyes met his. "It wasn't easy, but I learned to survive on my own and ended up somewhere I never expected—in the Thieves Guild. But Doni never stopped looking for me or..." she rubbed her eyes, "caring about me. It took him ten years, but he found me. I was a different person by then." She examined her half of the contract. "My life had taken a very different course."

"Scarlett, lass. If anyone can relate to that, it's me."

"Thank you, Jack." The gnome managed a smile through her pain and grief.

Jack's captain's voice rose. "Now, I don't need to do the whole, 'Doni would want you to continue' routine. You already know how much he loved you, and how dedicated he was to the guild." He leaned toward her. "*Quite* dedicated and... well, enthusiastic."

A gnomish laugh cut through the sniffles and sobs. She let out a long, cathartic sigh.

"You still up for this?" Jack looked her in the eyes. "No one is going to hold it against you if you aren't, lass." He glanced back at Marian. "Especially not me."

"I'll be fine," Scarlett said and folded up the burlap strip. She stood and walked to the bow, raising her hand overhead.

"No!" Jack rose and gripped her arm before she threw the pact overboard. "Not yet. Trust me, lass. That day may come, but it isn't today. Give yourself time."

Scarlett glanced back at Marian and then at her pledge to Doni.

"Don't wait too long, Jack." She tucked the burlap in her pocket. "Don't be a fool like me."

⚜

ON THE FOURTH DAY AT SEA, THE TINY WHITE DOT AT THE HORIZON had grown into a beacon of promise. By the time the merchant ship rounded the point and aimed its bow towards the harbor, Trusty Jack's anticipation had risen as high as the lighthouse atop the promontory into Benevolence Bay.

"Blow me down, Benevolence at last." Jack put a hand on Big Rig's shoulder.

"Fourteen years is a long time coming," the dwarf said and held out a cheroot.

Jack happily accepted the smoker and strode to the coal bucket, sparking it to life. In the noonday sun, the azure shallows glimmered with reflections. He inhaled the thick and spicy smoke, allowing it to drift from his mouth so he could savor the leaf's peppery flavors.

"Back at last, Cap!" Lana joined them at the railing.

A half mile ahead, Benevolence's shoreline teemed with activity. Smoke rose from chimneys and campfires. A random assortment of buildings, huts, and beachside cantinas lined the sandy shoreline. Jack followed the swarms of tiny specks dotting the coast. A mix of pirates, rogue entrepreneurs, former criminals turned business owners, and passing treasure seekers with dreams of life-changing scores, Benevolence was anarchy at its finest. Not a brute and crude barbarism, but an accepted and celebrated chaos where risk and reward, and pleasure and danger, danced across a ballroom of liberation and existential freedom.

"I don't see her," Big Rig said, standing on tiptoes at the railing. The dwarf peered across the still waters. "Lana, can you spot her?"

The half-orc clasped the rails, her green triceps flexing. "Not yet. But I do see that." She spat over the side and pointed ahead to starboard.

Trusty Jack blew out a puff of smoke. As it cleared, the familiar shape of the massive galleon, black as night, approached.

"*R.I.P. Tide*," Big Rig said.

"And who would that be?" Siân asked, joining them. The nocsi pointed at a large figure with a staff on the forecastle deck.

"That would be Captain Pitch," Jack said and took a pull on his smoker. "Most fearsome pirate in the Jewels."

"Is that a problem?" the nocsi asked.

"Not since she's heading to sea, no lass. But even if the galleon were anchored and its captain ashore, any resentment she might harbor against us for, oh say... souring the stew between us would be nullified in port." Jack tapped the ash from his cheroot. "Unless it's an argument over cards at Grumpy Jim's canteen or a formal duel. You see, lass, this here's Benevolence." He stuck the smoker in the corner of his mouth and spread his arms wide. "Welcome to the free zone."

Nevertheless, Jack made sure he stood behind a mast and rigging, out of the line of sight, as the ship passed. He was relieved, and not a bit surprised, to see Lana and Big Rig do the same. News had certainly reached the half-ogre captain that he and his companions were alive. The longer he avoided crossing paths with the vile sorcerer-pirate, the better.

"How do you enforce such a thing?" The otter-like species peered at the passing coral and abundant fish and plant life beyond the ship's wake. "I mean, who's the law here?"

"Ain't no law, lass," Lana said. "Come to think of it, I've never seen much of a need for it. You, Cap?"

Jack shook his head. "Things have a way of working themselves out here, Siân," he said. "You'll like it, just you wait. Lots of inspiration for your songs and verse."

The other Salty Scoundrels grinned.

Jack fixed his eyes on the prow of a ship breaking into view ahead from behind a frigate. As if under a spell, his mouth curved upwards and a euphoric wave ran through his limbs. "You see what I see, Rig?"

The quartermaster shaded his one eye with a thick hand. "Shiver me timbers!"

Jack felt the strong grip of the half-orc on his forearm.

"Cap... there she is!"

"*Lady Luck*!" Big Rig did a jig, smoker clenched between his teeth.

Jack followed the sloop's lines. Her full profile emerged from behind the other ship anchored in the bay. *Hello, old girl,* he thought. She looked spectacular. New trim, fresh masts, and a three-tone paint job that had given her a much-needed update.

"Well, Captain... how does she look?" Scarlett joined them at the railing.

Jack took a pull on his cheroot and grinned.

Scarlett looked at all four of them. "Don't all speak at once..."

Jack kept quiet, taking in his companions. Siân was scribbling on a small sheet of paper. Big Rig and Lana stood motionless.

"Just taking her in, lass," Jack said.

"How soon can we board her?" Big Rig asked.

"As soon as you like," the gnome said. "The notary can co-sign the deed when we're ashore."

Jack closed his eyes and relished the moment. So many memories. And a part of his past he wasn't sure he would ever revisit.

The merchant ship slowed. Jack followed the telltale signs of the crew preparing to drop anchor.

"You think Grumpy Jim still makes that Prickly Peach Twist?" Lana asked.

"Not sure," Big Rig said, "but *I* will let *you* know. When *I* have one. But *you*," he pointed at the half-orc, "will be drinking at the cantinas or campfires."

"What? Why?"

"Because you're banned, that's why!"

"What's this bilge? Are you cracked?" The half-orc stomped forward, towering over the dwarf.

"Aye, lass. I think your memory is the thing that's cracked," Jack said, easing her temper with a hand on her muscular shoulder. "And not from that knock to your head, but from all the rum you poured down your throat last time we were here."

"I don't remember doing anything of the sort!"

Jack cackled and eyed Big Rig.

The dwarf burst out laughing.

"What?" Lana said.

Both Scarlett and Siân were all ears.

"Let's just say we saw *all* of you, and so did everyone in Benevolence." Jack took a drag and blew out smoke with performative flair.

"Quite the dancer, you were," Big Rig added and gestured with his cheroot.

"Bollocks!" Lana's head went from the dwarf to Jack to Siân. She pointed a finger at the nocsi. "Don't you dare put that in one of them there songs, you hear me?"

"What's that?" Siân scribbled something quickly and put the paper away.

Jack didn't miss the smirk on their furry face.

Lana's grog-blossom cheeks had become a bouquet of roses.

"You'll go in and order one for me, won't you, Scarlett? I'll wait in the alley."

"I'm sorry, Lana. I have some business when we arrive. And I'll need the captain to join me." The gnome nodded in his direction. "And, we need to get you to a forge," she said to Big Rig.

"Aye." The dwarf puffed on his smoker. "If that's any sign," he pointed at a thick plume rising from a structure on a nearby hill, "there's an old acquaintance of mine hitting the hammer as we speak."

"Excellent." Scarlett clasped her hands. "I'll leave it to you and Marian to coordinate."

Trusty Jack checked on the mage. She stood about ten feet from them taking in the sights and sounds of the anarchic world that was Benevolence Bay. This would be new territory for her. He wasn't worried about her safety. She certainly didn't need anyone's protection, but he did hope the community's wild antics and hedonistic attitudes weren't a poor reflection on his reputation.

Marian caught him looking her way. Her eyes softened and she smiled.

His heart skipped a beat.

"Jack?"

"Huh, what's that lass?"

"Are you listening?" Scarlett stood, hands on hips.

"Sorry," he said a bit louder than necessary. "Something caught my eye."

Marian rolled her eyes.

That's progress, he thought.

"I was discussing the compass and forging the needle."

"Rig's got that covered, I'm sure. Right, mate?"

"Aye, lad. I was just saying that half-orc should still be hammerin' away."

Jack tracked over the buildings and activity along the shore. Memories of familiar locales returned. Grumpy Jim's Canteen, Tohalu Traders, the half-orc blacksmith Big Rig mentioned blanketed in more scars than a cutting board, and the market vendors... troves of flotsam and jetsam for sale that spoke of the far-reaching arm of pirates and adventurers in the Jewels.

How much has it all changed?

Pulled by the power of memory, his gaze moved across the shoreline until it landed on a two-story building made of white stone. Squinting, he spotted a young woman emerging from the entrance. With the aid of a walking stick, she crossed the playground and headed to the gate leading to the beach.

"I've heard stories of your philanthropy," Scarlett said.

Trusty Jack met her gaze. The gnome had a twinkle in her eye.

"What are you on about?"

"You did admirable work providing for the children at the orphanage through your... pirating ways."

Marian's blue robe crossed the corner of his eye. The mage settled herself at the railing within earshot.

"That's just talk, lass." His cheeks grew warm. "It wasn't much, and only when we had extra," he said.

"Right," Scarlett said.

Plunk!

Jack felt the tug of the ship as the anchor caught. The merchant swung to port and settled, its bow facing out to sea. He pivoted toward the shore and focused on the orphanage.

The young woman passed through the gate and stood at the shoreline. She raised an arm and waved.

Scarlett responded in kind.

"Who in blazes is that?" Jack asked.

"That, Captain Hawk, is my client."

23

ON THE LEE

❦

Benevolence was thriving.

Trusty Jack took in the sights and sounds of the pirate haven as they rowed ashore. The free port had doubled in size since he'd last sought refuge at the autonomous outpost. By the look of the lively businesses and copious amount of exchange occurring along the sandy streets, it had grown even more industrious over his fourteen-year absence.

"There's Ol' Tooth!" Big Rig pointed at a human woman.

"She don't look a day older." Lana shielded her eyes and focused on the ancient soothsayer. "It's downright uncanny, it is."

"Woman's pickled by the salt and sea," Big Rig said. "With a sour personality to boot."

"Half-sour." Lana elbowed the dwarf to laughter.

Trusty Jack followed the old woman's familiar, hobbled gait. Lana was right. Somehow the fortune teller had managed to defy death's grasp. She'd crossed eighty-five summers during their previous visit to Benevolence, making her the oldest resident in the anarchic town.

Counting the subsequent years that had passed, she would be nearing one hundred now.

Jack had every intention of giving the seer a wide berth while ashore. Last time, she'd been on his heels whenever he walked the town, rambling on about some portent nonsense.

What was it, again? he thought, watching as Ol' Tooth adjusted the beads and bones dangling around her neck. The fortune teller barked something to a passerby who hastened their pace toward a set of market stalls.

'Troubled destiny...' that's what she had called it.

Ol' Tooth's shrunken apple of a head rotated toward the bay.

Jack ducked.

"You alright?" Scarlett said.

Even Marian, at the end of the aisle, raised a brow.

"Superstitious to his bones, he is," Big Rig said.

"Bollocks," Jack said through gritted teeth.

"Been like this since I first met him," the dwarf announced for all to hear.

Trusty Jack shook his head. "Ain't true. Don't listen to him."

Scarlett smirked.

Jack didn't have the courage to check Marian's expression.

"Won't even bring a banana on board," Big Rig said.

"I ain't the only one, mate!" Jack said, staying low. "That there's a right superstition, that is."

"Bananas?"

Jack caught the familiar tutting of Siân's teeth.

"I must learn of this superstition."

"Oh, I'll tell you all about it," the dwarf said to the bard. "*All* about it."

Trusty Jack shook his head at Big Rig's enthusiasm.

A scraping along the hull brought them to a halt. Jack peered over the side.

No sign of Ol' Tooth.

He rose and hopped out, splashing in the shallows. With a heave, he pulled the boat forward so the others could depart without getting wet.

"Quite the gentleman," Scarlett said as he lifted her over and down.

He turned back as Marian stepped up to disembark.

"Allow me," he said and held out a hand.

Without hesitating, she accepted it.

Skin as smooth as marble ran over his coarse and roughened sailor's fingers.

The squeeze she gave him to steady herself sent a warm feeling up his arm.

He popped his tricorne up and down in a playful fashion. "Welcome to Benevolence. Enjoy your stay."

"Jack?"

"What?" He turned and eyed Lana, who waited on the rowboat.

She waved her hand delicately and fluttered her eyelids.

Big Rig giggled.

"You two get into town," he said in his best captain's voice. "Rig, do some preliminary work on a crew and supplies. And find out what that scallywag Captain Pitch was up to in port; something's afoot, or I'm Ropey Jane's uncle."

"Aye, will do." Big Rig jumped out of the boat into the shallows.

"And you," Jack held out a hand for Lana.

The half-orc took it and stepped off the boat like a boulder leaves a cliff.

"Stay out of trouble or by the gods of the sunken sea, I'll maroon you on the first shoal out of port."

"Whatever you say, Cap." The half-orc's attention was on the activity in town.

He poked a finger into her belly.

"Huh?"

"Listen up, Lana. Get yourself aboard *Lady Luck* and give her a once-over." He leaned close. "Take this." He handed her two gold pieces and checked on Marian and Scarlett. The two stood nearby on the sandy shore in earnest conversation. "Get us all some grub for tonight and get me two of them fancy meals from Trixie's and some palmberry wine."

"Oooo! We're drinking palmberry wine?" Lana rubbed her hands together.

"No, *we're* not drinking palmberry wine. *I am*." He thumbed his chest.

"And someone else." Lana grinned and pointed at Marian.

Jack snatched her finger and checked on the mage. Marian's attention remained on Scarlett.

"You and the others..." he dropped an extra few pence in her large green palm, "are drinking rum. Make sure you get enough for all of you, Lana. Not only you."

"So, lots of rum?"

He shook his head in defeat. *One of a kind. Come to think of it, let em' all get three sheets to the wind tonight.* If Lana was on board *Lady Luck* with a good patch of the bay between her and Benevolence, then she could let loose. A celebration was in order all around.

"Alright, lass," he said. "The scoundrels can splice the mainbrace this eve." He pulled another gold piece from his pocket. "As much rum as you can carry, you can buy."

The first mate's eyes lit up. "Yo ho ho, Cap!" She slapped him on the shoulder so hard he stumbled.

"By the gods, Lana..." His eyes narrowed and he put on his best captain's face. "Don't be poppin' any of them corks until you're back on our ship, savvy? If I so much as see or hear of you sippin' grog ashore—"

"Promise, Cap!" Lana curtsied with a pretend skirt.

Trusty Jack laughed. "Now off with ya." He watched as she stomped off, whistling a shanty.

Aye, he thought, looking around, *it's good to be back.*

"Jack." Scarlett approached. "Marian is joining us. I want her to meet my client."

"Fine by me, lass." He did his best to keep his expression neutral and hide the good news. "Lead on."

The three made their way along the sandy shore. Jack half-listened to Scarlett describing her first visit to Benevolence. The gnome's words were for Marian more than he, and she recounted her subsequent journey by charter to Mayrotten Island, where she had stepped into *The Dreg* and ignited the changes to his life that led them here. The words reached his ears, but his eyes were on *Lady Luck* in the bay.

An invisible force pulled at him to grip the ship's wheel. To call out to his companions for adjustments to the sails so she aimed true in the wind, and to feel the freedom of a destination-less rudder on an open sea.

Smack!

Jack halted, pain stinging his neck. Marian and Scarlett looked at him, eyes wide.

Gooey liquid ran under the collar of his shirt and down his chest. He wiped his neck and felt the familiar fleshy pulp of an Ulangi fruit. Hand covered with red juice, he gazed up at the edge of the palms and mangroves.

"Heea! Heea!"

A surge of embarrassment rose in his blood. As if through an alchemical change, it morphed into anger. Jack rushed to the edge of the jungle and shook his fist at the small black and white creature dancing along a branch. "I'll get you for that, mate!" he shouted.

The Galanki monkey danced along the branch and cackled.

Jack picked up a small rock and hurled it at the creature.

"Jack!" Scarlett shouted.

"Stay out of this, lass," he growled. "This is personal."

"Wait, you know this creature?" Marian asked.

"Oh, indeed I do." He spat in the sand.

The Galanki taunted him from the mangrove branches.

"This goes way back." He took a step forward. "We've got unfinished business, ya scallywag! I'll get the last laugh on you!"

Marian and Scarlett erupted in a chorus of giggles.

Jack swung about. "Something funny?" He eyed them.

They shook their heads.

"Heea! Heea!" The Galanki squatted and defecated over the edge of the branch before vanishing into the brush.

"Bloody monkey," he said. "You better steer clear of town!" he shouted.

"Come on, Jack," Scarlett said, "you can clean up at the orphanage." She waved them on. "You look like you've been stabbed."

Marian's hand covered a smile.

Jack spotted a group of children led by the young woman they'd seen from the ship making their way toward them. A boy, no more than five or six years old, broke from the pack and ran ahead. Sand kicked up at his heels as he rushed to reach them.

"Ahoy!" the boy shouted and waved his arms.

"Energetic lad." Jack reciprocated with a wide motion of his arm.

"Well, hello there," Marian said as the youth reached them.

The boy bent over, hands on his knees, panting. "Are you a pirate?"

"Me?" Marian said. "No."

"Not you, him." The boy pointed at Jack.

"Aye." Trusty Jack bent down so he was face-to-face with the lad. "I be a pirate. And a captain."

"Do you have a ship?"

Jack grinned. "Of course." Trusty Jack hoisted the youth up and aimed the child towards the harbor. "See that there ship with the fancy-colored trim?"

The boy shielded his eyes and nodded.

"That's me ship, that is. *Lady Luck's* her name."

"Do you need a crew?"

"As a matter of fact, I do. You interested?" He plopped his tricorne on the lad's head, leaning it back so as not to cover his face. In the corner of his eye, Jack spotted Marian looking at him, a sparkle in her eyes. He winked at her.

"I want to be a pirate," the boy said.

A memory flashed through Jack's mind. Even though it was brief, it stung.

"Well, you'll have to be asking permission from the headmaster for that," he said, as the young woman approached. Jack dropped the boy down but let him hold on to the tricorne. The youth joined the other children who surrounded him with curiosity as he displayed the pirate hat to his fellow orphans.

"You made it." The headmaster leaned down taking both of Scarlett's hands. "I received your latest message by albatross. I'm so sorry."

The gnome nodded.

Jack felt a strange aura about the young woman. Short for a human, she couldn't be more than twenty years old, yet a subtle authority emanated from her bearing and demeanor. *Makes sense,* he thought, considering her charges running about the sandy shoreline. Tanned from the tropical sun, her hair was shoulder length, crudely chopped, and deep chestnut with streaks of blond. It was the eyes that pulled him. Green, like emeralds. Something about them was familiar. Perhaps she too had been an orphan here, and he'd seen her about on one of their stops before the incident with Bonnie sent him drifting rudderless across the sea.

"There's been some changes since the last message," Scarlett said.

So, the thief's been sending secret missives. Not surprising, being a member of the guild. The gnome had done well hiding it from him and the others.

"We have our blood iron blade," Scarlett said. "And a new ally." Their mission leader gestured in Marian's direction.

"Marian Fitzwater." The mage clasped her hands together. "An admirable job you're doing with these children."

"Thank you." The headmaster rubbed the head of a small girl who had planted herself against her leg. "It's..." she looked at the orphans causing mayhem up and down the shore, "...challenging, to say the least."

"I can imagine," Marian said.

Jack felt the headmaster's eyes on him.

I do know you.

"It's been a long time, Captain Hawk," the young woman said.

"You two know each other?" Marian asked.

"Oh, yes," the headmaster said. "The good captain here saved my life. I'm in Benevolence helping these children because of him."

"Because of me?" Jack looked from Marian to Scarlett, seeking answers. The gnome's mouth curved upward in a sly grin.

"I've been keeping an eye on your ship." She nodded in the direction of *Lady Luck*. "Brings back memories."

"My ship?"

"I wanted to be a pirate once, too." The headmaster stepped forward with the aid of her walking stick. "But someone told me I would be better off learning my letters ashore."

"Shiver me timbers," Jack said, and took a step back. "Precious?"

24

CAT OUT OF THE BAG

"Please," the young woman gestured at chairs and a sofa inside the orphanage, "make yourselves comfortable."

Jack's mind swirled with confusion.

"Would you like a hand with that?" Marian asked as clanking glasses mixed with the soft rhythm of lapping surf and children's laughter outside.

"You're very kind, but no. I'm used to carrying far more than this with so many little ones around."

"Jack, are you going to sit?" Scarlett patted the empty section of sofa next to her.

"What?"

She repeated the action.

Motionless, Jack observed the once-little-girl now turned head-master as she returned from the kitchen with a tray of chilled coconut tea. Her limp was more pronounced without the walking stick. With her long cotton dress her legs were hidden, but by her gait he guessed she had taken a permanent injury to a knee.

Precious handed him a tea and smiled before doing the same to the others.

Removing his tricorne, Jack ran the glass across his forehead. Cool condensation on the surface dampened his sweaty skin. Even now out of the sun, the day's heat lingered. A bead of sweat trickled down his neck under his braided ponytail, tickling his backside.

"Please, sit." Precious indicated the open space next to Scarlett on the sofa.

Sink me, but this is a sight. Looking from the young woman to Marian and back again only added to his confusion. *The past's rushing back to me from every side...*

The headmaster took a seat in a worn and fraying reading chair.

"I suppose we should begin by properly introducing you," Scarlett said.

"Indeed. As they say here in Benevolence, 'the cat is out of the bag.'" The headmaster met Jack's gaze, a soft kindness glinting in her eyes. "My formal name, though no one here knows it and I've not used it since before I ended up in safe hands with you, Captain Hawk, is Orla Chen."

Marian gasped.

Precious nodded. "I apologize, Lady Marian, for not properly introducing myself on the beach but by the looks of our pirate here, it's better I do this slowly or else he's going to faint."

"Aye," Jack said, "Like a squall of sprites, this is."

"Please, call me Marian," the mage said. "I've signed away my family line."

"Then we are sisters of a unique kind." Precious smiled. "I've been without my family since I was shipwrecked in that storm all those years ago."

Jack's mind flashed back to *Lady Luck* when they'd found her. "Bloody brave and determined you were, lass," he said and turned to Marian. "Spent a full night and half a day at sea clinging to a scrap of *Endurance's* deck, she did. All alone... adrift."

Marian's expression made clear her respect for the young woman's courage and tenacity.

"Why do you go by Precious?" Scarlett asked.

"That was a nickname Captain Hawk gave me after they brought me on board. I don't quite remember why, though."

"The lass wasn't telling us who she was," Jack said. "My guess is someone told you to keep tight-lipped when the ship went down in case you survived. Out of want to protect you, mind. Regardless, you didn't have a name and I gave you that one. You was a wee little lass, you were. Precocious as a water sprite." He shook his head and laughed. "You strode about the deck telling this one and that one what you knew *and* what you wanted... and you got it." He smiled. "Charmed the pants off the crew."

The headmaster put a hand to her mouth, her cheeks red as roses.

"'Precocious' must've been sailing in my mind," he said, "because when you needed a name, 'precious' is the one that came out. You were cute as a daisy, you were."

He felt Marian's eyes on him and turned. "What?"

"Nothing," she said, smiling warmly.

"But Precious," Jack said, leaning forward on the sofa. "How in blazes did you manage it? Afterwards, if you take my meaning?"

"After they commandeered *Lady Luck*," the young woman said, "they brought her to Benevolence for repairs before sailing on to Redtown. I'd been hiding in the secret compartment in the galley, like you instructed. There was much activity on board between your fellow crew being shackled below deck and the sea elves running about looting inventory. Eventually, all went quiet on that first night in port and I took a chance and made my way off the ship."

"You were how old?" Marian asked.

Precious looked to him.

"Five, maybe six, I'd guess," Jack said, thinking back.

"I remembered that morning on *Lady Luck*," Precious said, "when you were racing down the ship... you hoisted me up on the railing and showed me the lighthouse. And you taught me a new word, 'benevolence.' I never forgot it. Nor the orphanage you talked about that was going to get new beds, funds for food, and even books with the money from... well, pirating."

Jack felt his face flush as all eyes turned to him.

Precious rose and went to a line of bookshelves. She ran a finger over the bindings and crossed from one end of the copious library to the other. "You told me to learn my letters rather than become a pirate. It's a humble collection but I hope I've made good on that advice."

"Lass, the fact that you're here talking to us, and doing the good work with the children, is admirable enough."

"I was raised here by the former headmaster. Being literate when I arrived, I was pushed to continue my education. The old dwarven woman used every opportunity she had with those passing through port to help procure books and increase my learning."

"Aye," Jack said. "Hilna was a rare soul, she was. Done righteous work with the children for many long years." He looked about the room. "She's passed on, I assume?"

Precious nodded. "Two years ago next moon... peacefully, surrounded by the children."

"I'll be sure to tell Big Rig. He'll be sad to hear she's gone to the endless mountains."

"And you took over?" Marian said.

"Not much choice, really. It's been interesting, to say the least. And exhausting." Precious laughed. "Now I know why Hilna always had bags under her eyes." She crossed to her desk. "Captain Hawk, I have something for you."

"Please, lass," he said. "Call me Jack."

"Very well." She opened a drawer and held out a tubular item.

"Is that?" Jack found himself unable to finish the question.

Precious approached and handed it to him.

"My spyglass." He clasped the scratched and faded golden tube, turning it over in his hands.

"The one your father gave you," Marian said.

Jack nodded and wiped his eyes.

The mage rose, adjusted her blue robe, and came and knelt next to him.

"Now look what you've gone and done, Precious," Jack said. His lips trembled. He did his best to hold back the emotions rising in his heart. "You're making me look a fool in front of these two."

"Nonsense," Marian whispered and put a hand on his knee. "Remember that day on Freeland Point?"

"How could I ever forget, lass." They'd picnicked on the treeless grasses of the peninsula overlooking Redtown. He'd let her use the spyglass, sitting behind her on the blanket and guiding her hand over a shoulder so she could view the ships and coastline. Spotting a Yarwhal breach and smack the sea in a dramatic splash, she'd turned around, their faces inches apart. Her lips were so close. Before he knew it, they were—

"I passed a sack of loot prepared by the sea elves that night when I snuck off *Lady Luck*," Precious said. "Your spyglass was poking out. I snatched it and hid it when I made the shore, hoarding it as a reminder of the kindness and care you showed me in my time of need." She joined them and put a hand on his shoulder. "It brings me great joy to see you reunited with it, especially now, knowing its familial origin and," the headmaster's attention turned to Marian, "the memories it holds."

Jack retracted the spyglass and gripped it tight. "Precious," he said as Marian returned to her seat, "how did you know I was alive?" He directed the next question at Scarlett. "And what's this all about, with you being the client of the guild and wanting to find me to captain a ship?"

"Quite right," Scarlett said, sipping her coconut tea. "It's time to take out that cat. Ms. Chen, if you would."

"Well, to start," Precious sat down in her reading chair. The fabric settled around her, molded to her body from years of use. "The legend of your death was oft recounted by the pirates in Benevolence, especially when the rum barrels were emptied in the wee hours. You became quite the tragic hero over the retellings."

"Indeed," Jack said, remembering Scarlett's version when she'd arrived on Mayrotten Island.

"But when I was stowed away on *Lady Luck*," Precious said, "I overheard the sea elves banter. Angry words of resentment were thrown around, directed at the commodore..." Precious paused and turned to Marian.

"Yes," the mage said, "my sister. Please, go on."

"They disapproved of setting you adrift rather than killing you outright. Mind you, Jack, I was young and as the years went by, I remembered this narrative more as a feeling than a memory of words spoken."

Understandable. To be that young and hear such things... Jack knew that the heightened fear and trauma of the event would cause it to persist, but even then, the years could cloud the veracity of something experienced so young.

"The official stories I heard over the years contradicted my version. And yet, I know what I heard," Precious said. "Did it prove you were alive?" She held up a hand. "No. But it didn't confirm you were dead either."

An uneasy silence settled over them. Jack's stomach tightened. All three were waiting for him to speak about the interim between Bonnie's banishment at sea and his return to the world.

He leaned back and folded his arms.

"Two years ago," Precious continued, "I was fetching the weekly produce for the orphanage downtown. An old, one-legged pirate stood in conversation with my least favorite, and luckily infrequent, visitor to Benevolence, Captain Pitch. The two stood under the shade of a palm outside Grumpy Jim's within earshot of the fruit cart. The old man spoke to the half-ogre captain, words spitting between pokes at his teeth with a toothpick. 'Saw me a sea dog on Mayrotten last run,' he said. 'Call me Ropey Jane's uncle if it wasn't the spittin' image of Trusty Jack. Uncanny it was.'"

Pitch, Jack thought. *Why is this pirate haunting me so? Something's a foot...*

"'Aye,' Pitch had said, with that raspy and wicked voice of hers." Precious shook her head in disgust. "'That island makes strange visions it does,' she told the old salt. 'You sure you don't be seein' things, Bandy?'" Precious edged up in her chair. "And then Bandy responded: 'I didn't hang around to be inquirin'. But I tell you, it was Trusty Jack or it was a ghost.' Pitch then asked if he followed up about it ashore to which Bandy replied, "Nay, never set foot on that cursed sand. Stayed on board and on the docks. No thank ye, but that island is downright spooky, it is.'"

Jack struggled to recall any one-legged pirates on Mayrotten. Too much rum clouded his memories of those long and wasted years. *Think, Jack.*

As if rising from the dead, a mental specter pushed through the drunken fog. "Was that stump of a leg made of mahogany, with a curvy knot for a foot?" He made a fist with his fingers in all directions.

Precious nodded.

"Aye, I know who that was."

"And so," she said, "when word arrived that Markus Fitzwater was approaching the allotted time to transfer from council-controlled regent to righteous king, something stirred within me. A need, a desire to act." She shook her head. "I don't know why it rose. I've always been resolute in wanting nothing to do with my Chen line, but it was like a dormant responsibility germinated inside of me... and it bloomed into a revolutionary flower."

"I understand this," Marian said. "I've felt it too."

"I apologize for my next words," Precious said. "They will not be flattering towards your father."

"I appreciate your candor," the mage said. "But you do not need to soften your criticisms. I am not proud of my family's actions since my aunt vanished at sea. Most likely, I stand alongside the accusations you will now name."

Precious lowered her chin in a gesture of thanks. "So many troubles had worsened since Markus Fitzwater took over at the palace. The endless rising taxes that burden the many to benefit the few. The displacement of entire communities for indulgence in delicacies, the ignorance of the beauty of the natural resources of the Jewels." She took a deep breath. "And, most importantly, the unnecessary return of an ancient and malignant magic."

"It's here?" Marian said.

Jack didn't miss the concern in the mage's voice, nor how the muscles in her forearm tensed as she gripped the arms of her chair.

"It is." Precious's face grew earnest. "And so, my desire to make a better government for the people in these islands crossed with the need to find a solution to a deadly fever. I knew that it was time for me to come out of hiding and accept my family line."

"To what end?" Jack said. "The regent's going to be sworn in as the absolute monarch in what... a little over a week now?" He checked on Scarlett, who raised an eyebrow.

"I can see by your expression, Marian," Precious said, "that you know where this is going."

"The Chens," Marian said, "have the same right to the throne as my aunt's line did. Long ago, they chose to pursue the judicial branch instead of governing from the palace and stuck to that claim until they were wiped out in the tragedy at sea."

"Therefore, Orla is the rightful heir," Scarlett said.

"Aye, but you've got no way to prove any of this, lass." He looked around the room. "Why are you all smiling?"

"Remember the dragon sculpture in Redtown, James?" Marian said. "The one in the fountain circle at the guild halls?"

Jack nodded.

"The magical firewater it breathes is red because the former Queen's line was the last to rule the Jewels. It reflects the associated hue of each familial royal line through an ancient spell. If Precious were to speak the arcane words, and the queen, my aunt, is truly dead, the fire would shift color."

"To blue," Scarlett added.

The color of the Chen family's crest, Jack thought, remembering that they had long presided as nobility on Sapphire Island.

"So why not go there now?" he asked. "Oust the bloody regent." He glanced at Marian. "Kick him out before it's too late."

"I'm afraid I can't do that," Orla said.

"Why not?"

"Because I have no intention of ruling the Jewels."

"You lost me, lass. I'm sailing blind here."

"I intend to take the more difficult, and therefore more rewarding route."

"What route is that?"

"Justice."

Jack followed Precious as she rose and grew animated. "If I can't demonstrate why the regent shouldn't become king or present a better life for those in the Jewels, then I'm just more of the same."

"But you're not!" Jack said. "You're one of us." He gestured at the others.

"Indeed, but I want to bring actual change to the Jewels. So, the people can decide on their own."

"Decide on what?"

"Who their leaders should be. I intend to halt Markus Fitzwater's rise from regent to king, hold a temporary reprieve while in power, and set up the first truly free elections in the islands."

Jack's mouth opened but nothing came out.

Precious smirked. "I do more than sit inside this room and read books, Jack. I live among pirates here in Benevolence. Though few, there are some redeeming aspects to buccaneer culture. The crew's voice in deciding who runs a ship, for example... Some others..." She swung her head back and forth.

Aye, he thought. *Can't deny those.*

"There are two things I want to bring with me when I go to Redtown. The first is evidence, beyond the obvious, that the regent is not only corrupt but has also actively manufactured his rise to power and eventual transcendence to king."

"What evidence do you have?" Marian asked.

"Jack, when that storm wrecked *Endurance* and sent me into the drink... I remember an image. As I was tossed about on the swells, in the dark and stormy night, a flash of lightning brought the sea to life. A short way off loomed a ship. Or rather... a ghost."

An uneasy feeling, like a haunting tide, rose in his belly.

"Black as the night its hull was," she added. "Laughter and cheers from its deck cut through the howling winds, reaching my ears."

"Shiver me timbers," he whispered.

"There were strange lights flashing overhead in the storm clouds. Indistinct and almost..."

"Magical," Marian said.

"I've spent years doing research to find out what they were. None I spoke with here in Benevolence could explain them. And I needed to be prudent about where and with whom I inquired. Through a trusted contact with connections to the Thieves Guild, I was introduced to Scarlett. With her help, I consulted an elderly

mage-turned-historian from Drakeland through secret corre-
spondence."

Scarlett nodded at the mention of her guild's role and resources.

"That was no natural storm, Jack," Precious said. "It was a
conjuration."

"Captain Pitch," Jack said, looking from face to face. "On the *R.I.P.
Tide.*"

"You mean..." Marian began.

"Aye," Jack said. "That was no accident."

"But why would a pirate want to end the Chen line?"

"I don't think Captain Pitch gave a pence about the Chens," Jack
said. "I'm sure there was gold and more involved in that deal."

Marian's face went white.

Blimey, Jack thought. *That means Master Rin was most likely in on the
ruse. Had that bloody mage played Bonnie as well?*

"With my family out of the way, and Marian's aunt, the Queen
Ricarda, lost at sea," Precious said, "along with her soon-to-be-born
son, it left only one line."

"The regency through my family," Marian said, voice crackling in
anger. "You don't think my aunt's ship—"

"All those years ago?" Precious shook her head. "I doubt that. As
our pirate here can confirm, there are many actual threats in the sea
besides sorcerous buccaneers."

"I am so ashamed." Marian put her head in her hands.

"Lass." Jack rose and went to her. He knelt by her side. "Ain't
nothing to do with you. You've done a world of good, serving the
common folk all these years."

He went to put a hand on her thigh but hesitated. In the corner of
his eye, Scarlett nodded encouragement.

His hand came to rest on her knee. "Marian?"

She lifted her head. "What makes those with power in the Jewel
Islands like this?"

"That's a riddle without an answer," he said. "Maybe when this is all
over one of us will find out."

"Or both of us," she said, placing her hand on his and squeezing it.

The energy of her touch sent indescribable waves through him.

"There's one more piece to this puzzle," Scarlett said. "As it turned out, Orla's situation proved advantageous for my organization." The gnome raised an eyebrow.

"The compass," Trusty Jack said. "But where in blazes did you get it?"

The thief shook her head. "Apologies, Jack. That is something I cannot share. But the guild saw an opportunity that was..." the gnome smirked. "Mutually beneficial."

"Aye," the pirate whispered. "Keep your secrets, then."

"And thus began a master plan that led us all here today to this orphanage," Scarlett said.

Silence fell as those gathered reflected on the complexity and cunning involved in the operation.

"I want to show you all something. Follow me." Precious led them down a short hallway. She paused at a wooden door. "Steel yourselves." She swung it open and led them inside.

No fewer than ten cots were filled with sick children.

"How are they?" Precious asked a half-elf at a bedside.

"No better, and a few are worse," the nurse said.

"I can help here, at least to slow the fever's progress," Marian said, already joining the half-elf. The two spoke in hushed voices as the mage withdrew items from a pouch.

"And this is the other solution we can bring the people," Precious said. "We can eradicate this malignant presence once and for all."

"It's moving fast," Scarlett said, looking around the room. "Over the sea by boat. At this rate..."

Precious gripped his arm. "You and I both know what is on that island in the mist," she whispered. "And, how to get it."

Jack scrutinized her eyes. *You have it still, don't you?*

"I had heard of your exploits for years at the bars and cantinas in Benevolence. Once, I even witnessed two pirates come to blows over who was the best navigator through the Jewels' dangerous waters."

Jack grinned. *Pitch always hated that it was me.*

"You were the only one I knew I could trust, unconditionally. And so, a long quest to hunt down the dead pirate began. With Scarlett's help and hard work, and endless hope, it seems we succeeded. And now we have a ship, a captain, the blood iron we need for the compass needle, and a means to halt the regent's rise to king."

"We just need to sail to Dragon Tail Island and survive," Scarlett said.

"Where is all the money flowing from?" It was Marian, returning to the group. "To fund this."

"The guild is providing financial support for a coup and free elections," Scarlett said. "And for the resources necessary to make it happen."

"Why?" Marian asked.

Jack could guess the answer.

"The truth of it is," Scarlett said, "the guild benefits from a system of representation far more than a monarchy."

Jack knew all too well why they would do it—it was easy to coerce and bribe representatives of the various levels and branches of government. And lots of new blood coming and old blood going to be groomed, wooed, or blackmailed to do their bidding.

Marian touched Precious's sleeve. "I'd like to do some prep work for these treatments. Is there somewhere with an open flat surface?"

"Yes, my intern will show you to the storeroom."

"I won't be long," Marian said. "Scarlett, I could use your nimble gnome fingers to do this more efficiently."

"Happy to help."

The three hastened off.

Jack looked over the sick children in the beds. His blood boiled at the sight. It broke his heart, spilling anger through his body and turning it to pity.

Once Marian, Scarlett, and the nurse had exited the room he turned to Precious.

"About the map, lass," he whispered.

"Safe and sound." Precious winked.

25

A SQUARE MEAL

Marian raised her hand but hesitated. *You're doing the right thing. After this, it'll be over.*

She knocked on the weathered door.

Lady Luck lay still, anchored in the bay. The setting sun cast a crimson glow over the harbor, its shimmering reflections dancing on the hulls of the surrounding ships. Waves of laughter, like the ebb and flow of crashing surf, came and went behind her on deck where the others had gathered at an outdoor makeshift table. Lana had heaved the ship's cargo crates into a line while the remaining Salty Scoundrels brought stools and candles up from the galley.

Marian glanced back as the sweet sounds of the nocsi's newly acquired lute came to life, adding melodic accents to the merry gathering.

Maybe we should join them and forget—

The door swung open.

"Evening." James smiled and gestured with an arm, inviting her to enter.

"Good evening to you as well." She stepped over the threshold, the weight of the conversation to come turning from anxious idea to tangible inevitability.

"May I take that?" The pirate indicated her bag with her spell preparations and herbal remedies.

She handed it off to him. "So, how does it feel to be back home on *Lady Luck*?"

"Needs a bit of decorating." He nodded around him, indicating the cabinets, desk, and dresser that had been vacated by the last seafarer to captain the ship. "I've not yet touched the helm." He put her bag down on a small end table. "Savoring that for when we weigh anchor." A boyish grin rose on his face.

James had cleaned up for the occasion. With a pair of loose-fitting trousers and a crisp freshly pressed white cotton shirt, the man exuded casual pirate, if such fashion existed. Clean-shaven, with his blond ponytail in a braid and mustache trimmed, she couldn't deny it: the man was still dashing.

"Give me a moment." He went to a cabinet to retrieve a set of glasses.

Marian surveyed the room. In the candlelight, the richly colored mahogany walls exuded an earnest, yet cozy comfort. To her left, a single bed ran flush to the wall, mirrored on the opposite side by a desk and chair. Here and there, nautical items lay scattered on surfaces. She recognized his spyglass resting on an unfurled map on the desk. Next to it, secured to the floor, stood a globe at waist height on a rotating mount. At the far end of the room, up a set of steps, a rectangle space was bordered by a low wooden railing. Three windows carved into the ship's stern, their glass bubbly and uneven, looked out onto the bay. A long table, set for two at the heads with four chairs in between, occupied the entire upper area.

James climbed the steps and took a bottle off the table, approaching with two wine glasses clasped in his other hand. "Now I know you're not a fan of rum," he said and held out both glasses.

"What makes you say that?" She reached for a stem, fumbling to release a glass without causing him to drop the other. Her fingers grazed his own, and deny it as she might, the heat inside of her rose.

"Hold on." He laughed. "This isn't something I do often." The pirate placed the bottle on the teak floor at his side. "Here you are, lass." He separated the glasses, one in each hand, and held one out.

"Thank you. And what makes you say that? About the rum?"

"Oh, come on now, Marian." He grinned while filling her glass. "Don't think I've forgotten all the little things."

Stop saying all the right *things,* she thought.

"You were a good sport of it with Lana in the safehouse in Redtown." He poured himself some wine and held out his glass. "What are we toasting to?"

"Aren't you the captain? Don't you usually do the honors?"

He bowed his head. "The honor is yours this time."

"To..." she searched about, looking for inspiration. "To... to old friends." She winced as soon as she said it. *Oof, Marian, that was awful.*

The pirate raised his glass. "Old friends it is."

She clinked his cup and sipped.

The undeniable taste of currant, hibiscus, and palm sap tingled her taste buds.

"You remembered," she whispered.

"Aye." His hazel eyes twinkled in the candlelight. "Was always your favorite."

This is not going in the right direction, she thought, fighting back a renewed, fiery desire to narrow the distance between them.

"What do you call this?" She crossed to his desk and pointed at a triangular metal instrument with a set of mirrors and a short telescope. "I've seen them in nautical depictions, but I've never known what they were or how they work."

"That," he said, joining her, "is a sextant."

Gods, I am making this worse.

"Sex," he said, "for sixty. Referencing degrees." He picked up the instrument and handed it to her. "Thirds of one hundred and eighty."

She examined the sextant. In addition to the large metal triangle, it had a series of small circular lenses with different degrees of shading and a miniature telescope in line with two square mirrors.

"You can measure the distance to an object, often using a star in the sky. Or, the sun."

He vanished from view behind her.

"You hold it like this..."

His hands fell over her own, guiding her on where to grip the instrument.

"Now look through that telescope."

A hand landed on her hip and turned her, so she faced the dining area.

"Align that candle on the table in the middle of the viewfinder."

She closed her other eye and scanned back and forth.

"Got it?" he asked, pushing up against her backside.

"Yes." She was half concentrating and half working to keep her body from responding to his contact.

The candle vanished and the view through the lens went dark.

"What happened?"

"Tell me when you see it again," he said.

She heard a click and the view through the lens brightened.

A second click and the candle returned.

"Now."

"Good. Those there shades protect you from the sun, if you be doing this during the daytime. That's how Big Rig lost his eye."

"What?" She turned in surprise.

When her gaze met his, it was as if they had been frozen in time on the hillside with the spyglass in their youth, the spell now breaking thirty years later.

His eyes pulled at her.

She felt herself leaning in and—

Knock knock!

Startled, she dropped the sextant. It plunked on the desk.

"Oh no. Did I break it?"

"Nay, it's fine. They make em' thick for that reason." He reached over and set it aside. "Now, who in bloody blazes is this?"

Knock knock! "Jacky boy!"

The muffled voice of Big Rig resonated through the thick wooden timbers. Marian didn't miss the slight slur to his words.

The pirate crossed the room and swung the door open.

"What is it, mate?"

The dwarf's head peeked inside. "Oh, excuse me (hiccup)... Evening, Marian."

She smirked. "Good evening."

"What *is* it, mate?" James growled.

"Well, it's like this, lad (hiccup). Lana wants to set up the mast swing (hiccup) to initiate Siân. And I said," he swayed in the doorway, "not without the captain's consent. Now, mind you, lad, (hiccup) she countered with—"

"Off with you, mate! Go crazy if you want. Scarlett can take a turn as well for all I care. But if any of you drown because you're three sheets to the wind, we're leaving you at the bottom of the bay." He pushed the dwarf back out and shut the door.

Marian chuckled.

"Sometimes, Marian... you have no idea." The pirate shook his head and came back over to the desk.

"They're good friends to have, James. They care deeply about you." She couldn't hold back the warmth in her tone. "And they respect you."

"Aye." He sent the globe spinning with a stroke of his palm.

The awkwardness of the previous interruption hung in the air.

Deep down, her rational mind told her it was meant to be. They'd been moving in the wrong direction from the one she intended before stepping through the door to his cabin.

"Shall we eat?" she said.

"Aye, let's." The pirate gestured for her to climb the steps. "Either side is fine."

She chose the left end of the table.

James went to a small serving cart in the corner. He filled a plate and set it down in front of her.

"Wow," she said, eyeing the variety of delicacies.

"Aye." He filled his own plate and sat at the other end. "Trixie, who runs *The Parrot's Palate*, used to be a chef in the capital on Topaz Island. The gnome got into a bit of trouble," he waved his hand as if how wasn't important, "and had to pack up right quick. She's been running the kitchen here ever since."

"Benevolence is filled with surprises," Marian said, taking up her utensils.

"Please," James gestured to eat.

The food was outstanding. Marian could have been at the palace with the quality of the culinary preparation. The meal passed with ease. They bantered about this and that related to Redtown. She gave updates about the goings on and people that James would remember from his early days. They even laughed so hard remembering one of his early attempts to scale the garden walls to see her that she'd spit out her food. That had caused James to almost choke on his wine. By the time they'd cleaned their plates and had another glass of palmberry wine, she was feeling sated and relaxed.

With the alcohol came an additional boost of courage.

"James?" she asked, shifting her tone.

"Aye, lass." The pirate dabbed his mouth with his napkin. In the flickering candlelight his hazel eyes were like emeralds in a treasure chest.

"I want you to know that I uncovered evidence related to your imprisonment."

He poured himself more wine but didn't respond.

"Through my connections with Sir Roderick and the Red Knights, I found proof that my father was behind all of it. You were, as you claimed, set up and framed for a crime you did not commit."

He took a long pull off his wine, saying nothing.

"I know I didn't believe you when you told me but—"

He held up a hand and shook his head. "You don't need to apologize, Marian. I would have responded the same way in your shoes."

Oh, thank the gods. Why hadn't she expected him to be the reasonable man he once was?

"If anyone needs to apologize here, it is me." He stood up straight in his chair, chin high. "After Rig and I escaped Longshore, I should have come back."

Now it was her turn to say nothing.

"It wasn't the worry of being caught, Marian."

"I know." The man was fearless in the face of danger, and he'd risk death for her, she had no doubt.

"It's just... you see..."

Now she held up a hand. "Your eyes tell me everything I need to know, James." He'd earned the exemption from finishing by the words he had spoken a moment ago. She might not have ended up in a long-term relationship herself, but she understood how difficult it could be for a proud man to express heartfelt feelings of weakness and shame.

The pirate fiddled with his napkin.

"I'm sorry this all happened," she said. "To both of us."

"Me too, lass."

She knew him as well as he knew her, and the look in his eyes said it all. Heartbroken by the course of their lives, but too proud to admit it.

"And what different paths we've both taken since then," he said, gulping wine.

"In some ways. In others, as you said when first approaching me in Redtown, we do share common purposes. Just from different ends of the spectrum."

His expression softened. That was as much as she could offer in respect to the honor embedded in his subsequent criminality.

"Aye, Marian. It's been a road."

"James." She set her wine down. "What about the road after that? I mean, after my sister set you adrift?" She was all jitters, but she had to inquire. She had the right to ask.

With a screech, the pirate's chair slid across the wooden floor. He rose and stepped down from the upper platform, approaching his desk. His hand went to the globe and spun it.

"I'm not ready to talk about that, lass," he whispered. "I may never be."

You poor man. The pain of whatever it was that had happened was palpable in his tone. She could still read that in him after all these years.

She rose from her seat and went to him. "I respect that," she said, placing a hand on his arm. "So much of all of this is not our fault, James. We were caught in a storm and did what we had to do to survive. My father, and you being framed and later sent to sea. Me, abandoned... unintentionally, lied to by my own family, and made to look a fool—"

"You are not a fool, Marian," he said, turning. "You've never been anything but perfect."

Her heart hit the floor. James's face went blurry as her eyes welled up.

"Let's just go from here," she said, wiping her eyes. "We can still work together, can't we? As friends?"

Do I want this? she thought. The protective side of her soul made its presence known. *You need this.* Feelings were stirring, but that was a lost dream, and more than that an island culture was on the line. What was the alternative? Become a pirate? She looked at James covered in tattoos. He wasn't going to give up the sea. It was in his blood now. She saw the way his eyes brightened on board a ship. It was as if a part of his spirit waited on deck, rising to meet him when they weighed anchor.

The pirate spun the globe a second time.

"It's best if we make peace. Okay?"

"Agreed." He faced her and smiled. "There's a lot on our plates now, no denyin' it."

She nodded, relieved at the light-heartedness of his tone. "This was nice, James. And thank you for being so gracious... both with the dinner and our conversation."

"You make it easy, lass. You've truly found your calling with the Order of Telathia."

Her heart was roiling. *You're almost through it,* she thought.

"One thing." He picked up her bag from the nearby chair and handed it to her.

"What's that?" She threw the strap over her robe.

The pirate made his way to the door, gripping the handle but not yet opening it. "I need to go inland in the morning. Only a short way. Come with me."

She stopped halfway to the door.

"It's nothing dubious, Marian. We've said our pieces here tonight. This is something I've wanted to show you for years."

"I don't know if it's a good idea, James."

"Consider it a peace offering and," his eyes softened, "a thank you for understanding and respecting my privacy." The pirate opened the door to raucous shouts and laughter on deck. "Plus, like me, I'm sure you could use a break from all of this." He nodded out the door, indicating the Salty Scoundrels.

A resounding splash echoed over the ship to cheers.

"Okay, why not?"

"That's the spirit. I'll meet you at ten o'clock at the end of Main Street on the far side of town."

"Ten it is," she said and exited. "I'll check on the others before I go down to my hammock."

"Better you be goin' straight to your cabin, Marian." He rolled his eyes like a madman. "Trust me, by the sounds out there, you're safer below decks." He pointed at her. "Captain's orders."

"Aye aye," she said and moved towards him but hesitated.

He too motioned forward and then halted.

"Okay, this is awkward," she said and held out her arms. "A hug?"

He laughed. "Hug it is."

Thick, muscular arms wrapped about her. She rested her chin on his shoulder and whispered in his ear. "You're a good man, James." She kissed him on the cheek.

"And you, Marian," he said and squeezed her tight, "are one of a kind."

She pulled back and held his hands a moment, mixed emotions swirling in her heart. *It's done, and it's for the best.* "Good night, James."

❧ 26 ❧

FOOTLOOSE

❧

Walking Benevolence's main thoroughfare had been an experience. Marian had heard accounts of the anarchic port, but to see it, hear it, and smell it was like spinning the focus dial on a spyglass. Sure, the wildness was palpable. And she sensed an edge of lawlessness. But there was also an exhilarating spirit to the unruly haven. People went about their business like most others throughout the Jewels. Everything she had witnessed among the common folk in Redtown existed here, only more... *raw,* she thought.

"Morning, miss." An old half-orc nodded from her rickety porch, whittling.

"Good morning."

"Morn's the best 'round here, lass. Sea dogs are all still sleepin' off the grog." The half-orc rose and lit her pipe. "Bit o' peace and quiet for the rest of us."

"This is quiet?" Marian said. Scratchy melodies from an old fiddle reached her ears from a nearby hut. The music mixed with the shouts of two merchants arguing over the price of fish. Behind it all were the harbor bells ringing out ten o'clock.

"Aye, a nice calm morning in Benevolence." She puffed on the pipe and pointed the stem in her direction. "First time?"

Marian nodded.

"Well, you got the look about you. You'll be fine." The old half-orc sat herself back down in the rocking chair. "Wouldn't want to go messin' with you, even in my prime." A large smoke ring rose from her mouth. "Takes one to know one." The half-orc's hand swirled and the smoke morphed into a skull and crossbones. "Don't stay too long lass, or you'll find yourself turning into a pirate."

"That would be a sight," Marian said. "Good day to you."

She couldn't help but be puzzled at how the residents had managed to keep the town from collapsing into chaos. And, without strict oversight or royal rule of law. While that meant a higher risk of unpredictability and less control, it added a strange and exhilarating freedom to the tropical air. Had her own demeanor changed since they'd arrived in port? She couldn't deny feeling the spirit of liberation saturate into her blood and bones, far more so than how she had felt in Redtown after freeing herself from familial obligations.

Marian spotted James standing under a palm tree at the end of the lane. She neared the corner as Big Rig lumbered up to the pirate, looking like a corpse risen from the dead. Her former lover, on the other hand, was glowing. His square jaw and muscular arms shone in the morning sun. It didn't hurt her newfound footloose ways in Benevolence that the handsome pirate had invited her on an excursion, even if they had reached a mutual understanding and put the past behind them.

She smiled as she joined the two pirates.

James had an aura about him this morning that she could only describe as "piratey."

"Top of the morning, Marian." His chin rose and he closed his eyes, aiming his face to the sky. Dappling sunlight peeked through the shade of the palm leaves. Shadows danced over his face. "And a fine morning it is."

"For you," Big Rig said. The dwarf's skin was beaded with sweat. His cheeks were more slate than onyx. "Good morning, Marian."

"Good morning," she said. "You must have had quite the night by the look of you."

"Bloody half-orc," Big Rig grumbled. "Lana managed to get me to finish off the rum in the wee hours."

James slapped his quartermaster on the shoulder. "Aye, mate. You done your Benevolence best!"

"Excuse me, Marian," the dwarf said. "I won't be a moment."

She stepped into the shade and adjusted her robe.

"Not many sea dogs ashore, Jack. Five or six at most that I'd trust with a rope."

"Where in bloody blazes are they all?" the pirate asked.

"Business is good." The dwarf shrugged. "New ships and new captains. Picking is lean."

"Is this bad?" she asked.

"Aye, we need a crew," James said. "And not only to sail but to defend ourselves should we run into trouble... be that navy or nature."

"Or, our less savory brethren," the dwarf added. "Grumpy Jim pulled me aside on my way here, Jack. He told me Captain Pitch was asking about you in port."

"Pitch?"

"Aye. News travels fast, it seems," Big Rig added.

"Is that also not good?" Marian asked.

They both nodded their heads.

"There's more," the dwarf said. "Slimy's contacts told Grumpy Jim that an albatross landed in Benevolence for Pitch and... get this, lad... *R.I.P. Tide* weighed anchor that very hour."

"What in blazes could be urgent enough to send that bilge rat sailing?" the pirate said.

Big Rig shrugged.

"I'll have a think on this," James said.

"In the meantime," Big Rig said, "I'll be heading to the forge. Scarlett's coming with me." His one good eye narrowed and he shook his head. "I don't want anywhere near that compass."

"Understood," Jack said. "You have the blade, Marian?"

She pulled the dagger from her waist and handed it to Big Rig. "I'd say don't damage it, but..."

Crow's feet around Big Rig's one good eye creased. "Well, let's hope my dwarven blood is still potent, because I ain't swung a hammer at an anvil in decades."

"Scupper that, mate," Jack said. He turned to her. "Don't listen to him, Marian. He's a mountain dwarf through and through. I've seen him shape molten steel once, way back. 'Twas magic in the music of it, there was."

The dwarf's hungover grey cheeks brightened with a rosy tint. "Lana's working on *Lady Luck*, getting her ship shape. Between chunkin' over the side, mind you."

Marian made a face.

"Sorry lass," Big Rig said. "I should've kept that to myself."

"And Siân?" James asked.

Big Rig shrugged. "Who knows. Last I saw her was in the wee hours... memory's hazy." He rubbed his eye, clearly struggling with the hangover. "But I remember her jumping from *Lady Luck's* crow's nest with a right impressive dive. After that, something about heading to Grumpy Jim's for last call. That nocsi probably brought in coin by spinning yarns with her new lute 'til the dawn."

"Well, maybe she'll turn up some news with those ears of hers." Jack took off his tricorne and hung it on a crudely painted sign nailed to the palm's trunk. "Thanks for the updates, mate." The pirate turned and the sun's rays highlighted his strong features, the blonde bristles on his chin alight like a cluster of candles. "Ready to go, Marian?"

"I am," she said. "Though I'm curious as to where?"

"Good," he said and winked. "That makes it all the more of a surprise." He motioned to follow him along the rising path that hugged the edge of the bay.

The sun beat down on her exposed skin as they left the shade of the palm for a stretch of open rocky grasses. Her mage's robe turned out to be a most beneficial garment. A soft breeze wafted up and under the fabric, cooling her skin. Out to sea, clusters of billowing clouds hovered over the cerulean water. Underneath their flat bottoms, shadows darkened the ocean to a deep blue.

After a short stretch, the path leveled off and hugged a small cliff with the jungle interior on its right.

A Galanki monkey cried out.

"Is that your friend?" she said, following behind him.

"Very funny," he said, panting.

She smiled to herself. Her anticipation rose with every step they took toward their hidden destination. *Stop it, Marian*, she thought, pushing down the wave of youthful exuberance. The exhilaration of Benevolence and of being around James again, on a high-stakes adventure no less, sent an undeniable rush through her. She eyed his back as they hiked uphill. The pirate's broad shoulders swung right and left as he strode along the path. The smile grew on her face and with it, déjà vu of the time they'd used his spyglass and—

"Did you sleep well on board *Lady Luck*?"

"Very well," she said. "Better than I have in a long time."

"Look at that," he said, pushing aside a branch extending over the path, "we'll make a pirate of you yet."

She laughed. *Why this noticeable ease this morning?* Whether it had something to do with their conversation last night or the surprise reunion with Precious, she didn't know. She had to admit, the idea that he'd accepted their personal treaty and moved on that quickly needled at her pride. *Is he not the least bit disappointed?*

The path veered into the jungle greenery.

Marian followed Jack's lead, feeling the humidity rise inside the densely shaded canopy. Unfamiliar sounds and smells rose. A bird she didn't recognize called out from somewhere in the branches overhead. Her senses came alive with each step forward through the moist soil. Rich and earthy aromas teased her nostrils.

James halted without warning.

"Sorry," she said, bumping into him.

"Hear that?"

"What am I listening for?"

He waved her forward. "Come on, it's just ahead."

Marian sought their destination through the verdant foliage but found herself distracted by the jungle's beauty. She lost herself in the beams of golden light penetrating the canopy, casting elegant shadows over the jungle undergrowth.

"This way." Jack left the path and motioned for her to follow.

Glimpses of the azure sea broke through the greenery over his shoulder.

He stopped and turned, extending a hand.

She hesitated. "What is this, James?"

"A demonstration of trust between us, lass. I brought you here because I've wanted to show you this special spot for years. Now I have an excuse because there's something I need to retrieve."

"What is it?"

"You'll see. Give me your hand."

"Alright." She extended her arm.

Calloused fingers tightened around her palm.

Marian, what are you doing? she thought, letting him lead her ahead.

"Following your road," her guild master's voice answered inside her mind.

"Close your eyes, lass."

"What?" She froze. "Why?"

"Come on, Marian. It's me." He squeezed her hand. "Trust me."

The soul of a man she knew once long ago shone in his eyes.

"Okay, James." The world darkened as she acquiesced.

A second strong hand landed on her hip, guiding her to step forward. With her eyes shut, the rush of falling water was unmistakable.

"A little more, lass. A half step forward. I got you."

Rugged hands pressed against her waist, sending a curious wave of desire through her.

"Open your eyes."

She yelped and swayed.

"I got you!"

The vertigo subsided in his strong grip and she found her visual bearings.

"What do you think?" His voice was hot air at her ear as he held her from behind.

Marian took in the spectacular circular cove from the ledge. The steep sides were alive with vines and blooming flowers in a variety of potent jungle colors. To her right, halfway around the pool, a thin waterfall plunged at least fifty feet. Where it struck the clear water, it sent out plumes of billowing mist that fed the tropical plants, adding an air of enchantment to the scene. With the morning light breaking over the edge of the cliff, a rainbow arced across the mist in front of the waterfall.

"It's beautiful," she said, mesmerized.

"That there narrow passage..." His arm appeared over her shoulder and aimed at a vertical slit in the rocks across the cove.

She spotted a thin band of water running through the chasm.

"Opens to the sea," he said. "They say of old that this was a private bathing pool for a Golden Elf queen."

"You're making that up," she said.

"No, Marian. I would never lie to you."

She turned.

"Never, lass."

His face was inches from her. Desire rose, despite her mind telling her to—

"There's more," he said, "come on." James led her away from the ledge and down a winding path. The roar of falling water echoed off the cliffs as they descended. Cool mist caressed her cheeks as they emerged near the falls.

The pirate waved her along the narrow shoreline to where a patch of sand large enough for a skiff to land formed a secret beach.

"Are those ruins?" she asked, spotting a broken statue half-consumed by a millennium of jungle growth.

"Aye," he said. "An old votive."

"It's Telathia." She clasped her hands in the direction of the stone fragment.

"I thought you would like that. Seems whoever this elven queen was, she was a devotee as well. Now, give me a moment. I won't be but a minute. Enjoy the view."

"Where are you going?"

He pulled off his boots. And then his shirt.

The sight of his bare chest, with the assortment of pirate tattoos and scars, sent blood rushing into her limbs.

"After treasure, of course." He walked to a nearby rock along the shore. "I *am* a pirate." He winked and dove into the water.

A minute passed. Then two. Marian took in the beauty of the waterfall. After three minutes an uneasy feeling came over her.

"James?" She went to the rock, peering down into the clear water.

Something's wrong.

"James!" His name echoed off the walls of the cove.

She knelt and looked under the surface. Twenty or so feet down, the shadowy figure of the pirate emerged as if he had passed through the subterranean rock.

He broke the surface.

"You scared me!"

"Ha!" He held up a small tube.

"What is that?" she said, angry on the surface though secretly relieved.

"That, my dear Marian, is a map." The pirate swam to the shore and sat down. He undid his ponytail and let his blonde hair fall freely to his shoulders.

She joined him on the sand.

He held out the tube.

"A map of what?"

"Dragon Tail Island." The pirate raised an eyebrow.

"What? How?"

"A long story for another time. Had it on me when your sister took *Lady Luck* and set me adrift." He leaned over, expression smitten. "I gave it to Precious to keep safe when she hid in the galley. And, by the sea's spirit, she did. The lass hid it here so no one would find it." He twirled the watertight tube in his hand. "This gives us the answers to the island's riddles and the layout of the tomb."

"Where was it?"

"There's a second cave below. You have to swim about ten feet under the cliff to get to it. A small opening overhead keeps the air fresh but it's far too small to see from above."

She shook her head.

"What?"

"James Hawk, the farm boy who became a pirate. Like a character out of a fairy tale."

"Am I now?" He stood and put his hands on his hips. "Well then, how about we celebrate with some rum?"

"And where are we supposed to get that?" She couldn't help but be charmed by his boyish exuberance.

"Now, let's see..." He looked about the cove and then raised his head and aimed it toward the sun. "Five paces to the east." He stomped his way in the appropriate direction. "Third stone up the wall." His fingers went up the rocks. "One, two, three."

To her surprise, he loosened a slab in the cliff. It came out and with a plunk he dropped it on the sand.

"If Lana's been here since we arrived, we're doomed," he said. "Otherwise..." He reached in. "Well, yo ho ho!" He pulled out a bottle.

"Fourteen years that's been aging in there." He examined the contents through the dark glass. "Now, I know you're not crazy about straight rum." He tossed the bottle over to her and scurried up the rocks until he reached an overhanging branch with bright red fruit. Marian didn't recognize the species.

The pirate shook the branch and several fell to the sand.

He climbed higher and shimmied his way along a ledge until he was at the boundary of the mist.

"James. Be careful." She stood. *Just like a boy.*

He vanished into the plume of spray.

"James!"

The pirate's legs and arms reappeared and he made his way across the ledge and jumped down, a flower stem between his teeth.

"What in the name of the Jewels are you doing?"

"Now hold on, Marian." He picked up one of the fruits and took out a small dagger. Around the sphere, he cut and halved it, scooping out the flesh on one side. Then, he squeezed the other half so the juice fell into the open makeshift cup. He picked up the rum bottle, which he uncorked with his teeth, grinning at her.

Marian rolled her eyes at the classic pirate move.

James poured a hearty portion into the fruit juice and placed the flower stem into it as a garnish and handed it to her.

"What..." As much as she was confused, the effort and the beauty of the flower held sway over her.

"Go on, try it." He took a heavy swig from the bottle of rum.

She raised the drink to her lips and sipped. Sweet, berry-like juice mixed with the savory rum, sending a pleasant clash of flavors over her tongue.

He slapped a knee and carefully touched the fruit cup in her hand with the bottle to cheers the occasion. "Not bad, aye?"

"What is it?" She took a bigger sip. "The fruit, I mean." She held up the halved portion and examined it. The skin looked like dragon scales, red with tinges of purple.

"Heart fruit. Proper name, I don't know. But that's what we pirates call it. This here drink is called a Bleedin' Heart." He took another long pull on the rum bottle.

"That name's certainly familiar to both of us," she said and sipped.

"Ain't that the truth."

She edged closer to him. *What are you doing, Marian?* she chastised herself.

She let herself lean against his strong torso. When his arm reached around, pulling her in close, the last of her resistance melted.

"I never want to see you in pain, Marian," he said, looking in her eyes. "No more bleeding hearts for either of us from here on out."

She grabbed the back of his neck and pulled him in. "Kiss me already." Their lips met, and everything fell away. The past. The present. The future. She didn't care about any of it. She wanted this, and she wanted it now. It could all be damned.

She ran a hand down his chest, over his iron muscles. The tension in his neck eased against her grip and their kiss deepened.

Her breathing grew heavy and lustful. She undid her robe and pulled him down onto the sand.

"Marian," he said, his strong arms running over her.

"Just this once," she said. "For old time's sake."

27

TOUCH AND GO

❦

Scarlett took her time on the descent from the forge back into Benevolence. She reached the last curve along the meandering path and halted to relish the vista. The climate and topography on the isolated isle fell somewhere between the northern tip of Ruby Island, with its semi-arid coastline, and the lush and humid tropical shores of Emerald Island's south coast. As much as she identified with the gritty quality of Longshore's surrounding landscape, Benevolence took the top spot of places she'd visited in the Jewel Islands. A strange comfort was to be had in seeing the limits of one's surroundings amidst a vast and empty sea. It took no more than two hours to cross from one end of Benevolence to the other, and any rise in elevation not blocked by the jungle offered a three-hundred-and-sixty-degree panorama of the isle's hook-shaped coastline. Curious as it was, something about that put her at ease. The fact that the rogue isle was home to an anarchic community didn't hurt its ranking, especially for a professional thief with a penchant for skirting the law.

Scarlett's nostrils tingled as the scent of heated metal wafted down the hillside. She gazed up at the forge nestled in the greenery. Big Rig had been right about the blacksmith; the half-orc was a character. Between his hearty beard like an avalanche of dirty snow, gregarious personality, and penchant for raunchy jokes, the smithy could hold court amongst the best entertainers in Drakeland's underground cabarets. The patchwork of scars riddling his body was like nothing she'd seen before. Nicks and lines of various shapes and sizes spoke of smelting burns, but others stood out as obvious traces of sword slashes and dagger thrusts. The source of those battle wounds had been left to her imagination. When she inquired with Big Rig as to their origin, the dwarf shook his head. His one eye went wide with concern that the blacksmith might hear her question, and the pirate had returned to gathering materials and polishing the anvil in preparation for crafting the compass needle.

Clang! Clang! Clang!

Commotion on the streets of Benevolence drew her attention downhill. A crowd had formed at the docks, with additional townsfolk scurrying toward the bay. Shouts from a nearby mooring caused her to gasp. *Felicity* sat anchored dangerously close to shore. Scarlett dashed down the path, taking the dusty switchbacks with what would count as long strides for her small gnomish legs.

"Scarlett!"

She turned as Jack and Marian emerged from a path leading out of the jungle.

"What's happening, lass?" Jack said, catching up and motioning for Marian to trot with them downhill.

"I don't know," she said. "But *Felicity's* dropped anchor!"

"*Felicity?*" Jack snatched his hat from the sign on the palm trunk and they hustled down the dusty street.

Scarlett focused her vision, attempting to make out the commotion's source. "I see a stretcher," she said.

Precious limped at a brisk pace next to two sea elves hauling a body towards the orphanage.

The gnome's stomach wrenched when she recognized the outfit. "God's no! It's Ashana," she said.

"Who?" Marian asked, running next to her.

"Captain of *Felicity*," Jack said, panting. "The ship that brought us to Redtown."

They caught up to Precious and Scarlett almost gagged at the sight of the sea elf. Her face and exposed skin were a festering and burned mess.

"What in blazes happened?" Jack said.

"We were intercepted sailing south," the sea elf at the rear of the stretcher said, hustling along the sandy shore. "Bloody *R.I.P. Tide*."

"Pitch?" Jack said.

"Aye. The captain did her best to save the ship. We lost half the crew before fleeing. She took the brunt of a vicious spell from that sorcerer protecting us... put herself on the line to save us all."

Of course she did, Scarlett thought, her heart sinking.

"A pox on that witch!" The tone of Jack's anger held no bounds. "Is she going to make it?"

Precious made a face that didn't send the message Scarlett had hoped for.

"You bloody well try, Precious." The pirate turned to Marian as they trotted along. "Will you—"

"Of course," the mage said.

They hurried into the building. Scarlett, running with her small legs, was the last inside. By the time she entered, Ashana had been transferred to the sofa.

"Let's start here," Precious said to Marian. "We can move her later."

Each of them began assessing the woman's injuries.

Scarlett watched in amazement as the two worked in tandem, sharing their observations and diagnoses as they passed over her body.

The sea elf muttered something inaudible and her body started convulsing.

Scarlett turned away.

Jack's strong hand gripped her shoulder. "She'll be alright, lass," the pirate said. "She's a fighter."

"Try and relax, Ashana." Marian's voice was measured and gentle. "I am going to ease your pain."

Scarlett dared to look and found herself mesmerized by the soft glow that radiated from the mage's fingers. The healer ran a hand in small circles over the sea elf's face and neck, chanting at a whisper.

"There," Marian said, as the convulsions eased.

"I'm going to get a salve," Precious said.

Marian nodded and began loosening the buttons on the captain's shirt. "Jack." She gestured for him to go outside.

The pirate nodded as they undid Ashana's top.

Scarlett gasped and covered her mouth. The lesions that had formed from the dark magic had come to life. Like malignant centipedes, they writhed about under the surface of her skin, singeing and poisoning her flesh as they roamed her torso.

"You might want to wait outside, Scarlett," Marian said.

"Jack..." Ashana whispered. Her arm rose like it was under another's control.

"He's with the others on the porch," Scarlett said, finding her courage and approaching. "What is it?"

"Jack," she whispered.

"He'll be in later," Scarlett whispered.

She caught Marian's concerned expression.

"Get him now, Scarlett." The mage covered up the sea elf's chest so she was decent for him to enter.

"Is it that bad?"

The mage nodded.

Precious returned with the ointment.

"I think the soothing spell is all we can do," Marian told the headmaster.

Precious looked over the sea elf and acquiesced.

Marian grasped the captain's hand. "She's no longer in pain, Scarlett. But hurry." Precious took the sea elf's other hand and clasped it between both of her own.

"You're not alone, Ashana," Marian said, voice gentle and soothing. "We're here with you. Your crew and ship are safe."

What nobility and grace, the gnome thought, observing the healer.

"Scarlett." Marian's tone was urgent.

The thief shook herself free of the sight and went to the entrance.

"... Pitch was looking for you, she was. And, I think—" a sea elf from *Felicity* halted his words when she stepped through the doorway.

"Jack," she motioned him inside.

The pirate strode forward. "Marian?"

The mage shook her head.

"Bloody Pitch!" Jack punched the wall.

"James!" Marian's voice shook the interior.

He nodded and held up a hand in apology. The pirate knelt. "Ashana, lass. It's Jack," he said near her ear.

"Jack..."

"Aye, you done gone and turned yourself into a hero, you bloody fool." He shook his head. "You're going to Davy Jones Locker lass, with pride."

Felicity's captain reached up and grabbed his sleeve. Scarlett winced as the sea elf's face leaned towards the pirate. Almost no flesh remained, only eyeballs and lips surrounded by squirming lesions over bone.

"Jack..."

"Aye, lass." Trusty Jack leaned closer. "Let go... you don't need to fight this no more. You're in Benevolence."

"Navy," she whispered.

"Aye." The pirate nodded. "They're in our sights, too. I'll take a ship down in your name, I will."

"No... over the horizon," she whispered.

"What's that, lass?"

"Here... tomorrow."

With a final gasp, the sea elf's grip fell from the pirate's sleeve and her body settled.

"Be at peace, Ashana," Marian whispered and took the sea elf's other hand from Precious. She placed them both across the captain's chest.

Silence descended over the room.

Scarlett's lips trembled. *This can't be happening.*

"I'll get my helpers to prepare a grave," Precious said and rose.

"No," Jack said. "I'll bring a hammock. I want her sewn inside with a boulder at her feet." The pirate stood and put a hand on a shoulder of each of the two sea elf sailors who had carried her in. "We're burying her at sea."

⚜

"SORRY TO INTERRUPT."

"What is it?" Scarlett turned from the view of the captain's lifeless body.

"I think you both should come see this," Precious said.

Scarlett tugged on Trusty Jack's sleeve.

The pirate didn't respond.

"Jack?"

"Aye," he said. The muscles in his jaw tightened and he gritted his teeth. "Pitch will pay for this, she will."

"Precious says we need to see something outside."

Scarlett allowed the pirate to go first. She took a last look at Ashana's body wrapped inside the canvas hammock. "I'm sorry this happened to you," she whispered. "Be at peace."

The gnome hastened to the entrance.

"What's this, then?" Jack said as they stepped onto the beach.

Scarlett stopped dead in her tracks. The remaining members of *Felicity's* crew had gathered in front of the orphanage, a mixture of sadness, pathos, and anger painted on their faces.

The quartermaster, who had been in the fray during the incident with Bonnie Fitzwater's galleon, stepped forward.

"You be sailing south, then?" Trusty Jack said. "I can understand wantin' to be gone from the Jewels."

The sea elf held out a length of rope. He tied a knot and handed it to the pirate. "We've all voted and it was unanimous."

Trusty Jack examined the knot.

Like Scarlett, he too seemed to be unfamiliar with its significance.

"Voted on what?" the pirate asked.

"You've got a crew, Captain. If you'll have us."

Scarlett's eyes went wide.

"Blow me down," Trusty Jack said, removing his tricorne and placing it over his heart.

"All we ask is that if we cross paths with that bloody pirate, you seek revenge for what she did to Ashana."

Trusty Jack's hands balled into fists. "On that we're agreed." The pirate's head swept left to right over the twenty-odd sailors. "Brethren of the coast," he said, addressing *Felicity's* crew. "If we spot that bilge-hearted sorcerer a'sea we'll take down the *R.I.P. Tide* with no quarter and rid the Jewels of her bloody filth, so help me and all me mates!"

"And if not?" Scarlett stepped forward. Much as she didn't want to ask, prudence dictated they be clear on terms.

"We're with you either way, Ms. Tanash," the sea elf said. "Aren't we lads?"

The crew nodded and shouted out hearty "Ayes!"

"It'd be an honor to sail under you, Captain Hawk," *Felicity's* quartermaster said.

Trusty Jack spat on his palm and extended his hand. "The honor's all mine."

The quartermaster reciprocated in kind on his suction-cupped fingers and shook the pirate's hand.

"Welcome aboard *Lady Luck*, lads!" Jack shouted to cheers from the sea elves.

"We'll get on the water and settle in," the quartermaster said. "We don't have time to waste, with the Navy a day out of Benevolence."

"Aye." Trusty Jack looked her way. "Much as I hate to, we need to leave right fast to avoid them."

We can't leave, Scarlett thought. *Not yet.*

"I understand you lost your cook a while back?" the sea elf said.

"Aye," Jack said. "'Twas a good friend, Myron was."

"Well, seeing as you already have a quartermaster..."

"You're good with a pot, are ye?"

"It's something of a hobby, is all."

"He's being modest, Captain!" A sailor shouted from somewhere in the crowd. "He's got the gift, he does! Roasts a hare crispier than a witch's temper!"

The rest of the crew shouted affirmations.

"Well, with that kind of enthusiasm, who could say no?" Trusty Jack slapped him on the shoulder. "The galley's yours to command."

Precious stepped up next to Trusty Jack, pointing her walking stick down the beach.

Scarlett shifted left and right, trying to see what drew their attention. At her height, the view was a sea of legs from *Felicity's* crew. "What is it?" she said, approaching her companions.

"Speaking of quartermasters, the dwarf is back," Precious said.

Big Rig pushed his way through the crowd of sea elves, wiping sweat from his brow. He held out a hand.

In his palm was a wrapped cloth.

Scarlett sighed with relief. *The compass needle.*

"It's done," he said.

28

HOIST THE COLORS

"**W**ell, this is it," Precious said, leaning on her walking stick. She looked at the faces around her on deck. "If all goes well, we'll meet again in Redtown."

Trusty Jack nodded with the others. *Lady Luck's* hull creaked, as if she too were eager to depart.

"Do you have a bearing?" the young woman asked.

"East, for now," Trusty Jack said. "Once we pass Mayrotten Island it's up to that there compass." He indicated the device in Scarlett's tiny hand.

All eyes went to the gnome.

The group huddled around the thief, shielding her from the crew.

Scarlett popped open the lid.

Big Rig had done his work well. The needle, forged with sharp angles, hovered on its post as if it were crafted alongside the original.

"We have a week until the inauguration." Precious pulled her attention from the compass and Jack found himself the focus of her gaze. "Sail fast, sail safe."

"Aye," the pirate said. "We've got the Navy to skirt first, then the magic rising near the mist."

"I can cast a shield ward on the compass once we're in range of the mists," Marian said. "It won't hold long against the dark magic, but it might get us into the fog without the device attracting spirits and creatures of the deep."

"Anything helps," Big Rig said.

Scarlett pressed the button and flipped it shut.

Jack sighed with relief alongside the dwarf, who flung a coin into the bay as they broke the huddle.

Precious went from one to the other, saying her goodbyes.

Jack stepped aside and waited. He gripped the ship's railing and peered down. The harbor boy in the dinghy nodded, waiting at the skiff's oars.

"Farewell for now, Captain."

Trusty Jack took off his tricorne and bowed. "Safe journey to you, Precious. Until we meet in Redtown."

"When this is all over, I'd welcome more time to get to know one another. I know it sounds strange, but you feel like... family."

"Aye," he said, feeling a bit embarrassed. "I'd like that. But it'll depend on your new government's attitude toward pirates."

"Not *my* government, Jack. The people's."

"Aye." He placed the tricorne back on his head. "I'm proud of you, lass."

"As am I of you."

"For what?"

She glanced over at Marian. "You know for what."

So, he thought, *the two had talked.*

She took a step forward and leaned on her walking stick.

"Be safe, Jack." Her face grew earnest. "Bring everyone back, promise?" Precious's expression softened. "You once told me that honest folk always keep their promises... even pirates."

"I can't do that lass, you know that," he said, voice low. "But I'll bloody well try."

"Aye," she said, making a piratey performance of her response. "I savvy." She dropped her walking stick to the harbor boy. The lad caught it and set it down in the dinghy.

"A hand, lass?"

"Please," she said.

Jack helped her descend the rope ladder.

"You didn't need to come on board, Precious. Coulda' done said our goodbyes ashore."

"And miss a chance to be back on *Lady Luck* with her rightful captain?" She climbed down the netting. "Wouldn't miss it for the world."

The harbor boy pushed off from the sloop's hull.

Precious waved goodbye and Trusty Jack popped his tricorne up and down. He took one last look at Benevolence. The town had proved its worth yet again, the refuge a reminder that there were places left in the Jewels where he could find solace and safety.

"James?"

"Aye, lass."

"A word before we depart." Marian checked to make sure no one else was within earshot. "About yesterday... I was rash and—"

"Lass, I wanted it as much as you did."

She smiled, the amber shards in her mahogany eyes catching the morning light. The mage opened her mouth to speak but looked away.

"Hey, Marian." A finger turned her chin. "I'm no farm boy. I understand how the world works."

"It's just... I meant what I said in your cabin. Our mission can't fail and—"

"No, it can't," he said.

"It was wonderful, don't get me wrong." Her cheeks flushed and she bit her bottom lip.

"Aye." He smirked. "Like old times."

"We needed it... you know, to close the door."

He nodded.

"So, friends?"

"More than friends, lass. You're everything to me. Always will be."

The soft touch of her fingers squeezed his hand.

"Thank you, James." She looked about the ship. "So, to sea then?"

"To sea." He inhaled the salty air as a morning breeze kicked up. "Good day for sailing."

"I leave that to our captain's competent hands," she said. "I'm looking forward to seeing the legendary Trusty Jack at the helm of *Lady Luck*."

Her hips swayed gracefully as she strode to where Scarlett stood along the starboard railing.

Friends it be, then, he thought with a forlorn sigh.

The deep, distinct humming of a dwarf rose behind him.

"Bit eager, mate." Jack inspected the quartermaster. Big Rig wore a set of ragged leather armor with two hand axes crossed on the chest.

"Gettin' the feel of it again. Been a long time." He wiggled his hips and swung his thick arms. "I left this extra set with the smithy going on fourteen years." The mountain dwarf adjusted the straps around his waist. "Bit tight on me sides..."

Jack chortled.

"Be happy I'm a planner, mate!" Big Rig eyed him with playful annoyance. "Had some extra blades and bows stored at the forge as well." The dwarf tapped a finger to his temple as if to say, "Smart."

"Enough for the crew?"

"Almost." Big Rig took the twin axes in his hands and swung them. "Scarlett and me dropped into town this morn' and closed the gap. Our sea elves will have bows and cutlasses, all." The dwarf glanced in the gnome's direction. "The lass was like a kid in Slimy's shop, she was... couldn't believe the contraband the night elf had in the back room."

Good, Jack thought. At least they were all geared up.

"That elven bow of yours is in your quarters." The dwarf reattached the axes onto his leather chest armor. "Got you an extra quiver of arrows."

"Cedar shafts?"

"Aye," Big Rig said. "With sea hawk feathers."

"Good man." Jack motioned to follow him to the helm. When they reached the wheel, the pirate took a moment and surveyed the deck. The crew scurried about, preparing for departure.

As if born twins, the pirate and his quartermaster lifted their chins in unison and let the wind caress their cheeks. They examined the cloudless sky.

"Blowin' east-southeast," the dwarf said. "Light and steady."

"Aye, looks like a broad reach until we turn north." Jack placed his hands on the helm. *Hello old girl,* he thought, letting the worn wood handles greet him. *Been a long time.*

The dwarf met his gaze, a childish anticipation in his eye.

"Weigh anchor, Mr. Riggins," Jack said with purposeful formality.

"Aye aye, Captain." The dwarf lumbered forward on deck. "Weigh anchor, lads!"

Like a beast waking from a long winter's sleep, *Lady Luck* came alive. Sailors hastened about, climbing the riggings and checking sails.

"Raise the main!" Big Rig barked as the ship lay dead into the wind.

The music of canvas and rigging in motion reached Jack's ears. He spun the wheel to aim them out of the bay. With *Lady Luck's* rudder right full, the sloop's slow rotation added to his anticipation. Then, with a snap, the mainsail caught the breeze and the sensation of the ship pulling forward ran through his limbs. Jack spun the wheel in the opposite direction and found the sweet spot to steady their course.

"How does she feel, lad?" the dwarf asked, stomping over to him.

"Like I never left."

"Clear lane, Cap'n!" a sailor shouted from the crow's nest.

"Hoist the colors, Mr. Riggins," Jack said. "Let's do this like the pirates we are."

"Salty words to me ears!" Big Rig slapped his chest, rattling his axes. He repeated the captain's orders to cheers from the crew.

Jack smiled as the skull and crossbones rose and fluttered in the breeze.

"Passing fathom buoy!" a sea elf reported.

"Unfurl the headsail!" Big Rig shouted.

Trusty Jack relished his old friend's voice booming over the deck. *Just like old times.*

"Ease sheet to broad reach!" the quartermaster directed the sea elves at the sail.

Trusty Jack adjusted the tiller to the middle as the ship edged free of the harbor. The sloop drifted downwind, the headsail flapping, blocked from the breeze by the larger mainsail. The pirate swung the rudder in the opposite direction and *Lady Luck's* forward sail found the breeze and tightened.

"Sailing broad reach, Mr. Riggins," the pirate said.

"Sailing broad reach!" the dwarf repeated for the deck hands.

With the prow aimed to sea, and without a landmark as bearing, Jack checked his compass and noted their course. The rhythmic pulse of splashing water bounced across the deck as the hull cut the sea, adding a musicality to the rolling motion of the heeling ship.

"She's sailing right clean, Captain!" Lana shouted, gripping a rope and leaning over the starboard railing amidships.

Nearer to the prow, Marian stood with Scarlett. The two smiled at him.

Trusty Jack winked.

"*Lady Luck* is back!" Big Rig shouted to more cheers.

"Give us a shanty, Cap!" It was Lana, leaning dangerously far overboard, her muscular arm flexing as she held a rope line.

"Aye, Captain!" Big Rig echoed her request. "For old time's sake."

Jack's eyes went to Marian, the phrase a reminder of their tryst the previous day.

The mage blushed and approached, her steps uneasy as the heeling ship rolled on the swells. "Yes, Captain Hawk," she said. "Give us a shanty."

"Come on, Jack," Scarlett added, joining them.

Siân appeared from below deck. The nocsi swung the lute strapped around her torso to her backside and gestured dramatically as if introducing him on stage.

Jack took a moment and let the ship and the wind inspire.

Aye, that's the perfect one it is, he thought.

He puffed his chest and sang:

THE TIDE WAS HIGH, AND THE MORN WAS PALE,
    When we stepped once more 'neath the sail.
    The rum was stored, the anchor weighed,
    The view of land began to fade.

With a cheer for the life we'd missed,
We set our course where the sunrise kissed...

"So, HEAVE AWAY!" HE SHOUTED.
"Heave away!" the crew repeated.

LET THE WHOLE WORLD HEAR,
We're bound for lands both far and near,
With Lady Luck we've naught to fear,
So, heave away lads, let the tides decide!

THE TIDE WAS HIGH, AND THE WIND WAS NEW,
The ship found the breeze, her captain his crew.
The colors were raised, the sails were—

"SHIP HO!" A VOICE FROM THE CROW'S NEST BROKE INTO HIS VERSE. "Nor'northeast, Captain!"

Jack halted the shanty and peered to port. His arms maneuvered the wheel left and right, responding to the wind to keep the sails tight on their broad reach.

"Blimey they've got good eyes, sea elves do," Big Rig said, approaching.

"Take the helm, Rig."

"Quartermaster has the wheel!" Lana shouted for all to hear.

Jack pulled out his spyglass and steadied his feet on the heeling ship. An empty sea greeted him through the circular viewfinder. Left and right he scanned, following the horizon.

"You see it?" Big Rig asked.

Jack shook his head. *Where are you?*

"Is it the Navy?" Scarlett's voice, a few steps away, reached his ears.

Trusty Jack swept the spyglass over the horizon a second time. A smudge crossed the circle. He reversed direction and tracked back until he found it. A hazy mast and hull grew legible. Hints of dark blue and red, the Navy's colors, dappled the ship's forward mast.

"Aye," he said. "'Tis the Navy, it is."

"Ships ho!" the sea elf shouted. "Two more, Cap'n! Asides the lead!"

Jack eased the spyglass left and then right. *Blimey, that lad's got eagle eyes*, he thought. Sure enough, two more indistinct hulls manifested from the haze, one on each side of the advancing ship.

He slapped the spyglass shut and gave Scarlett a salty grin. "The race is on."

✣ 29 ✣

WALK THE PLANK

✦✦✦

For three days, *Lady Luck* sailed east. Trusty Jack was smitten with their progress. Despite cutting an angle to intercept out of Benevolence, the Navy frigates had never closed the distance. That first day had dealt Jack and his companions the most tenuous hand in their card game of nautical cat and mouse. With each setting sun, through a combination of his own cunning seamanship, the salty wisdom of Big Rig, and the keen senses of the sea elven crew, they'd managed to increase the distance from their pursuers. Their greatest boon was the simple fact that the sloop was smaller, leaner, and faster than the Navy vessels, and once again Trusty Jack thanked the tides that the class of ship under his feet was a favorite amongst pirates.

"Land ho! Port horizon!"

Lady Luck rolled with the swells on a following sea. Hands gripping the helm, Jack kept her tight on the lee, the wind blowing over his shoulders. All three headsails bloomed in wide arcs, opposite the main-sail, as if the ship were flexing its nautical muscles. *Lady Luck* felt alive under the midday sun, like a racehorse galloping with nostrils flared.

"Passing Mayrotten Island, Captain," Big Rig said, lumbering over to the helm.

"We're close, Rig." Trusty Jack spun the wheel back and forth to maintain their bearing. Though he dreaded it, soon they would need the Dragon Tail Compass to point them through the mist to their cursed destination.

"Feels good watching those Navy rats lose distance." The dwarf cackled. His thick fingers patted a nearby post, thanking their ship. "She always liked the lee." The dwarf inhaled deeply and let out a hearty, audible, and fully dwarfish exhalation. "It's good to be a pirate, ain't it?"

"Aye, mate," Jack said, half-listening.

"What's got you, lad?"

"Nothing, just..." He glanced back at the frigates. "Fairy Jenny's a'swirling in me head, is all."

The quartermaster's eye widened. "You got the Jenny's?" He reached into a pocket of his leather armor. Then another. And another. "Bollocks, I'm out of coins."

"It's nothing, Rig. Been at the wheel too long, is all," Jack said, though he failed to convince himself. He'd had the Jenny's twice before, and both times had proven prescient.

"Let me take over, lad. You've got the ship tight on the lee and the wind's holding course."

The pirate handed *Lady Luck* over to his quartermaster and arched his body so the crow's nest appeared overhead. His spine and back muscles thanked him.

"Maybe I'll go below and sneak in a half hour of shuteye," he said. "Don't want to be eyein' that bloody island with its tainted spirit anyway." He spat to port, Mayrotten a distant line over the rolling sea. He grimaced. *Plus, too many memories.*

Not long and they'd be at the edge of the mists. Once that happened, he would need to be at his best—senses alert and on his top sailing game.

Captain's instincts sent his hand reaching for the spyglass in his pocket. His fingers touched the metal tube and he hesitated. *Bah*, he thought. *Let it go. Sea elf in the nest's got the best eyes on the ship.* Jack withdrew his hand and gazed ahead over the ship's prow. Nothing on the horizon by his naked eye.

"Alright, Rig," he said. "I'll be in my quarters getting me a bit of shuteye. Have Lana wake me in—"

"Come on, ya scallywag! You're gonna answer to the captain, you are!"

He and Big Rig both swung their heads at the half-orc's authoritative tone. There'd been nothing but clean behavior aboard since departing Benevolence. Jack couldn't imagine a lack of discipline unfolding with the sea elves, especially under their current circumstances.

"Is that... a boy?" the dwarf asked, head twisting back and forth from an approaching Lana to the helm as he steered the ship.

Blow me down, Jack thought, as the first mate pulled along a resisting child. When he caught sight of the lad's face, he let out a hearty laugh. "Lookie here, Rig... we've got ourselves a stowaway!" Trusty Jack knelt so he was eye level with the rascal from the orphanage. "And a hungry one, too."

"I'll be a bloody pirate, I will!" The boy yanked against the half-orc's grip and wiped what Jack took to be jelly from his cheek.

"Whoa, there lad." He held up a hand. "Not with that kind of language you won't."

"I've heard you sayin' all sorts of dirties for days," the child said.

"Have ye, now?" He motioned for Lana to release him.

"Found him in the galley, Cap," the half-orc said. "With his face in the jelly jar," she growled. "And you scallywags been blamin' me for the missing grub!"

"Aye, lass. Our bad," Jack said. "You're cleared."

Lana, smug with her acquittal, eyed Big Rig who had glanced back. "Don't think I'll forget this, mate!" She pointed at the dwarf.

"Steady on, Lana," Jack said. "Dismissed. And my apologies."

The half-orc hmphed and strode off, chin high.

"Alright, lad." Jack stood, towering over the boy. "What's your proper name?"

"Billy." The boy folded his arms and puffed his chest.

I like him already, Jack thought, but did his best to maintain an earnest exterior.

"Well now, Billy... stowaways who are caught by pirates usually walk the plank."

The boy's eyes went wide.

"But seein' how we're short-staffed, maybe I should let you work off what you've eaten?"

"And what he owes for three days at sea," Big Rig added, adjusting the helm to and fro.

"Good point, Mr. Riggins." Jack folded his arms, mimicking Billy.

"Deck needs scrubbing," the dwarf added.

"Aye, it does. So, what'll it be lad? The choice is yours. Walk the plank or..." He knelt so the two were eye to eye. "Work the planks?"

"Awful close to Mayrotten Island to be in the water... all sorts of spirits down there."

Trusty Jack bounced his eyebrows as punctuation to Big Rig's words.

"I'll scrub the planks, I will!" Billy said, unfolding his arms. "Please, Captain Hawk, sir..."

"Aye, I think we savvy one another." Jack held out a hand. "Welcome aboard, Billy."

They shook hands.

"Lana!"

The half-orc returned. Billy took a step back as she towered over him.

"Now, Billy... the first mate here will take you down and show you where you'll hammock. Then, you get that jelly off your cheeks and make yourself presentable to be on deck... by pirate standards."

The boy's eyes brightened and so did Jack's mood, the Jenny's in his mind blown away by the boy's enthusiasm.

Trusty Jack stood and put on his best Captain voice. "First Mate Luholi, take Billy below and hammock him as part of the crew."

"Aye aye, Cap'n." She gave a mock thumb salute.

Thankfully, Lana's temper had simmered, and she too was charmed by the youth's exuberance.

Jack joined his quartermaster. He and Big Rig had their fun, and neither had any intention of putting the young lad to work. "Alright, mate. Let me try this again. I'm going below for a bit of shuteye before—"

"Mist ho!"

Jack's spyglass was out on instinct. He scanned ahead past the ship's prow. "Shiver me timbers," he whispered. A grey mass approached like a sandstorm composed of billowing and dark magic.

"Will we make it inside before the Navy reaches us?"

"Aye," he said, responding to Scarlett's voice and peering into the mists. "They never had a chance, lass." *And that's what's been giving me the Jenny's.*

"And they won't follow?"

He closed the spyglass and shook his head. "Never. No one in their right mind would."

"Cap'n!" A sea elf to stern called for his attention.

"Sink me," Jack said, checking on the frigates. The lead ship remained in line behind them, but the other two had split off, aiming out to sea in the opposite direction to where Mayrotten Island formed a boundary.

"Ship ho!" a sea elf cried out from the crow's nest. "Dead ahead. Edge of the mists!"

Jack dashed to the bow and flung open the spyglass. His eye on the lens went wide.

"What's happening?" Scarlett's urgent voice broke the spell of shock that had fallen over him.

"Scourge of the Jewel Seas," he muttered, the Jenny's in his mind mocking his foolishness.

"What?"

It's a bloody trap, he thought, and glanced at the frigate behind him. *Hounds to the hunters.*

Jack lowered the spyglass and locked eyes with the gnome. "R.I.P. Tide."

30

SCOURGE OF THE SEAS

"Beat to quarters!!"

Scarlett stood dumbstruck as Trusty Jack's command sent *Lady Luck's* deck into a frenzy.

Deckhands dashed to their posts. Archers scurried up ropes to shooting stations.

"Quartermaster!" the pirate shouted.

"Aye!" Big Rig appeared at his side.

"Get every bloody ounce of canvas on the wind," Trusty Jack said. "Give her all she's got."

"Jack." Scarlett stepped forward. "What are you doing?"

"Making good on my promise, lass." The pirate adjusted the wheel as the crew let out more sail.

"You're taking on that ship?" She pointed at the *R.I.P. Tide*. The galleon, a fierce skull protruding as a battering ram, bounced across the sea on a line for *Lady Luck*.

"Ain't going back on my word, lass. Made a promise. I owe it to them and to Ashana."

"We *need* to get to Dragon Tail Island." Anger and concern vied for dominance in her veins.

"Trim sails!" Trusty Jack focused on their bearing.

"Jack, lad." Big Rig reappeared at her side. "You're losing the lead. Ain't we making a run for the mist?"

"You too, now?" the pirate barked.

"James, what are you doing?"

Thank the gods, Scarlett thought, as Marian joined them. *She'll talk some sense into him.*

Trusty Jack gazed at the approaching galleon, eyes afire with revenge.

"You intend to take on a pirate ship and the Royal Navy?" Marian asked. "Have you lost your mind, James?"

"I am bloody captain of this ship!" he shouted. "I won't go back on my word."

"That's what this is about?" Marian spread her arms wide in desperation.

"And what about your word to us?" Scarlett indicated herself and Marian. "You'll stake your reputation over our quest? Over the lives of children? The future of the Jewels?"

"Hasty now, lads!" The pirate called to the sea elves handing out cutlasses. "Let's be ready."

"Mr. Riggins..." Scarlett pulled the quartermaster aside. "We can't take on *R.I.P. TIDE*, let alone the Royal Navy. This is madness."

"You have to intervene," Marian said, joining them.

The mage was right. Scarlett knew it and by the look of the dwarf, so did *Lady Luck's* quartermaster. Jack's pride was like an avalanche. Triggered by the smallest disturbance to his name and reputation, it grew more reckless with every passing moment. After everything that had happened since they'd set out from Redtown, Scarlett knew that the pirate's closest and oldest companion was the only one capable of quelling his rising tide of revenge.

"Aye," Big Rig said. "It's folly. He knows it, too." A thick dwarven hand squeezed Scarlett's shoulder. "Let me try." The quartermaster approached the helm.

Scarlett and Marian exchanged a look of uncertainty as the *R.I.P. Tide* bore down on them.

"Can we reach the mists?" Marian asked.

"I don't know," she said, voice hesitant. Scarlett checked the pursuing frigate. The ship hadn't closed the distance, but it hadn't lost any ground either. To her left, the two naval vessels had split and spread out, closing the route of escape southward. The gnome swung her head right. Mayrotten Island's shoreline left no means to run heading north. She didn't have enough sailing knowledge to determine if they could outrun the galleon and vanish into the mists before it intercepted them.

"Captain," Big Rig said.

"Rig, get Lana to put a line of sea elves on the port railing," Trusty Jack said. "Keep us out of range as long as you can. We'll hit her with arrows on the cross, then come around her stern and—"

"Jack!" Big Rig's voice held an authority Scarlett had not encountered during their time at sea. Thicker and bolder, it resonated as if meant to traverse a mountain chasm. "This is not the time to do this, lad." The dwarf's voice dimmed to its usual volume and tone. "Not with the Navy out there and certainly not with our commitment to those on our ship."

"Not your call, mate."

"With all respect, Jack. It's not yours, either."

"I'm the bloody captain!"

The quartermaster shook his head, the wrinkles on his face creasing. "You leave me no choice. First Mate Luholi!" Big Rig shouted.

Scarlett understood enough nautical protocol by now to grasp that something official and serious had been set in motion.

"We're not engaged yet, Jack," the dwarf said, as Lana arrived at his side.

"What exactly are you gettin' at?" The pirate's grip on the wheel tightened.

Big Rig puffed his chest. "I'm saying this isn't your call, Captain. This warrants a collective decision." The quartermaster turned to *Lady Luck's* first mate. "Lana, are we currently engaged with the enemy?"

The half-orc looked to the galleon. "No, we are not."

"Then I am calling it to a vote," Big Rig said. "Pirate code's in play."

Thank the gods, Scarlett thought.

"Captain intends to engage the buccaneer's galleon... along with the Navy frigates," Big Rig said to Lana. "I respectfully disagree. We should run for the mists. We cannot win this fight, and we have a standing commitment to our fellow passengers that takes priority." A thick dwarven hand gestured in her direction. "What say ye, First Mate?"

"I'll need to consult the crew."

"There's no time, Lana," Big Rig said. "Per the code, you need to represent them based on existing knowledge of our mission."

Scarlett examined the half-orc. The former monk had already mustered herself for battle. Her pre-fight juices were flowing, veins bulging in her neck and eyes surging with bloodlust.

Come on, Lana, she begged. *Don't be a fool.*

The half-orc stared at the approaching galleon. Her eyes shifted to the pursuing frigates, and finally, Mayrotten Island. The first mate's brawny green frame rotated and faced the mists.

"Agreed, Quartermaster," Lana said. "Ain't a winnable fight, Cap. All due respect. Plus, we should honor our existing pact. On behalf of the crew, I support the quartermaster."

"Scupper all of it!" Trusty Jack spun the wheel back to their broad reach run and the flight to the mists.

Big Rig jumped onto the helm and righted the ship as Lana shouted out orders to trim the sails.

Scarlett followed the pirate's long strides as he stomped his way aft, muttering under his breath.

"James?" Marian said as he passed.

"Not now," Trusty Jack grumbled.

"Don't look like good odds, Rig," Lana said, eyes going from the *R.I.P. Tide* to the mist wall and back to the black galleon.

"No, it don't, lass," Big Rig said, working the helm.

Scarlett checked on Trusty Jack.

The pirate stood on the stern deck, spyglass aimed at the *R.I.P. Tide.*

She scurried up the stairs.

"You better get below deck, lass." He snapped the telescope shut. "It's nothing personal; it's for your safety."

"Jack, I can help."

"I know you can. And something tells me you will, despite that order." The pirate checked their course. "*R.I.P. Tide's* got the wind, and at the rate she's sailing, even if we make the mists without engaging, they'll be raining arrows on us as we pass." His jaw muscles tightened. "Make sure you stay close to something that can shield you."

Scarlett had marked potential shelters on deck, both forward and aft, as soon as they departed Benevolence. Call it a Thieves Guilder's way of moving into a new home. Identifying exits, potential hiding spots, blind points for sneak attacks... those were her profession's equivalent of a sailor's pre-departure rituals or a healer's prepping of spell pouches before setting off for the sick ward.

"And if we're boarded?" she asked.

Trusty Jack raised an eyebrow. "Chaos. You'll need to keep one eye on the opponent in front of you and one on everything about you... and above you as well." He aimed a finger up at the masts and sails. "It's a balance of melee and evasion, along with a hearty dose of luck."

That gave her pause. Most of her skills resided in tracking, infiltration, and pilfering with a focus on solitary targets. The idea of a tempest of combatants, on a confined deck with all sorts of obstacles, and the ship heeling, sent an uneasy sense of vulnerability through her that she didn't welcome.

"Stay out of sight, lass," the pirate said. "Let us pirates take care of things if they board us. You'll know when it's comin'. Grappling hooks and ropes will sound. Or," Trusty Jack's face grew earnest, "it may be magic."

Captain Pitch. She bit her lip. It was worrisome enough to have a ship over two times the size of *Lady Luck* chasing them down, but add in a powerful sorcerer with the strength and size of an ogre? Her hand went to her vest pocket. *Only as a last resort,* she promised herself.

"They're pulling bows, Captain!"

The pirate turned at the warning from the sea elf in the crow's nest. "Get to cover!" He dashed off.

Scarlett ducked behind a crate halfway between the main mast and the stairs to the poop deck.

"Brace!" a sailor shouted.

The twangs of arrows penetrating the deck mixed with the pitter patter of shafts deflecting off surfaces. One scream punctuated the first movement of the nautical combative symphony.

Lady Luck rolled on the swells, determined and intent on speed and haste. A tingle of moisture cooled her cheeks as they edged closer to the mists. She guessed it would be no more than five minutes until they vanished inside the ominous magical fog.

"It's no good, Jack." Big Rig's voice reached her ears. "They're comin' broadside."

"Aye, bring us about. Let's try and skirt the hooks," Jack responded, a bit closer to her position.

"Coming about!"

That's Lana, she thought. Roles were adjusting under combat conditions.

Her back to the crate, Scarlett eased the pressure of her feet pressing into the deck as the heeling ship swung around. Like a shadow, the gnome slid around the box, shielding herself on the opposite side in response to the change in course.

"Blades at the ready, hearties!" Trusty Jack shouted. "Cut the lines when the hooks land!"

The hiss of projectiles reached her gnomish ears.

Clank! Clank! Clank!

Scarlett planted her palms on the deck for additional ballast as the ship leaned from the pull on its hull.

"Cut em' free!" Jack's voice echoed above a crescendo of shouts from what she knew were enemy pirates from the *R.I.P. Tide* running parallel to them.

Bows twanged.

A chorus of pitter patters sounded as shafts landed on deck.

"Board em' lads!"

Scarlett's muscles tightened at the sound of the dreadful voice. *Captain Pitch.*

Thumps of feet landing on deck.

Shouts and cheers.

The clang of clashing steel.

Death cries.

Crack!

Silver light flashed to her right. A scorching line smoldered along the wooden deck. Three sea elves from *Lady Luck's* crew sizzled, their corpses charred and smoking.

Scarlett peeked at the mayhem. The half-ogre captain stood in black leathers decorated with stark white bones. At least three heads taller than the half-orcs supporting her, she stood out like a queen among pawns. Her anatomy was like mashed potatoes sculpted into a thick and lumpy mass of flesh and bone. Pitch's half-orc blood was evident in her angular brow and tusks, but the rest of the sorcerer looked like coarse mud hardened into an intimidating menace. Worst of all, to Scarlett, were the braids that fell down her back from under her tricorne. Swarms of flies circled them, drawn to the sorcerer's sinister magic.

Captain Pitch raised her skull-tipped staff and aimed it across deck.

Scarlett tracked to her target: Big Rig at the helm! She rolled out into the open and flung a dagger.

The sorcerer arced her body and grunted as the blade dug into the back of her thigh. She dropped to a knee, head swinging left and right in search of the source.

Scarlett ducked back behind the crate.

"Bloody tricksters!" the sorcerer shouted.

Jack had been right. It was chaos. The entire deck was a frenzy of combat.

She chanced a second look.

The legendary captain of *Lady Luck*, who had climbed halfway up the mast, drew his cutlass and leaped in the air. His free hand caught a rope rigged through a pulley and he descended, boots landing with a thud in front of the sorcerer.

"Well, well, well." Pitch yanked the dagger from her thigh and tossed it aside. "If it ain't an old man thinkin' he's still a pirate worthy of his salt." The wicked captain of the *R.I.P. Tide* stood, teetering from the injury to her leg.

Trusty Jack dropped into a sword fighting stance and thrust his blade. Pitch parried with her staff and struck him on the cheek.

The pirate staggered, dazed.

"You're an old man now, mate. You should be ashore." She swept low to take out his feet.

Jack jumped over the staff and spun, swiping his cutlass across Pitch's chest. The blade rattled the bones on her leathers but failed to penetrate the black armor.

"Ship's free!" the sea elf in the crow's nest shouted.

Scarlett wanted to be relieved, but even with the galleon drifting away, the handful of crew from the vessel and their captain fighting onboard left her full of dread.

She peered over the rails, seeking the naval frigates. The lead ship was closing, but still a fair distance behind them. The other two had dropped sails and were holding position.

Crack!

Pitch shot a bolt from her staff at Trusty Jack, who rolled out of the way and came up with a one-two slash combination. The sorcerer went to dodge but stumbled from the leg injury and Jack's second swing slashed her free arm, sending blood across his cotton shirt.

"Ain't that slow yet you bilge rat!" *Lady Luck's* captain reset his stance. "You're gonna—"

The pirate tumbled as a barrel collided with his torso.

"Jack!" Scarlett dashed closer behind a post.

"You're insulting my prize!" Pitch cracked the half-orc who had tossed the barrel with her staff. "Leave him to me, idiot!" The sorcerer sent a swift kick to Trusty Jack's ribs, sending him off his knees. The butt of her staff came down into his gut.

Scarlett winced at hearing the pirate's cry of pain.

"Ain't even started in on you yet, mate," Pitch said.

Jack struggled to rise, gasping. His knees gave out and he collapsed back onto the deck.

"I'll take the ship and then deal with you, Captain Hawk." The skull at the top of the sorcerer's staff sparked to life. Captain Pitch snickered and aimed the glowing weapon at Big Rig.

Scarlett reached into her pocket. Her fingertips landed on her last resort. Without it, they would have no way to get through the magic barrier and enter the tomb on Dragon Tail Island. That meant no dragon's blood. *Unless we survive this*, she thought, *none of it matters*.

She withdrew the scroll and unfurled the parchment. Stepping out from behind the crate, she read the spell's elegant script aloud, summoning its magic. The inked letters came to life, glowing red.

A bolt of lightning shot from the sorcerer's staff.

With a poof the scroll vanished. Like a comet, a majestic eagle shot from between her hands. As if crossing a "t" with a feather quill pen, the magical bird of prey snatched Pitch's lightning bolt with its beak as if it were a snake.

"What in the blazes?" the half-ogre captain shouted.

Scarlett pulled her eyes from the bird's flight up and away from the ship.

The *R.I.P. Tide's* captain homed in on her. "Well, what have we here?"

Scarlett froze, paralyzed by the sorcerer's wicked gaze.

"A gnome with pesky daggers and fancy scrolls?" Pitch's staff came alive, sparking with deadly light. "I'll cook yer hide and eat it for—"

"Argh!" The curving tip of Trusty Jack's cutlass poked through the half-ogre's chest.

Pitch dropped to her knees, the staff falling from her hand.

Jack lifted a leg and kicked the sorcerer's back, freeing his blade and sending her face first onto *Lady Luck's* deck.

"That's for Ashana, you lily-livered scurvy dog," the pirate growled.

⚓

"BOUNTY ON YER HEAD'S HIGHER THAN A CROW'S NEST, JACK." THE half-ogre cackled as she lay splayed out on her back. Blood from the open wound saturated the stark white bones decorating her leathers.

Big Rig brought *Lady Luck* about amidst the mayhem on deck. Jack's boot stopped the sorcerer from rolling overboard on the heeling ship.

Captain Pitch reached for her staff, wincing from the pain of the mortal chest wound.

Trusty Jack lifted his boot and brought it down on her warty, rough-skinned forearm, halting her from seizing the magical weapon. "A high price on my head?" he said. "For breaking out of Longshore?" He pointed the tip of his cutlass at the sorcerer's face. "Guess I've built me quite the reputation of late."

"That ain't the half of it, mate." Pitch's bulbous and sickly eyes locked on Marian.

Jack glanced at the mage, who ducked behind a crate to avoid an arrow from the nearby *R.I.P. Tide*. She shook her head to indicate she had no idea what Pitch referred to.

"You don't know do you, lass?" Captain Pitch coughed blood. "Oh, that's a treasure, that is." Jack's nemesis laughed through the gurgling liquid rising in her throat.

Shouts and battle raged around them on deck as sea elves fought the last of the *R.I.P. Tide's* crew.

"Kill her now, Jack!" Big Rig shouted from the helm, ducking an arrow. "There's no time!"

"Know what, Pitch?" Trusty Jack let the tip of his blade push against the skin under the pirate's lumpy, grotesque chin. "You talkin' about the storm you brewed to take down *Endurance*?"

"Aye, I done that and I would bloody well do it again, I would. But that ain't it." The half-ogre's fists clenched from the pain of the cutlass wound. "I'm going to Davy Jones Locker, I am..." she grinned. "I'll be taking the other secret with me."

"Out with it!" Jack put his boot on her chest wound.

Pitch's scream of pain morphed into mortal laughter, her imminent demise undeniable. "Oh, that is sweet irony, that is..." The sorcerer let her head roll over to view the *R.I.P. Tide*. "Looks like you lost this one, mate," she said. "I ain't makin' it, but neither will you."

Jack glanced out to sea. They'd managed to gain some distance after repelling the broadside but random arrows still crossed the water. A ship that size had at least one squad of longbows and they were sending potshots. He checked their course and the wind. *The bloody rat is right*, he thought. *R.I.P. Tide* was coming around and had the weather gauge. *Lady Luck* was cut off. The battering ram on the galleon's prow would drive right into them and sink them.

Captain Pitch's breathing grew labored. Jack followed a line of blood that ran like a pioneering river across *Lady Luck's* deck.

"Speak, you scurvy dog!" Jack's frustration usurped his anger and he slashed the cutlass, slicing the sorcerer's ear clean off.

The sorcerer's gnarly and wart-ridden face rolled back toward him, seemingly numb to the pain. "The dead tell no tales."

The half-ogre's fingers loosened their grip, her clenched fists easing. With a final rasp, the massive body went limp.

"Bloody nonsense!" The pirate kicked the corpse for good measure.

"Jack," Marian said, peering over the crate. "I—"

The galleon bore down on them. He couldn't find the words for what he wanted to say, so he just looked in her eyes.

"Something's happening!" Scarlett dodged a pair of pirates engaged with blades and ran forward holding the Dragon Tail Compass. "It's vibrating."

"Brace!" Big Rig shouted. "Brace for impact!"

"We need to hunker down," Jack told them. "That ship's going to hit us and—"

Whoosh!

A cluster of tentacles burst from the deep. Jack dove, grabbing Scarlett at the waist and throwing her to safety alongside Marian behind the crate.

An ominous groan, as if the sea itself had been disturbed from slumber, boomed across the water.

Jack dared to peek over the crate. Titanic suction-cupped limbs spiraled around the galleon's masts. As *Lady Luck* drifted into the mists, he caught glimpses of the enemy ship smashing and breaking as the beast squeezed its hull.

"To port! To port!" Big Rig's shout was nearly drowned out by the groans of the monster and the screams of the *R.I.P. Tide's* crew.

"Blimey." Jack recognized the fleshy fangs that broke the surface at the center of a slimy and bulbous head. "'Tis another like the creature from Mayrotten harbor!"

Scarlett joined him, peering over the crate.

Jack's head went from the galleon to *Lady Luck's* sails.

"What is it?" Scarlett said amidst the mayhem.

"Reverse course!" Trusty Jack cried out. "Rig!" He pointed. "To starboard!"

The quartermaster looked up and nodded understanding.

Marian gasped. "Gods, it's going to hit us."

The beast yanked and tore at the galleon, dragging it in an arcing collision course with *Lady Luck*.

"Come on, lass," Jack said, encouraging his sloop to rotate clear of the approaching ship. "Turn."

Sea elves dropped their weapons and did all they could to address the sails and rigging, following the quartermaster's order.

"It ain't going to work." Jack slammed a fist on the crate. "Bollocks all!" He scanned about, seeking another solution.

Marian stood and made for the stern.

"Marian!" If Jack had it right, the collision would be to the rear of the sloop.

Scarlett dashed off, joining the healer.

Bloody fools! he thought and followed. "Marian, get to the front of the ship. What in the blazes—" The now familiar spell pouch in the mage's hand told him all he needed to know. As much as he wanted to lift her up and dash for the bow, he reached for a coiled rope. Tying it off on a post, he wrapped a safety loop over Scarlett and himself. "I'll grab her when it's time," he said to the gnome, "I won't let her go overboard."

As soon as the words left his mouth, the *R.I.P. Tide's* hull snapped in half, sending a deafening crack over the sea. The galleon's back portion swung around, still gripped by the beast, making directly for them.

Marian stood fast, speaking inaudible words.

What are you doing, lass! he thought.

Cobalt light sparked from her fingertips.

Goosebumps ran up his neck as the air chilled.

The mage's index finger flowed in a graceful circle, pointing at the water between *Lady Luck's* stern and the approaching broken hull of the galleon gripped by the monstrous kraken.

"Look!"

Jack followed where Scarlett was pointing over the side. A chasm was forming in the sea, surrounded by swirling and churning water.

"I don't believe it." The pirate looked at the helm. "Keep her to starboard, Rig!" If he had the calculation right, and the whirlpool grew stronger, *Lady Luck* would rotate in the opposite direction of the *R.I.P. Tide* when they both contacted the spiraling current. If luck were with them, they would miss colliding, narrowly skirting each other stern to stern.

Marian's motion grew wider, her entire arm rotating.

"Hold fast!" Jack shouted as the sloop edged the spell's boundary. He kicked the last remaining pirate from the boarding party, a vicious looking half-orc, over the side with the heel of his boot.

Lady Luck swung.

R.I.P. Tide entered the opposite edge of the swirling water. The halved hull in the grip of the kraken's tentacles shifted and began to shoot away, but the creature yanked back, holding it from rushing off with the current. The kraken pulled the broken ship across the eye of the whirlpool.

Like a sling shot, the galleon caught the closer side of the spiraling current.

"It's going to hit us!" Scarlett shouted.

Jack lunged and tackled Marian as the *R.I.P. Tide* slammed into *Lady Luck's* backside.

Screech!

"I got you, lass," he whispered, using his body as a shield over top of her.

"James," her lips were near his ear. "I—"

"I got you."

The resistance and vibrations eased. Jack stole a glance at the stern. The galleon spiraled rapidly, descending into the vortex. Flailing tentacles the size of masts writhed above it, gurgling and splashing mixed with the cracks of snapping wood.

And then, silence.

"You alright, lass?"

"Yes." Marian's breath was hot at his neck.

"What did you do?" Scarlett asked.

Jack stood and helped Marian to her feet.

The mage wiped her hands on her robe. "An energy funnel. I wasn't sure it would work at sea. It's usually done with atmospheric elements on land."

"Jack..." Scarlett said his name as if it stretched over time.

The pirate turned as the lead naval ship, no more than a few hundred yards away, vanished.

The mist enveloped them.

"Rig, bring us about into the wind to assess the ship and the wounded." Jack looked around the deck. Pitch's body lay dead, surrounded by a group of sea elves. Others, from *Lady Luck* and the sorcerer's crew, were scattered about, dead or injured.

Marian hastened down to where the closest of the hurt sailors lay. She knelt and began tending to them.

An eerie silence overtook the ship.

Jack wiped sweat and blood from his forehead and squinted. He could barely see beyond the ship's railing.

Crossing the deck, his gaze met the one eye of his quartermaster. The dwarf had a strange look on his face. *Why isn't he turning?* He strode down the stairs.

"Mate, turn her into the wind," he said.

Big Rig only shook his head.

𝕏 31 𝕏

THE DEAD TELL NO TALES

࿇

Adrift.

Trusty Jack gripped *Lady Luck's* helm, as if he could still control their fate. An eerie silence had swept across the deck, broken only by the splash of the dead body of his rival pirate being tossed overboard.

Suffocating banks of fog closed about the ship. Occasional breaks in the mist exposed an empty sea enveloped in a thick gloom. Jack's pirate instincts told him the chill that ran through his blood wasn't natural; magic was at work with a dark cunning.

"Captain." Big Rig gestured for him to join him at the ship's stern.

Jack hesitated, looking about for Lana to take the wheel.

"Leave it, lad," the dwarf said. "Ain't going to make a difference."

Jack followed the quartermaster as he lumbered up the flight of steps to the poop deck. Marian, Scarlett, and Siân halted their hushed conversation, their eyes tracking his steps. He had nothing to say, and so, he said nothing.

"It's bad, lad," Big Rig said, when they reached the railing.

Jack peered over the side. The collision with *R.I.P. Tide* had torn the rudder free. Only the post and a small plank above the water line remained. *Lady Luck's* stern looked like it had been swiped by massive claws. Thankfully, the ship's structural integrity remained.

Jack sighed. "I'm all ears, Rig."

"Current's pulling us, where to, I don't know," the dwarf said. "The sooner we make repairs, the better."

Jack checked the sea along the hull. His quartermaster was right. It hadn't been palpable on deck, but a wake of bubbles trailed from *Lady Luck's* stern. "A replacement rudder is out," the pirate said. "We don't have the time. And I don't like the look of it out there." He spat over the side.

"I say we jury-rig her," Big Rig said. "Get a sail and tie some heavy objects to the cleats to keep it under. We can rope her to port and starboard stern and bridle the ship."

Jack craned his neck, checking the strip of fabric atop the main mast: no wind, only the current's motion fluttered the cloth. "It's something at least. We can't tack but we'll have about a sixty-to-eighty-degree range of motion in the direction we're heading."

The pirate waved to Scarlett who stood, dazed, at midship.

"How bad is it?" she asked, scurrying up to join them.

"It's not good, lass. What's the bearing to the island?"

Jack and Big Rig leaned in as the gnome flipped open the compass. The blood iron needle spiraled before settling to the southeast.

"Well, that's one bit of luck," Big Rig said.

"Is it?" Scarlett closed the device.

"Aye," Jack said. "We're going to jury-rig a rudder. We should be able to steer that course, or close to it."

"Lana!" Big Rig's voice boomed across the deck, echoing through the surrounding mist.

Both Jack and Scarlett glared at him.

"Sorry," the dwarf said, cringing. "I'll pass on word to keep orders to hands and ears."

"This is a right mess, ain't it, Cap?" The half-orc took the steps two at a time and stomped across the planks.

"Aye, it is. Listen up, lass. I'm putting you in charge of this here jury rig. Get some sea elves to help. We want a sail in the water for direc-tional drag. Tie some pots and pans on it to keep it under."

"On it," Lana said. "We bridling it port and starboard?"

Trusty Jack winked, thankful for his first mate's salty wisdom.

"I can take one rope myself, Cap." She curled an arm and flexed her bicep. "I'll get three of the uninjured sea elves to work the other side." She dashed off to inform the crew and start on the solution.

"Will this work?" Scarlett asked.

"It will," Big Rig said, "but it'll be slow on the response. Everything you'd do with a real rudder will take three-times as long."

"Rig," Jack said, "recruit anyone on the crew who is good with a saw and wood. Have them haul that post up and start on repairing what's left of the rudder. And mate," he put a hand on the dwarf's shoulder, "it don't have to be pretty. It just has to work."

"I don't know what you did back there, lass," he said to Scarlett as she approached. "But it was a bloody sight, it was."

"Counter magic scroll," the gnome said. An uncomfortable pause followed, where she opened her mouth to speak but no words came out.

"What is it, lass?"

"We needed that for what's to come." She shook her head. "I don't know what we'll do now."

"Aye, I'm getting used to that sentiment on this here adventure." He sighed. "One step at a time, lass."

"I'll see to the wounded with Marian," Scarlett said, her expression easing. "Do you want this?" She held out the Dragon Tail compass.

Jack eyed the device. *Do I?* He hesitated but accepted it from her tiny hand. He stared at the ornate cover as it lay in his palm. "Strange, that is," he whispered.

"It's growing stronger," she said. "As if humming but making no sound."

Big Rig took a step back, shaking his head with hands out as if to shield him from its magic.

Trusty Jack shrugged and put the compass in a pocket. At this point, it was one more thing on a long list of concerns. He scanned the view about the ship, an uneasy feeling in his bones.

His pirate senses whispered in his ear. *Something's out there.* It wouldn't be the Navy. There was no way they'd dare enter the mists. His thoughts returned to the nautical trap that ended in near disaster. And his own actions at the start of the ruse.

What in blazes was Pitch doing there with the Royal Navy?

He gripped the dwarf's shoulder, stopping him from walking off. "Listen, Rig," he said, "about what happened back there..."

The quartermaster shook his head. "Nothing to apologize for, lad. That's why we're a democracy. Can't let one of us make decisions for all. The ship under duress, withstanding. Then it's your call." He winked. "Checks and balances, mate." The quartermaster glanced down to the main deck. "They get it, lad." He nodded in the direction of the sea elves. "There's trust and honoring one's word and then there's ego. Can't let pride overshadow self-preservation."

"Well, for what's it's worth, thanks, Rig. It's good to have you at my side." He glanced over at Marian. The mage faced away from him, in an animated conversation with Siân. Jack sighed, a pang of regret tightening his belly. He had a second apology to attend to; it was a matter of when the right time would be.

"Worked out in the end, ironically," the dwarf said. "Through a twist of fate, the crew got their wish. That bilge rat captain and her ship of scurvy dogs is sunk."

"Irony's off the charts," Jack said, patting the pocket with the magic compass. "We have a bearing, but no rudder. Not the way I thought this would play out."

A rabble of sea elf voices rose amidships. One broke from the group and hustled up to the poop deck.

"What is it?" Jack asked.

"There's something out there, Captain."

I knew it.

The three ran down and joined the crew at the railing.

"I seen it or I'm a troll's uncle," a salty sailor said.

"Seen what, lad?" Trusty Jack peered out to sea.

"A ship. But mind you, not quite true, Captain."

Jack took out his spyglass and scanned the layers of fog.

"What do you mean, 'not quite true?'" Big Rig's voice was a whisper.

"It looked... well..."

"Out with it, lad," Jack said, searching the mists. "Nothing would surprise us in this bloody place."

"Ghost-like, she was."

Jack snapped the telescope shut.

"Captain." Another sailor pointed at the sea under the ship.

In the haunting waters, faint and eerie wisps of light swirled in the deep.

"By the gods," Big Rig said. "Those be sunken sailors." The dwarf's eye went cold. "We're in the sea of spirits, we are."

"Captain!" A sea elf pointed at the billowing mists. "There... wait for that patch o'fog to pass. 'Twas there again."

Jack leaned forward with the others, his naked eyes homed in on the area the sailor indicated. Greenish light flashed in the fog.

"There, Captain! Did you—"

"Aye, I saw it," Jack said. He followed its implied track, waiting for the ship to emerge from the fog bank.

They all gasped as a majestic and spectral galleon materialized a short distance from *Lady Luck*.

The ship, and all its riggings and sails, were aglow with an eerie transparent green.

"'Tis a ghost ship of legend," the dwarf whispered.

Jack's eyes tracked across the hull, the masts, and the banners. His eyes widened. *I know this ship.*

By now, everyone had joined them at the railing. Gentle splashing broke the silence as the galleon neared. With unnatural grace, it turned and lined up next to the sloop, weightless over the sea. Without aid of hand or body, a gangplank lowered.

Gasps echoed amongst the group as a ghost of a man crossed to *Lady Luck*.

"That be a Navy uniform..." Big Rig said.

"Everyone back." Trusty Jack waved to the crew and his companions. "You two stay with me," he said to Lana and Big Rig.

"You're a long way from the world of the living," the ghost captain said. Undead sprites like wisps of smoke swirled around his commodore's hat. The man's voice was a rasping echo, soulless and hollow, as if it traversed immeasurable distance to reach the ears of the living.

Jack scrutinized the officer. A navy man for sure, and a decorated seaman. *That uniform... it's old.*

"Captain Hawk of the *Lady Luck*," Jack said, nodding politely. "We've no gripe with the realm of the in-between, mercy on your souls." Like all pirates, he knew the legend. Trapped by dark magic, those under its spell had left the world of the living but were denied their final resting place. And so, they drifted as specters, left to suffer eternal unrest. "We wish only to pass to the hidden island. We mean no disturbance."

"Your very presence is a disturbance." The voice came from the gangplank. "And a most welcome one."

A ghost of a woman, her belly laden with child, and dressed in royal garb, made her way down the gangplank.

Blimey, Jack thought, the ship's identity ringing true.

"Queen Ricarda." Marian stepped forward. The mage bowed formally in front of the ghost of her aunt.

Spectral sprites danced about the woman's dress, illuminating her movements. Even beyond life, the queen's presence held a noble and elegant aura. Jack noted the resemblance to Marian's features in the spirit's eyes and angular cheekbones.

"You are not here by accident, dear niece," the former Queen of the Jewels said, her form ethereal and flowing.

Jack's mind was racing, conflicted with the horror of standing before these two ghosts and what the implications of their presence in the mists suggested.

"No," Marian said. She looked over at him, hesitating.

Jack nodded for her to continue. *By all means, lass,* he thought, stunned beyond words.

"How is it you are here, your Grace?" Marian asked. "What happened to you?"

Jack could hear the grief in the mage's words. It had been over thirty years since the queen's ship had vanished. As a boy, he had been one of the last people to see the galleon, through the very spyglass gripped in his hand.

"A tale of tragedy and woe." The queen's voice carried the same soulless sorrow as the captain. "And one that you will not take kindly to hearing, dear niece."

Marian's jaw muscles flexed as she bit down, steeling herself for her aunt's words.

"Our ship was attacked off Topaz Island," the queen said. "Despite Commodore Henlop's best efforts, we were taken by force."

"By whom?" Marian asked.

"Captain Pitch," Jack said, putting it together. "Commanding the *R.I.P. Tide.*"

"Indeed," the ghost commodore said. "We were taken as a prize and towed to the mists, our rudder removed along with all supplies and cargo and set adrift."

"It was the sinking of the *R.I.P. Tide* on the edge of the mists this very hour," the queen said, "that drew us here."

"Pitch did this for amusement? For..." Marian glanced toward Jack and the others. "Piracy?"

"No, dear niece." The queen shook her head. "Captain Pitch took it upon herself to gloat before sentencing us to eternal suspension."

Jack's stomach curdled. He could already guess what the queen's next words would be.

"Your father hired Captain Pitch."

Marian swayed.

Jack got to her before she went down.

"James... no."

He held her close. "I got you."

It all made sense. Everything that had happened had been part of a master plan by Markus Fitzwater to secure his family's place as the next ruling line in the Jewels. Nothing was off-limits with his ruthlessness; the man's evildoings knew no bounds.

Trusty Jack sat Marian down on a crate. "Hey." He looked her in the eyes. "This is why we're here. Why you're here. To make this right. Savvy?" He lifted her chin. "You are not your father."

The mage nodded.

"My son and I..." The queen's hand went to her belly. Ghoulish fingers passed through the surface of her dress. "We were all that stood in the way of my half-brother from inheriting the throne."

"Not all, your Grace." Scarlett stepped forward and bowed. "A Chen, who survived a similar action by the regent, is making her way to Redtown as we speak."

Marian rose. "I'm alright, James," she said and squeezed his arm in thanks. "Orla Chen will claim the right to rule and speak the ancient words at the fountain. The dragon's flames will shift hue and she will set a course for change. For a new era in the Jewels."

The queen smiled. "Even as a precocious child, you had a way about you, Marian."

"We sail to Dragon Tail Island to bring the aid and support she needs," the mage said, "to heal the pestilence from the lingering dark magic plaguing the islands, and to sway the people to end this corruption, shameful deceit, treachery and...."

Jack's eyes widened as the mage's face shifted. The panther turned furious.

"Murder."

"I cannot feel comfort, dear niece," the queen said, "not now as one of the soulless. But I remember it as a fading sensation, and your words would bring it over me now were I still alive."

"If we succeed and lift the curse from the island..." the voice was Siân's, who approached Marian. "These people will be freed from their in-between suspension; it is the same dark spell that holds them."

"How do we prove this, your Grace?" Marian asked, placing a hand on the nocsi's shoulder to acknowledge her words. "How do we present the people of Redtown with evidence of this injustice... this treason and betrayal?"

"Before Captain Pitch sent us to our fates, the sorcerer took something from me."

Jack's ears, along with Scarlett and the others, perked up.

"The Ruby Pendant," Marian said, "of the royal line."

The queen nodded. "I suspect it was meant to go to your father, to be kept hidden and secret, but the pirate desired it. Its powerful magic can be harnessed and... corrupted."

Aye, crafty, Jack thought. Pitch managed to maintain a hold over the regent and keep herself safe. *And squeeze him for who knows what over the years.* The description of the conjured storm that sunk *Endurance* and left Precious adrift flashed in his mind. The pirate sorcerer had most likely tapped additional forces with the pendant to conjure a tempest of that magnitude and terror.

"We dumped the body, Jack," Big Rig whispered. "I had the lads kick her over the side. She's in Davy Jones Locker."

"Then your proof is lost," the queen said. "Swallowed by this hallowed sea."

"Captain Hawk, sir."

Jack, along with the rest of his companions and crew, swung around.

Billy stood, arms clasped behind his back.

"What is it, lad?" Jack said.

The boy, seeing the ghosts for the first time, went sheet white.

"It's alright, Billy." The pirate strode to him and knelt. "They be spirits, aye. But not of the dead."

"What are they?" the boy whispered.

"Unfortunate souls. Cursed to a life neither living nor dead. But we can do right by them, we can. Now what's it that's got you coming out from hiding?"

The boy shook his head.

Jack grinned. He knew that look. "Oh, I see. Something tells me you're worried you'll get in trouble?"

Billy nodded emphatically.

"You have my word, boy. You've got a pass." He winked.

"Well," Billy said and made a circle over the deck with a toe, "when Mr. Riggins wasn't looking, I went over to that half-ogre captain."

"And?"

"She was just lyin' there dead and stinky. So, I went through her pockets. I heard Mr. Riggins say they were going to dump her overboard and I thought rather than let any coin go down with her..."

"What did you land, lad?"

Everyone gasped as the boy pulled out a large ruby gem dangling from a chain.

"The pendant." Marian approached and reached for the necklace.

Billy pulled his hand away. "Finder's keepers."

"Now, lad," Jack said. "You agreed to be part of this crew." He raised an eyebrow in earnest. "That means we all divide up any and all booty found amongst our brethren, per the terms."

Billy folded his arms. "I never seen no terms."

"Here's the score, lad," Big Rig said, his voice holding a quartermaster's edge. "You can keep that there necklace or you can hand it over and you'll get your finder's share *on top of* your crew share when we get back to Redtown and divide up all the gems and gold."

The boy's eyes went wide.

"Oh." Big Rig crouched down. "Did ye think we're running around in these godforsaken mists for a good time?" He winked his one good eye. "There be treasure on that cursed isle lad... chests full of it."

Billy's face glowed with desire.

Jack snorted. Aye, *he's got the pirate's curse as good as the rest of us.*

"But," the dwarf stood and shrugged, "if you want to deny us that there necklace that's your right. We'll be doing the same when it comes to the treasure on the island."

"What?"

"Can't have it both ways, lad," Lana said, joining in. "It's nothing personal, Billy. It's the pirate code."

"Fair is fair," Big Rig said and shrugged again.

Billy kicked the deck, scuffing it with his shoe in defiance. He held up the necklace and sighed, handing it over.

Jack leaned down and put a hand on the boy's shoulder. "You learned an important lesson today, Billy." Jack gestured with his hand in a wide arc, sweeping past the others around him. "We be mates, lad. Trust is built from the deck up."

"He'll be a Salty Scoundrel before long with this kind of piratin'," Lana said.

Easy lass, Jack thought. He caught Marian eyeing him, a strange parental air to her stare. "Let's not get hasty. Billy's got a full life in front of him and can make his own choices when we get back to Redtown." Pushing off his knees, Trusty Jack rose. "I do think someone's earned them a right nickname today."

The boy grinned.

"Fair Billy," Jack said to ayes of approval from the Salty Scoundrels. "One's deeds and actions define who they are, lad. You done gone and maybe saved the Jewels by playin' fair and square." He winked. "Not a bad first run at sea."

"Come close, boy." Queen Ricarda's hallowed voice sent a shiver up Jack's spine. "I can glimpse the regret that my soul might have had, seeing such a generous young man. My own child never saw the sun's light. He remains trapped here," she indicated her belly, "and never will."

Ricarda's ghostly eyes shifted and Jack found himself the focus of her stare. "You have a difficult road ahead of you, Captain. The island is close, but to reach it you must pass through the wailing wights."

A haunting silence fell over the deck. Mist passed overhead, obscuring the mast and torn sails. Jack swore the moisture formed into shapes of fell beasts and spirits.

"Captain Henlop can lead you on a safe course through the shoals, but you must stay true to yourselves against the wights. If they succeed in seducing you with their foul magic, you will join us, for we fell prey to their alluring song... and are thus doomed to roam this in-between world so long as the dark magic remains in the world."

A haunting silence fell over the group.

"Follow in our wake, avoiding the rocks," the ghostly form of Captain Henlop said, "and keep sight of us at all times."

Trusty Jack nodded, thoughts already focused on the makeshift rudder and how it would fare with such a request.

"Be resilient and defiant against temptation and terror," Queen Ricarda said. The specter drifted across the deck until she hovered before Jack's eyes.

He held her stare.

"You, most of all, Captain Hawk."

32

BATTEN DOWN THE HATCHES

❦

"Port heave!" Jack stood on the poop deck, doing his best to shout orders and keep *Lady's Luck's* prow aimed at the ghost galleon's stern.

Lana's grunt as she pulled on the rope echoed over the misty sea.

"Ease it a bit, lass," he said. *Lady Luck* drifted back on course. "That's it." Trusty Jack checked on the sea elves. The three struggled to hold the starboard line against the pull of the sea. "Keep her tight, lads."

"It's time," Big Rig said, stomping up the stairs from the main deck. Jack too, had seen the galleon signal that they were entering the shoals.

"I want everyone below deck save for you, Lana, and the elves on the rope," Jack said. "No exceptions, Rig. Have 'em batten down the hatches. Not one soul leaves the lower deck, no matter what they hear."

"Understood." The dwarf started off.

"And Rig." Jack motioned him back. "Give me your hand."

The quartermaster hesitated when he reached into his pocket.

"Come on now, muster up, mate." The pirate eyed him.

A thick hand rose and Jack slapped the compass down into the dwarf's palm. "Give that to Scarlett. If something happens to us, tell her she's got enough crew below to sail *Lady Luck* back to Redtown. And the pendant is in Marian's safe hands."

"James?"

He jumped at the sound of his name. "Blimey, lass," he said, turning. "You put the fright in me. Bad enough already out here."

"I want to stay on deck," Marian said.

"Absolutely not."

"What if something happens and one of you requires healing?"

He shook his head. "Too much relies on you. I won't risk it."

"But—"

He pointed at his tricorne. "Need I remind you that I'm the captain? That's an order."

Soft hands gripped his calloused fingers. "Be careful."

"The dead don't scare me, Marian. It's the living I fear."

"So, you're a philosopher now, too?" She smirked.

The urge to grab her close, and kiss her, lost out to discipline and respect for their pact.

"Lass, I'm sorry for the way I—"

Her finger touched his lips, silencing him. "I understand," she said, eyes sparkling.

"Don't come out, Marian. No matter what you hear, savvy?"

The mage ran a hand through her salt and pepper hair, fingers trailing through the thick and wavy strands like a fleet of ships cutting the sea. "See you afterwards." The mage walked down the steps, opened the hatch, and disappeared below.

No sooner had the top shut than a howling rose about the ship. The mist thickened and grew dark. Trusty Jack shivered. He squinted, struggling to keep sight of the galleon ahead of them.

"Rig?" The dwarf was no more than a silhouette near the main mast. "She still in your sights, lad?"

"Aye. But it's getting..."

The unfinished sentence hung in the air like a bard waiting to deliver the final words of a haunting tale.

"Cap!" Lana's head went to and fro, her grip tight on the makeshift rudder's rope.

Ghoulish merfolk swirled about the ship, their motions elegant and alluring. A seductive song, sweet as summer cherries dipped in honey, reached his ears.

"Hold fast, lads!" Big Rig shouted amidships in the gloom. "To port! To port! Shoals ahead!"

"To port, Lana!" Trusty Jack fought through the dancing specters, making his way to the half-orc to aid her in turning the ship. Mere steps from the first mate, a ghostly merfolk crossed his path.

"James..."

It was Marian. The specter whispered in his ear, words traveling to his heart.

"Come with me, James."

This is real, he thought.

"Captain, no!" Lana shouted.

"Steady on, lass." Trusty Jack leaned back as the half-orc reached for him, avoiding her grasp. "Don't you see, Lana? We're being fools, we are. This... it's *real.*"

The merfolk swirled around him, a chorus of voices adding forbidden words to the illusion. A specter's arm reached for his and he took it. The spirit led him to the railing.

"Jack, no!" Big Rig's voice cut into the dream.

Trusty Jack swung a leg up and over the rail.

"Come down, James. Down into the deep..."

Yank!

Jack crashed down on deck.

"It's the wight's call, that is!" Big Rig said, pulling him up. The dwarf shook him, hands clenched on his cotton shirt. "Snap out of it, mate!"

Blow me down, he thought, and brushed off the spell. *Lady Luck* and the harsh reality of the haunting specters returned into focus.

"Hold the ship steady," Big Rig said. "We need to keep the galleon in sight!" He dashed forward.

The howling rose to a fevered pitch. Jack looked about. A carnival of ghosts danced on deck. One passed near to him, and a flash of its face sent a deadly chill down his spine.

"No... it can't be!" He stumbled back.

Again, the specter crossed his path. This time its appearance left no doubt.

"To work with you, filth," the ghoul said, face turning into the all-too familiar orc king that had haunted his living dreams for ten years. "Torture and pain await."

Jack squeezed his eyes shut, mustering every drop of courage to stave off the trauma and memories of his time as a captive of the orc tribe. *"You remember the beatings, Jack?"* The ghoul cackled with the orc king's malicious voice. *"Work, work, work. That's all you're good for."* The hideous laugh that mocked him in his darkest hours under ball and chain deep in the southern island's foreboding jungles pierced his conscience. He screamed in horror and fell to the deck. Arms and legs scrambled backwards across the planks.

"Overboard with you...." The ghoul took on the features of the thick and muscular beast, stomping towards him, tusks dripping. *"Into the deep!"*

A flash of memories swirled... adrift on the makeshift raft after Bonnie's ruse. Storms, lightning... pitching about. The dark island. Marooned... in need of water. Hiding from the glowing eyes. And then, caught. Enslaved. Years of forced labor. Torture. Pain. Finally, opportunity. Escape... blood from his victims on his hands. More blood. More deaths. A savagery embraced to survive. And then, the skiff. He was free. Alone on the sea. Back where he'd started. Until a passing ship heading north to the Jewels... Destination: Mayrotten Island.

"Jack!" Strong, stubby hands pulled him off the deck.

Crack!

His cheek stung with pain.

"Snap out of it!"

The pirate focused his eyes. Big Rig stood before him.

"We're off course!" The dwarf pointed ahead.

Trusty Jack's eyes went wide at what lay in their path. "Shoals!" he shouted, coming back to his life, his role as captain, and his charge over the others. "To starboard!" The galleon lay three ship lengths off the right side of the railing, sailing away. Through the swirling voices and dancing merfolk, a cluster of rocks and broken water loomed dead ahead.

Lady Luck eased to port, aiming further into the dense cluster of rock-filled waters.

"No!" Big Rig pushed him aside and made for the stern. Two of the sea elves crewing the rope had released their grip. They stood on the rails, teetering, ghoulish wights caressing their faces. In unison, both sailors jumped overboard and vanished into the darkened deep. The third elf struggled against the pull of the sea, but it was too much for her alone. She flew over the stern, unable to hold the line.

Trusty Jack lunged for the remaining lead. The rope shot across the deck toward the sea. He snatched the knotted end inches before it went over the railing.

"Hold it, lad!" Big Rig shouted.

The rope eased as the quartermaster yanked from above his grip and brought in more line.

"Let some out, Lana!" Jack shouted, struggling to aim the ship to starboard. He glanced through the dancing wights. The galleon had vanished in the mists.

"We're done for!" Big Rig said.

"Heave!" Trusty Jack shouted.

The two struggled.

The rope resisted.

Jack glanced back.

They were on a direct course for the rocks. Once the hull hit the angular boulders, they were sunk.

"Rope's caught!" Big Rig peered through the railing.

Jack pulled but there was nothing for it. "We need Lana's strength!"

The half-orc fought off a pair of wights, swatting with her free hand and cursing while holding the line. When she saw them struggling, she made for them.

"No!" Both he and Big Rig shouted through the chaos. "Stop!"

Lana halted in time to keep enough line in play so as not to lose the canvas to the sea.

"We're doomed, lad." Big Rig shook his head.

"Bollocks, mate!" Trusty Jack pulled, one final futile attempt. He fell over backwards. "Heave, Rig! It's free!"

The two yanked on the line, working to correct the ship's course. Tiny fingers emerged from under the row of rails, gripping the deck. A small hand reached up and grabbed a post, pulling upward.

Billy's face appeared.

"Get out of here, lad!" The pirate shouted. "Get back below!"

Billy struggled up and onto the railing. Just as he was atop the post about to drop on deck, *Lady Luck* grazed a rock. The hull shook like a small earthquake.

"Billy!" Jack shouted.

Through the screams of wights, he watched as the boy splashed into the sea.

"No!" Jack tumbled to his left as something pushed him aside. A blur of gray fur arced into the air, lunging overboard.

Siân!

He and Big Rig heaved.

Lady Luck turned.

Jack checked the shoals. They were running parallel to the rocks. The pirate and his quartermaster pulled hand over hand, holding tight to continue the ship's rotation. He peered overboard. A mass of merfolk had surrounded the nocsi, who treaded water, holding the boy. With every passing second, the two drifted farther from the ship.

"Billy!" Jack shouted, desperate to do something. "Siân!"

He locked eyes with the nocsi, who nodded slightly as if in farewell. An unworldly glow rose in the bard's eyes.

What's she doing?

The bard lifted Billy out of the water, paws holding him over her head.

Boom!

Jack flew across the deck and tumbled down the stairs, crashing into a stack of crates near the main mast.

He shook off the fall from the psionic blast and stood. The rush of sudden motion sent dizzy waves through his body and he stumbled. He focused his eyes on the passing shoals. The ship was moving... fast!

"Siân!" Big Rig shouted from the stern, searching left and right. The dwarf tied off the line. "Siân!"

Jack dashed up the stairs.

"I got him, Cap!" Lana said, holding Billy on her bicep like a tree branch. "Caught him clean out of the air!" She kept the port line tight with her free hand.

Jack peered overboard. The wights, the shoals, and the thick mists drifted away from the ship.

The nocsi was nowhere to be seen.

"Where is she, Rig?" Trusty Jack searched the cursed waters in desperation. The nocsi was the best swimmer he'd ever seen. *She'll make it.*

A thick hand gripped his arm. "Jack, lad."

The pirate followed the dwarf's gaze down into the murky depths. Siân's body descended, pulled down by the hands of ghoulish wights.

Trusty Jack took off his tricorne and held it at his chest, lament and sorrow rising like a tide.

He glanced over at Billy. "What in blazes got into you, boy?"

"I was hidin' in your quarters, like I was told," the boy said. "Out the window I seen the rope caught on the leaden frame." He lowered his gaze. "Don't be angry, Mr. Hawk, but I had to break the glass to get out and pull it loose."

"Angry? Scupper that, lad. You done saved us," Trusty Jack said. "And, Siân saved you." He nodded in the direction of the deep. "Pirates true. Both of you."

"Aye," Lana and Big Rig said, heads bowed in the calming seas.

"She'll never be forgotten," Trusty Jack said. *We'll tell your tale, Siân,* he thought. *It'll be worthy of the highest verse.*

Lana lifted her head and gasped.

"What is it?" Jack had never seen the half-orc's eyes so wide.

She pointed behind him.

"Shiver me timbers," he whispered, turning. "Dragon Tail Island."

33

X MARKS THE SPOT

Scarlett wrapped her cloak about her. The ominous sight off *Lady Luck's* bow sent a gloomy chill deep into her bones.

Dragon Tail Island, she thought, taking in the baleful destination that had consumed her waking hours and haunted her nightmares, for over a year. It wasn't an island, so much as an islet—stacks of craggy black rocks jutting from the sea. Mist swirled around its rising peak like lingering smoke. With the shoreline in sight, she knew why the island was so named. A jetty extended in a wide spiral, creating an artificial cove. The rocks diminished in scale as they curved to a small tip, forming what looked like a dragon's tail.

"Now that we're here, I am not sure this was a good idea."

Scarlett nodded at Marian's words but kept her eyes on the approaching island.

Lady Luck glided through the entrance between the jetty's narrow tip and the steeper black rocks along the opposite side of the cove.

Big Rig called for the crew to drop anchor, his voice bouncing off the surrounding stones.

"We'll row ashore," Trusty Jack said, joining them. The pirate pointed to stairs carved from the living rock that rose straight out of the sea.

Scarlett followed the steps until her eyes came to rest on a shimmering archway flush with the island's black stone. "I have bad news," she said, willing herself to face the pirate and the healer. "According to my sources, legend speaks of an ancient magic blocking the chamber's entrance. I used the scroll that was our one chance to dispel it in the fight with the *R.I.P. Tide*. I'm sorry. I should have said something earlier, but—"

"Aye, that is a lack of social tact, isn't it Marian?"

"Yes, James." The mage's lips tightened, as if holding back a smile. "Quite unbecoming of our gnome friend."

Scarlett furled her brow at the sarcastic and oddly lighthearted exchange.

The pirate withdrew a scroll and unrolled it, his eyes going back and forth from the island's shore to the page.

"What is that?" she asked. From her height and angle, she couldn't read the parchment.

"Oh this?" Trusty Jack said. "'Tis an ancient map. Copied from an original long ago. It has some diagrams, a few phrases and instructions... that kind of thing." He winked. "Strangely enough, there's also an 'X' that marks the spot."

Marian's resistance broke and she smiled.

"You have a *map*!" The gnome snatched it from his hand. *By the gods,* she thought, eyes running over the parchment. A crude version of the island, with instructions of how to enter the chamber were scribed in an elegant and fading ink. *And blow* me *down.* The pirate wasn't lying. Right there in the center of what looked like the tomb, was a literal "X" marking the spot.

"I don't understand," she said, handing it back. "How? When?"

"We all have our secrets, lass." He grinned, rolling up the map. "You can bet your last pence I wasn't sailing to this curse-ridden isle without knowing what I was getting into..."

"You've had this all along?" Her cheeks grew hot. *How dare he?*

"Not all along. Retrieved it in Benevolence. Quite the outing that was." Trusty Jack smiled at Marian, who reciprocated and blushed.

"But it had been in my possession since way back when *Lady Luck* was first lost." The pirate's calloused hand came to rest on her shoulder. "Precious kept it safe all these years. I gave it to the lass before Bonnie boarded *Lady Luck*."

"You knew at Mayrotten Island... in The Dreg?" Scarlett said, more to herself than to the pirate.

"Aye. You've kept your secrets too, Scarlett Tanash. Ain't no denying that. Them nighthawks and albatrosses flying about sending secret messages here and there. And, I've kept mine." He thumbed his chest. "What matters is between the two of us, we've made it here." He sighed, eyeing the island. "Not without losses... hard ones. Now, it's time to get this done."

"Pirates and thieves." Scarlett shook her head. "Two sides of the same coin."

"Here's hoping there's a lot of coins in that there tomb." The pirate licked his lips in a show of a lusty appetite for treasure. "Rig!" he barked.

The dwarf lumbered up to the bow.

"Everyone stays on board *Lady Luck* except the four of us and Lana."

"Understood." The quartermaster nodded. "The lads will get to work on that rudder post-haste. And I'll put a sailor on Fair Billy. Don't want him setting foot on that island."

"Wise, that is," the pirate said. "Have them teach him to play bones."

Scarlett followed the dwarf, who led them to the rope ladder down to the dinghy.

"Knowing the boy's luck," Big Rig said, as he offered Scarlett a hand, "his pockets will be full-up by the time we're back."

Scarlett stared at the uninviting island. *If we come back.*

⚜

SCARLETT GAZED UP AT THE SHIMMERING WALL THAT WAS THE entrance to the tomb. "It's odd," she said, holding a tiny hand out, careful not to touch the surface. "It looks like glass."

"The ward is source magic," Marian said, examining the archway. The mage pointed at a set of designs that Scarlett recognized as elven symbols. "It's an ancient binding that can't be broken by non-divines, unless they possess the words and gesticulations of the original spell." The mage held out her hand for the map.

Scarlett hadn't yet shaken off her surprise at the turn of events.

Judging by how Marian reviewed the parchment, the thief discerned that she had studied it closely beforehand.

Much afoot between these two, she thought, eyeing the pirate.

Ghoulish bands of mist clung to the surrounding rocks, blanketing the island in a dim and endless dusk. As if called forth by a charmer's music, slithers broke free and snaked through the group standing at the entrance to the tomb.

"I don't like this one bit," Big Rig said, looking down at the serpentine fog between his legs.

Scarlett glanced back. A porthole here... a railing there... and the top of the mast poking through the magical shroud, were the only signs that *Lady Luck* lay anchored in the shallows.

"Here goes nothing," Marian said, taking a step closer to the archway.

"Alright, mates. Let's all get back." Trusty Jack's strong arms guided everyone down a few steps.

"Keep your eyes open for trouble," he said to Lana and Big Rig and stepped up to join Marian.

"Asilar..." The mage's hand moved in elegant swirling motions. "Hanatha..." Her fingers twisted in a strange configuration. She swept her hand left and up. "Li-requi..." Keeping to the same finger positions, she emphasized a downward motion. "Yilan." This time her hand went right, index finger switching from up to down. "Ka-tá." Both hands rose overhead and with a slow arcing motion, the mage formed a semi-circle around her until her arms came to rest at her sides.

Scarlett, like everyone else, held her breath.

The gentle lapping of the sea against the black stairs broke the haunting silence.

"Nothing's happening," Jack whispered.

"I don't understand," Marian said, re-reading the words inscribed on the parchment.

Scarlett bit her tongue, not wanting to say it out loud. Had they any way of knowing the map was authentic?

"Try it again, lass," Trusty Jack said.

Marian repeated the ritual. Again, nothing happened.

"I know my ancient elven," the mage said. "I'm speaking the lines as written."

Scarlett stepped up and joined them, craning her neck to examine the arch. "What are those symbols?" She pointed at a series of designs carved between the words.

"Decorations, I assume," Marian said. "Filling the empty spaces."

"Each one is different. Let me see the map."

Marian passed it to her.

Scarlett scrutinized the verses, her eyes travelling from the page to the arch and back again. "These," she pointed to the decorative symbols between the lines on the parchment, "are the same as those." Her finger aimed at various symbols separating the words over the entrance.

"Aye," the pirate muttered. "You're on to something there, lass."

Marian took back the map, eyes running over it.

"Try it again," Scarlett said, her thieving mind's penchant for puzzles gaining momentum. "Speak each of the words on the arch at the end of each line of the spell with the coordinating symbol."

The mage uttered the now familiar incantations while her hands moved in the associated patterns. Scarlett recognized the new inclusions at the end of each line. Marian's arms made their slow arcing motion, and again she rested her hands at her sides.

"Rish-osar." The mage spoke the final word from the archway.

An eerie silence fell over the group.

Nothing, Scarlett thought. *We made it all the way here and—*

"*Halith*..." an ethereal voice whispered.

Scarlett's jaw dropped. Unlike the ghostly words of the specters in the mist, this had a calm and welcoming tone.

"*Ilan-tá.*"

Marian grabbed Trusty Jack's arm as the icons on the arch glowed bright as the morning sun. For a moment, Scarlett was certain a face passed over the entrance, elvish in features with long, flowing blonde hair.

"Now that's a sight I ain't never seen," the pirate whispered as the boundary dissipated.

"We're in!" Lana rubbed her hands and stomped up the stairs to the entrance. "I've been practicing my countin', Rig." She giggled. "Working on me thousands." The half-orc pushed past Scarlett. "You think it'll be in the thousands, Cap? The gold, I mean?"

Trusty Jack blocked her with his arm like a ship's beam.

"Easy there, lass. Slow and steady we're takin' this. Our thief's going first."

Scarlett stepped up and, feeling bold and rather excited by the prospect of achieving their goal, passed through Lana's legs to chuckles from Big Rig and Jack.

"Keep me in sight," she said, taking out her glow stone. "Let me see that map."

The pirate handed it to her and she marked it to memory before offering it back.

"Come on, let's go get ourselves the dragon blood." She nodded at the half-orc. "And a pile of treasure." *And then get off this island as quickly as we can*, she thought and scurried down the musty steps.

Scarlett slipped down the stairs in silence, hand dragging along the cold stone wall. She felt like a thief in her element again. *Well, at least the sneaking part*. As for *where* she was, no one back at the guild would ever believe it. A pang of regret accompanied the thrill running through her veins. *Doni would have loved being here...*

The passage descended with strict precision into the heart of the island. No turns.

"There's shadows ahead," she whispered, turning back to send her voice up the steps. Using her glow stone, she edged her fingers apart, allowing small cracks to pass light through and guide her descent.

Click.

She froze.

Moving only her eyes, she scanned around her foot. Her fingers edged apart, risking a fraction of light. With the patience of a tortoise, her neck rotated so she could examine the step's surface.

Crafty, she thought, the slight bulge running at its middle to the opposite wall undeniable.

"You alright down there, lass?" The pirate's question echoed off the ancient stone walls.

"That's a matter of interpretation," she said. "Don't come down. Give me a moment." Her hand went to a pocket, fingers finding the one grindle-windle marble she had left. "I wanted to keep this to remember you, Doni," she whispered. "Sorry, but I need it."

She tossed it down the steps.

Bounce after bounce, it descended.

"Come on," she said, urging it on. She needed it to hit one of the bulges and—

Like a clap of thunder, a shock wave blew past her and rushed up the steps. Dust fell from the ceiling and she sneezed but managed to maintain pressure on the step's trigger.

"Lass?"

"I'm alright!" she shouted, peering around as the view cleared.

An otherworldly glow of ancient magic pulsed in the corridor below. The walls shimmered with what looked like some kind of enchanted broken glass.

"That would have been unpleasant," she said, and pushed harder on the trigger under her foot to make sure it didn't happen in her section of the corridor.

Scarlett aimed the glow stone around, examining the walls and ceiling. "Where are you? Damn the elves of old and their cleverness." She let her head fall back and sighed in exasperation. The ceiling two slabs back came into view. Relief washed over her.

"There you are," she said. "Hey! I need help," she shouted. "Send down Lana and..." she gauged the height overhead, "Big Rig."

"Get down there, mates."

The pirate's words bounced off the stone walls.

Scuffling echoed down the stone passage.

"What was that?" Big Rig asked as the two neared.

Scarlett held up a hand. "Do *not* take another step." She twisted her neck and made out the edge of the half-orc's hulking frame two stairs up. "Lana, I need you to put Big Rig on your shoulders and hoist him up to the ceiling."

"You need her to do what?" the dwarf said. "Isn't there some other way to—"

"Quiet!" Her order bounced through the chamber. "Sorry, just... do what I say or you can forget about treasure and any other—"

"We're listening lass," Big Rig said. "Go on."

"Do you see that small bulge in the ceiling a third of the way over to the wall?" She pointed up and to her right.

"Aye, of course," the dwarf said. "Been annoying me since we got down to you. How anyone could craft a stone tomb and leave an imperfection like that and—"

"Big Rig, please..."

"Steady on, mate," Lana said. "Let Scarlett talk."

A dwarvish grumble reached her ears.

"When Lana hoists you up. I want you to push it."

"The stone?"

"Yes. It's an elven pass-safe switch for the trap."

"Right," the half-orc said. "Come on, Rig. Get up on me shoulders."

Grunting ensued, followed by mumbles and curses.

"Hold me steady!" Big Rig barked.

"I got you, mate. No worries."

"You're wobbling back and forth like you done had too much grog."

"Bollocks! If I had too much grog I'd be swaying like this."

Big Rig uttered several phrases that challenged even the most gutter-talking thieves in Drakeland's sewers.

"Are you ready?" Scarlett asked.

"Aye. Pushing it now."

Clangs and screeches, as if machinery had been re-started after an age, boomed and echoed inside the stone walls. When it went silent again, Scarlett checked the step.

The bulge was no more.

"Good job, thank you. You can put him down, Lana."

"Easy!" Big Rig shouted. "I'm not a cask of grog!"

Thunk.

Strong fingers gripped her shoulder.

"You good now?" Lana's voice was in her ear.

"Yes." *I think.* She slid her foot off the trigger. In the silence and stillness, she let out a sigh of relief.

"Again, thank you both." Scarlett wiped the dust from her clothing. "You can all come down now!"

When the others reached her position, she nodded down the passage. "I'll signal from the bottom. Wait here until I tell you to come down. And whatever you do, don't touch the glowing walls."

According to the map, the stairs should open into a main chamber. What she didn't understand, and what left an uneasy feeling in her stomach, was the round eyeball drawn dead center in the room parallel to the "X" that Jack had so eagerly mentioned.

Nearing the bottom, the gnome slowed her steps. Patterned stone tiles, made of black and white marble, edged into view. *That's natural light*, she thought, examining the illumination's effect on the floor. She put away her glow stone and mustered her courage to peek inside.

So, that's the eye. A domed ceiling, three stories high to where the island's peak rose from the sea, was topped by an oculus. The circular portion open to the sky cast a flat white light into the chamber. Scarlett tracked down, following the beam.

A rectangular stone slab, altar-like, lay directly under the soft light. Resting on top was an object that caused her to pause. It looked like—

"Uncanny that is," Jack whispered, joining her.

"I don't see anyone," she said. "You can wave the others down."

"What in blazes is that?" The pirate pointed at the object.

"I don't know."

Scarlett stepped onto the first tile and held up a hand. "Just a moment." The thief edged her foot down onto the white section and pushed. Then, she did the same on a black portion. With a rogue's grace, she snuck her way about, scanning for traps or other sabotage. Her eyes went to the strange object on the tomb-like stone table. *What is that?*

At the edge of the light, a series of recesses along the walls glimmered. When her gnomish eyes adjusted, the sight brought a smile to her face. *Now that's a lot of treasure.* "It's clear," she called back to the others. "You can all come in."

Scarlett stayed put on the tiles, about halfway between the altar and a wall, as the others tiptoed their way inside the chamber.

Lana, who had lit a torch, stomped forward and looked up. "Bloody weird, that is."

"It's an oculus," Marian said. "Allows natural light in."

"What about the rain?"

Before the mage could respond, the half-orc bounded off. "Rig! Ha ha!" The half-orc danced about as if holding up a skirt. "I'm a booty baby, sure and true! Lookie here matey, some loot for you!"

The dwarf's one eye widened. Scarlett could see that deep in his soul, a treasure lust rose.

"We're rich, lads!" Big Rig slapped a knee and barreled over to the shimmering alcove. "We're bloody rich!"

Lana handed the dwarf her torch and began tossing handfuls of gold coins into the air, letting them rain down on her companion. Occasionally, a red or blue gem mixed in with the currency sparkled in the torchlight. The half-orc lifted a gem-encrusted necklace and held it up to her chest. "Oh, this is right pretty, this is..." She reached down into a pile of jewelry. "Here, mate." The half-orc offered Big Rig a tiara with a large white stone set in its golden bands. The dwarf put it on and the two danced in a circle, arm in arm, laughing and cackling.

Scarlett joined Marian and Jack at the stone slab.

"This is a burial tomb," the mage said, squatting and reading the ancient symbols carved into the thick stone sides. "It holds the ground-down bone dust of the ghost dragon slain by Nimárwe."

Scarlett shivered. To think, an actual dragon of old... its remains, at least, within reach of her living body.

"And this?" Trusty Jack pointed at the device resting on the tomb's lid.

The three examined the object. Rising on metal legs shaped like dragon's talons, a white orb swirled with a magical haze. From Scarlett's height, she couldn't see more than the sphere's underside. A symbol, indistinct in the shadows, lay at its bottommost point. She placed her tiny hands onto the lid of the tomb and pulled herself up.

Marian and Jack's eyes went wide.

She shrugged, standing on top of the slab. "Have to do it more often than you think in my line of work."

The pirate leaned closer to the sphere, peering inside.

"There's a flask in there," he said.

"Thank the gods," Scarlett said.

"That's the dragon blood, then?"

"Yes." It was Marian who had leaned close. The mage's eyes ran over the lower section of the orb. "Let me see the map, James."

Giggles mixed with exclamations of joy echoed across the chamber as Big Rig and Lana discovered additional treasures.

"Do we break it open?" Scarlett asked, feeling uncomfortable with the idea.

"Definitely not," Marian said, eyes running over the parchment. "But..." The mage handed the map to Trusty Jack and placed her hands onto the orb.

"Marian, be careful," the pirate said. "Are you sure—"

"I know what I'm doing, James, thank you."

Exes, Scarlett thought and smirked.

"Compass..." Marian said.

Scarlett took out the magical device.

"Sorry, I meant a standard one."

The pirate reached into his shirt pocket and removed his own.

"When I ask, give me the orientations," Marian said.

To Scarlett's surprise, the mage flexed her arms and the orb rotated. A familiar sigil appeared from the underside where it had been lurking amidst the talons.

"That's the ghost icon, that is," Trusty Jack whispered. "Same as on the Dragon Tail Compass."

"Yes," Marian grunted and set the sphere's bottom upwards so the symbol aligned with the oculus.

Soft, strange words whispered from the mage's mouth. Scarlett knew by her tone and inflection that they were old elvish.

"James, tell me which way is west."

"What in the blazes?"

"What's the matter?" Scarlett asked.

The pirate rattled the compass and leaned down so his eyes were inches from the device. "Bloody thing isn't working. It's spinning like a top."

Not good, Scarlett thought. She checked the Dragon Tail Compass. It too spun frantically.

"I need to know which way is west," Marian said. "Otherwise, this isn't going to work."

"Mate!" Trusty Jack called out to Big Rig. "Which way you think is west? I'm thinkin' it's about... there." The pirate aimed his arm to the right at a forty-five-degree angle.

"Have you turned into a landlubber?" the dwarf said, the tiara sparkling on his forehead. "It's that way." He thumbed toward them, an emerald-encrusted necklace in his grip jangling.

"You two are both cracked," Lana said. "It's more like... there." She aimed in a completely different direction.

"By the gods," Marian said. "You call yourselves pirates?"

"Now hold on there, lass," Jack said and gazed about. "Give me a moment and I'll get it." The pirate wet a finger and held it up.

Despite being in a windless underground chamber, Scarlett kept her mouth shut.

"Aye," he said. "It's gotta be that way." He aimed his arm across the chamber.

"If you say so," Marian said. More arcane words left the mage's lips and she rotated the orb.

Scarlett jumped as a massive slab crashed down, blocking the exit.

Everyone froze.

"Wrong way, mate," Big Rig said, breaking the silence. "I told you." He thumbed in the direction he had pointed a moment ago.

"Well, we've got a serious problem," Scarlett said, peering at the trap door that closed them in. "Unless someone is going to grow a pair of wings, we're in for a long stay on this island." She examined the oculus, their one remaining means of exit.

"We get one more chance," Marian said, re-reading the lines on the parchment. "And if we fail a second time, my guess is that the oculus is going to close us in..." She looked at Trusty Jack. "Forever."

"I was certain that was west." The pirate shook his head.

"Well, you better be *more* certain this time," Marian said.

"Lad!" Trusty Jack got Big Rig's attention a second time. "You sure, mate?"

The dwarf thumbed in the same direction again, insistent.

"Nothing for it," the pirate said. "Me second-in-command gets the call."

"Always said you were a smart one, Jacky boy." The dwarf went back to frolicking in treasure with Lana.

Are they mad? she thought. Treasure lust had cast a spell over two of the three Salty Scoundrels.

"Here goes nothing," Marian said, and shifted the orb where Big Rig indicated.

"Well, look at that," the pirate said as the mist inside the sphere stirred.

"We're far from land, lad!" the dwarf shouted. "I told you back at the Home of Rest not to question my bearings at sea." Big Rig tapped the side of his head with a finger.

"And now south?" Marian said.

Trusty Jack indicated the direction, based off his quartermaster's accurate choice of west, and the mage rotated the sphere, aligning the pattern with the cardinal point. The mist accelerated its spiral and vanished.

"By the Jeweled Deep," the pirate whispered.

With a slow creaking, the slab blocking the exit rose.

"Thank the gods," Scarlett whispered.

Marian removed her hands from the sphere.

The three examined the orb's contents. A red flask with a black cork rested on a small base.

"So that's golden dragon blood, then?" Trusty Jack said.

"According to the tales," Scarlett stepped closer, eye to eye with the relic. "Now what?"

"Now..." Marian took back the map. Her eyes ran over a line of faded text in elegant script. "We get this flask and get out of here."

Musical words left the mage's mouth, of the same type spoken at the entrance to the tomb.

As if it had never been there, the orb shell vanished.

"Well, I'll be a troll's uncle!" Jack swatted his tricorne against a knee. "You done it, lass!"

Scarlett reached for the flask and wrapped her tiny fingers around the bottle's neck. She jiggled it and felt the distinct back-and-forth weight of liquid. "There's blood in there."

Marian let out a sigh of relief.

"Pack it up, mates!" The pirate shouted to Big Rig and Lana. "Stuff as much as you can in those sacks. I'll let you have two runs to the ship and then we're getting off this bloody isle and back to—"

Boom!

With a thunderous crash, a large slab plummeted from the western wall to the floor. It shattered, echoing through the chamber like thunder at sea.

As if emerging from the void, an armored foot, tinged in a purple-black radiance, stepped into the world of the living. Another followed, and with it came the shadowy form of a helmeted warrior in an unworldly glow.

Scarlett's spine chilled. "What is that?"

"A guardian spirit," Marian said. "It has questions for us."

34

LONG SHOT

✦

"You trespass."

The warrior halted opposite the stone tomb. Only a horizontal sliver at eye level broke the full helmet atop their head.

Scarlett could see nothing inside the opening but a faint red glow. Odd as it was, she wasn't frightened. The presence felt as if it were so beyond her own reality that whatever happened couldn't, and wouldn't, influence the events of her own life and world. And yet, deep inside her heart, she felt great power radiating from the spirit. Perhaps it was so great that it was... *unfathomable,* she thought, growing suddenly terrified.

"We are here by rights, Guardian of the Divine," Marian said. "We have survived the trials of the mists and opened the archway to the tomb."

"You still trespass."

"We are only here for what is needed." Marian indicated the flask in Scarlett's hand.

"That shall not leave the chamber."

"It must be taken," Scarlett said. "You don't understand, we need—"

"It is forbidden."

"Why?"

"That is of no concern to you, mortal. It is for the greater order of divines that this island remain unaltered."

"The gods have left us to fend for ourselves for a thousand years," Marian said, her voice calm but firm. "But the corruption of the defiant one, Hanis-tá, lingers in the isles. A plague ravages the young. It spreads. And where have our gods been?" She held out her hands. "All we can do is use the lingering traces of magic to protect ourselves, along with our own intellect and cunning. And that has brought us here, with great sacrifice. We have *every* right to the dragon's blood, for the same reasons your master chose to sentence the remains of dark magic to this island."

"Your tongue is eloquent," the guardian spirit said. "And, your history since the sundering has run a course both surprising and impressive to the divines."

"Would've been nice of them to stop by and tell us," Trusty Jack muttered.

"What will it take for you to allow us this boon?" Marian said.

"It is not yours to take. I will not say this again."

"Then we are at an impasse," Scarlett said. In the corner of her eye, a muscular form made its way in the shadows across the chamber. *Lana*, she thought.

"Indeed," the spirit said. "And there is no leaving."

"What?" Trusty Jack stepped forward. "Ain't no one telling me what I can and can't—"

Marian gripped his arm.

"We are free people," the mage said. "Neither bound by you or your divine."

"You have trespassed and entered the mists. There is no going back."

"What are you sayin'?" Trusty Jack said.

"You are sentenced to eternal in-between, to roam the sea of souls with your brethren who have ventured across the threshold."

Scarlett's feet slid back on the tiles as the guardian spirit walked *through* the stone tomb, reaching for the flask in her hand.

"Spread out," Jack said, voice low.

The spirit increased its pace towards her, the red glow in its helm igniting into a fiery radiance.

Oh no... not good. She gulped and backed up.

"Argh!" Lana hurled a golden shield from the treasure pile. It passed through the spirit's form and smashed against the side of the tomb, sending bits of carved stone flying in the air.

Whoosh!

A goblet crossed from the other direction where Big Rig stood and passed through the spirit with the same ease.

"It's no use! Run!" Jack shouted and dashed for shelter behind a column.

A flash of blue light illuminated the chamber. Marian stood, arm outstretched, a curving translucent barrier creating a shield for Big Rig and Lana to find cover.

The guardian spirit reached out its hand, aiming it at Marian's spell, and pulled inward. The shield's radiant beams funneled into the spirit's fingers. Blue magic swirled and crackled in the spirit's palm, shifting hue and turning red.

"Get down!" Marian shouted.

Scarlett dove behind a pillar. If not for her small size, she would have been incinerated by the burst of fire that shot forth.

"Lass!" Jack shouted from a nearby column, pulling on his shirt, indicating her clothes.

She patted out the flaming tips of her cloak.

"Make a run for it, Cap!" Lana shouted from across the room. "I'll cover for you!"

"No!" Trusty Jack yelled back.

Scarlett followed the ominous footsteps of the guardian spirit as it stomped across the chamber.

"I can hold this thing off, Cap! Give you all time to get out!"

A shadowy version of the pirate behind the column smashed a fist into the floor in frustration.

A half-orc battle cry rang out.

"Damn it, Lana!" the pirate shouted.

Again, the radiant light from the healer rose.

Scarlett peeked around the pillar. Another shield spell flared from the mage. This one saved the charging half-orc from certain death as the spirit shot streams of fanged serpents at a charging Lana.

This is madness! Scarlett thought.

"None shall live. None shall die. You will stay bound in the mists."

Ignoring the guardian's doomspeak, Scarlett dashed to the wall and stealthed her way around to Marian.

"What are we going to do?" she asked, finding shelter behind the mage's kneeling form.

"What is that?" Marian nodded at Scarlett's vest.

A crimson glow pulsed in her pocket. Scarlett pulled out the Dragon Tail Compass. The needle had gone blood red with an otherworldly light. "I don't know why it's doing that."

Big Rig's form flashed past, making for Jack at the nearby pillar.

"Lana's in a mood, she is!" the dwarf shouted. "You know how she gets. Nothing's going to stop her. Now's the time to get out."

"I got a better idea, mate," Jack said.

From her position with Marian, Scarlett followed the pirate's movements as he stood and leaned around the pillar.

"Lana!" the pirate called out. "Remember how we took down Hairy Harry and his lily-livered lackeys?"

Marian snatched the compass and smashed it against the ground.

"What are you doing?" Scarlett said.

"Saving us, a second time." Marian yanked out the needle and slapped it into her palm. "Except you're the one who's going to do it."

"Do what?" Scarlett examined the needle. The sharp-edged double-sided stone pulsed, as if alive with magic.

Marian grabbed her with both hands and looked her in the eye.

"I savvy, Cap!" Lana shouted. "Me and you. On three..."

"Throw it, Scarlett. Now!" Marian's panther eyes were afire. "Kill it!"

It's the dagger blade, she thought. *Marian's right! The weapon was made to do this.*

Scarlett cupped the compass needle in her palm like a two-sided throwing dart.

"You got one shot and you get it now," the mage said. "I'll give you an opening."

"Two!" Lana's voice boomed across the room.

"Wait, Marian... I need—"

"Now!" The mage shoved her into the open.

"Three!" Lana said.

Marian leapt from behind the pillar and spoke a spell. Her hand swirled with a series of mesmerizing spectral butterflies. The guardian spirit switched course from the charging Lana to Marian, lured by the charm magic.

The avatar raised its hand. Ethereal fingers crackled with red energy. Through a powerful conjuration, a glowing blade manifested a few inches in front of their sparkling fingertips.

Scarlett's vision narrowed. She thought of her guild training. Of the thousand times she'd thrown a dart at the hay bales as an apprentice. Of the long road to get here. Her wins. And losses along the way... Tingle, Siân, and all the others. *This one's for you, Doni.* She flung the dagger.

The needle spun through the air like a glowing, sharp-edged comet. It crossed paths with the conjured blade that shot forth from the spirit's hand.

Crimson and purple fireworks exploded from the spirit's chest as the blood iron needle struck home.

Air surged inward towards the guardian's form.

Dark mist in the skies above the chamber swirled like a vortex, entering through the oculus.

Scarlett clutched her throat, gasping as the pressure tightened. A deafening roar of wind ravaged her ears.

Spears of red light rose around the guardian, circling the room like an army of spirits.

Scarlett shut her eyes in terror.

Hanis-tá inath katan. The haunting words penetrated the divine tempest, echoing off the walls of the chamber.

Then, silence.

Scarlett knelt, panting.

"Ha ha!" Lana shouted. "I didn't do anything, but someone did. Was it you, Cap?"

Big Rig's strong grip yanked Scarlett up. "You alright, lass?"

"Yes, I think so," she said, wiping dust from her cloak. His gray beard and slate face blurred and she stumbled. "Steady on," the dwarf said, his stout arms grabbing her before she fell. "Take a moment."

"Wasn't me, mate!" Trusty Jack shouted. His strong hand slapped Scarlett's back, making her lose her balance a second time. "A shot worthy of song, that was, lass."

"Well, I'd be lying if I said I wasn't relieved," Big Rig said. "Even if we don't know our way back through the mists without the compass."

"One step at a time, lad," Trusty Jack said. "I'm relishing this victory for a moment."

"We don't need no magic compass, Cap!" Lana shouted pointing up at the oculus. "Look!"

Scarlett, along with Jack and Big Rig, peered through the opening. Blue sky filled the view.

"The mist is gone!" Lana said, "And so is that bloody curse."

"Yo ho ho!" Big Rig said. "We can wait for nightfall. The stars'll guide us back to Redtown." The dwarf's eye grew wild with excitement. "And, with *Lady Luck* laden with treasure!"

Scarlett shook her head, working to clear the lingering chaos of the encounter. *If it wasn't for Marian,* she thought, *we would have never—*

"Where's Marian?" Jack said.

⁂

"MARIAN!"

The healer slumped against a pillar, legs splayed out across the stone tiles.

Jack ran to her side. He lifted a hand off her stomach, exposing a mortal wound. "Scarlett!"

"I'm here." The gnome's tiny fingers clasped the mage's other hand.

"My bag," Marian whispered, eyelids fluttering. "Quickly."

Jack held her cheek, "Oh gods, Marian." His heart sank at the flow of blood from her belly. He'd seen it many times as a pirate. And this blade wound's source wasn't a cutlass or a saber. She'd been hit by divinely cast magic. "Don't leave me, lass. Please... not a second time." His gut wrenched.

She raised a bloodied hand to his lips. "Hold... you need to hold it for me." She coughed up blood.

He clasped her hand.

The mage shook her head and pulled back.

"What, lass?"

"She means this, I think." Scarlett emptied a pile of spell preparations onto the stone floor.

"Marian, what do we do?" Desperate to make sense of the bundles of herbs, feathers, and other sundry items scattered on the tiles, he sifted through them.

The healer cried out in pain, her body seizing.

"Marian!" Jack held her close, pressing his face against hers. "Don't leave me..."

She coughed more blood and shook her head. "It's too late."

"No. No. No... Scarlett's got the spell pouches." He snatched up a cluster of herbs and feathers tied with string and placed them in her bloodied hand. "Here!"

The mage shook her head, eyes rolling back. "I know... better than anyone when it's over," she said, her focus returning for a moment. "I'm going..."

"No!" Jack screamed. "Marian... please stay with me." He looked around the chamber, desperation in his eyes. "This can't be happening!"

The pirate's words bounced off the hallowed walls.

"Use the dragon's blood!" He gripped Scarlett's cloak. "Give it to her!"

"I can't," the gnome said. "It'll kill her unmixed."

"Someone, do something!" he shouted, checking on Marian. The mage's eyes had closed, her body fallen against his, lifeless.

Smack!

A blow to his shoulder sent him tumbling.

He slid across the stone tiles. Shaking off the impact, his ears picked up a faint and raspy voice chanting strange words. *Lana?*

The former monk knelt in front of Marian, a spell preparation gripped in her green hand. The half-orc's fist transformed into a glowing ball of light. The first mate thrust it against the mage's belly.

Marian gasped, her back arching. She cried out and slumped against the pillar, eyes shut.

"Marian!" Jack dashed back and held her lifeless body close. "Marian!" He eyed Lana. "What did you do, you bloody fool!"

"Jack, she was in pain," Scarlett said, reaching for his shoulder.

He swatted her hand away. "I'll bloody—"

Marian gasped.

"Marian.... Marian!" Jack softened his grip on her body and checked her stomach. As if time rolled back, the red stains faded and with it went the hole in the robe where she'd been wounded.

"James."

"Oh, Marian!" He squeezed her tight. "I thought I lost you," he whispered in her ear.

"You did," she said.

The pain that had shattered his soul resealed, and waves of joy surged through him. He looked in her eyes to be sure it wasn't an illusion. The familiar amber shards sparkled and greeted him, capturing his heart as they had so many times before.

"I love you, Marian."

"I love you, too, James."

As if in an amorous duet, they reached for one another and kissed.

"Oh sure, don't say thank you or anything," Lana grumbled.

Jack managed to settle himself enough to break free of his one true love and look at Lana. The half-orc stood, arms folded, grinning.

"Mate, I'm sorry for barkin' them words at you," he said. "I don't know what you did or how you did it..."

Lana shrugged. "Ain't nuthin', Cap. I learned me a thing or two at the Home of Rest. Never thought it'd come in handy."

"It took skill to cast that spell," Marian said. "Your connective magic is strong, Lana."

"The monks at the monastery were always on about that. Thought it was creepy, if I'm honest. Prefer me fists and feet." She winked and smacked her knuckles against her palm. "I recognized the red-eared fiddle feather in that stack of dried herbs. Figured that chip tied with it had to be white quartz?"

Marian nodded.

"The headmaster used a similar combination once when a younger resident hurt themselves real bad." She shrugged. "I took a chance. Guess I guessed right."

"You certainly did," Marian said. "That's the most powerful spell I had prepared. Anything less, and I wouldn't have made it."

Lana pointed a finger at Jack. "You owe me *big time*, Cap."

"Mate," he said, "you can have all the Molly's Molasses in the Jewel Sea when this is done. I'll see to it."

The half-orc giggled, licking her tusks. "And toasts whenever I please?"

"Whenever you bloody well want, Lana." He looked Marian in the eyes. "Everything I need is right in front of me."

Marian squeezed his hand.

"I'm the luckiest man in all of Arsel," he whispered.

The mage blushed and lowered her eyes.

"Music to me ears, that is," Lana said. "*And* me belly."

"With the amount of treasure here," Big Rig said, stuffing a sack across the chamber. "You can buy your own bloody distillery."

The half-orc skipped like a schoolgirl across the chamber to help her shipmate with the booty.

The soft touch of a finger turned Jack's chin.

Marian's eyes held him under a spell.

"It's going to be different, this time," she said, and kissed him again.

A wave of desire rushed through him. "We'll make it work, lass," he said. "I'll learn to be better at everything. That's a promise. Living without you is unthinkable." He kissed her, running a hand through her salt and pepper hair.

"Jack..." Scarlett said.

He kissed Marian, ignoring the gnome.

"Jack..."

Marian's hand clasped his neck and they deepened their embrace.

"Jack!"

"What, lass?" Both he and the mage turned their heads.

"We've got a problem."

The thief stood under the light of the oculus, her body a shadow. Smoke rose, snaking its way up and out of the opening. Ghostly streams danced with an unworldly elegance, climbing like a serpent responding to an enchanter's music.

He and Marian were up and next to Scarlett in seconds. Big Rig and Lana dropped the sacks of treasure, eyes wide.

A pool of black liquid where the guardian spirit had withered bubbled at their feet. Next to the shield that Lana had tossed during the fight, a steady stream of bone dust drained from a crack in the tomb like a sand clock, mixing with the spirit's essence and transforming into white smoke.

"James..." Marian squeezed his wrist and nodded at the oculus.

Through the opening, the fumes spiraled like an ethereal whirlpool, growing wider and thicker with each rotation.

As if manipulated by a divine hand, the cloudy mass pulled and stretched, taking shape.

A chill tingled Jack's spine.

"Gods, it can't be..." Marian muttered.

The entire party gazed skyward.

An otherworldly screech shook the chamber.

Jack's hands covered his ears. His knees buckled and he collapsed under an invisible force wave.

The chamber blurred.

And then, silence.

Trusty Jack lay on the tiles, gasping.

Marian was the first to rise, the flowing fabric of her robe catching the light.

Jack pushed himself to his knees, shaking his head. The spinning image of the tomb settled.

Whoosh. Whoosh. Whoosh.

Waves of air surged through the oculus.

A white form passed overhead.

Scarlett dashed out of the chamber.

Jack followed, taking the steps two at a time, his long strides overtaking the gnome. He emerged on the stairs outside and leapt onto the black rocks.

"What have we done?" Scarlett asked, pulling herself up the craggy boulders behind him.

As they suspected, the skies had cleared. A calm sea lay free of mist and magic.

Jack struggled up to a flat perch.

Above the turquoise waters, a white drake flapped its massive wings with slow, hypnotic rhythm. Its ghostly scales shimmered against the sun like a lone animate cloud over the sea.

Jack stared in disbelief, gauging the beast's scale at its distance. *It's three galleons if it's a foot.*

"Zarlak," Marian said, joining them on the precipice.

Jack's blood went cold. The painting at the palace, the one Marian had shown him years ago, returned in terrifying clarity. The ghost dragon of old, sent by the defiant god Hanis-tá to destroy the Jewel Islands and spite his divine sibling, Telathia. Defeated at great cost by the only one with the power to stop it, the Golden Elf wizard, Nimárwe.

"Resurrected from the tomb," Marian said. "An ancient terror returned to the world of the living."

Tiny gnomish fingers gripped Jack's sleeve.

The pirate pulled out his compass. Thankfully, the needle spun and settled, functioning as it should. He aimed himself north and marked the drake's flight path on the dial. *Cursed luck*, he thought. A shaky hand removed the tricorne and held it at his chest.

"James, which way is it heading?" Marian said.

The three stood on the precipice, eyes following the diminishing creature of legend.

"Redtown."

35

OVER THE BARREL

❧

Marian stood at *Lady Luck's* bow as the ship rose and plunged over the swells. The night sky was alive with stars, as if a god's hammer had crushed a diamond and with divine breath, blown the dust over an empty and infinite cosmos.

For three days and nights they had sailed a course for Redtown, following the haunting trail of disease and death in the wake of the fell drake, Zalark. An endless line of floating fish, withered plants, and corrupted sea life had run parallel to the ship. Two days prior it had veered southwest. Marian knew what the change in course meant. The otherworldly creature, whether driven by whimsy or earnest intention, had diverted to the nearest Jewel Island. James had convened with his quartermaster and first mate, and the quorum agreed it best to stay on a direct line to Ruby Island. Marian didn't want to think about the dragon's ire and what it could do to the agricultural communities on Topaz Island. As awful a circumstance as it was, if the beast had chosen to ravage the nearest landmass, it might offer enough delay for them to reach the capital and prepare for what might come.

A strange and quiet hope had risen amongst the crew and companions the following day. She and Scarlett had debated over whether the drake had left the Jewels, perhaps seeking distant lands over the sea and avoiding the mainland entirely.

Their conjecture, as it turned out, was moot. This morning, Marian awoke in the cramped single bed of the captain's quarters with James and peered out the broken window. The familiar line of deathly corruption trailed in *Lady Luck's* wake once more. They'd followed its path through the day until, at sunset, the edge of Ruby Island broke the horizon.

Telltale signs that Zarlak had indeed chosen the Jewel's capital as its destination lay before her eyes. But it wasn't smoke that rose from Redtown; the city lay blanketed under a familiar ghoulish mist.

Why and to what purpose the drake had targeted the capital was obvious. Hanis-tá was a vengeful spirit. Zarlak had but one purpose: to eradicate all traces of civilization in the Jewels. To erase the legacy of the Golden Elves and the society that had risen after their leave-taking. Anyone who had been a member of the Order of Telathia knew the extent of animosity between the two divines. This was to be the final chapter in a saga a millennium in the making. What broke Marian's spirit was that its coming had been hastened, even prompted, by their actions. An attempt to do good, to make the islands a better place, with a democratic system of government and a cure for the ailing and sick had led to the unthinkable. Loathe as she was to confront it as truth, she wasn't even sure there would be a future for the Jewels.

"What is that?" Scarlett's crimson locks appeared at her side. The gnome climbed up onto a crate and peered ahead. "It looks like a blue—"

"It's a shield," Marian said, recognizing the defensive magic. Her eyes scanned the semi-circular illumination covering one of Redtown's middle districts. "That's the guild circle and the fountain."

"I hope they're sheltering citizens in there," the gnome said.

Crack!

A sickly purple bolt flashed in the sky, illuminating the surrounding mist and cityscape. It crashed against a second shield dome, this one green and higher on the rising hillside.

"Gods," Marian whispered, spotting a ghostly form swoop down and circle the magic protecting the palace. "It's Zarlak."

"Hazard to port!" a sea elf shouted.

A half-sunk naval vessel passed as they sailed into the harbor.

"There's more on this side," Scarlett said.

Sure enough, three frigates lay floating in pieces to starboard. Eerie mist clung to the timbers and half-sunken masts.

"That new galleon's gone," Big Rig said, lumbering up to the bow. "Must've put to sea."

Is Bonnie not here? Marian thought and examined the approaching docks. As angry as she was at her, so much had happened that they needed to talk and find a way forward.

Boom!

She, along with Scarlett and Big Rig, peered up the hill. Through the misty night, Zarlak pummeled the magical barrier around the palace with a second round of dragon lightning.

"Is that going to hold?" Scarlett asked.

"Not forever," Marian said. Judging by the spell's color and resistance to the dragon's breath, it had to be the work of Master Rin and whomever she had in there with her from the mage guilds.

A burst of flaming balls soared like comets into the misty skies. The drake veered, avoiding the attack, its ghostly white skin reflecting the fiery magic cast by the mages.

"There're no soldiers fighting back." Big Rig gripped the rails, peering through the mist. "What in the name of Gin Tanny is going on?"

The dragon let out a mighty screech.

Struck by fear, Marian and the others cowered.

The drake turned and set its sights on the harbor.

"Look out!" a sailor shouted.

Zarlak passed overhead and arced back across the wharf. With a whoosh, a gust of wind heeled *Lady Luck*, sending everyone who wasn't prepared tumbling.

Marian's stomach grew nauseous from the passing traces of dark magic. She checked on Scarlett. The gnome's skin had gone a sickly white.

With slow but earnest determination, the drake flapped its massive wings and rose over the buildings in the lower district.

Gods, Marian thought, the ill-feeling passing. *The size of it.*

Zarlak cried out, its wings sending timbers and shingles free from Redtown's buildings. A glow filled the drake's ghost white neck.

Marian gasped. *No...*

The beast's jaws gaped wide and a violet bolt shot forth, shattering Eel Town's clock tower. Screams of townsfolk echoed over the water.

The reality was all too clear: Redtown was in the throes of a life-and-death struggle. The capital would prove to be the pivotal battle for the survival of the Jewel Islands.

"What's the plan?" The familiar commanding voice of James broke through the tumult and chaos of the city's fight against the fell creature.

"Get out of here!" someone shouted from the docks. "Put to sea, you fools! And take as many people as you can."

I know that voice, she thought.

"Sir Roderick!" Marian ran to the gangplank and disembarked.

"My lady..." the Red Knight took a step back, his armor a mess of blood and soot. "I..."

"Did you follow my orders?" she asked.

"Of course, my lady." With a wave of his hand, Roderick sent his unit back to aid nearby citizens. "The inauguration was underway today and then this..."

"Are the defenses holding?"

"We can do nothing, my lady!" He kicked a sword from a fallen comrade. "Blades and arrows are useless against this cursed drake. They pass right through as if it were a ghost."

"It's worse than I thought," Big Rig said as the others disembarked and joined her on the dock.

"The mages are trying to take it down, but..." Roderick shook his head. "We're shepherding as many citizens as we can to the guild ward. Those who can make it are safe under the magic, but with the way things are going... my lady, those spells aren't going to hold."

"Where is my father?" Marian asked.

"No idea."

"What?" she stepped forward.

"In the palace, I think." The knight shrugged. "He hasn't sent orders or been seen since the attack. I've been leading the evacuations and defenses."

"Bloody coward!" Trusty Jack said, joining them. "When we find him—"

Marian held up a hand, signaling for the pirate to be silent. "What about my—"

"Your sister?"

Bonnie hastened toward them in full naval uniform, blotches of red spattered across her waistcoat and pants.

"It's not mine," she said, indicating the blood.

Marian looked from the admiral to James and then back again.

"Sir Roderick gave me your message." Bonnie went to embrace her sister but hesitated.

Thank the gods, Marian thought, and pulled her in.

"We have a lot to talk through," her sibling whispered in her ear.

Marian nodded, her chin pushing into her sister's shoulder. "There's more, Bonnie." She pulled back and reached into her robe, withdrawing the pendant. She held it up for all to see.

Sir Roderick gasped.

Bonnie cocked her head.

"You wouldn't believe me if I told you... either of you."

Boom!

Like a flash of lightning, the docks came alive for a brief instant with an eerie glow as the drake pummeled the magic ward at the palace.

"Come on," Bonnie motioned them over to a half-destroyed building along the wharf. "Get out of the street."

"Bonnie," Marian said, and glanced back at James who followed with the others.

"He's the least of my... of *our* problems right now," her sister said.

"My lady." Sir Roderick pointed at the pendant. "How—"

"I don't have time to explain. All I will say is my..." the thought of calling him a father made her want to vomit, "the regent had our expectant aunt, Queen Ricarda, and her ship..." *How do I say this?*

"Gods," Bonnie whispered, picking up on the implication.

"He will pay, my lady!" Sir Roderick's one eye burned in fury on his scarred face. "He will pay for this with his—"

"Listen to me! All of you." Marian motioned James and the others over. "I'm only going to say this once. Right now, the city needs us. The Jewels need us. All of Arsel needs us. I don't care what you," she pointed at James, "and you," she pointed at her sister, "and you," she pointed at Sir Roderick, "have running through your blood. Right now, we need to all work together. Show me you are better than... than... him!" She pointed up at the palace.

"What do you need?" It was Bonnie who stepped up and nodded at the pirate and the knight.

"Scarlett!" Marian shouted.

The gnome joined them.

"Scarlett, I need you to get to the healer's guild. Make your way up the hill to the fountain. Use your skills and stay alive." She knelt and gripped the thief's shoulder. "Precious should be there, gods willing."

The gnome nodded.

"Find the headmaster of the healer's guild, Scarlett. Tell her who you are and give the dragon's blood to Desdianté."

"Desdianté?"

Marian checked with the knight, who nodded, affirming he'd followed her orders in the note she'd given him before departing Redtown. "Yes, a night elf. He knows you're coming and he's the one person with the knowledge to mix the elixir so it can heal the sick safely." The mage stood. "Go and be safe."

The gnome wrapped her cloak about her and was off, vanishing in the shadows.

The dragon shrieked again.

"Get down!" Bonnie screamed.

Marian dove in the open doorway of the merchant's shop, tumbling inside as a bolt destroyed a navy ship docked in the harbor. Like an angry tempest, the flash illuminated the ship in the mist as it shattered into hundreds of pieces, raining down debris.

"My ship!" Bonnie rose from behind a barrel and kicked a nearby crate. "That was our last remaining frigate!"

"Is there any hope, my lady?" Sir Roderick asked. "Or do we stand defiant to the end?"

"Nothing is stopping it," Bonnie said. "The mages don't have the power of the elves of old."

The image of Nimárwe standing tall and proud, in the painting celebrating the defeat of Zarlak rose in Marian's mind. Victorious in her gleaming gold armor, armed with bow and quiver, the wizard warrior stood over the drake triumphant. *Are we doomed?* she thought.

"We are mere mortals," Sir Roderick said. "The warriors of old had powers of an ancient magic. None but the golden elves and their dragons can face down Hanis-tá's demon."

As if transported back in time, the past returned in vivid clarity. Marian stood in Master Rin's office before all of this began. Before everything had turned her life upside down. Gazing at the majestic painting in the morning light, her eyes ran over the masterpiece in a potent and vicarious memory. *Nimárwe held a bow.* From the weapon gripped in Nimárwe's hands, Marian's eyes traveled the canvas, down the elf's torso and legs, over the neck of the felled beast, to the wizard's gleaming boots. *That means she used an—*

"Marian?"

Bonnie gripped her arm.

The force of the solution hit like a powerful spell. She stumbled.

"Marian?" Bonnie caught her and helped her steady her balance. "Are you hurt?"

"I know how to defeat it," she said, looking at the faces around her. "At least, I think... I need to get to the palace!"

"The palace?" the knight said. "Why?"

"Trust me. I need your safe escort, Sir Roderick."

"You have it, my lady."

"James?" Marian waved him over.

"Can *Lady Luck* be ready to push off at a moment's notice?"

"Aye, lass. Pirates be savvy on quick exits, especially from the Navy." He smirked in Bonnie's direction.

"I need you not to be on it when it does."

"What?" the pirate grimaced.

She squeezed his arm. "Trust me, James."

His eyes softened.

"Bonnie," she said. "Come here, please."

Marian took a breath. *Here goes nothing.* "James, I want you to let Bonnie sail *Lady Luck*."

"Are you mad?" He stood tall and pointed at her sister. "This bilge rat?"

"I need her expertise, along with your crew's, to pull this off." Marian turned to her sister. "That is, if you are willing?"

The admiral nodded. "This mess is bigger than all of us. You and I have played our parts in it, Jack, especially with Marian."

The pirate grumbled.

"I will do what is right by her and our city." The admiral's eyes narrowed. "That's as good you'll get from me you bloody pirate, even if you were framed... which was unbeknownst to me." She held her hands up in her defense. "Let's not forget, you stabbed me in the leg back when this all started."

"And you sent me off to sea in a bloody storm!" Trusty Jack barked.

"I could have killed you." Bonnie smirked, returning the gestural volley.

"And why didn't you, aye?" The pirate stepped forward so the two were eye to eye.

Marian examined her sister's face. She pursed her lips the way she had as a child when wont to share her feelings.

"Well, blow me down," the pirate bellowed out a hearty laugh.

"Don't flatter yourself," Bonnie said. "I hate you, Captain Hawk. But I love my sister."

Marian's muscles eased. *Good enough.* "James, are we in agreement?"

"This here's one topsy turvy parlay," he said. "But aye." He grinned. "Agreed." The pirate pointed a finger at the admiral. "But keep your filthy Navy paws off that helm, you hear me? Big Rig's the only one allowed to touch the wheel."

"Fine by me," Bonnie said. "Wouldn't want to risk the scabies."

"You bloody—"

"Enough," Marian said, stepping between them. "James, I need you to find somewhere along the harbor with a view in all directions. High up... either a tower that still stands or somewhere along the hillside."

"What's this all about, lass?"

"Just do it!" Marian pulled him in and kissed him. "And be careful. I need you alive or we can't do this." She looked in his eyes. "And *I* need you alive afterwards... if this works."

"I don't know what kind of schemer you got workin', lass, but I'll be here when you get back. That dragon and a whole dread army won't keep me from you." He put a hand on her cheek. "You make sure you come back, savvy?"

"I savvy," she said. "Sir Roderick has never let me down."

She heard the old knight's fist slam against his plate-armored chest in answer to her claim.

"And James, bring your elven bow."

36

HOLD FAST

Marian dashed down the palace hall. Through a line of open windows, the ward's eerie glow sent green light shimmering across the tiles.

"Hurry!" she called to Sir Roderick, who was falling behind.

She turned two corners, passing a guard coming the other way.

"My lady," the half-orc said, "we've cleared that wing. You are better—"

"I'm fine!" She kept going, intent on the door at the end of the hallway. "Actually," she halted. "Come with me."

Sir Roderick rounded the bend and the guard's head went back and forth between them.

"You heard Mage Marian!" the knight barked. "With us!"

She dashed to the door and flung it open.

"Like I said, my lady." The guard followed her inside. "Everyone's been evacuated to the..." The half-orc halted mid-sentence as Marian ran her hands along the wood wall.

She pushed against a plank and a fake bookshelf swung open.

"Get up," she said.

"Marian?" Regent Fitzwater sat huddled in the safe room, wielding a dagger.

"Get up you pathetic coward."

"Marian, what's happening? I—"

"Sir Roderick." Marian stepped aside and let the sergeant enter.

"What are you doing?" her father cried as the knight heaved him off the floor.

Sir Roderick ripped the dagger from his hands and flung it aside. "Captain," he said to the half-orc, "on my orders as head of the Red Brigade, and defender of the city and people of Redtown, you are to take the former regent to the holding cells downstairs."

"Holding cells?" Markus Fitzwater said, struggling. "Wait, did you say 'former'? What is going on?"

"You are under arrest." Sir Roderick shoved him into the burly arms of the half-orc.

"Marian? What is this about?"

"You want to know what this is about?" She surged forward so they were face to face, her cat-like eyes burning a hole through his whimpering expression. "This is about a dead queen, murdered on your orders. This is about a framed man and a betrayal of a daughter, done on your orders. This is about corruption, and greed, and about hundreds of innocent children's souls gone, on your orders. This is about suffering that you can't begin to understand because you..." She stepped back. "I have a city to defend. You don't deserve another breath."

Markus Fitzwater's eyes were alive with fear and confusion. "I don't... I don't understand..."

Marian pulled out the pendant. "I heard the tale from Captain Pitch herself!" She clenched the chain tight. "You make me sick." She turned to the half-orc. "Get him out of my sight."

Her father cried out, pleading and rambling excuses, as the captain dragged him away.

"More lies," she said. "Come on, Sir Roderick, there's no time."

The two backtracked through the corridors and up a flight of steps until they reached the treasury.

As her foot touched down in the museum, a thunderous boom

rattled the display cases. The green light of the magic ward flickered against the drake's renewed assault.

"It isn't going to hold," the Red Knight said.

Marian approached the display case. The one she'd passed so many times over the years that she'd lost count. That was, until she'd decided to leave the palace and her father's corrupt and poisonous presence. And now, she was back. This time, as her gaze landed on the object inside, she smiled.

The pain had blown away. Now, it represented hope. Love lost and found. Heroism and a romantic declaration in her youth.

She bashed the glass with an elbow and snatched the golden arrow off the velvet fabric.

"Back to the docks?" Sir Roderick said.

"One more stop." She hustled out of the treasury and up the steps to the next floor. Down the hall and around the corner and she stormed into Master Rin's office.

"What are you after, my lady?" Sir Roderick asked, on her heels.

"This." Marian approached the painting. She held the golden arrow up and checked its design against the one embedded in Zarlak's neck. The fletchings matched. With a twist of her wrist, she angled the shaft so it aligned with an arrow lying on the grass at Nimárwe's feet.

"How did we never see it?"

She smiled at the sound of the old knight's voice behind her.

"It was right there, my lady. All these years..."

"Yes, quite the heirloom," she said, taking in the majestic elf depicted by an ancient hand. "Something tells me it was left for us... perhaps for this very purpose."

Crack!

Marian darted to the window and peered down. Master Rin and five of the ten mages who had formed the band of spellcasters lay on the grass. The look of their mangled bodies left no doubt that the drake's dark magic had taken their lives.

"Master Rin has fallen," she said.

The remaining magic users attempted to reform the circle and recast the ward, but Marian knew that without the arch mage, and with the injuries sustained by those who yet stood, it would be futile.

"The barrier is down, Sir Roderick," she said. "We have to hurry."

⚜

THE YEARS MARIAN HAD SPENT IN THE PALACE GARDENS HAD PAID off. She and the knight navigated through the lush trees and plants with impressive haste, clearing the arboretum's lower boundary and re-entering the city's Kiha-Olo district.

The Palmetto Club was still intact, but much around it had taken severe damage. So much had been turned upside down with the drake's invasion, and so much more had been upended in her life over the last few weeks.

"If we can reach the harbor," she said, running along with the knight through the streets, "then you can take the guards and help with—"

The ground shook as if struck by an earthquake. She and Sir Roderick tumbled to the street. The golden arrow rolled out of her hands and down the cobblestones.

Marian's ears nearly exploded at Zarlak's cry. The drake landed across the open square, crushing a building with its rear talons.

The ghost dragon shot its long neck forward, its spectral head and glowing eyes confronting her with a haunting undead bloodlust. Mist fell like ghostly waterfalls from its gaping jaws.

Give me the jewel...

Frozen in fear, her limbs paralyzed by the dragon's speech, she lay dumbstruck.

The pendant... give it to me.

The hypnotic words swirled in her mind, disrupting her thoughts.

Sir Roderick's gleaming armor appeared in front of her. "Return to the darkness of death!" he shouted, protecting her from the beast's stare.

The knight's impenetrable courage sent a wave of inspiration surging through her veins. She shook off the sublime terror and rose. A hand went to her pouch and pulled out a spell preparation. Uttering the incantation, Marian conjured her strongest attack spell, *Telathia's*

Spear. Her hand shot forth, sending a glowing shaft straight into the dragon's head.

The radiant spear struck, but the ghostly scales deflected the magic. Sparks shot into the air, illuminating the nearby buildings on the square. Marian caught sight of the golden arrow near the dragon's front talon.

"Go, my lady." Sir Roderick unsheathed his massive two-handed sword. "While there's time."

"Roderick, no!" Marian took a step forward.

"Go!" he commanded, his one eye fierce with the order. The muscles in his cheeks and jaw softened. "It has been the honor of my life, serving you."

Zarlak raised its head into the sky and let out a second wail that shook the city.

"See my blade, fell drake?" the Red Knight shouted, his voice rising in a tone she'd not heard since he was young but no less proud. "You shall feel its wrath!" With noble grace, the knight shifted to the right side of the street, drawing the dragon's ire and opening a passage for her to retrieve the arrow and flee.

Marian paused, a mixture of awe at the immense power of the beast and the tragedy and honor of the knight's selfless sacrifice.

"Trelatia Unia Licara!" Sir Roderick's enchanted blade burst into flames at the sacred words uttered in the ancient tongue.

"Run, my lady," he said. "Save our city."

❧

"LANA, ROUND UP ANYONE WHO'S NOT INSIDE THAT MAGIC WARD." Jack pointed up to the guild circle on the hill. "Staying out here is certain death."

"Aye, Cap," the half-orc said.

One had only to look at the damaged buildings to know there were wounded everywhere, many unable to walk. For certain, more would be trapped under debris and fallen timbers. Lana was the only one among them with the strength to lift heavy obstacles and a bottomless well of endurance to carry victim after victim through the city to safety.

"We'll be sailing *Lady Luck* out with Big Rig, then?" a sea elf asked.

The dragon's thunderous screech prevented Jack from answering.

The pirate, the crew, and his fellow Salty Scoundrels, all crouched in response to the drake's cry. All except Lana. The half-orc eyed the ghost dragon hovering over the palace and growled.

"Go with Lana, lads," Jack said. "Help ferry anyone who needs assistance. That's an order."

A chorus of "ayes" called out from the crew.

"Here she comes!" Big Rig lumbered his way down the street.

Marian emerged from the mist, taking long strides. Her robe flowed behind her, interrupting the darkened backdrop of the devastated cityscape.

What's that in her hand?

The drake broke through the mist high on the hill. Jack tracked the creature as it dove and slammed into the palace. The low rumble of stone blocks, carved and set by elvish hands a thousand years ago, echoed across the harbor.

"The palace," he said as Marian reached them, pointing behind her.

The mage didn't turn.

"Are you ready to prove once again you are worthy of this prize?" She held out her hand.

"Is that..." His eyes ran over the golden arrow. Memories flooded back. He hadn't seen it since...

"Made of golden dragon bone," Marian said. "From the quiver used by Nimárwe that slayed Zarlak a thousand years ago."

The mage put it into his hand. "And will do so a second time this night."

Marian's eyes were alive, fierce and shining bright. "You get one shot, James."

"We're ready," Bonnie said, approaching. Big Rig, close behind, joined them.

"Alright, what's the plan, Marian?" Jack said.

"My father has been arrested. He's sulking in a cell." She looked at her sister. "That's a story for later."

"Something tells me I won't be surprised," the admiral said.

"*Lady Luck* will sail out into the harbor and lure the drake." Marian looked to Big Rig, who nodded affirmation.

"How?" Jack asked. "Drawing the dragon from the city, I mean."

Marian held up the pendant. "Zarlak spoke to me. It was..." her words trailed off. She shook herself free of whatever spell the memory had over her. "The drake wants the pendant. Something about the magic it holds... an essence of the divine, perhaps. Whatever it is, Zarlak desires it."

"Where's Sir Roderick?" Jack said, looking about.

"He was a good man, James. And it was his sacrifice that helped me reach you with that arrow." She gritted her teeth.

Jack sensed the wave of emotion held back by the mage. He'd known the knight in his younger years. The man was nothing short of noble, loyal, and proud.

"Your innocence was proven through Sir Roderick's willingness to believe in me. Through his efforts and unwavering belief in honor, and the rights of the people of Redtown, and across the Jewels..." she paused. "Including you... we've made it this far. Let's finish it. For Sir Roderick, and for all those who have sacrificed life and livelihood in the cause of justice."

If ever Marian had inspired him to admiration, respect, and love, it was now. The woman was as extraordinary as everyone claimed.

"With that arrow?" Bonnie said, raising a brow.

"The painting, sister. The one in Master Rin's office."

"Of course," Bonnie said. "Nimárwe."

"Yes," Marian put a hand on her sibling's arm. "Master Rin fell shielding the palace."

The admiral shrugged. "Better that way than what might have come if she lived through this."

No love lost between those old flames, Jack thought.

A bolt flashed in the night sky. Again, the magical ward above the guild halls flickered, waning in strength.

"We're out of time," Jack said. "Give the pendant to Bonnie and get somewhere safe."

"I'm going on *Lady Luck*."

"Marian, it's not safe."

"As if any of this is... or has been?"

"But—"

"This city is my responsibility." The mage clutched his hand. "You may be my one true love, James, but you don't get to tell me what to do. No one does."

"That's my sister," Bonnie said. The admiral folded her arms and eyed him, smugly.

"You jump off that ship and dive down as deep as you can when that thing comes for the pendant," Jack said.

Marian pulled him close. Her warm lips met his, sending a rush through him. "I will."

"I'm all for chewin' the fat," Big Rig said, "But if I'm going to Davy Jones Locker tonight as some bloody ghost corpse from that drake, I want it over and done with. You all be givin' me the Jenny's with this talking and lip smacking. My bones are achin' and it's either going to be mead in the mountain halls with the spirits of my forefathers or Molly's Molasses in the ruins of this city with Lana tonight." He spat. "At this point, I'll take either."

"Aye," Jack said. "I'll be joining you for a clap of thunder, mate."

"Hit the neck, James," Marian said. "On its underside. Aim for the halfway point between head and body. That's where Nimárwe's arrow protruded from Zarlak's corpse in the painting."

"Hope that wasn't artistic liberty," Big Rig grumbled.

"Where will you be, Jack?" Bonnie asked. "So we know how to lead the drake and maneuver the ship."

"Up that there hillside," he pointed. "Past the docks."

"Cheroots tonight, lad," Big Rig said, landing a hearty slap on his arm. "If we make it out of this."

Trusty Jack winked at his old friend.

"Good luck, Jack." Bonnie held out her hand. "Or, should I say, 'Hold fast, ya scurvy dog'?"

"Your pirate talk is terrible." Jack shook her hand. He was loathe to admit that her callouses and grip were as salty as his own. "Stick to naval formalities. Suits you best. Especially in that ridiculous hat."

Marian's sister muttered under her breath and hurried off with Big Rig towards *Lady Luck*.

"James, before you go... I..." Marian's eyes softened.

"I know, lass, me too." He pulled her close, clutching her against his chest. "You're an inspiration." He kissed her head and picked up his bow. "Now off with you, Mage Marian. Let's save this city."

Jack waited until Marian stepped on board *Lady Luck* and then made his way across the docks and up the hill. No sooner had he reached the small rise with a view of the surrounding harbor than a crimson glow sparked on the ship's deck.

Marian had summoned the pendant's magic.

The ghost dragon cried out, turning from its relentless attack on the magical barrier protecting Redtown's citizens.

"Blow me down," Jack said taking in the scene. "If you'd have asked me a year ago where I'd be today when I was three sheets to the wind in *The Dreg*, it would've never been anything this cracked."

He picked up the bow and ran his hand over the ornamental leaf pattern. "Elvish spirits in you better be alive and awake this night." He set his stance and waited, the golden arrow stuck in the ground at his feet.

With a roar, Zarlak spread its wings and glided over the city's descending streets. The titanic drake soared above the ruined lower district, eyes aglow and trailing a ghoulish mist from its mouth.

Jack checked *Lady Luck*. Big Rig gripped the helm, with Bonnie calling out to him from the bow.

He tracked the ship's path and the beast's intercept course.

So far so good.

A deafening whine rose. The drake soared past, sickening his stomach. Trusty Jack gritted his teeth against the dark magic trailing in its wake.

A bolt shot from its mouth, illuminating the harbor. With a crack, *Lady Luck's* mast split and broke, collapsing over the side with a splash.

Marian, Bonnie, and Big Rig all dove for cover as the beast rushed past. The sloop heeled from the trailing wind tunnel, pitching to its rails.

Jack's fingers reached for the golden arrow. "Come on, you scurvy beast! Turn!"

Zarlak arced away.

"Bollocks!" His hand stopped inches from grabbing the shaft.

With wings spread wide, the drake rotated and aimed towards Redtown. The beast sent a bolt crackling towards the magic barrier. Its impact shattered the blue bubble and broke the mages' spell.

"Gods," Jack whispered. "They're in the open now."

Zarlak cried out in victory. The fell creature flapped its wings in earnest, rising towards the now exposed masses.

He had no shot! The drake would destroy the city and every remaining citizen.

Cobalt light passed his position, expanding over the wharf and up into the city streets.

Jack's eyes went wide when he looked at the remains of *Lady Luck*. Marian stood at the prow of the injured ship, clutching the pendant. An azure radiance spread with divine power from her hand.

She's using the gem's power. For a moment, he stood transfixed. The mage held an otherworldly aura, as if a godly spirit channeled through her.

Spectral butterflies, like those the mage had summoned in the chamber on Dragon Tail Island, flowed from her hand in a magnificent charm spell.

Zarlak neared the guild circle. The spell's spectral creatures passed over the dragon's ghostly skin. The beast spun its neck and eyed the source. Two fierce eyes brightened and it cried out, banking back towards the harbor.

"Drake, ho!" Jack said.

This was it. One more chance!

Trusty Jack surveyed *Lady Luck's* course. Big Rig and Bonnie were doing their best to angle the ship so he'd have a shot.

"Come on, ya salty dogs! You can do it!"

Zarlak tucked its wings and increased speed.

Jack's stomach dropped as the beast passed like a spear shooting through the sky.

"Dive! Dive!" he shouted, out of earshot of his companions.

To his relief, Big Rig abandoned the helm. The dwarf charged across the deck to Marian and tackled her, plunging over the side with the mage still holding up the pendant.

The drake pitched away, as if sensing the ambush, angling its descending flight.

The bloody underside! he thought. *I can't hit it!*

Miraculously, *Lady Luck* turned. He spotted a figure at the helm.

Bonnie, he thought. The admiral spun the helm, muscling the wheel arm over arm to rotate the rudder.

Trusty Jack gauged the dragon's path and the turning ship.

She's going to—

Marian's sister peered up the hillside. For a moment, their eyes met. The admiral nodded as the dragon smashed the hull, shattering *Lady Luck* to pieces.

Zarlak rose, twirling in triumph. The drake arced back for the city intent on the final decimation.

Bonnie had set the angle!

The dragon's head aimed up to the stars. The beast rotated, intent on a dive to gain speed.

A ghostly underside broke into view. Jack grabbed the arrow and nocked it. He drew the bowstring. Like old lovers reunited, the pair synchronized with an ancient magic, glowing with divine light.

Jack narrowed his eye and aimed, compensating for the distance. The air around him glittered. An elf in gold armor materialized as a specter. Nimárwe's finger touched the underside of his hand gripping the bow and raised his aim ever so slightly.

Jack exhaled and let the arrow fly.

Like a beam of sunlight piercing the night, the enchanted arrow cut through the darkness. For a moment, the entire island went still. It arced over the harbor on a path toward the ghostly drake. The mirage that was the elven companion vanished, as if blown away on an invisible breeze.

Thud!

Zarlak shuddered, releasing a deafening shriek. As if a knife cut the sky, a void opened over the harbor. The drake's body contracted, sucked into the seam. The mist clinging to the city pulled over the harbor and into the magical opening.

Jack felt his skin tighten. His ears popped.

The divine portal contracted to a single point of light and—

Boom!

Jack dove. Golden light cast a divine radiance over the city. It passed over Ruby Island. Over the Jewel Archipelago. Over the open sea, reaching as far as the shores of Drakeland and the northern Fjords of Raulkulnen.

Lying on the grass and panting, Jack scanned the harbor. To his relief, Big Rig and Marian tread water near the remains of *Lady Luck*.

He looked back at the city.

A starry night hung over a ravaged but liberated Redtown.

In the newfound silence, his ears picked up cheers rising from the guild district.

37

EVEN KEEL

✦

Scarlett pushed through the crowd. Shouts from the city guard competed with raucous cheers as soldiers ordered squads to search unprotected districts for survivors.

The thief squeezed through a group of Redtowners and climbed the fountain's circular ledge.

"Scarlett!"

Trusty Jack's tricorne bobbed up and down among a sea of heads. The dragon fountain's watery flames tinged the hat's fabric with a reddish glow.

Scarlett waved and Marian, who walked with the pirate arm in arm, pointed in her direction. The mage's face spoke of weariness. She'd spent enough time with the healer to know the weight was physical and emotional.

"Marian!" A red-robed mage pushed through a mass of Redtowners. "Are you alright?"

"Alara, thank the gods." Marian pulled away from Jack's support and embraced her friend.

"It's done, lass," Trusty Jack said, approaching. With the boost from the ledge, Scarlett and the pirate stood eye to eye. She peered over his shoulder, seeking others from the docks.

"Bonnie didn't make it," he said, voice low.

Scarlett glanced at Marian. The healer's colleague tightened her hug as Marian fought back tears.

"Neither did Sir Roderick," Trusty Jack said. "Damn noble acts by both of them."

"And *Lady Luck*?"

"Bah," he said and took off his hat.

Scarlett had to smile. Something had changed at the heart of the man. The pathos and burdens pulling the pirate down during their first encounter that fateful night in The Dreg had lifted, as if his soul had weighed anchor.

"I'm sorry, Jack. I know how much that ship meant to you." The sloop had been everything to the pirate. The lynchpin to a second chance. To his freedom. His escape from worldly woes.

"Ain't about the ship, lass." He glanced at Marian, who said goodbye to her fellow mage and joined them.

"Desdianté?" the healer asked.

"The night elf has the dragon's blood," Scarlett said. "I didn't even finish my greeting before he was off, scurrying down the guild hall stairs with the flask."

"Good," Marian said. "Let's hope his years of knowledge and research prove worthy."

"I met Marge, by the way. Quite the sprite you have overseeing things." Scarlett's stomach tightened, but not as much as it had when previous memories of Tingle rose.

"Indeed, she's a character," the mage said.

"I'm sorry about your sister, Marian."

The healer's lip pursed and her cheeks trembled. "Thank you, Scarlett. I only wish we'd had time to talk."

"Aye." Jack put an arm around Marian. "There's been too many losses on this here adventure."

"How did you do it?" Scarlett said. "The dragon, I mean?"

"Marian's the one to be given credit," the pirate said. "She figured out the arrow was of golden dragon bone. From Nimárwe's quiver of old."

"We *all* did it," the mage said, "and James made a remarkable shot." Marian kissed him.

"Had a bit o' magic guiding me." The pirate winked.

"You did it!" Precious pushed through the crowds.

"We all did, lass," Trusty Jack said, and plopped his tricorne on the woman's head. "And now you've got work to do, Captain."

"My lady!" A plate-armored half-elf, her face smudged with dirt and soot, pushed through and saluted Marian. "I am Dayo, at your service. We mourn the loss of Sir Roderick. I am next in command of the Order." The woman pulled off her helmet, revealing a flattened plume of tight-wound braids between sides of shaved and sweaty umber skin. "Your father is in custody. He's being brought down."

"Thank you, Dame Dayo."

"You should speak, Marian," Precious said. "If you are able?"

"Of course."

Scarlett jumped down from the fountain's ledge to make room for the mage.

"Attention! Attention!" Dame Dayo smacked her sword against her plate armor.

Marian stepped onto the stone railing.

"Attention!"

The crowds of Redtowners hushed.

"My fellow citizens," Marian said. "Many of you know me, but for those who do not, I am Marian Fitzwater, healer from the Redtown guild and member of the Order of Telathia. We have persevered through a most tragic day and night, rivaled only by the attack a thousand years ago... by the very beast now banished to the void."

Gods, Scarlett thought, watching the mage. *What an orator.* She was born to speak, to draw eye and ear. And yet, that fact was made more noble by her choice to shun its potential power and humbly serve her brethren rather than rule from the palace.

Scarlett glanced at Trusty Jack.

The corner of the pirate's mouth broke into a smile.

"But not without cost," Marian said, her tone earnest. "Too many lives have been lost this day. And in the days leading up to this tragedy."

A commotion on the side of the square turned everyone's head.

"What is it?" Scarlett asked the pirate.

"That bilge rat's being brought in."

Marian waited until her father stood in the strong arms of two Red Knights at her side.

"There will be no inauguration today," the mage said. "Nor ever."

Gasps from the crowd.

"The former regent, Markus Fitzwater... my father." The pain and rage in the mage's eyes at his mention was plain for all to see. "Is not worthy of the throne."

"How dare you?" her father shouted. "I am the rightful ruler of these islands!"

"Not anymore you aren't," Marian said. "You are nothing short of a traitor to the people."

More gasps from the crowd.

"This is an outrage!" Markus Fitzwater struggled against the guards holding him. "Empty accusations. That's all this is. Now let me go!"

"I have evidence," Marian said. "Terrible deeds mark the trail leading to this day." The mage's panther-like eyes were afire. They burned into her defiant father. "Our beloved queen, my aunt, and her unborn child, were sent to their deaths in a ploy by Markus Fitzwater to seize the throne." She thrust the pendant up for all to see.

More gasps.

The regent's eyes went wide.

"The plot has been uncovered," Marian continued. "The regent stands accused of murder, of political assassination, of treason, and of downright greed. All on the backs of hard-working citizens, our islands and their resources, and... the children."

"Shame!" someone shouted.

"Bloody taxes!" another called.

"And the sickness! That's his fault, that is!"

Marian held up a hand to quiet the crowd. "There is more, sadly."

Unsavory expletives and angry shouts reached Scarlett's ears.

"She has no authority here!" Markus yelled to the crowd. He turned to his daughter. "You signed away your rights as a noble, *daughter*."

"Yes, I did," Marian said. "And the next in line, my sister..." The mage's lips trembled. "Died saving this city."

"No!" The regent's body collapsed. The guards kept him from falling.

"You should take charge!" a voice shouted. "You've always done right by us!"

Applause rose in support of the claim.

Marian shook her head. "I have no desire but thank you. Luckily, there is one among us this day who is of the ancient line and can rightfully claim that role."

The crowd hushed.

"This," Marian, with Jack's aid, helped Precious onto the ledge. "Is Orla Chen."

Scarlett peered through a sea of legs at the former regent. Markus Fitzwater's defeated and slumped body came to life. He looked to his daughter in shock.

"Orla Chen suffered through the regent's attempt to destroy all royal lineage threatening his power. And yet..." Marian locked eyes with her father. "She lives. Thanks to none other than an innocent man falsely charged with murder."

Scarlett peered up at the pirate. Trusty Jack mumbled something and shook his head.

"Captain James R. Hawk," Marian said. "Known to all of you as Trusty Jack!"

Cheers from the crowd.

The pirate waved his hat to applause.

"Three cheers for Trusty Jack!" a voice shouted. "Dragon slayer!"

The pirate waved off the crowd that had erupted in cheers.

"This fountain," Marian said, quieting their fervor and gesturing to the magical water rushing from the dragon's mouth, "has flowed red since Queen Ricarda's line first ruled the Jewels." The mage gestured to Precious. "Orla, if you please."

The woman turned her back to the crowd, red light highlighting the edges of her form in the night. Scarlett's gnomish ears picked up words with an uncanny resemblance to those spoken on Dragon Tail Island when they had entered the tomb.

An eerie glow rose on the stone dragon.

"Shiver me timbers," Trusty Jack said.

Crimson reflections dappling Marian's robe went blue as the fiery water shifted hue. The mage handed the pendant to Precious and stepped down from the ledge.

"I am but a simple islander from Benevolence," Precious said, nodding at the mutterings of surprise in the crowd. "My life has been lived as a commoner. I've run an orphanage since I was rescued by the good pirate, Trusty Jack." Precious pointed at Captain Hawk with her walking stick.

"What of the regent?" a voice called out.

"Hang 'em!" another shouted.

"Put him in the stocks!"

"No!" Precious held up her hands. "Please... fellow citizens, hear me out. We can rebuild this great city and the island chain that houses it." Her gaze rose to the palace ruins. "It is time to let a legacy surrender to history," she said. "With your blessing, I suggest we take down what remains of the palace and rebuild a new seat of government. The royal gardens, a haven of the nobility, should be a public park... accessible for all."

The crowd, as Scarlett expected, was more than approving.

"As for the former regent, we must respect a code of civility lacking under the previous regime. We are better than that. Therefore, he will be placed under arrest and given a fair trial, with evidence presented and sentenced by a..." Precious looked at Trusty Jack, "group of fellow citizens through a democratic process."

Mixed words, both for and against, rose in the crowd.

"They're peasants!" the former regent shouted. "Fishmongers and farmers... you're going to let them decide the fate of—" He halted at the sight of Dame Dayo approaching.

The two guards lifted a cowering Markus Fitzwater and forced him to face the crowd. "By rights decreed and with the authority vested in me as head of the Red Order, protector of this city and all its subjects,"

Dame Dayo said, voice bold and carrying over the crowd, "you, Markus Fitzwater are hereby removed from office and placed under arrest until trial and sentencing. You will be housed in Longshore prison until that date."

"Oh, that is sweet irony, that is," Jack leaned down and elbowed Scarlett. "McHardy's and Flounders are going to have a grand ol' time with him."

"Citizens, it may surprise you to hear this, but I have no wish to rule these islands," Precious said. "Such divides between us are old and tired, and unjust. Instead, it is my wish that we establish a temporary government to restore order and treat the wounded. Once that is accomplished, I intend to step aside. We will hold free elections and *you* will decide who represents you and your interests."

Cheers from the crowd.

"Particulars can be ironed out through the local councils but rest easy fellow islanders. Each district in Redtown, and each community on Ruby Island and throughout the Jewels, will have a voice!"

A celebration ensued. Redtowners hugged and shouted.

Scarlett caught Precious's eye and nodded. *Well done.*

"Before we disperse and leave this long and tragic night behind us, there is one more piece of news," Precious said, quieting the crowd. "The dragon that ravaged this city arrived from the legendary isle over the eastern sea. That cursed destination and the mists that kept it at bay are no more. We are free of the dark magic and its sickness, but the children afflicted by its disease suffer still. The price we paid to rid the Jewels of that dark force and save the future for our children is the havoc and destruction around you in Redtown." She swept a hand from left to right. "I do not look upon this lightly. It breaks my heart to see such reckless hate and death, and the cost of an end to evil in our land. But that hard price did yield a reward."

"Let him through!" Dame Dayo shouted and pushed aside Redtowners.

"Jack? Do you mind?" Scarlett said and held out her arms.

The pirate heaved her up and held her so she could see. "Aye, lass. You want to witness this part, I'm sure."

The night elf that Scarlett handed off the dragon's blood to at the guild hall approached the fountain. Hooded, his purple eyes aglow, the magical water's reflections flickered off the folds of his robe.

Marian spoke a word with the reclusive healer and then joined Precious on the ledge.

"Through the never-ending work of the healer's guild, and Mage Desdianté in particular," Marian nodded at the night elf, "we have a cure for the sickness."

"Blessed gods!" someone shouted.

"Yes, an ancient recipe has been remade. The elixir of old has been mixed using the dragon's blood," Marian said. "It is being administered to the afflicted children in Redtown as we speak. Ships will be sent in the morning to all other islands. We are asking for those of you with vessels capable of sailing to volunteer to help get these out as fast as possible."

"Welcome to a new dawn, Redtowners!" Precious shouted, to cheers. "May the Jewels shine bright and prosper!"

"Anyone capable of aiding with the wounded," Dame Dayo said, "see the city guards posted at the edges of the square."

As the citizens dispersed, Lana and Big Rig pushed forward and joined the group at the fountain. Each had a large sack over a shoulder.

"Captain," the dwarf said, "a word?"

Trusty Jack joined his fellow Salty Scoundrels. A brief exchange ensued, followed by hearty nods amongst the three.

"Precious," the pirate said, approaching. "Me mates would like a word."

Big Rig and Lana stepped forward.

The half-orc bowed formally.

"You don't have to do that, idiot," Big Rig said.

"She's royalty now, Rig," Lana spat back.

"Indeed, it's quite unnecessary." Precious smiled and patted the half-orc on the arm.

"It's like this, it is," the dwarf said. "There's enough booty in these here sacks for us Salty Scoundrels to live like royalty ourselves for the rest of our days. But we wouldn't feel right with it."

Lana nodded emphatically. "We put aside a wee bit for ourselves."

She leaned down and winked. "But this is all yours... meaning for Redtown."

Marian met Trusty Jack's gaze. The pirate was aglow with pride for his crew's generosity.

"Thank you," Precious said to the three pirates. "That is very self-less of you."

Lana blushed. Big Rig bowed his head and grumbled. Trusty Jack took off his hat and placed it on his chest. "Aye, lass. We want it to go to right good use."

Scarlett found herself wiping an eye.

As if hearing the end of the city's plight, golden light shone on the ruins of the palace as dawn broke over the sea.

"A new day for Redtown," Scarlett said, peering up the hill.

"And for the Jewels." Precious smiled.

"That's him!" A citizen pointed at Big Rig.

"Get your filthy paws off me!" The dwarf fought back as two city guards grabbed him.

"What is the meaning of this?" Precious said.

"He's one of them fugitives, he is," the Redtowner said. "Escaped from Longshore."

"Now wait there a moment," Trusty Jack said. "First off, that salty dog's responsible for part of the good that's happened here tonight, and to the point, the lad was to be serving a ten-year sentence. He'd been in fourteen years when we broke him out. It was only because of that bilge rat regent and his dirty friend, the warden, that they pushed it to life in prison." The pirate strode to Markus Fitzwater, still held by two Red Knights. "Ain't that right, Markus?" Jack grabbed the man's shirt. "Out with it, ya scurvy dog!"

"Yes, yes," the man said, defeated.

"He's free as anyone else, he is," the pirate said. "Now let him go."

The city guards looked at Dame Dayo, who nodded.

"And as for me," Jack thumbed his chest. "I was on year eight of ten when I broke out. Jailed for a crime I didn't commit so you can take down them bloody posters. This one here," he pointed in Scarlett's direction, "is the reason why you have a leader willing to make change in the islands. And our other companion sacrificed herself to save a little boy in the mists. I think that's time served on all accounts."

Scarlett's heart sank at the mention of the bard, Siân. Another companion lost on their tumultuous adventure.

"We're square now," Trusty Jack said, "ain't we?"

"Indeed, we are. Please nullify all wanted statuses," Precious said to Dame Dayo.

"Lana's remaining contract ain't worth the bother," the pirate added, "not with everything else in play."

Precious nodded. "Well, glad that is done with."

Me too, Scarlett thought, her concern easing. The last thing she needed was to end up in jail after all they'd been through.

The temporary leader of Redtown turned to the pirate. "What will you do now, Jack?"

"No idea, lass, but there's plenty o' work to do here for a start, that be certain." The pirate looked at Marian.

"And there's a fleet to rebuild," Precious said. "Ever think of a post in the Navy?"

"Do you offer me insult?" Trusty Jack barked to laughs from his salty companions.

Precious held up her hands in defense.

Scarlett, being a master thief, had one eye on everyone and everything in the square. Right now, her focus was Lana, who gazed at the distant harbor. The gnome stepped onto the ledge and squinted. "Looks like the Navy managed to send that new galleon out to sea before everything went to pieces," she said.

Big Rig hopped up next to her. "Aye, and what a beauty. You've got one ship at least, Ms. Chen." The dwarf pointed at the majestic galleon lowering its sails and turning into port.

"No, we've lost that one too, I'm afraid." Precious smirked. "Dame Dayo?"

The Red Knight stomped over.

"My first official act as interim leader," the woman said. "I want you to have the deed to that galleon signed over to Captain Hawk."

"I'll see to it."

Trusty Jack swung around. "Blow me down, lass! You take me for Ropey Jane's uncle?"

"Not in the least." Precious, leaning on her walking stick, put a hand on the pirate's shoulder. "You lost *Lady Luck*, didn't you? It wouldn't be right to downgrade. Plus," Precious met Marian's gaze. "I imagine your quarters could use with a bit more room these days."

"Well, honk my hooter!" Lana threw the dwarf up in the air, catching him. Big Rig was too elated to be angry.

Scarlett giggled as the two pirates danced in a circle, arm in arm, like when they had discovered the treasure on Dragon Tail Island.

"Private quarters, mate!" Lana slapped the quartermaster as they danced, "for both of us!"

"Aye! I don't need to hear your snorin'!"

"I don't snore!" Lana said.

"And those retractable masts," the dwarf said. "What a sight!"

"You and your riggings, Mr. Riggins." The half-orc halted. "Aye, that's a punner, that is!"

The two erupted into laughter.

"We be sailing away on a galleon!" the dwarf sang, pulling out a cheroot and sticking it in the corner of his mouth.

Scarlett didn't miss the tension, unnoticed by the others, between Trusty Jack and Marian.

"We have so much work to do." Desdianté said, approaching the mage.

"Where is the headmaster?" Marian asked, "she must be thrilled with your research outcome."

Her guild companion shook his head. "I'm sorry, Marian. I know you two were close. If it wasn't for the old elf, the shield wouldn't have held as long as it did."

The mage's lip trembled.

She's lost so much in all of this, Scarlett thought.

"It means new guild leadership is needed." Her fellow mage raised an eyebrow.

"Let's take this one day at a time," Marian said.

Scarlett stepped down from the ledge.

Well, that's that, she thought. *Done, but with a heavy cost.* Good news for the Ten Fingers at the Thieves Guild back in Drakeland.

The coastline around Redtown alighted with a honey-like glow as the sun rose further.

I will miss the islands, she thought.

An audible sigh turned her attention to the pirate.

"You alright, Jack?" she said.

"Aye, lass. One day at a time."

❧ 38 ❧

DOWNWIND RUN

THREE WEEKS LATER...

❧❧❧

The Salty Scoundrels had frothy feet. All three showed signs of the sailor's malady. Big Rig had taken on an irritable impatience, barking at the crew during walk-throughs and inspections on the galleon. Twice in the last week, Jack had bailed Lana out of the brig for brawling. And just this morning, he and Marian had their first major row.

And over what? he thought. *A bloody piece of toast.*

Deny it as he might, it was time to put to sea.

The galleon was shipshape and Redtown had reached a steady hum of repairs and rebuilding. Precious and community leaders had established working groups to run elections. Local representatives would be the first and, she claimed, most important step in reshaping the city's government. Word had gone out by land and sea inviting community leaders and governors from the surrounding islands for a major council, one that Jack imagined would be celebrated in years to come as a pivotal moment in the history of the Jewel Islands.

As for the fever, the dragon's blood had proved to be the cure-all of legend. Mixed in the appropriate and exacting ancient formula, thanks to the deft hands and scholarly knowledge of Desdianté, the elixir had reached all but the most isolated and remote settlements with a one hundred percent success rate. Marian had gotten word yesterday that within the next week or two, at most, the archipelago would be rid of all traces of the ancient sickness.

"Welcome aboard," Trusty Jack said as Scarlett walked up the gangplank.

"Quite the ship." The gnome peered at its multi-tiered decks. "I approve of the new name."

"Aye, credit goes to Lana for that," he said. The galleon's title, *Royal Patriarch*, a nod to the now incarcerated former regent, had been replaced with a similar honorific, but with a more noble and worthy figure memorialized in the ship's bones.

"*Song of Siân*," Scarlett said. "It rolls off the tongue with sweet poesy."

"Been meanin' to ask, lass. What happens now with that guild of yours? How exactly do you expect to take root in the Jewels?"

"Delicately and slowly." The gnome winked. "They'll give it a year or two to let things germinate. Keep to the shadows. When the time is right, they'll start planting seeds."

"We'll miss having you around, Scarlett. Like you said, pirates and thieves be like siblings... of a kind."

"Who knows, Jack. You may see me again sooner than you expect."

He raised an eyebrow.

"I've gained a new perspective spending time with pirates." She glanced back at the view of Redtown. "The Jewels have captured a portion of my heart. It may be best that someone with keen and intimate insight into the islands and its new politics oversees our enhanced presence."

"How would the Thieves Guild take to that?" he asked.

The gnome smirked. "After this win, my voice will matter more than ever. Perhaps I can convince the higher-ups of the benefits of discrete underground tactics that challenge our longstanding traditions."

"Well, lookie here," Trusty Jack said, leaning down. "Scarlett Tanash, the good-hearted thief."

A tiny hand pushed him. The pirate toppled over on deck, laughing.

"Aye," he said, rising and adjusting his cotton sleeves. "I'd be eager to see that, I would."

"Careful with those, you landlubbers!" Lana barked a short ways down the deck.

"Sink me, she's got more?" Jack followed a cluster of wooden casks roped together being hauled on board with a pulley.

"Is that rum?" Scarlett said.

"Apparently Redtown's run dry of Molly's Molasses," he said, shaking his head. If *Song of Siân* went down at sea, the famous drink would turn to legend, spurring treasure seekers and rummeliers alike to expeditionary voyages seeking lost barrels.

"What is that?" The gnome pointed at a canvas wrapped over the ship's prow.

"Some trick Rig and Lana have up their sleeves. Won't let me near it until we weigh anchor."

"Is Marian on board?"

"No, she's on a round to the guild hall. Harbor boy'll row her out when she's finished. Should be here by now, come to think of it." *Why was she taking so long?* The fight they'd had this morning didn't help the uneasy feeling in his stomach. The thought of leaving without things settled between them wouldn't do. He owed her an apology. Bonnie's funeral had been hard on her, and now he'd gone and added a trivial layer to her emotional burdens.

Jack stepped to the railing and eyed the dock. No sign of her.

"It's how long a sail to Drakeland?" Scarlett said.

"Can't be sure, lass. Not until I cozy up to the personality and particulars of this here galleon."

"And we're stopping in Benevolence on the way?"

"Aye, figure three days to Benevolence if the winds are fair. Four or five in port to do this and that. Need enough time to brag on me new ship to the sea dogs at Grumpy Jim's." He grinned. "Then another two weeks for the crossing. We'll spend a week or so in Drakeland seein' the sights before we sail back to Redtown."

"And then?"

"Sorry?"

The gnome narrowed her eyes.

"What are you gettin' at, lass?"

"Jack, I think you and I have spent enough time together to consider one another friends?"

"Aye."

"I am asking about you and Marian. Two months is a long time to be apart"

He opened his mouth but found himself short of words. His heart, on the other hand, had plenty it was willing to share.

"How is it going to work?" Scarlett said. "With the two of you."

Jack checked the shoreline. The harbor boy sat in the dinghy, waiting along the dock. *Where in bloody blazes is she?* he thought, remembering his stupidity that morning in raising them to words over a trivial difference of opinion. The pirate removed his tricorne and ran a hand through his blonde hair. "Don't know, lass. One day at a time," he said.

"Can I give you some advice?"

"I'm all ears, Scarlett. It's a right fix, it is." That was putting it mildly. The city needed a mage of her caliber and leadership, especially in this time of rebuilding. Yet, like his salty companions, the pirate's life had settled deep in his bones. Even now, with three weeks on dry land he was on edge. The shadow of their future relationship had lurked in the background since they'd officially reunited, but earnest discussion had been kept at bay by the ongoing adventure and subsequent activities during the first weeks of recovery in the capital. Now, there was nothing left to keep it hidden. An on and off, time together and time apart, approach had become a default solution. The idea of it, of spending even one night away from her tore open his insides. He wanted every second of every remaining day he had to live and breathe to be by her side.

"I almost threw this away after we lost Doni." A tiny hand withdrew the scrap of burlap, her half of the marriage pact with the gnome they had made as children. "You told me not to, and now I know why." She raised an eyebrow.

"I'm not following your meaning, lass," the pirate said.

"Letting something go can be easy, Jack. Holding on to it is much harder."

"You be talkin' in riddles, Scarlett Tanash."

"You know exactly what I mean," she shot back, playfully. "It's your advice."

"Turned against me," he mumbled. "But I savvy your meaning. Thank you, lass."

"Cap!" Lana waved from the front of the ship.

"Come on." He gestured for Scarlett to follow him forward. "Let's see what this nonsense is all about."

"We're all ready, Jack," Big Rig said as they approached. "Just waiting on Marian to board and say a farewell."

"Aye, Rig. Thanks. Now what's this rubbish all about?" Jack nodded at the canvas over the prow.

The half-orc giggled and rubbed her massive green hands together. "Rig and I spent a wee bit of the booty on—"

"Without consultation and vote?" Jack said, looking from his first mate to the quartermaster.

"Now hold on, mate," the dwarf said. "Lana and I agreed we'd take this from *our* cuts."

"Fair enough, then," the pirate said. "A bit shifty not seeking my approval, seein' as it's ship related..."

"Well, wait until you see it, Cap. Then you can decide if it's still got you addled," Lana said. "Ready?"

"Aye." Jack checked the dock. Still no sign of Marian.

"Come up to the railing, both of you," Big Rig said.

Lana signaled to the sea elves holding ropes tied to the canvas. The cover rushed back, revealing a polished and expertly carved figurehead.

Jack removed his tricorne and held it at his chest. "Blow me down, me hearties. It's a right sight, that is." The likeness of Siân, strumming a lute, was nestled in swirling patterns of rushing swells.

"You like it, Cap?" Lana asked.

Trusty Jack put a hand on her shoulder and smiled. "Aye. A master carving."

"'Inspiring' was the word I told the carver when asked to describe the nocsi," Big Rig said. "Sculptor's an old forest dwarf. Lives up in them there hills on the underside of Roundhorn Pass." He pointed up at the twin volcanic peaks beyond the new foundation of Redtown's soon-to-be civic center. "Retired and reclusive that forester is... wasn't sure the lass still lived and breathed, not to mention if she was capable of carving."

"That's where you went for three days?"

"Aye," Big Rig stroked his beard. "I *was* hunting," he said, "just not for game." He winked. "Made from the finest mahogany in the isles. And, from a naturally fallen tree. Not one cut to purpose."

Jack put a hand on his old friend's shoulder. "Siân would have appreciated that, Rig."

The quartermaster lowered his head. "Wordy as she was, I admit to missing her."

"Ship's all done and ready now, Cap," Lana said. "Although we could do with a bit more rum."

"Steady on, lass," Trusty Jack said. "What I saw come aboard will have us heeling all the way to Redtown."

"More like halfway if I have anything to do with it!" The half-orc licked her tusks.

"Aye, I must admit, I can't wait to put to sea," the dwarf said.

"It's beautiful." A hand touched Jack like no other could and wrapped around his waist.

"Marian," he said, meeting her eye.

She kissed him. "Sorry I'm late."

Why was I so worried? he thought.

The others made their way aft, leaving them alone at the bow.

"That was very nice," she said, examining the figurehead. "A heartfelt gesture."

"Aye. Marian, I'm sorry I've been—"

She put a hand on his lips.

"But I want to apologize for—"

"Shhhh..."

426

"I know you, James. It's not easy to change course when you've been sailing in one direction for so long."

"Them be salty words for a landlubber."

She laughed. "Maybe your sailor ways are rubbing off on me."

"I'd follow any course for you, lass."

"Such romantic words from a pirate," she said, and playfully ran a hand over his chest.

"Bah, stop with that talk." He felt his cheeks flush.

She pulled him close.

"Is this going to work, Marian? Meaning time away and..." He held her cheek. "Being honest, I don't want to spend another moment without you."

"I sent the harbor boy away, Miss," a sea elf said.

"Thank you." The amber shards in Marian's eyes sparkled.

Jack turned his head but a hand pulled it back.

"Your bags are on deck?"

She nodded.

"You're... you're coming with us?"

"I'm coming with *you*."

Of all their kisses, only the first, when their lips met on the hill overlooking Redtown, rivaled the one on the bow of the newly christened galleon, *Song of Siân*.

"No more bleeding hearts for either of us," she whispered.

"Let's get sailing, Cap!" Lana shouted, followed by cheers from the crew.

Marian pulled back and smiled.

"What about the guild?" he said.

"The guild will be fine. There's plenty of other mages capable of taking a leadership role."

Jack's heart swelled with emotion.

"Plus, I want to check on the children at the orphanage and make sure they're in good health."

"Aye, and we can drop off Billy." Jack nodded down the deck.

The boy trailed behind Big Rig as if he were a scaled-down twin. The quartermaster spat and Billy mimicked the action.

Jack grinned. *Boy's got pirate bones.*

The two passed Lana, who worked a set of ropes. The half-orc held out a palm and Billy punched it with an undeniable knuckler's form. The first mate adjusted his fist, making him repeat the action.

"Actually, I was thinking maybe he could stay," Marian said. "With us." The mage put her arm around his waist. "He reminds me of someone."

"Does he now?"

The two made their way back to the others.

"Do we need to sail back after Drakeland?" Marian said.

"Lass, we don't have to do anything except what our hearts desire." Jack strode boldly, his full pirate pride on display.

"I packed some warmer clothes. I remember you talking about visiting the Fjords of Raulkulnen one day."

"Aye, to get me one of them glow stones," he said. "I'll bet Billy would fancy one, too."

"Change of plans, mates," Trusty Jack said with his best captain's voice. "Marian's coming with us."

A round of hearty pirate exclamations rose from the Salty Scoundrels.

Jack caught Scarlett's eye. The gnome nodded her chin ever so slightly.

"Benevolence is our first port of call," Jack said, gripping the helm. "Then, across the open sea to the mainland to drop off Ms. Tanash. That's the plan."

"Scupper plans, Cap!" Lana said. "We be pirates!"

"True, that is!" Big Rig said.

"Well, you need to drop me off in Drakeland, please," Scarlett said.

"Aye, we'll stay true that far, we will," Jack said.

Ship has a good feel, he thought, tightening his grip on the wheel.

"And from there?" Scarlett said.

Trusty Jack took pause, the thief's question lingering on deck. He inhaled the scent of the sea. Big Rig and Lana waited eagerly and respectfully, being companions true. The pirate locked eyes with Marian, the long road and trials of their love conquered, and his broken heart mended.

A pirate's pride welled in his chest like the rising tide.
"Only the wind can tell, lass."

A NOTE OF THANKS

Thank you for taking the time to read my books!

If you enjoyed *The Curse of Dragon Tail Island*, and have a moment to leave a rating, it would make my day! It helps me reach readers and share my stories.
Many thanks, Jonathan Nevair.

ALSO BY THE AUTHOR

AGENT RENAULT SPY-FI ADVENTURES

Escape into a world of galactic espionage in this fun and fast-paced spy-fi adventure series featuring a tough yet conflicted secret agent, cloak and dagger intrigue, and a charming cast of alien characters.

Agent Renault Adventures (link)
High-stakes thriller excitement meets space opera adventure.

SEA SHANTY: HEAVE AWAY!

*The following sea shanty was written especially for this novel by the Scottish author, Rowena Andrews.

The tide was high, and the morn was pale,
When we stepped once more 'neath the sail.
The rum was stored, the anchor weighed,
The view of land began to fade.
With a cheer for the life we'd missed,
We set our course where the sunrise kissed...

So, heave away (heave away!), let the whole world hear,
We're bound for lands both far and near,
With Lady Luck we have nothing to fear,
So, heave away lads, let the tides decide.

The tide was high, and the wind was new,
The ship found the breeze, her captain his crew.
The colors were raised, the sails were full,

435

The waves gave way 'neath eager hull.
With a laugh and a toast, our course was set,
Bound for the point, where sea and sky met.

So, heave away (heave away!), let the whole world hear,
We're bound for lands both far and near,
With Lady Luck we have naught to fear.
So, heave away lads, let the tides decide.

The tide was high, and the harbor behind,
Benevolence Bay where the land is kind.
Where the taverns are full, and the rum flows free,
But away we must go, away to the sea.
Away on the wind, to the far horizon,
Away, away until our adventure is done.

So, heave away (heave away!), let the whole world hear,
We're bound for lands both far and near,
With Lady Luck we have nothing to fear,
So, heave away lads, let the tides decide.

The tide was high, and our Lady Luck smiled,
The ship, the crew, her captain beguiled.
No bones were tossed, no dice were rolled,
An adventure, a story, left to be told.
Beyond the horizon, away beyond the ocean swell,
Where legends, and secrets, and treasure dwell.

So, heave away (heave away!), let the whole world hear,
We're bound for lands both far and near,
With Lady Luck we have nothing to fear,
So, heave away, lads, let the tides decide.
Heavy away, lads! Heave away!

AUTHOR'S NOTE

This novel is something of an homage to the adventure stories I read, watched, and imagined in my youth. I am sure readers recognized similarities to the legend of Robin Hood. Inspiration for many of the characters in this novel came from *The Merry Adventures of Robin Hood* by Howard Pyle (1883), as well as earlier sources such as Thomas Love Peakcock's 1822 novella, *Maid Marian*. In fact, you might call this novel an imaginary retelling... or, at least, one strongly inspired by that story and characters. If the emphasis on a "good pirate" stealing from the rich and giving to the poor, Jack's talent as an archer, and the very on-the-nose, "Mage Marian," weren't enough to make it obvious, the Salty Scoundrels were inspired by the Merry Men of Sherwood Forest: Lana, a nod to Friar Tuck, Big Rig an ironic twist on Little John, Alan-a-dale the source of Siân, and the origin of Scarlett Tanash coming from Will Scarlet.

Add to this character foundation a book that became my childhood favorite, *Treasure Island* by Robert Louis Stevenson, and you had the beginnings of my love of pirates and the cultural setting for this story. That short novel, along with *Kidnapped* and others, whisked me away on imaginary adventures, and reenforced a love of the sea in a setting akin to my childhood home on Long Island. N.C. Wyeth's illustrations for *Treasure Island* are rooted in my mind—who can forget Blind Pew making his way down the path at night from the Admiral Benbow Inn? Closer to home, back in the real world, Gardiners Island, with its tale of Captain Kidd's treasure, was a short drive east along the North Fork. Not to mention all the other connections to seafaring and pirates that linked Long Island to swashbuckling adventure (full disclosure: I leaned far more into the myths, rather than facts, of pirates in this novel).

Finally, there was Dungeons & Dragons and a spate of related fantasy films. Way back in the 1980s, I began playing D&D with a small group of friends. I drew my own characters, invented backstories, and left our world for an adventurous alternative filled with swords, sorcery, and monsters (believe it or not, Trusty Jack started as an incarcerated criminal, freed by a divine charge and turned into a paladin, in a recent D&D campaign with friends during the COVID lockdown. I liked him so much I turned him into a pirate and gave him new life in literary form). From there, in my youth, it was a short hop to books like *The Hobbit* that started me on a lifelong road of reading fantasy and watching films (special shoutout to Erol Flynn and Tim Curry as models for Trusty Jack). In short, a lifelong love of fantasy blossomed alongside a penchant for stories of adventure and the sea.

Thus was *The Curse of Dragon Tail Island* born. This book came easy, and I would be lying if I said it didn't give me a means to escape the difficulties of the real world around me. If nothing more, I drifted off into a secondary world and stood on *Lady Luck's* deck every time I sat down to write—an invisible companion alongside a merry troupe of adventurers.

I won't lie, me hearties, I enjoyed every minute of it.

ACKNOWLEDGMENTS

As a boy, I spent many a day walking the shores of Long Island Sound, dreaming of adventure. Growing up on Long Island, NY, I was surrounded by water. The beaches along the Long Island Sound and the South Shore, with its ocean waves, made for easy and cheap entertainment for my family in the 1970s and 1980s. When my father came home with a small two-person, single mast, sailboat on the roof of our station wagon (a Snark for those of you who may remember the brand), a new dimension was added to my love of salt and sea. I remember the day when we drove down to a nearby secluded bay and embarked on the first of what was to become many summer sailing adventures. Sure, it was just simple tacking (and several tumbles overboard requiring us to fumble our way back into the boat and bail water with a milk carton), but when we caught the breeze and sped across the cove without the noise of a motor something stirred inside of me. Part of that nautical wonder is set into the pages of this story. Thanks, Dad, for making that happen.

As for this book's crew, well... it's a salty one. So many writers, readers, and friends have helped me with this foray into the fantasy genre.

My first mate on this journey was my mother, Nancy. She patiently read incoming chapters as I wrote them and braved a new genre... ("Jonathan, what's an orc?"). Mom, your feedback and enthusiasm was, as always, more valuable than any buried treasure.

My wife Mallary, ever willing to support me, provided a stack of books about pirates for my birthday when the novel was underway. That, along with her patience in listening to me share plot roadblocks and offering solutions, and encouraging my obsession with writing fiction more generally, makes her my ever-faithful life companion.

I was in new literary territory with not just fantasy but also romance. I want to thank my editor, Tina S. Beier, for making the manuscript stronger and tighter, and ensuring I was on the right path to make a second-chance romance blossom anew in a convincing and realistic way.

Special thanks go to my fellow writer and trusty advisor on all things Scottish and sea-related, Rowena Andrews. Not only did they offer feedback to the manuscript, but they graciously agreed to write the sea shanty, *Heave Away!*, that Trusty Jack sings as *Lady Luck* departs Benevolence. Thank you, Rowena, for writing those verses and sprinkling Scottish salt on the pages of this story.

Beta readers... my trusty companions ever ready to tackle rough versions of the story—thank you. To my writer pal, Peter Hartog, who stepped in and answered the call with author-seasoned suggestions to improve the details of the story, and as my resident "fantasy RPG consultant" to make sure I was keeping true to the worldbuilding, magic, and other aspects related to secondary fantasy—a hearty "Yo ho ho!" Thanks, mate. To reader and podcaster/reviewer extraordinaire, Laura Morgan, I appreciate you once again joining in the beta experience by reading this novel. Your ongoing support of my writing and books, and your suggestions for improvement, are most valued.

The cover for *The Curse of Dragon Tail Island* was created by my friend and work colleague, Steve Wood. I sent Steve a series of book covers and images, along with some notes, and got back a sketch that was so on-point my jaw dropped. From there, an amazing final cover quickly followed. Thanks Steve. Your spirited scene of the Salty Scoundrels on the deck of *Lady Luck* influenced the direction of the story (most particularly, Lana's love of Molly's Molasses rum and the ever-present cask tucked under her burly green arm).

Lastly, I am very thankful for the gracious generosity and support of the following writing community individuals, who continue to support me as I navigate my way through this creative journey: Jean-Paul Garnier at Space Cowboy Books, Rex Burke, Adrian M. Gibson and everyone at SFF Addicts, Shannon Knight, Tessa Hastjarjanto,

Trudie Skies and the gang at the Read Indie Fantasy Discord, Dani Finn, Lynda Engler, Andrew Jackson, Alex at Spells & Spaceships, Jamedi (Jamreads), Jodie at W & S Bookclub, Isabelle W. at The Shaggy Shepherd, Sue Bavey, Lorraine Bondi (The Book & Nature Professor), Laura and Hannah at OWWR Podcast, Sara and Lilly at Fiction Fans Podcast, The OG Bookbeard, Scarlett at Scarlett Readz & Runz, KDS, Gogs Herriott, Tufty McTavish, Ziggy Nixon... There are many more. Know that I see you and appreciate all of you.

I wish you all fair winds and following seas.

ABOUT THE AUTHOR

Jonathan Nevair is an award-winning writer and educator originally from Long Island, NY. After two decades in the classroom, he finally got up the nerve to write fiction.

For more information visit: www.jonathannevair.com

Join the mailing list: sign me up!

www.ingramcontent.com/pod-product-compliance
Lightning Source LLC
Chambersburg PA
CBHW020005120726
47903CB00004B/1144